Robert Goddard's first novel, *Past Caring*, was an instant best-seller. Since then, his books have captivated readers worldwide with their edge-of-the-seat pace and their labyrinthine plotting. He has won awards in the UK, the US and across Europe, and his books have been translated into over thirty languages. In 2019 he won the Crime Writers' Association's highest accolade, the Diamond Dagger, for a lifetime achievement in Crime Writing.

Also by Robert Goddard

THE FINE ART OF
INVISIBLE DETECTION

Robert Goddard

CORGI BOOKS

TRANSWORLD PUBLISHERS
Penguin Random House, One Embassy Gardens,
8 Viaduct Gardens, London SW11 7BW
www.penguin.co.uk

Transworld is part of the Penguin Random House group of companies
whose addresses can be found at global.penguinrandomhouse.com

Penguin
Random House
UK

First published in Great Britain in 2020 by Bantam Press
an imprint of Transworld Publishers
Corgi edition published 2021

A CIP catalogue record for this book
is available from the British Library.

ISBN
9780552172622

Typeset in Times NR MT by Integra Software Services Pvt. Ltd, Pondicherry.
Printed and bound in Great Britain by Clays Ltd, Elcograf S.p.A.

The authorized representative in the EEA is Penguin Random House Ireland,
Morrison Chambers, 32 Nassau Street, Dublin D02 YH68.

Penguin Random House is committed to a sustainable
future for our business, our readers and our planet. This book
is made from Forest Stewardship Council® certified paper.

For my mother-in-law, Thelma North

ONE

UMIKO WADA WASN'T A PRIVATE DETECTIVE. SHE JUST WORKED FOR ONE.
She answered his phone, managed his accounts, kept his records,
talked through problems with him, greeted his visitors, fetched
him bento-boxed lunches and made him tea, which he'd taken
to drinking virtually all day now he'd supposedly given up
smoking.

The sign on the door of the seventh-floor office in the
Nihonbashi district of Tokyo where Wada spent her working
days described it as the premises of the Kodaka Detective
Agency. But there was only one detective in the agency: fifty-
eight-year-old Kazuto Kodaka. There'd been several detectives,
apparently, when Kodaka senior was in charge. But his son preferred to operate alone. What would happen if and when his
body collapsed under the strain of his unhealthy habits and
chronic overwork was easy to predict. Wada would need a new
job. Which wasn't a happy thought. She liked this job. It
suited her.

She always thought of herself as Wada rather than Umiko
because that was how Kodaka referred to her. It had seemed
disrespectful at first. Now she was rather fond of it. It reinforced

1

an image of herself she'd honed over years of being alone. Simple, strong, independent. That was Wada. Umiko was a girl she'd once been. The Wada she'd become was nearly forty-seven, though she looked younger, probably because, as her mother regularly reminded her, she'd never had children to raise and worry over.

That wasn't Wada's fault, as her mother used to acknowledge but now seemed inclined to forget. She was a widow. Her husband Tomohiko – Hiko, as she'd called him and still did, in the privacy of her own thoughts – had been killed in the sarin gas attack on the Tokyo subway back in 1995, though technically he hadn't actually died until twelve years later. The decade and a bit he'd spent in a coma froze Wada's life. Her mother had still hoped, when he finally expired, that Wada would find somebody else to marry. But it had never happened.

Sometimes, though she'd never have admitted it to anyone, she was glad she hadn't gone on in the world with Hiko, bearing his children, keeping house for him, cooking, cleaning, deferring, conforming. She was as sorry as anyone could be that he'd died as he had. There was a time when she'd been sorry on the same account for herself. But that time had passed. That was why she'd finally dropped his surname and gone back to the one she was born with: Wada.

She'd met Kodaka because of the sarin attack. He was gathering evidence to use against members of Aum Shinrikyo, the murderous cult responsible, on behalf of relatives of other victims and wanted to know if Hiko had said anything to her, before lapsing into his coma, about Yozo Sasada, the cult member who'd released the gas in the train carriage Hiko had been travelling in that fateful spring morning in 1995. No, was the answer. Hiko was already unconscious when she'd reached the hospital. He'd said nothing. To her or anyone else.

She was working as an English translator when Kodaka first contacted her, earning money the only way she knew how. She enjoyed speaking and reading English. It took her to a mental space half removed from the Japanese world she didn't quite have a firm stake in any more. She felt freer there, better able to be herself.

It was a surprise when Kodaka contacted her again a few months later, this time inviting her to apply for a job as his secretary. Her fluency in English was something he reckoned would be valuable in dealing with foreign clients. Not that he actually had any foreign clients. But he was optimistic about expanding the reach of his operations and there were quite a few occasions when an improvement on his halting grasp of the international language was called for.

She took the job, which she described as personal assistant rather than secretary. It often involved working late or at the weekend for no extra pay, but she didn't mind and Kodaka rewarded her with occasional bonuses when business was good.

The business itself was biased towards commercial matters. There was a lot of vetting of potential recruits for companies or identifying which of their employees might be responsible for leaking sensitive information to competitors or the media or the tax authorities. Kodaka senior had sited the agency within easy reach of the Tokyo Stock Exchange to attract such business. Divorce and missing persons, the other staples of the profession, were less significant at the Kodaka Agency, though Wada enjoyed them when they came along. She found the tangled problems of other people's lives grimly fascinating.

Most of the time, her involvement with those lives was confined to putting Kodaka's notes and other records in order and compiling reports to lawyers, which she was much better and quicker at than Kodaka himself, whose talents lay in ferreting out information, staking out addresses and piecing together evidence. More than once, after pulling his bottle of Suntory whisky out of the bottom drawer of the scratched green filing cabinet behind his desk and pouring them both a glass as the lights of the city danced in the night beyond the office windows, he'd say they made a good team.

Sometimes, very rarely, Kodaka asked her to go out into the field and follow someone. This occurred when only a female tail was likely to escape detection. She proved to be rather good at it. Without intending any insult, Kodaka said she had the gift of being invisible. No one noticed her. She was anonymous. She attracted no attention.

Kodaka was unmarried. Wada's mother had suggested, in her desperation for a grandchild that only grew as her daughter progressed into her forties, that he might be a suitable husband, even though she'd never actually met the man. The idea was absurd. Kodaka found all the female company he desired in his late-night forays to assorted bars and clubs. He often arrived at the office in the morning with the rumpled, unshaven, red-eyed look of someone who'd barely slept, let alone in his own bed. He'd never made any kind of overture to her, probably because he valued her services too highly to risk losing them. He was right. The overtures wouldn't have been well received. That would have been unfortunate. Because they were a good team.

Yozo Sasada, the Aum Shinrikyo member responsible for Hiko's death, had finally been executed twenty-three years after the attack, along with the cult's founder, Shoko Asahara, and twelve others. Kodaka made no reference to their hangings, though when the day came Asahara's blank, heavy-lidded face was all over the newspapers and the giant TV screens that Wada passed on her way to work. She interpreted her employer's silence on the subject as an example of his sensitivity, which as ever could only be detected by what he didn't say rather than what he did.

The twenty-fourth anniversary of the attack had passed now as well, again unremarked upon in the offices of the Kodaka Detective Agency. Spring was advancing. Cherry blossom viewing spots in Kitanomaru Park were hard to come by. The world went on its way. It was business as usual.

Until it wasn't.

Wada made most of Kodaka's appointments for him. Most of his office appointments, anyway. He fixed personal rendezvous for himself. An unenthusiastic convert to modern technology, he recorded these in an old-style pocket diary and insisted Wada keep a paper diary for the office as well. He made occasional joking references to his reluctance to embrace paperless procedures, though Wada suspected he was also worried about the security of information committed to the virtual world. And there was no doubt many of his clients valued security so highly that his old-fashioned methods appealed to them.

That Friday, when Wada reached the office, she was mildly surprised to see an afternoon appointment with someone identified only by the hiragana み and た written in the diary in Kodaka's inelegant hand. It must have been made after she'd left the previous evening. She mentioned it to him when he arrived. He was looking far from spruce but by no means unusually dishevelled. All she learnt from him was that み た was one Mimori Takenaga, her name recorded in traditional albeit abbreviated style with the surname first and the forename second.

'She caught me on the telephone just before I left last night,' Kodaka explained.

'Husband trouble?' Wada enquired.

'Not the way you mean.'

5

And that was that. He didn't elaborate. And Wada didn't press him to. That was one of the things that made them a good team.

Mimori Takenaga arrived promptly at four thirty. She was a woman of about Wada's own age, but smaller and more delicately built. She would have looked perfect in a kimono, whereas Wada, on those ever rarer occasions when she wore one, felt lumpy and awkward. In the fashionable western clothes she was actually wearing, Mrs Takenaga looked smart and affluent but somehow ill at ease. There was an impression of someone playing a part she wasn't suited to, which the large, well-filled Mitsukoshi carrier bag she left in the waiting area failed to dispel.

She was closeted with Kodaka for about an hour, their voices reaching Wada as an indistinct murmur often drowned out by the telephone or traffic noise from the street below. The length of the consultation suggested the matter was both delicate and complicated. Kodaka asked for tea halfway through and Wada only caught a brief snatch of the conversation as she delivered it. Her curiosity was aroused, but she had no difficulty hiding it. Hiding her feelings came easily to her.

Eventually, Kodaka showed his new client out. Mrs Takenaga cast Wada a long frowning glance as she collected her Mitsukoshi carrier bag along with her umbrella. It was faintly disquieting. Wada could think of nothing she had done to merit such attention.

It had started to rain during the hour Mrs Takenaga had spent with Kodaka. The sky was unnaturally dark for the time of day and the rain, coursing down the window, appeared from Wada's place behind her desk to be coursing down Kodaka's forehead and cheeks as well as he stood close to the glass, gazing down, waiting, it was soon apparent, to see his visitor emerge on to the street.

'Hasui could have painted this,' he said at length, just as watery sunlight began to wash over his face. His interest in art, whenever it revealed itself, always came as a slight surprise to Wada. She was fond of Hasui's work herself, though she'd never mentioned this to Kodaka. 'He might have called it *Spring rain in Nihonbashi*. Takenaga-san has a traditional umbrella. Did you notice? Dark red.'

'Maroon.'

Kodaka smiled. 'Why do problems always seem simpler when I discuss them with you? I wonder. Perhaps your precision is the reason.' He turned towards her. 'Please lock the outer door and come into my office. Oh, and more tea would be welcome.'

The play of cloud and low sun was casting eerie variations of light across the walls of Kodaka's office when Wada delivered the tea and sat down, facing him across his desk. The green-shaded lamp wasn't on. Shadows were being given free rein, as Kodaka often seemed to prefer. There was cigarette smoke in the air, adding its own layer of haze to the atmosphere.

'Takenaga-san asked if she could smoke,' Kodaka said with an apologetic shrug. 'She was a little . . . nervous.'

Kodaka looked a little nervous himself, which was unlike him. But it was clear to Wada that he wanted to tell her why Mrs Takenaga had come to him. 'What is the nature of the case?' she enquired gently.

'The nature of the case?' Kodaka frowned pensively and took a sip of tea. 'Certainly this is not a normal problem. It is . . . complicated. And not just because of Takenaga-san's position. I will explain. Takenaga-san's father, Shitaro Masafumi, died when she was five. He committed suicide. Officially. She has never believed that. She believes he was murdered.'

7

'With good reason?'

Kodaka sucked his teeth. 'Hard to say. Masafumi died in Showa fifty-two.' 1977, fifty-second year of the Showa era, was more than forty years ago. Wada realized at once that the statute of limitations ruled out challenging a suicide verdict at such a distance in time.

'Too long ago for criminal or civil redress,' she remarked simply.

Kodaka nodded. 'Takenaga-san wants to know the truth, though. What she will do with the truth . . . I do not know. I am not sure she knows.'

'Can you get it for her?'

'Maybe it is already known. Masafumi was not a respectable man. He lived expensively, but the source of his income was unclear. He was suspected by the police of having sokaiya connections.'

Wada didn't need to be told anything about sokaiya. They were criminals who traded in commercial secrets, threatening to reveal damaging information, often at a company's AGM, unless they were paid off. Some had yakuza affiliations, some not. Kodaka had often been employed by companies to neutralize sokaiya threats.

'To escape arrest, which he is thought to have believed was imminent, Masafumi left the country, supposedly on holiday. He joined a tour party visiting Europe. Other members of the group described him as . . . distracted. He made many telephone calls and often sent telex messages from the hotels they stayed in. He looked worried all the time. He chain-smoked. He did not join in light conversation. They went first to Rome, then Paris, then London. While they were in London, Masafumi hired an English student who spoke good Japanese to act as his translator. He knew very little English himself, it seems. The translator was seen with him a lot. Sometimes they were in telephone boxes together, with the translator talking on the telephone while Masafumi stood beside him. Suspicious behaviour, certainly. The translator said he was "helping Masafumi-san do business".'

'What kind of business?'

'Unknown. But probably not legal. We can guess Masafumi was trying to raise money to get himself out of trouble. The translator could tell us. But he disappeared straight after Masafumi's death.'

'That is also suspicious.'

Kodaka nodded. 'I agree.'

'How did Masafumi die?'

'He used a plastic laundry bag in his hotel room to suffocate himself. Or . . .'

'Someone else used it to suffocate him.'

'Takenaga-san believes the translator killed him. Or knows who killed him. That was also her late mother's belief. Other members of the family believe he killed himself because he knew he would go to prison if he came home and may have wished to avoid bringing shame on them.'

'What do we know about the translator?'

'Very little. His name: Peter Evans. Estimated age: mid-twenties. A student, perhaps. Never traced. There was also a photograph.'

'Of Evans?'

'Of the tour party, standing in a group near St Paul's Cathedral. Masafumi was in the back row, with Evans standing beside him. But Evans moved just as the photograph was taken, so he was . . . blurred.'

'Takenaga-san showed you the photograph?'

'No. She no longer has it. It was sent to her mother by the member of the party who took it after they returned to Japan. It was later destroyed by Takenaga-san's uncle because . . .'

Kodaka paused to assemble his thoughts, then continued. 'Her mother gave her the photograph shortly before her death from cancer twenty-seven years ago. After her death, Takenaga-san, who was still unmarried then, arranged for a cropped portion of the photograph, with only Evans in it, to be printed in the personal advertisements page of the London evening newspaper, offering a reward of one thousand pounds to anyone who could identify him. The notice stated that this person had worked for her father in London in late August and early September of 1977. Anyone who *could* identify him was asked to write to her. This outraged her uncle, who was at that time supporting her financially and considered the matter of her father's death, *his* brother, best forgotten. So, he destroyed the photograph and forbade her to reply to any letters she received.'

'Did she receive any?'

'It was not likely she would, was it? A blurred photograph. Fifteen years after the event. With scant information. And all on the chance that someone who might know something would read that particular newspaper.'

'On that particular day.'

Kodaka smiled. 'Actually, the notice ran twice a week for a month.'

'But, still, she heard nothing?'

'Not at the time.'

'Nor since?'

Kodaka's smile broadened. He couldn't stop himself taking pleasure from such twists of fate as his clients sometimes brought him. And clearly there'd been such a twist in the matter of Mimori Takenaga. 'She had a letter . . . last week.'

'After twenty-seven years?'

'Remarkable, no?'

'Very.'

'The letter was sent on to Takenaga-san at her current address by the occupant of the house the Masafumi family had lived in back then. It was from an Englishman called Martin Caldwell. He said he had only recently seen the advertisement and believed he knew who Peter Evans was. That was not his real name, apparently. Caldwell did not say who Evans really was, but he implied there was a mystery surrounding him. Caldwell was willing to meet Takenaga-san to discuss the matter. Could she come to London for the purpose? He was not interested in the reward, but he *was* interested in helping her discover the truth, if she still wanted to pursue the matter.'

'As she does.'

'Oh yes. But she cannot go to London. Her husband takes the same view as her uncle of her father's long-ago supposed suicide. He would not allow her to go. She can contact Caldwell and arrange a meeting, since he has supplied her with his email address, but *she* cannot meet him. Even coming here had to be done under the cover of a shopping expedition. However, since Caldwell has never met her, there is no reason why someone claiming to be her – a woman of about her own age, suitably briefed and fluent in English – could not go instead.'

Silence fell. The implication was obvious. Kodaka had a mission for Wada. One more challenging than anything he'd previously asked her to do. She waited for him to make the request specific, but he seemed reluctant to do so. He sipped his tea and smiled weakly at her. Eventually, she took pity on him. 'You want me to go?'

He nodded. 'If you are willing.'

TWO

IT WAS A COOL, STILL, FITFULLY BRIGHT AFTERNOON IN LONDON. Commuting home by clipper ferry was one of the pleasures of Nick Miller's day. It was more pleasurable than usual this Friday because it was the start of the Easter holiday. He had three weeks of leisure to look forward to. No teaching. No commuting. And nothing to stop him doing some serious painting, especially for the first week, when his wife would be away with her friends in Tuscany.

The trimmed beard, unstructured jacket and loosely knotted tie marked him out as some kind of artistic professional. The tinted monoliths of Canary Wharf the ferry cruised past clearly weren't his natural territory. He surveyed them from the aft deck as he took sips of black coffee he hoped would clear his head after one end-of-term drink too many. And he wondered if Kate would be at home when he got there. It was end of term for her too, but she'd said something that morning about going round to Harriet's after leaving school to finalize arrangements for setting off the following morning.

She'd also asked him to buy some Parmesan cheese on his way home. As far as he could recall from a hustled conversation as they were both leaving the house, the cheese was the full extent of the shopping expected of him, which suggested dinner would be some pasta dish. He thought he might buy a bottle of wine to wash it down. Something Tuscan, maybe, to put Kate in the mood for her trip with the girls.

They were pleasant, simple thoughts for a spring afternoon turning towards evening. Then he realized, with something of a jolt, that he hadn't thought about his mother all day.

That had to be some kind of milestone, even though, in a sense, he'd done most of his mourning before she'd actually died, just after Christmas. And she wouldn't have wanted him to feel guilty about moving on with his life. No longer having to worry about her condition, her prognosis – how much of a future she had and how it was going to end – was a relief he hardly wanted to acknowledge, even to himself, though she'd told him that was how it would be. She'd worked as a psychotherapist, after all. She'd known how such things worked.

'I'm OK, Caro,' he murmured. She'd weaned him off 'Mummy' when he was about ten and insisted, in keeping with her New Age principles, on his using her first name. He took a deep breath of the crisp river air as he pictured her smile in his mind's eye. 'Forty-one and a stone overweight. But OK.'

Most of the passengers still aboard left with Nick at Greenwich. He headed for the shops, bought the cheese and wine, then ambled through the grounds of the old Royal Naval College and crossed Trafalgar Road. He was in no hurry. Whether Kate was home or not, he anticipated a late supper, in the kitchen, relaxing and swapping expectations for their different weeks ahead.

Greenwich Park rose ahead of him, long shadows stretching across its grassy slope, as he walked along Greenwich Park Street towards home. He led a privileged life. He knew that. Without Kate's family money they'd never be living in such a lovely part of London. The park, the college, the river. There was nothing to dislike about Greenwich except the hordes of tourists. Caro had often reminded him just how privileged he was. And, if she didn't, April, her partner of forty years, could be relied on to do it for her. Well, at least she was still there in his life to chip away at any signs of complacency.

He bounded up the steps to the yellow front door of their Georgian house and let himself in. The beeping of the alarm and the slew of post on the mat told him Kate wasn't home yet. No surprise, really. He silenced the alarm and carried the shopping into the kitchen, where he noticed the green message button flashing on the landline phone as he stood the carrier bag on the marble worktop. He went back to the front door to collect the post, then returned to the kitchen, sifting through the envelopes as he went. None of it looked very interesting.

He pressed the button on the phone. There was only one message, which, subconsciously, he assumed would be something trivial, since he'd have heard about anything important via his smartphone.

'Nick, this is . . . Martin Caldwell.'

Martin Caldwell? What did he want? They barely knew each other. He was a friend of Caro's from student days. And of April's. They'd shared a house in Exeter with several other students during their last year at the university. He'd come to Caro's funeral and Nick recalled meeting him a few times before that, spread over a lot of years. They'd exchanged a few words during the wake. But there'd been nothing to suggest Nick would ever hear from him again.

'You're probably wondering why I'm phoning you . . . out of the blue . . . like this.'

Nick was wondering exactly that. Caldwell's voice – soft, hesitant, unassertive – summoned for Nick a clear memory of his appearance at the funeral. Lean and hunched, with a narrow

14

face and grey hair worn too long, he was one of the few mourners who'd opted for black suit and tie, even though the suit didn't fit properly. He'd kept saying he couldn't believe Caro was dead. 'She was always so alive.' After a short while, Nick began to find him annoying and slipped away, leaving Caldwell . . . alone. Was that it, perhaps? Was he simply lonely?

'It took me a long time to find your number. I jotted it down after . . . you called me . . . about Caro's funeral.'

Nick had forgotten doing that. But he'd phoned quite a lot of people at the time, to take some of the load off April. He had no recollection of their conversation. There was no reason why he should.

'The thing is, something . . . rather surprising . . . has happened. And it, well, it's . . . something I think you need to know about. I mean . . . really need to know about.'

It was hard, if not impossible, to imagine what he could possibly be talking about. Nick waited, wondering if Caldwell was actually going to say what it was in the message.

'Could you phone me back as soon as possible, please? It's really . . . well, rather urgent. I'm going to be in London early next week. Could we, er . . . meet? I, er . . . seriously think we should. Give me a call . . . when you get this.' He recited his number.

Nick didn't think Caldwell lived in London. He seemed to recall someone saying, perhaps Caldwell himself, that he'd never actually left Exeter after university and had spent his working life in the city. And Nick had been told something else about where Caldwell lived that lay just out of his memory's reach.

'Leave a message if I don't answer and I'll get back to you as soon as I can. I'll, er . . . look forward to hearing from you.'

The message ended. Nick pondered what to do. It seemed unlikely he really did need to know what Caldwell had to tell him. But he was going to have to find out, just to put his mind at rest. And it would be easier to do that before Kate got back. He brewed some coffee and carried it upstairs to the study.

Sitting down at the desk, he listened to the message again, which made no more sense second time round, then dialled Martin Caldwell's number.

It rang a long time before Caldwell answered. Then, 'Hello?' came the doleful voice, quite suddenly.

'Martin? This is Nick Miller.'

'Ah. Nick. Yes. Er, thanks . . . for calling back.'

'How can I help you?'

'Well, can we meet, as I suggested? I'm, er . . . going to be in London on Monday. I'm guessing you've just started your Easter holiday. You teach, don't you?'

'Yes.'

'So, could we . . .'

'What's this about, Martin?'

'About?'

'Yes. Whatever it is, can't we discuss it now, over the phone?'

Long pause. 'No. No, I don't think that would be . . . a good idea. It's . . . complicated.'

'Can't you give me some inkling of what this is about? You said in your message something surprising had happened.'

'Well, it has.'

'And what is it?'

'I can't . . . Look, Nick, I don't want to tread on any toes, but I think you're entitled to know.'

'Know *what*?'

'Well, it's . . . about your father.'

'My *father*?' What *was* the guy talking about? Nick had never known his father. Geoff Nolan, another occupant of the shared house in Exeter, had refused to have anything to do with Nick's upbringing and had died of a drugs overdose before he was thirty. A long time ago Nick had tried to track down Nolan's family, without success. All he had to remember his father by was one fuzzy snapshot given him by Caro.

'Yes. Like I say, it's . . . complicated. I'd be much happier . . . talking about it face to face. *Is* Monday any good for you?'

'You're going to have to give me something more now you've mentioned my father, Martin.'

'And I will. On Monday. We really shouldn't . . . discuss this on the phone.' The hint of cloak and dagger irritated Nick. In fact, Martin Caldwell was pretty irritating all round. 'You live in Greenwich, don't you?'

'Yes. But—'

'Shall I come there? Around . . . mid-afternoon?'

Nick took a moment to think. He could continue badgering Caldwell into telling him what the hell this was all about right now or he could just let him have his way. In the end, the easiest course was to give in. 'OK. If you really think it's important.'

'Oh it is. Yes. Definitely. I can't really . . . overestimate its importance.'

No? That seemed unlikely. But Nick supposed there was an outside chance it would at least be interesting. Perhaps it was something Caldwell had felt unable to disclose while Caro was alive. Nick couldn't help being curious. Caldwell had undeniably known his father, after all. They'd lived under the same roof for a year. 'Monday it is, then. Shall we say four o'clock?'

'Yes. Let's say that. What's your address?'

After the call had ended, Nick leant back in the chair and thought about the father he'd never known. According to Caro, she'd still been confused about her sexuality during her time at university. Geoff Nolan had inadvertently helped her decide that men weren't for her. He'd always been a hopeless case, heading for early burn-out and wanting to know nothing – absolutely nothing – about his son. So why should Nick want to know anything about him?

There was no good reason. He pulled out from one of the desk drawers the old cigar box in which he kept assorted mementos of his childhood, including that solitary creased photograph of Geoff Nolan, aged twenty-one or so, sitting astride his motorbike at a kerbside and looking up at a first-floor window where Caro, presumably, was poised with the camera. He was in black biking leathers, one hand resting on a crash helmet, propped on the fuel tank, while his other hand was raised in a strangely lordly greeting. Long dark hair flopped over his forehead. His smile was somehow not genuine. It seemed calculated to mock something or someone, possibly himself.

Nick wouldn't have wanted to admit how often he'd looked at that photograph when he was younger, trying to draw some clues to his father's personality from his posture and expression. But there were none to be found. It was just a snapshot of a headstrong young man who'd had no idea he wasn't going to see out his twenties. It was just a picture. Geoff Nolan wasn't really there. He never had been.

Nick put the photograph back and replaced the box at the back of the drawer. Then he heard a noise downstairs – Kate's key turning in the front door lock. On a sudden impulse, he picked up the phone and deleted Caldwell's message.

'Darling?' came Kate's voice from below.

'Up here,' he shouted in reply.

'Did you remember the cheese?'

'I remembered.' Caldwell's message was gone now. Removed from the log. Kate would be in Tuscany all next week. There was no need for her to worry about what Nick was or wasn't going to learn from the guy. He'd tell her when she got back – if there was anything to tell.

'There's a bottle of red wine down here I'm tempted to open.' She was in the kitchen now.

'Succumb to temptation, then.' Nick put the phone down, stood up and headed for the door, confident he could put Martin Caldwell out of his mind. Until Monday.

THREE

MIMORI TAKENAGA HADN'T YET REPLIED TO MARTIN CALDWELL'S invitation to meet in London, so the first item of business for Wada, having agreed to go to London on her behalf, was to contact him. She kept the message brief but courteous and signed herself off as Mimori Takenaga family Masafumi. The swiftness of Caldwell's response took her and Kodaka aback. Within an hour, after a few more email exchanges, they had an appointment for the following Tuesday morning, at the British Museum tea room.

There was no denying, though Wada would have denied it, that she was excited about her mission to London. She'd only been there once before, with Hiko, during a honeymoon holiday in Europe. All she remembered of the city were the traditional picture postcard scenes: Big Ben, Buckingham Palace, Tower Bridge, Trafalgar Square. It would be interesting to discover how returning to somewhere she'd only ever been with Hiko would affect her. And even if it turned out to be a waste of time, Mrs Takenaga had already paid Kodaka more than enough to cover the cost of the journey, so there was nothing to be lost by it.

There was, however, something Kodaka didn't mention to her until after she'd made the appointment with Caldwell. And the timing of his disclosure struck her as suspicious. Had he wanted her to commit herself before he revealed this additional element in the Takenaga case?

'You should know that Takenaga-san also made accusations against a man her mother told her had been her father's business partner back in Showa fifty-two. He was never under police investigation, but she claims, again according to her mother, that straight after Masafumi's death this man took all the money from a secret bank account they had been operating. There was supposedly a lot of money in the account, accumulated through sokaiya activities. Masafumi had spoken to his wife of a figure in the tens of millions of yen. So his death could be seen as . . . highly profitable for his partner.'

'Do we know who the former partner is?' Wada asked.

'Yes.' The time for tea had passed. Evening was encroaching. The shadows within Kodaka's office were deepening. He pulled out the whisky bottle and poured them both a glass. 'Hiroji Nishizaki,' he said quietly.

Wada said nothing for a moment. If one of the country's leading entrepreneurs, founder and chairman of the Nishizaki Corporation, was somehow implicated in the death of Shitaro Masafumi, then the need to tread carefully – very carefully indeed – hardly needed stating. The Nishizaki Corporation had grown over recent decades into an investment and consultancy giant, prospering initially by buying and selling stakes in other companies, usually at just the right time, and more recently by dispensing expensive advice to those convinced they needed their expert guidance. The corporation had split into two supposedly autonomous branches to avoid any perceived conflicts of interest, Nishizaki Investment and Nishizaki Consultancy. But not everyone was convinced about their autonomy since

Hiroji Nishizaki was firmly in charge of both. Was he a leech on the commercial efforts of others? Or a shrewd judge of what was and wasn't profitable? Opinion was divided, but there was no doubt about Nishizaki's success. He'd become staggeringly wealthy. And the Nishizaki Corporation was a fixture near the top of the Nikkei index.

'Do not mention this to anyone,' Kodaka continued. 'The fact that Shitaro Masafumi knew Hiroji Nishizaki more than forty years ago – if it *is* a fact – proves nothing, particularly in relation to the circumstances of Masafumi's death. We should regard it as background information, nothing more. All you have to do in London is listen to what Caldwell says and report what you learn from him.'

'I will do that.'

'Good.'

'Still, this could be . . . a complication.'

'Potentially, yes.' Kodaka drained his glass and refilled it. Wada had so far taken only the tiniest sip of her whisky 'But our efforts for the moment should be confined to identifying Peter Evans.'

'A copy of his photograph would be helpful.'

'I agree.'

'I will try to access the archives of the newspaper in which the advertisement appeared.'

Kodaka squinted at the notes he'd made while talking to Mrs Takenaga. He had to turn the desk lamp on before he could decipher them. His whisky glistened like gold in the pool of light it cast. 'The London *Evening Standard*,' he read. 'May, 1992.'

'I will start straight away.'

'Leave it until tomorrow, Wada. A tired mind finds nothing.'

'When shall I fly to London?'

'When you like.'

'I will book for Monday morning if I can.'

'I may have more information for you by then. Tomorrow I go to Fukuoka. Takenaga-san gave me the name and address of the tour party member who sent her mother the group photograph. If the lady is still living . . .'

'It is a long time ago.'

'And it is a long way to go. But I might learn much. I will be back in time to manage the office while you are away.'

Wada paused to think about that, then said, 'Please leave most things as they are.'

Kodaka smiled. 'Of course.'

On her long subway journey home that night, Wada found herself thinking about the Nishizaki connection in the case more and more. There'd been something in Kodaka's tone of voice when he spoke of him that suggested he knew a little more about Nishizaki than he was willing to disclose. He often kept information to himself and there were things he did Wada was happy to know nothing about. For that matter, there were innumerable cases he'd handled before Wada started working for him that might for all she knew have involved Nishizaki. Sokaiya were a specialty of Kodaka's. And Mrs Takenaga had alleged that Nishizaki had once been sokaiya himself. Wada didn't feel entirely certain she was being told all she needed to know. Which, rather to her surprise, she found more intriguing than disturbing.

At her small apartment, she consumed a frugal supper and then, ignoring Kodaka's advice, immediately went online to see if there was an accessible digital archive for the London *Evening Standard*.

The result was frustrating. It seemed she could view copies dating from 1892, but 1992 was a different matter. Physical copies of papers could be inspected at the national newspaper archive, but that wasn't in or even near London. She abandoned the effort and moved on to more straightforward matters, starting with the booking of a flight. She found a seat on an eleven o'clock Monday morning departure, with flexible return dates. Next she booked herself a room for four nights at the Envoy Hotel, chosen because it was the hotel where, according to Mrs Takenaga, the tour party had been staying at the time of Shitaro Masafumi's death back in 1977. Now she was set.

Normally a sound sleeper, Wada woke several times that night and eventually rose early but by no means refreshed. Meditating, which she tried to do every morning, proved almost impossible. She decided to go in to the office.

She'd been planning to spend a few hours there anyway, albeit later in the day, to clear a few administrative tasks she'd otherwise have attended to in the week ahead. Peace reigned in Nihonbashi on a Saturday morning in spring. Birds skittered and chirped in flight. The air seemed to sparkle. Now she was up and doing something, she felt calmer, more in charge of herself.

The lobby of the office building was quiet, the porter behind the desk registering surprise at her arrival with the merest twitch of his eyebrows. She smiled and said good morning. He returned the greeting.

Then, as she approached the lift, there was a ping, the doors slid open and Kazuto Kodaka stepped out.

It was at once obvious to Wada he hadn't expected to see her. There was a flinch of dismay before he reordered his expression. 'Wada,' he said. 'Back so soon?'

'I have rather a lot to attend to.'

'Ah yes.' Kodaka was wearing a light raincoat over his workaday suit and was carrying a small travelling bag as well as a bulging shoulder bag. 'Of course.'

'Did you forget something?'

'My notebook.' He patted his jacket pocket. 'It was stupid of me to leave it here.' It was also unlike him.

'When is your train?'

'I am on the nine ten Nozomi.' He glanced at the clock behind the reception desk. 'There is time.' He seemed suddenly to relax. 'Will you walk with me to the station? We can talk on the way.'

Tokyo Station was an easy walk from their office, easier than usual, in fact, so early on a Saturday morning. They moved at an expeditious clip past the towering headquarters of assorted Japanese financial institutions. Wada suddenly realized she didn't actually know where the Nishizaki Corporation's HQ was situated. It could be just round the next corner for all she knew.

Kodaka seemed to read her thoughts. 'Nishizaki's head office is in Ginza,' he said. 'More places to entertain clients, I guess.'

'Have you ever handled a case involving Nishizaki before, Kodaka-san?'

'Maybe this case does not involve him.'

'Maybe.'

'And maybe I have not answered your question. Is that what you are thinking?'

'I had no luck with the photograph.'

'You have already tried?'

'Waiting would not have helped.'

'You have booked your flight also?'

'JAL, Monday morning. As we discussed.'

'And the Envoy Hotel?'

'I have a room there.'

'Much will have changed in forty-two years. I am not sure staying at the same hotel will tell you anything.'

'I have to stay somewhere.'

'You have a brother in New York, I think you told me once.'

25

'Yes.' Haruto was, if anything, more of a disappointment to their mother than she was. At least she'd been married. Haruto had never even managed that. 'He is with Nomura Securities.'

'When did you last see him?'

At their father's funeral was the answer. But she preferred to be less specific. 'Three years ago.'

'Too long. You should arrange a visit.'

'Perhaps when we are less busy.'

'Ah yes.' Kodaka looked up at the sky as they waited to cross the next street. Wada looked as well. Whether she saw what Kodaka saw she couldn't have said. 'I wonder when that will be.'

No more was said about Nishizaki. Kodaka's silence on the subject hung between them, not as an awkwardness so much as a suspended question.

Tokyo Station was already busy with weekend travellers. Wada and Kodaka were two inconspicuous figures in the bustle. Kodaka squinted up at the Shinkanzen information board for news of his train.

'On time,' said Wada. 'Platform sixteen.'

Kodaka smiled. 'Thank you.'

'I wish you a successful trip.'

'You also. Proceed carefully with Caldwell. Give him nothing. We need information. We do not need to give *him* information.'

'That may be difficult.'

'Regarding Nishizaki . . .'

'Yes?'

'There have always been rumours about sokaiya connections. It could explain his ability to predict so accurately whether a company had a prosperous future ahead of it or not. There are other, darker rumours also. But that is often so with successful people. Rivals tend to attribute their success to . . . underhand methods. Some cases I have handled . . . bore his shadow. I do not know how else to put it. Implications of Nishizaki Corporation personnel being involved in the background. But never the foreground. Nothing I could ever tie down. Still, if this is another such case . . . caution is required. You understand?'

'I am always cautious.'

Kodaka nodded. 'So you are. That is why I employ you.' He glanced up the stairs towards the platforms. 'I must go, Wada. Keep in regular contact, yes?'

'I will.'

The hint of a bow. And Kodaka was gone, hurrying towards the stairs.

Halfway up them, he turned and gave her a chopped little farewell wave. She couldn't be sure if he was smiling or not. But she was as she raised her hand in response. Even though she wasn't certain there was actually anything to smile about.

Wada returned to the office, turning over in her mind the question of what it was Kodaka had taken with him. She dismissed the idea that he really had forgotten his notebook. No, he'd come in to collect something quite specific, possibly connected to Hiroji Nishizaki. She'd certainly been intending to look through the cabinets where he kept the files of closed cases to see if there was something relevant in one of them. But now she rather suspected there was no point in making the effort.

She decided to try even so. Kodaka was a poor manager of paperwork. But she found nothing about Nishizaki.

For that, of course, there was an obvious explanation.

Kodaka had removed it.

FOUR

KATE HAD LEFT FOR HER TUSCAN HOLIDAY, BUT NICK DID NOT HAVE the rest of the weekend to himself. Hearing from Kate that he'd be alone, April asked him over for Sunday lunch.

This was no ordinary Sunday lunch. It was the first of the traditional boozy gatherings of her and Caro's friends since Caro's death and as such an important milestone in April's recovery from the loss of the woman she'd loved and lived with all of Nick's life.

Growing up with two mothers and no father was rarer in Nick's childhood than it had subsequently become. To him it was just normality, of course, though some of the other boys at his school hadn't seen it that way. But Caro and April had never mollycoddled him. In fact, April used to joke that if there wasn't a father in his life at least there was a father *figure* – her. Looking back from the perspective of early middle age at the often chaotic nature of family life chez Caro and April, Nick couldn't help being surprised by how they'd somehow managed to be passably good parents.

Many of the friends who would be at the lunch party were fellow veterans of the Greenham Common women-only anti-cruise missile protests of the 1980s. In Nick's childhood, Caro and April had virtually taken turns being arrested for trying to scale the fence at the RAF base. He supposed he should have been grateful one of them always stayed home to look after him.

Feminism, pacifism and socialism, augmented in many cases by vegetarianism and more recently veganism, were the elements that bound this now ageing sisterhood together. Nick was tolerated despite being a man, an unapologetic meat-eater and a floating voter largely because of sentimental memories of him as a little boy. One of the protests had involved hanging photographs of the women's children on the fence and, as one of those children, Nick enjoyed a special status.

It was a fine morning, so Nick decided to walk. He headed up through Greenwich Park, stopped for coffee in Blackheath, then ambled on south-west through Lewisham. As he approached Caro and April's house – just April's now, of course – he wondered, not for the first time, how they'd managed to handle money so badly over the years that they'd drifted steadily down the London property ladder, from a gabled semi in Dulwich that was the site of his earliest memories to a large but comfortless house not quite far enough west of the centre of Catford to be called Forest Hill. 'Because money was never our thing,' Caro would have told him. And there was certainly no disputing that.

When he arrived, the party was already underway. April, who'd lost weight during Caro's illness, was beginning to put some back on. She was more like the April Nick always pictured in his mind's eye: fleshy, flush-cheeked and sparkling-eyed, with short blonde-grey hair and a ready grin. The colour in her cheeks was partly due, he suspected, to the amount of gin she'd already drunk.

'God, Nicky,' she confided as they hugged, 'I had a good cry this morning thinking about times like this in the past when Caro was the life and soul of the party. But it's onwards and upwards, so have a drink, socialize and stay cheerful. That's an order, OK?'

Nick grabbed a bottle of beer and started circulating among the guests, most of whom he'd known for years. They were mostly in their sixties, politically committed Baby Boomers horrified by Brexit and global warming who tended to live in more select neighbourhoods themselves but heaped praise on Caro and April for choosing – as if it had been a choice – to settle some-where 'authentic'. Teaching in the private sector, as Nick did, meant he always had to endure a certain amount of sarcasm. But at least he taught art, which somehow excused a lot.

Most people had taken their drinks out into the garden, where the fitful sunshine made it just warm enough to stand around. Glancing back at the house while he listened smilingly to several old friends of his mother as they chatted about themselves and their children, he saw April tasting a dish that was simmering away in the kitchen. She was with Nan, a younger woman Nick had already been fleetingly introduced to. Something in their body language – he couldn't have said exactly what – made him think they could be more than just friends. He was surprised to realize he was neither horrified nor delighted by the thought. April had every right to seek happiness wherever she could find it. But it was another milestone measuring the passage of time since Caro's death. And it was a sobering one in its way.

The afternoon went well. The wine flowed and the world was set to rights in bittersweet debates that somehow failed to identify the secret foe who'd frustrated their high hopes for a better future. They were good people. They thought good things. And

Nick liked them, most of all because they brought him as close to his mother, who thought and spoke and *believed* as they did, as he was ever going to get now she was gone.

When the party broke up, April encouraged Nick to linger. Over coffee and brandy, she soon began to talk about Caro and Nick saw a chance to ask about Martin Caldwell.

'Do you remember exactly when you first met Caro?'

'You must have asked me that before, Nicky. What did I say?'

He smiled. 'I'm not sure.'

And she smiled too. 'Probably because I'm not sure either. But meet we did, I'm glad to say.'

'Before you lived in the same house?'

'Definitely. One of the reasons I moved in there was to be close to Caro and persuade her she wanted to be close to me.'

'I was speaking to Martin Caldwell after the funeral. He lived there too, didn't he?'

'Marty? Yeah. What did he tell you?' Was there something more than natural curiosity to the question? Nick wasn't sure. April wasn't always the open book she claimed to be.

'He didn't say much about it.'

'Marty never really fitted in. Too . . . tightly buttoned. Always a bit of a loner. I'm not sure he's ever been really happy. The last few times I've seen him, I've got the impression he's . . . adrift. There's no one in his life. Never has been, as far as I know. And he's retired now, of course, so he doesn't see many people from day to day. It's not a good way to end up.'

'How many people lived in the house?'

'Oh, six or seven. It was difficult to keep track with all the boyfriends and girlfriends who came and went.'

To avoid giving the impression he was obsessed with Caldwell, Nick threw in another name he'd heard mentioned. 'Miranda Cushing was one of your co-tenants as well, wasn't she?'

'Yeah. But that was before she set her sights on higher things.'
Those higher things had eventually taken Miranda Cushing into Parliament, where she'd outraged Caro and April by voting in favour of the Iraq invasion. Tony Blair had rewarded her with a junior ministerial post and later a peerage. Caro and April had rewarded her with withering accusations of treachery and warmongering. Nick had never met the woman, but he'd certainly heard a lot about her, whether he wanted to or not.

'And Marty? Was he a good friend of . . . my father?'

April started with surprise. 'Christ, Nicky, it's a lot of years since you mentioned *him*.'

'I know. But I'm an orphan now. It makes you think.'

'Only a child can be an orphan. Besides, luckily for you, you've still got *me*. And I'm not going anywhere any time soon. So come over here and give me a hug.'

And so, Nick didn't fail to notice, another question was dodged.

Half an hour later, as Nick was preparing to leave, he decided to chance one last enquiry about Martin Caldwell. 'There was something he said to me after the funeral that I can't quite remember. About the house you all lived in in Exeter. He still lives in the city, doesn't he?'

'Yeah.' April seemed to debate with herself whether to expand on the point, then decided to go for it. 'The daft bugger doesn't just live in Exeter, Nicky. He lives in the house we all shared. Well, in a flat in it, anyway. The same fucking house. Can you believe it?'

That was it. That was what Caldwell had slipped into their brief conversation. 'Maybe he wants to be reminded of his student past.'

'If you ask me, he wants to *live* in his student past. Which is plain unhealthy.'

'You think so?'

'We all have to move with the current, Nicky. That's what living is. And that's what I'm trying to do, as best I can.'

He put his arm round her shoulder. 'Today went well, April. Caro would be proud of you.'

Tears welled in her eyes. 'She'd be proud of you too. She always was.' She thumbed the tears away and gave him a stern look. 'You're not going to mope while Kate's away, are you?'

'Of course not.' He grinned at her. 'I've got plenty to keep me busy.'

Indeed he did. But early the following morning, however, as he was brewing his first coffee of the day, things took an unexpected turn. The phone rang. When he answered, he heard Caldwell's distinctively soft voice on the other end of the line. Though there was an edge to it that hadn't been there on Friday. He sounded either nervous or excited, or both. Nick had given him his mobile number, but it seemed he preferred to use the landline.

'This is Martin Caldwell, Nick. Are you . . . alone?'

'Sorry?'

'I mean . . . are you free to talk?'

'Just go ahead, Martin. What's the problem?'

'I'm not going to be able to keep our . . . appointment . . . this afternoon.'

'You aren't?'

'I'm terribly sorry.'

So was Nick, to his surprise. 'That's a pity.'

'Could we postpone it . . . by twenty-four hours?'

'I, er, don't see why not.'

'Something's come up . . . that complicates my travel plans.'

What might that be, Nick asked himself, in the reputedly empty life of Martin Caldwell? 'OK. So, tomorrow afternoon, then?'

'Yes. That . . . should be all right.'

'You're sure?'

'I'm really sorry . . . to mess you around.'

'Never mind. By the way, I've remembered since we last spoke that you told me at the funeral you still live in the house you shared as a student with Caro and April and . . . my father.'

'Not *still*. There was a gap of quite a few years . . . before I moved back in again. And . . . it had changed a lot.'

'I guess it would have.'

'We could arrange for you to see it . . . if you wanted. It might help you . . . get a clearer picture.'

'A clearer picture of what?'

'Did Caro ever talk about the other people who lived there?'

'Not much. There was Miranda Cushing, of course.'

'I wasn't thinking of Miranda.'

'Who, then?'

'Peter Ellery and Alison Parker. Have their names ever cropped up?'

'No, I don't think so.'

'No. Neither do I.'

'What do you mean?'

'I can't . . . say any more right now. I'll, er . . . see you tomorrow. Say . . . five o'clock. Yes?'

'I'll be here.'

'It's, er . . . possible I might be . . . a little late. But, er . . . Well, I'll see you tomorrow.'

'Is there something wrong, Martin?'

Long pause. Then: 'I'll explain everything . . . when we meet.'

And that was it. He'd hung up.

As he drank his coffee, Nick began to wonder whether Caldwell was playing some kind of perverse game, trying to make himself seem mysterious and important with all this switching of

34

times and days and implications of great revelations to come. Exeter was only a couple of hours from London by train. What exactly was his problem?

That thought prompted Nick to check whether Caldwell had phoned from Exeter. But another surprise awaited him. Caldwell had withheld his number. And Nick could think of no reason why he would do that. Other than the obvious one, of course. He wasn't in Exeter. And he didn't want Nick to know where he'd gone. Or maybe . . . he couldn't risk Nick knowing.

What the hell was going on? And who on God's green earth were Peter Ellery and Alison Parker?

FIVE

WADA VISITED HER MOTHER ON SUNDAY AFTERNOON. SHE GENERALLY substituted a lengthy telephone conversation for an actual visit until Haha's complaints about never seeing her daughter became so insistent there was nothing for it but to turn up in person.

It would have been impossible for Wada to explain that the primary reason for her reluctance to visit the tiny house in Koishikawa wasn't a wish to avoid her mother but the depression that always settled on her when she went back there. She didn't quite understand why returning to the scene of her earliest memories dragged her spirits down, but certainly it did, despite many of those memories, particularly if they involved her father, being happy ones.

Wada steered well clear, as ever, of a mother and daughter heart-to-heart. 'You are a mystery to me,' Haha often lamented. Which was as Wada preferred it. As she'd grown older, she'd found more and more comfort in the privacy of her thoughts. On this occasion, she was also able to plead professional confidentiality as a reason why she couldn't say anything about her trip to London beyond the fact that it was taking place. Conversation was therefore largely confined to Haha's complaints about inconvenient alterations to the ward refuse collection arrangements and confusing changes of stock location in her local minimarket.

Wada wondered if Kodaka would call her at some point on Sunday to report on what he'd been able to find out in Fukuoka. But no call came that day and she knew better than to call him. If he needed to be in touch, he would be.

No call came the following morning either. Still Wada wasn't concerned. Kodaka always kept as much information as possible to himself. She was confident she'd hear from him after she reached London. He'd said he expected to be back in Tokyo by Monday evening at the latest.

Wada had decided to put the long flight to London to good use by brushing up on her English. She'd bought an English translation of her favourite novel, *Sasameyuki*, by Junichiro Tanizaki, to read on the plane. The title in English was *The Makioka Sisters*, which didn't capture any of the allusive subtlety of the Japanese original. Understandably, the translator had failed to find any way to convey in English what the word *sasameyuki* – lightly falling snow – conjured up for a Japanese reader.

This didn't surprise Wada. She found the differences between the two languages fascinating even when they were also frustrating. As for *Sasameyuki*, she'd first read it aloud, to Hiko, during the early months of the coma he'd never woken from. The doctors had told her recovery was out of the question, but it had taken her a long time to believe them and, during that time, Tanizaki's leisurely tale had been the only source of consolation she could find.

She started reading the book on the train to Narita airport and continued after the plane had taken off. She felt too alert

37

to follow the example of many other passengers and snatch a few hours' sleep before the scheduled mid-afternoon arrival in London. Her view of jet lag was dismissive. She intended simply to view Monday as an unusually long day, but her resolve didn't sustain her much beyond struggling through disembarkation, baggage reclaim and immigration checks at Heathrow. She actually fell asleep on the train into London and reached the Envoy Hotel, just off Russell Square, yawning uncontrollably and with her eyes watering in the spring sunshine.

The Envoy was a conventionally smart hotel for tourists and business travellers. As she checked in, Wada managed to register the fact that it had been thoroughly modernized. As Kodaka had surmised, she wasn't going to learn much about what had happened there forty-two years in the past simply by being a guest in the present.

Her room's bland but comfortable furnishings told the same story. Even if she could learn the number of the room Shitaro Masafumi had died in, it would make no difference. The Envoy Hotel of 1977 was out of her reach.

She'd checked her phone on landing for a message from Kodaka, but there'd been nothing. It was past midnight now in Tokyo, so it was likely he'd wait till morning to contact her.

That gave her the chance to get some of the sleep she needed. She could barely keep her eyes open by now. Unpacking could wait. She closed the curtains and lay down on the bed.

When she woke, it took her a few seconds to remember she was in London, not Tokyo. She had no idea what time it was. Checking her phone, she was appalled to discover she'd slept for more than seven hours. There was a glow of street lamps beyond the curtains and a shushing noise of traffic on wet tarmac. It must have rained while she was asleep.

38

There was a message on her phone, but not from Kodaka. She didn't recognize the number. She opened it, even so.

It was a text message, from the lawyer Kodaka used whenever one of his cases became legally sensitive. Wada had never actually met Norifusa Dobachi, though she'd spoken to him and his secretary on the telephone quite a few times. Her impression of him was that he was a cautious, meticulous man. She was surprised he had her phone number. And she was even more surprised by his message.

Please excuse mode of contact. Please call as soon as possible. Very urgent.

If Dobachi said something was very urgent, Wada was inclined to believe him. She put a call through to his office number on the hotel phone, fearing her own phone mightn't have enough charge left to sustain a lengthy conversation at international rates.

She half expected to be greeted by a recorded message, since it was only just past eight o'clock in the morning in Tokyo. But the phone was answered promptly, by Dobachi himself.

'Dobachi-san. This is Wada.'

'Wada-san. You are not calling on the number where I left the message?'

'No. This is a hotel phone. I am not in the country.'

'I know where you are. Kodaka-san notified me of your trip.'

'He did?'

'I will explain shortly. But in the present situation your choice of telephone is probably wise. You should take all precautions that Kodaka-san may have taught you.'

'What has happened?'

She heard him sigh before replying. It was almost a groan. 'Kodaka-san is dead.'

For a moment, Wada couldn't speak. How could it be true? She'd seen and spoken to Kodaka only three days ago. How

39

could his life – everything he amounted to – have ceased to exist since then?

'Hit-and-run,' Dobachi continued solemnly. 'Near his apartment, last night. The police contacted me because they found my card in his wallet. He was crossing a street after leaving his local minimarket.'

'I do not know what to say. This is . . . terrible.'

'Indeed. Very terrible. According to the police it may have been deliberate. The car hit him twice. Witnesses said it knocked him down, then stopped and drove over him before speeding off. None of them recorded the registration number. Nor could any of them describe the driver, though they thought there were two men in the car.'

'Why would anyone do such a thing, Dobachi-san?'

'I cannot say. But a private detective makes enemies. It is the nature of the profession.'

'There has been no threat to him that I am aware of.'

'If he had been threatened, would he have told you? Knowing him as I do, I suspect not.'

'When did he tell you I was leaving the country?'

'Yesterday afternoon. After you had left. He came here to see me, without an appointment. He was . . . extremely anxious. He had just returned from a business trip to Fukuoka, he said, and had gone straight to his office. It had been broken into and searched. The computer had been stolen. Along with various paper files. He did not think it was a simple burglary. I asked about you, which was when he told me he had sent you to London . . . for reasons related to his journey to Fukuoka. This is true?'

'Yes.'

'You must judge whether it is wise for you to continue with whatever he asked you to undertake. You are no longer working for him, sadly. There is no contract you are bound by. Legally speaking, the Kodaka Detective Agency is no more. I will, of course, attend to the formalities of winding up the business. It would be easier to do so with your assistance, but . . . I would understand if . . .'

'Did Kodaka-san tell you about the case that took him to Fukuoka?'

'He gave me no details. But my impression was that he regarded the break-in at his office as a clear sign of danger. For himself . . . and you.'

The implications of what had happened swirled in Wada's mind. Kodaka was dead. The office computer and assorted files had been stolen. And she was alone, on the other side of the world, with an appointment fixed for the following morning with a stranger. The shock of Dobachi's news solidified into dread. What should she do? How should she react?

'He mentioned another person, Wada-san. Mimori Takenaga. You know her?'

'A client.'

'*The* client? In the present case?'

'Yes.'

'I will make discreet enquiries about her present situation. As for you . . .'

'If the danger is real, I cannot ignore it.'

'You could . . . make it obvious you have abandoned the case. Go somewhere . . . for a holiday . . . before returning home. I will take no steps to cancel your company credit card.'

Was that why Kodaka had mentioned her brother Haruto to Wada during their last – their very last – conversation? To plant in her mind the idea of taking refuge with him in New York if she needed to? If so, he must have known they were playing with fire by taking on Mrs Takenaga as a client. Which surely meant he'd known far more about the background to the case than he'd revealed.

41

'There is one other thing I have to tell you, Wada-san. While you consider what to do.'

'What is it?'

'Kodaka-san left a file with me. He took it with him to Fukuoka, so it was not there when the office was broken into. I received the impression that he had taken it with him to guard against such an eventuality.'

So much for the forgotten notebook, Wada reflected. This file was what he'd gone back to the office for on Saturday morning. Which meant it was central to the case. 'What does the file contain?'

There was a delicate pause before Dobachi replied. 'Numerous documents. I have not inspected them. Kodaka-san did not authorize me to do so. But he did authorize me to pass the file on to you. If you want me to.'

Wada assumed the file was one of the many bulging manila folders Kodaka lodged in his filing cabinet. 'What is written on the front of the folder?' she asked. Something always was, in Kodaka's scrawled hand, though not always something helpful. Kodaka played little shorthand games with himself when it came to record-keeping.

In answer, Dobachi used the word *kage-boshi*, which meant a shadow, specifically a shadow of a person. And Wada instantly remembered what Kodaka had said to her about Hiroji Nishizaki and his business activities. *Some cases I have handled bore his shadow.* 'You know what this means, Wada-san?' Dobachi asked.

'I think so, yes.'

'You can direct me what to do with the file. Kodaka-san was very clear that it would be a matter for you . . . in his absence.'

A matter for her. Wada might have been angry with Kodaka for putting her in such a position. But anger never came easily to her. Her mother had often complained she was altogether too calm for her own good. Well, that was her nature. Just as obliqueness had been Kodaka's.

'If you wish,' Dobachi continued, 'I can store the file in my safe here. Or . . . I can destroy it.'

'Please do not destroy it.' Her reaction to the idea was instinctive. She couldn't bear to think of the material Kodaka had carefully amassed being shredded or incinerated.

'I will store it, then. Unless . . .'

'Can you send it to me?'

'Of course. Kodaka-san gave me the address of your hotel. But please consider carefully, Wada-san. You are not obliged in any way to pursue this matter. It could be argued that it is not even appropriate for you to pursue it now the Kodaka Detective Agency is no longer functioning. It might be altogether wiser for you to . . . drop it.'

'By wiser you mean safer?'

It took Dobachi several seconds to summon an answer. But, when it came, it was unambiguous. 'Yes.'

Wada thought for a moment, then said, 'May I call you back later with a decision?'

'Please do. I will be here most of the day.'

'Thank you, Dobachi-san.'

Wada set her phone to charge, took two miniatures of gin and a can of tonic water out of the minibar and poured the contents into a glass. She turned off the bedside light and opened the curtains. Rain was slashing across the glass in random tear-tracks. She sat down on the bed and took a deep swallow of the gin. Then she leant back against the headboard, cradling the glass in her lap.

She felt safe here, in the dark, in a hotel room, in a city where no one knew her. But safe for how long? If they'd gone as far as murder to stop Kodaka, wasn't she likely to suffer the same fate

43

once she returned to Japan? If Nishizaki had sokaiya connections, commissioning another hit-and-run or something similar wouldn't be too difficult. In fact, it would make sense, as insurance against the possibility that she knew too much.

She worked her way steadily through the gin. The alcohol stilled some of her anxiety and helped her see her situation more clearly. She didn't know too much. She knew barely anything, in fact. That was what she had to change. That was her only recourse.

She picked up the hotel phone and dialled Dobachi's number. There was a gulf of silence before it began ringing.

Then he answered. 'Wada-san?'

'Yes.'

'Have you made your decision?'

'Send me the file.'

Wada barely slept for the rest of the night. By asking Dobachi to send her the file, she'd committed herself to remaining in London for several days at least. And, in effect, she'd committed herself to continuing what Kodaka had so fatefully started. Every time she thought it through, it seemed that was what she had to do. Every course of action, even *in*action, held its hazards. Yet still the timid, unassertive part of her longed to run away and hide. It might work, after all. It was possible Nishizaki didn't even know she existed. It was *possible* Kodaka had been run over by some drunken salaryman – or the aggrieved husband in one of the divorce cases he'd been handling.

Yes, all of that was possible.

But she didn't believe it.

And, come morning, she still didn't believe it.

Her appointment with Martin Caldwell was for ten thirty. The British Museum was only a short walk from the Envoy Hotel.

She wondered if Caldwell had arranged to meet her there for that very reason. He thought he was meeting Shitaro Masafumi's daughter, after all. He probably reckoned she'd want to see the Envoy, even though, as Wada now knew, there was little to be gained by it.

Wada still felt safe, reasoning no one could know where she was. But she was aware that could change when she met Caldwell. His affiliations and intentions were unknown. Plenty of people might know where *he* was. Their rendezvous was a moment of risk.

But it was a risk she had to take.

She entered the British Museum at ten o'clock, brandishing a Japanese language guidebook to London she'd bought at Narita airport. She wandered round a few rooms full of ancient statues. A memory surfaced of walking round the same rooms with Hiko, but the memory felt so distant it could have belonged to someone else, not Wada as she was now. She went to the café specified by Caldwell – not the main one, in the Great Court, but the small Montague Café near the museum's rear entrance. There she sat sipping green tea and leafing conspicuously through her book. No one paid her the smallest amount of attention. This was reassuring in its way. She'd always been someone others found easy to disregard. And, just now, being disregarded was what she preferred to be.

She kept an eye out for a solitary middle-aged Englishman matching her mental picture of Martin Caldwell as ten thirty came and went and became ten forty.

No solitary middle-aged men of any nationality came in. No one glanced meaningfully in her direction. She checked her phone, to see if Caldwell had sent her a message saying he'd be late. He hadn't. She sent him a message of her own. *Where are you?* There was no reply.

And there was no Caldwell.

She'd flown thousands of miles to meet this man. To learn what he knew about Peter Evans and the death of Shitaro Masafumi.

But she wasn't going to meet him. Not here. Not now. By eleven o'clock, she knew, though she stayed another half an hour. He wasn't coming.

There was still no message.

She walked out into the courtyard at the front of the museum, turning over in her mind all the contingent possibilities at play. Kodaka was dead. Was Caldwell dead too? Everything seemed and felt normal, this spring morning in London. Pigeons. Tourists. Red buses. Grey clouds.

But something wasn't normal. *Something* had happened. And might still be happening. Beyond her grasp. Out of her control. The file was going to take at least a couple of days to reach her. Until then, she knew nothing. She was helpless. And quite possibly in danger as well.

Think, she told herself. *Reason it through.* It was what her father had often told her to do with a troublesome piece of school homework. He'd tap the side of her head and say, 'You have a brain in there. Use it.'

She pulled her shoulders back and strode out through the gates into Great Russell Street. She was alone. She was vulnerable. But she wasn't resourceless.

And she wasn't giving up.

SIX

NICK COULDN'T SETTLE TO ANYTHING, CERTAINLY NOT THE LANDSCAPE he was trying to finish in Kate's absence. The mystery of Martin Caldwell's intentions and the hint of defensiveness in April's account of their time together in Exeter niggled away at him. Until, by Tuesday morning, he'd decided to do whatever he could to find out more about Caldwell before meeting him.

Tuesday morning was Pilates morning for April. He took a guess on the timing, reckoning he could come up with some kind of cover story if she hadn't left by the time he arrived or came back while he was still there. But since, as he recalled, she usually adjourned to a coffee shop in Catford Broadway afterwards with some of her classmates, he was confident he'd have the place to himself.

And he was right. As he let himself in after the short drive from Greenwich, he knew at once that the house was empty. And silent. Though, if he let it, the silence would fill with memories of his mother's voice.

He went up to her bedroom. There were still strands of her hair in a brush, though whether April had left them there deliberately or not he couldn't have said. He willed himself not to be sucked into thinking about such things.

He'd come for the old hatbox Caro kept at the bottom of her wardrobe, containing not a hat but cards, letters and messages received from friends and relatives during her illness, including daubed paintings of smiling faces from her niece's four-year-old daughter. It was a poignant collection. And, somewhere in it, Nick felt sure, was the letter Miranda Cushing had sent her a few months before her death.

'Don't tell April Miranda's written to me, Nicky,' Caro had said to him when he popped round one afternoon and she showed him the letter. 'She'll have a fit. She's always thought she was some kind of traitor to the class struggle for accepting a peerage.'

'You were pretty down on her yourself,' Nick had said.

Caro had smiled gently at him. He could picture her smile exactly, and the way the sunlight shafting through the window had fallen across it. 'Letting politics come between friends seems ever so slightly ridiculous when you look at the world from my current situation.'

'What does she say in the letter?'

'Oh, what everyone says. How sorry they are. How much they hope I'll be better soon. She's not really a bad person. I haven't actually met many of those. Still, vellum paper and an embossed letterhead would be too much for April. So, can it be our little secret?'

'Sure.'

Caro had held the letter out for him to see. He'd glimpsed large, curlicued handwriting and an address in SW10. 'She talks about the crazy times we had when we were all living together in Exeter. God, we were young then. And we did some stupid things. Some were worse than . . .'

Her words had tailed off there. She had fallen silent and leant back thoughtfully against the cushion behind her. Her gaze had drifted to the window. And the blur of sunlight beyond it.

When, eventually, she'd looked back at him, all she'd said was, 'Why don't you make some tea, Nicky? Camomile for me.'

And there was the letter, in his hand again. With address, telephone and email details printed at the top. His eye drifted down across the sentences.

I was really sorry to hear . . . I know we've had our differences . . . It seems desperately sad to me now that we let political disagreements come between us . . . I often think about the year we all lived together in Exeter . . . There are a lot of memories tied up in 18 Barnfield Hill, aren't there – the good, the bad and the downright incredible? . . . Can you believe all that madness was more than forty years ago? . . . Do you ever think about Peter and Alison? . . . Do you ever wonder if it could have turned out differently? . . . You don't have to reply to this letter . . . I just want you to know you're in my heart, Caro.

Nick had intended merely to lift Miranda's contact details from the letter, but after reading it he decided to take it with him. Certainly April didn't want it. She probably didn't even know it existed.

Back in his car, after pondering the matter for a few moments, he decided to chance his arm. He rang the mobile number printed on the letter.

Unsurprisingly, it went to voicemail. 'This is Nick Miller. Caro's son. We met . . . well, a long time ago. I'm hoping . . . Well, I need to talk to you about Martin Caldwell and I know Caro was very touched by the letter you sent her a few months before she died and I thought you'd be able to help me understand what's going on with Martin. He's contacted me, you see, and, er . . . Well, it'd be really great if you could spare me a few minutes on the phone. I'll hope to hear from you.'

The landline number went unanswered as well. Nick recorded a slightly better organized version of the same message. He wondered if Miranda would decide to ignore him. A sympathetic letter to a dying friend was one thing. Getting involved with the friend's unknown quantity of a son after her death was quite another. He looked at the heading on the paper. *Miranda, Baroness Cushing.* That would have been a red rag to a bull where April was concerned.

He'd started the car and was about to move off when his phone rang. It was Miranda.

'Nick. How nice to hear from you. And surprising.' She sounded unfazed by his call. Her voice had the firmness of someone who'd given more than a few speeches in her time.

'I'm sure it must be a surprise, yes. Thanks for calling back.'

'No problem. I'm sorry I wasn't at Caro's funeral. I just thought . . . it might be difficult.'

'Caro always thought of you as a friend.'

'I know. She phoned me. Not long after I wrote to her. We had a good chat. But she warned me April was still sticking pins in my effigy.'

'She has her principles.'

'I wouldn't argue with that. Anyway, I gather you didn't call about April.'

'No. Martin Caldwell.'

'Has he been bothering you?'

'Not exactly. But he wants to meet me and, well . . .'

'He came to see me recently. He was in a bit of a strange state. Nothing new there, to be honest.'

'Why did he come to see you?'

'I think he's lonely. Simple as that. Did he give you some special reason for meeting?'

'Yes. But, er, I wanted to check him out beforehand with someone who knew him when he was a student.'

'He's harmless. Good-hearted, in his way. A bit prone to fantasizing, that's all.'

'Fantasizing about the past?'

'Is it the past he wants to talk to you about?'

'Yes. Something to do with . . . my father. Geoff Nolan.'

'Well, you certainly shouldn't believe everything he says. About Geoff or anyone else. When are you meeting him?'

'Late this afternoon.'

'Mmm.' Miranda paused for thought. Then she said, 'It'd be nice for *us* to meet, don't you think? You could tell me all about yourself. I'd like that.'

'OK.'

'Can you make it to Chelsea for lunch? There's a lovely Italian just round the corner from me.'

Miranda Cushing – Baroness Cushing – was tall and elegant, with delicately tinted hair, blue-grey eyes, high cheekbones and a mischievous smile. She was waiting for Nick when he reached the restaurant, where ladies who lunch were in some abundance. Her clothes looked expensive and she wore them well. She was halfway through a glass of Prosecco and more or less insisted he have the same.

Even if Nick had wanted to dislike Miranda for April's sake, it wouldn't have been easy. She had a ready laugh and a self-deprecating twinkle in her gaze. She seemed genuinely interested in what he'd done with his life and was disarmingly frank about what she'd done with hers: early marriage and divorce – from an Italian, which explained her fluency when ordering from the menu – single motherhood, politics – with more than a hint that she'd backed whatever policies were calculated to advance her career – and now part-time participation in the House of Lords, leaving her a lot of free time in which to enjoy herself, which Nick had the impression she was adept at doing.

When he showed her a few of his paintings on his phone, she noted the stylistic resemblance to Morandi. This only confirmed him in the belief that she was hiding a wide-ranging intelligence behind a frivolous façade, heightening his interest in what she had to say about the Exeter household she'd been a part of in her student days.

'It was a long time ago,' she began, as a third glass of wine lubricated her memory. 'We were young. We were wild. It's not a new story. There was a lot of bed-hopping and dope-smoking. We were badly behaved boys and girls. And most of the time it was enormous fun. I'm sure Caro and April must have told you what sort of scene it was. And what they haven't told you I expect you're able to imagine, based on your own time at university. Where did you go?'

'Liverpool.'

'Where you didn't lead a monastic existence, I assume.'

'Not exactly, no.'

She looked thoughtful. 'I can't really imagine what Marty plans to tell you about Geoff.'

'What can *you* tell me?'

'Well, he was very good-looking. My mother would have called him dashing. In fact, I think that's what she did call him after catching sight of him on graduation day. Definitely dishy. Girls flocked to him. But he never knew where to stop – with anything. I mean, we smoked a lot of cannabis, as I say. But Geoff moved on to cocaine. And he got hold of some LSD at one point. He did drugs the way he drank. To excess. I couldn't keep up with him. Neither could anyone else for long. When I heard how he died, it wasn't a huge surprise. He had a self-destructive streak that was part of his attraction. But you

52

couldn't rely on him or trust him or expect him to think about anyone except himself.' Miranda shrugged. 'Sorry.'

'No need to apologize. I've heard it before.'

'I never knew Caro had a thing with him, even though I was under the same roof at the time, until she told me years later he was your father. It can't have lasted long. Just long enough to produce you, I guess. It wouldn't have meant anything to Geoff, I'm afraid. That's how he was.'

'So what's Martin Caldwell going to be able to add?'

'God knows. He and Geoff didn't get on very well, as I recall.'

'How many people lived in the house?'

'Eight. There were three floors and lots of bedrooms.'

'So you, Caro, April, Martin, Geoff. Plus?'

'Well, there was Vinod. Vinod Hardekar. His curries were something else. He became an accountant, I think. We lost touch.'

'In his phone call, Martin mentioned Peter Ellery and Alison Parker.'

'Yes. They were the other two.' She grew momentarily solemn. 'The two who didn't make it.'

'Didn't make it?'

'They drowned. Early June, 1977. Not long before the end of term. It was a terrible thing. I often think of them, Alison in particular. She had so much life in her it's hard to believe it was over at twenty-one. Haven't you ever heard about this from Caro and April?'

'No. Not a word.'

'Well, it was a painful episode. I suppose they thought it was best forgotten.'

'What happened?'

'It was a bank holiday weekend. In fact, Tuesday was a holiday as well, for the Queen's Silver Jubilee. I wasn't there. I'd

53

taken off to France for a few days with my latest boyfriend. Anyway, Peter, Alison and Marty decided to go down to Cornwall. A spur-of-the-moment thing. That was on the Sunday. Peter had a camper van. He was older than the rest of us. Did I mention that?'

'No.'

'Oh. Well, actually Peter owned the house. He'd inherited it from his parents when they were killed in a car crash. He'd been to Cambridge. Quite the brainbox. He was doing a master's degree at Exeter. Don't ask me what in. Something ancient historical. Probably Oriental. He could speak Japanese. He even had some books in Japanese. Which I always thought odd, because he once told me his father had been a prisoner of the Japanese during the war. But then he *was* odd, in lots of ways. Still, he didn't charge us any rent. We just chipped in to cover the utility bills. So . . . no one was complaining. Least of all Alison.'

'They were an item?'

'Towards the end, yes. Much to Marty's chagrin. He had the hots for Alison. I suppose that's why he went to Cornwall with them. To see if he could prise them apart.'

'How did they drown?'

'No one exactly knows. They were drunk. They were high. They were on the beach. Night fell. They went in for a swim. Well, Peter and Alison went in. Marty had fallen asleep. They left him behind. After that . . . it's anyone's guess. But they didn't come back. And two days later Alison's body was washed up.'

'What about Peter?'

'His body was never found. It's probably in a sea cave somewhere, trapped between rocks. And that's always been the problem for Marty. Without a body, he's never managed to convince himself Peter's actually dead. I'm not sure he's ever really wanted to.'

'But you're in no doubt?'

'We were at first, of course. We all wondered if somehow he could have survived. But, if he had, where was he? And the longer it went on, well, the more obvious it became. He'd drowned too.'

The conversation paused as their plates were removed. They asked for time before considering dessert.

'A tragic accident is what it amounts to,' said Miranda musingly. 'But Marty's never been happy to leave it at that. And now . . .'

'Now what?'

'This hasn't got anything to do with your father, Nick. Geoff didn't go on that Cornish jaunt. I guess Marty's mentioned him because he thinks that'll get you to listen while he sets out his latest theory. Maybe he hopes you'll give it more credence than I did.'

'And what is his latest theory?'

'Somehow, he's got hold of an advert that appeared in the *Evening Standard* back in the early nineties. A woman in Japan – yes, Japan – was seeking information about a young Englishman called Peter Evans who'd worked for her late father in London in September 1977. There was a photograph printed in the advert. Of Peter Evans. And, well, he looked a bit like Peter. Our Peter.'

Nick looked intently at her, studying her face to see what *she* believed in all of this. 'You're saying Peter Evans was Peter Ellery?'

'I'm saying there was a *resemblance*. In a blurry newspaper photograph. That and the similarity of the names was enough to convince Marty Peter hadn't drowned in Cornwall. He was alive and well three months later, working for a Japanese businessman in London.'

'But what did you think?'

'That I couldn't be sure. The photograph just wasn't distinct enough. It looked like a blow-up, cropped from some larger picture. Peter Evans had a beard. He was thinner than our Peter. He looked, I don't know, a lot more than three months older. Plus I've got no photograph of Peter to compare it with. Marty has, but he hadn't brought it with him to show me, which suggested to me he wasn't confident it would stand up to examination. Exact memories of faces fade over the years, just like other memories. If I'd chanced on the newspaper photograph without Marty leaning over my shoulder, it wouldn't have occurred to me it was Peter. But is that because I'm sure he drowned in Cornwall? Is it all down to what you want to believe?'

'And Martin wants to believe it's him?'

'Absolutely. My scepticism had no effect on him whatsoever. He said he'd written to the woman in Japan, offering to help her identify Peter Evans. Did I want to know what came of it? Naturally, I said yes, although I suspected very little would. But last Friday evening—'

'Friday?'

'Yes. Why?'

'That's when he phoned me.'

'Mmm. Well, he'd obviously decided to involve you for some reason. He told me the Japanese woman had been in touch and was coming to London this week to meet him. Did he mention that to you?'

'No. He just said he wanted to talk to me about my father.'

Miranda shook her head. 'I don't know what he's up to. To be honest . . .'

'Yes?'

'I wasn't sure the Japanese woman was really coming. I even wondered if he'd made the whole thing up.'

'But you saw the advert.'

'I did. It's an actual newspaper cutting. With a date printed on it. It looked genuine. And faking it would have been an enormously complicated exercise. Out of the question, really.'

'Do you think maybe Martin's lost it?'

'You tell me. After you've met him. Now, they're hovering with the dessert trolley, Nick. I suggest we put them out of their misery and order something.'

They parted in the street, halfway between the restaurant and Miranda's house. The tumult of King's Road wasn't far away, but it was quiet and still in this corner of Chelsea. In the end, they'd skipped dessert in favour of coffee. Nick hadn't wanted to risk getting home late for his appointment with Caldwell.

'Where did you say your wife's gone?' she asked suddenly.

'Tuscany.'

'Are you going to join her there?'

'It's girls only.'

'That's a pity.' She looked at him thoughtfully for a moment, then said, 'I imagine never knowing your father plants a lifelong curiosity about him in your mind. But you'll learn nothing of value from Marty. Geoff's been dead more than thirty years. Peter and Alison more than forty. It's all ancient history.'

'Are you sure Peter Ellery's dead? A hundred per cent certain?'

'How can I be? His body was never found. But, if he didn't drown, why did no one ever see him again?'

'Perhaps he didn't want to be seen.'

'That's a bit extreme, isn't it? And, in the wildly improbable event he's still alive, why should it matter to you anyway?'

'I don't know. Maybe Marty will tell me.'

'He'll tell you some kind of story, I'm sure.' She lowered her voice as she stepped closer, inclining her head slightly, as if sharing a secret. 'If you let him.'

*

It was only after he'd set off back for Greenwich that Nick realized he'd failed to ask Miranda where in Cornwall Alison Parker's death – and presumably Peter Ellery's as well – had occurred. There were a lot of beaches down there to choose from. He could ask Martin Caldwell, of course. And he meant to, if Caldwell didn't volunteer the information.

As far as Nick was concerned, though, it was put-up-or-shut-up time for Caldwell. Nick was going to listen to what he had to say, about Geoff Nolan, about Peter Ellery and Alison Parker, about the Exeter household in general. He was going to listen very carefully. And if, as he expected, it all turned out to be nothing but a lonely man's desperation to relive his youth, then that would be it. He would send Caldwell packing, then return no more calls or messages and draw a line under the whole business.

With any luck, he'd soon be able to get back to his painting. Leave ancient history behind. And re-engage with the present.

But Caldwell had a surprise in store for Nick. He didn't turn up. Not at five o'clock. Not at six. Not at all. There was no apologetic phone call this time. And he didn't answer when Nick phoned him or respond later to the message Nick left. As an aimless evening in front of the TV drifted by, Nick realized he'd somehow been had. What Caldwell had been trying to achieve, or whether this broken appointment was part of it, he couldn't for the life of him imagine. And, for the moment, he couldn't be bothered to try.

'To hell with Martin Caldwell,' he said as he poured himself another glass of wine.

SEVEN

WADA WAS ON THE SEVEN THIRTY TRAIN TO EXETER WHEN IT PULLED out of Paddington station the following morning. She tried to read some more of *The Makioka Sisters*, but the news of Kodaka's death had robbed her of her normal powers of concentration. The words on the page floated disobediently before her. The refuge she was accustomed to finding in Tanizaki's writing was denied her.

She'd been tempted to travel to Exeter in search of Martin Caldwell the previous day, following his failure to meet her as arranged at the British Museum. But she'd decided she should wait in London for a message from him. None had come. Nor had there been any further news from Dobachi. The afternoon and evening had passed in an agony of inactivity. She'd tried not to think too much about Kodaka's final moments, which had turned out to be impossible. Sleep had come late and fitfully.

Dawn, though, had brought clarity if nothing else. She wasn't going to do what was easiest or, at least in the short term, safest. She was going to do what, in all the circumstances, she judged to be best. Because that was her nature. And fighting against her nature was, as she well knew, futile.

*

The English countryside rolled gently past the train window for the next two and a half hours. The final approach to Exeter took her through lush water meadows. The sunlit scenery, refulgent with spring growth, made her wish she and Hiko had seen more of England than London, Windsor Castle and Stonehenge during their whirlwind European tour all those years ago.

Once she'd arrived in Exeter, she followed directions on her phone from the station to Caldwell's address, 18 Barnfield Hill. Even on foot, she was blocked and diverted several times by building work and found herself wondering why such an ancient city seemed still to be under construction.

Barnfield Hill itself was tranquil enough, though, a gently sloping road of detached villas that looked as if they dated from the nineteenth century, or maybe the early twentieth. Number 18 was large, red-bricked and bay-windowed like its neighbours, though not quite as well maintained, with window frames clearly overdue for repainting. A gentleman's residence when originally constructed, no doubt, but divided into flats now. In one of which lived Martin Caldwell.

Wada walked up the brick-stepped path to the front door and inspected the bell-pushes. She pressed the one marked *CALDWELL* and waited, wondering if he would answer. There was a speakerphone next to the buttons. But it remained silent, even when she gave the bell a second, longer push.

Her intention, if she got no answer, was to press a few other bells until she did, then try to talk her way in and see where that took her. Before she could try the tactic, however, she heard someone walking up the path behind her.

She turned to find a woman of seventy or so approaching, overdressed for the weather and carrying a bulging supermarket bag, panting as she came. She had grey, curly hair, a round face and a rather lovely smile. 'Can I help you, dear?' she asked.

'Perhaps,' Wada replied. 'I am looking for Martin Caldwell.'

'I don't think he's back.'

'Back . . . from where?'

'I really don't know, dear.' The lady squinted at Wada. 'If you don't mind me asking, are you Japanese?'

'Yes. I am.'

'That's odd.'

'It isn't odd to me. I've always been Japanese.' Wada smiled to make it clear she was trying to be humorous.

The lady chuckled. 'Of course you have. I'm sorry. What I meant was . . . Martin said he was going to London to meet a Japanese woman, so it's odd a Japanese woman turns up here to see him.'

'I am the Japanese woman he was going to meet. My name is Mimori Takenaga.' Wada wondered if Caldwell might have mentioned the name. The lady's reaction suggested not. 'He didn't turn up for our appointment. And I have heard nothing from him.'

'Oh. Really? That's . . . unlike him.'

'I travelled here this morning because I couldn't think of any other way to find out why he didn't meet me as planned.'

'I can't explain that, dear. But, since you've come all this way, why don't you come in for a cup of tea?'

As she opened the front door, the lady introduced herself to Wada as Joan Stapleton. She led the way into a wide hall, with the doors to flats 1 and 2 on either side. The stairs ahead of them were panelled off. They had to go through another door to reach them. Then Mrs Stapleton began a breathy climb to the next floor.

There were the doors to three flats off the landing they reached, one to the rear of the house, two at the front. Mrs Stapleton lived in flat 4. 'It doesn't look as if my husband's back yet,' she said, opening the door. 'Come along in.'

'Which flat does Mr Caldwell live in?' Wada asked.

'Six. On the top floor. He's all on his own up there.'

They entered flat 4. The rooms were well proportioned and high-ceilinged. China rabbits of all sizes eyed Wada from shelves, cabinets and tabletops as she followed Joan through to the cluttered kitchen, which looked out on to a fire escape and part of the rear garden.

'You'll have some tea, dear?' asked Joan, filling the kettle and opening the caddy that stood beside it.

'Thank you.' The two tea bags that were tossed into the teapot made Wada's heart sink.

As the kettle boiled and, after that, as the tea brewed – for what Wada judged to be far too long – Joan gently interrogated her about why she – or rather Mimori Takenaga – had travelled all the way from Japan to meet Martin Caldwell. It became apparent that she regarded Caldwell as someone who occasionally needed saving from himself. It also became apparent that the theory she and her husband Wally had come up with to explain Caldwell's rendezvous in London with a mysterious Japanese woman was some kind of internet romance.

Wada explained that romance had nothing to do with it. She'd come to see Martin Caldwell in order to shed light on the circumstances of her father's death in London in 1977.

'Oh, Martin knew your father, did he, dear?' Joan asked quizzically as she finally poured the tea.

'It's more likely he knew someone who knew him, Mrs Stapleton.'

'You can call me Joan, dear. Biscuit?'

'I'm not hungry, thank you.' Indeed she wasn't. But she was observant. And the removal of the biscuit tin from a shelf had disturbed a key, hanging on a hook above the worktop. She was also blessed with good eyesight, which revealed there was a

62

number written on the cardboard tag attached to the key ring. The number was 6.

'They're shortbreads. Delicious. I don't suppose you can get them in Japan.'

Wada smiled, thinking of the vast selection of Scottish shortbreads she'd seen in the food hall at Takashimaya. 'You've persuaded me,' she said.

Bearing a tray, Joan headed off into the lounge. Wada debated the issue with herself for a fraction of a second, then took a sidestep to the worktop, lifted the key off the hook and slipped it into the pocket of her trousers. She removed a glove from another pocket as she did so and dropped it on the table. The plan she'd improvised was to come back later to retrieve the glove, surreptitiously returning the key at the same time.

'Martin must have been living here in 1977,' Joan continued, as Wada caught up with her. 'He was a student at the university, you know. He's told me this was quite a lively place then. It wasn't divided into flats until later. I suppose him and his student friends lived in some kind of commune, if you know what I mean.' She pronounced the word *commune* as if the concept of such an arrangement was deeply sinister. 'Nothing like that now, I can assure you. Quiet as the . . . well, quiet is what it is. Which is how Wally and me like it. Martin too. You don't want noise and carryings-on at our age, do you?'

They sat down. Wada stifled a wince as she sipped the tea. It was even stronger than she'd feared. She took a bite of shortbread. 'When did you last see him, Joan?'

'Not sure. Friday, I think. He'd gone by Saturday. Early start for London, I dare say.'

'And you have not heard from him since?'

'Not a word. Though we wouldn't expect to. He keeps himself to himself.'

'What does he do for a living?'

'Well, he used to work for an insurance company. But he retired a few years ago. He keeps busy, though. So he says, anyway. I wonder why he didn't meet you. He seemed to be looking forward to it. Where can he have got to?'

'That is a good question.' Wada managed another sip of tea, aware she was going to have to drink it all before leaving. And aware that the sooner she left the sooner she could try her luck in Caldwell's flat. 'I wish I knew the answer.'

It took Wada another half an hour to extricate herself from the Stapletons' flat. Joan promised to contact her as soon as Caldwell returned and said she would tell him he should contact her himself with an explanation *and* an apology. Meanwhile, she was very interested in what Wada could tell her about the practicalities of wearing a kimono and was clearly disappointed when Wada said they were completely impractical, which was why she never wore them. 'But you'd look so lovely in one, dear.' Really, it was impossible to dislike Joan Stapleton. She and Haha would have got on famously.

Eventually, Wada made an exit, hastened by a telephone call that prevented Joan detaining her further. She waved and smiled as Wada let herself out.

The call was fortuitous. Joan didn't strike Wada as someone who indulged in brief telephone conversations. Which meant there was no chance of her looking out of the window and being puzzled by not seeing her visitor walk away along the street.

As soon as the door of flat 4 closed behind her, Wada turned and hurried up the stairs leading to number 6.

She moved with a quiet, soft-footed tread as she approached Caldwell's door. She slid the key into the lock and turned it slowly and carefully, then gingerly pushed the door open. She listened for a moment before stepping inside.

As she closed the door behind her, shutting out the rest of the building, the particular atmosphere of Caldwell's flat disclosed itself in a succession of sensations. The angle of daylight was different up here, because the windows were dormers. That and the fact that there were no carpets, just rugs of various sizes laid across the floorboards, gave it the feeling of an attic. It wasn't cluttered or untidy. The place felt both masculine and solitary, but not excessively so. Caldwell was in control of his world.

As Wada moved cautiously through the rooms, she was alert for tiny flexions of the boards beneath her feet. She didn't want Joan hearing any creaks overhead. But she'd always been light on her feet. She remembered how impressed Hiko had been by her ability to walk across the famous nightingale floors at Nijo-jo in Kyoto without making a noise. There weren't going to be any creaks.

The lounge told her nothing, beyond confirmation, by the positioning of a single armchair directly in front of the television, that Caldwell lived alone. The kitchen was neither manically clean nor conspicuously dirty. A rear door led from there out on to the fire escape. A wall calendar next to the door had the word *DENTIST* and a time – 10 a.m. – written on the line for the following day. But it had been crossed out. There was no rubbish in the pedal bin. It looked as if Caldwell had expected to be away for several days at least.

Some herbs were growing in pots on the windowsill: basil, coriander, oregano. The earth in the pots felt moist. Wada guessed watering them was something Joan did in Caldwell's absence. Turning away from them, she caught a sudden reflection of movement in the glass door of the oven, but, wheeling round, she saw nothing beyond the window except trees and sky. A bird in flight, she concluded – nothing to be alarmed about.

Next stop was the study, furnished with desk, computer, landline phone, bookcases, a two-drawer filing cabinet and a stack of cardboard boxes in one corner, with papers piled on top.

Wada clicked the mouse, but the computer didn't respond. It had been switched off at the wall: another sign Caldwell didn't expect his visit to London to be a day trip. The desk drawer contained nothing but stationery: pens, envelopes, paper clips, a stapler, a calculator. She tried to open the top drawer of the filing cabinet, but it was locked and there was no sign of the key.

A small red light was flashing on a button on the phone. *Message waiting.* Wada pressed it and the monitor button.

You have one new message. First new message received today at nine twenty-nine hours.

'Marty, this is Miranda. Nick Miller tells me you never showed up for your appointment with him. Are you all right? I'll help if I can, you know. Give me a call when you get this.'

Miranda? Nick Miller? Friends, presumably. The display gave her Miranda's number, which she recorded on her phone. Then, as she switched off the monitor, she noticed a peel-off jotting pad standing beside Caldwell's phone. A telephone number was written on the top sheet in pencil, starting with two zeros. She peeled off the sheet and put it in her pocket.

Next she took a look at the papers piled on top of the boxes. It was all household stuff as far as she could tell: utility bills, bank and credit card statements, dating back years.

Leafing through them exposed the lid of one of the boxes in the corner. Suddenly, as her glance slid across it, Wada froze. Somebody had written on the box with a black felt-tipped pen:

サリン

Sarin. In Japanese katakana.

For a moment, Wada couldn't seem to breathe. She stepped back and stared at the characters. She'd seen them often enough, in newspaper reports following the Tokyo subway attack and later coverage of the trials of Shoko Asahara and other members of the Aum Shinrikyo cult. サリン. *Sarin.* The cause of her husband's death and the deaths of many other husbands like him. But that was far away. That was in Japan. What did that have to do with Martin Caldwell? Why did this Englishman have a box with the word written on it – in *Japanese*?

She pulled the box out and crouched down beside it. Originally it had evidently contained twelve bottles of Cossack vodka. There were remnants of Sellotape on the folded-together flaps and, in faded red lettering, the rubber-stamped demand *Ban the Bomb*. Plus those three Japanese katakana that could only have one meaning. Written by hand. Written by someone who knew the language. Caldwell? Or Peter Evans, Shitaro Masafumi's translator? Was that how Caldwell knew Evans? Because they'd been friends?

Wada prised the flaps apart and looked in. The box was full of papers and documents. She began leafing through them. There were lots of photocopied newspaper cuttings dating from the 1970s, mostly from a paper called the *Western Morning News*, written by a reporter called Barry Holgate. There was too much material to take in at a glance, but various words sprang out at her: nerve gas; chemical warfare; sarin. Several of the headlines referred to somewhere called Nancekuke. Some of the articles included grainy photographs of industrial buildings in an isolated, coastal location and, in one case, a photograph of a sign attached to a chain-link fence: *MINISTRY OF DEFENCE CDE NANCEKUKE RESTRICTED ENTRY PERMITS MUST BE SHOWN CAMERAS NOT PERMITTED*. There was a map as well, folded over to show a stretch of coastline with the runways of an airfield marked out near a village called Porthtowan.

As Wada continued to delve, she came upon a Kodak-yellow wallet of photographs, slipped in between the documents about halfway down the box. She lifted out the wallet and opened it. There was a sheaf of snapshots, their colour slightly faded. Judging by the age of the people in the pictures and the seventies style of their clothes and hair, Wada reckoned they were snaps of Caldwell and his friends from university days – members of the commune, perhaps, that Joan had said lived in the house when he was a student at the university. On that basis, one of them could be Peter Evans. But which one it was impossible to say.

Some of the pictures had obviously been taken in the garden of 18 Barnfield Hill. Wada recognized the house in the background. In one a group of eight was standing outside the front door: four young men, four young women. One of the women was spectacularly beautiful, with flowing blonde hair and a direct, luminous gaze. The others were attractive in their youthful way, but she stood out as someone apart. She appeared in several of the pictures, including the half-dozen or so taken at a beach party, where the light was softer and thinner with each shot, as evening advanced, somewhere long ago on a broad sandy shore.

Wada suddenly noticed an object that had been slipped into the wallet along with the photographs. To her surprise, she found it was a computer stick. There was a tiny label stuck to it, on which was written, in a minute hand, *facetrail*.

Wada was squinting at the word in bemusement when the telephone started ringing, so loud in the silence of the flat that it made her jump. She turned and looked across at it. What to do? Let the caller leave a message? She waited for the answerphone to kick in.

But she changed her mind before it did. Slipping the computer stick into her trouser pocket, she moved across the room to the desk and picked up the phone.

She didn't speak. At first, neither did the caller. Then there came a male voice at the other end of the line. 'Martin?'

She didn't reply.

'Martin, are you there? This is Nick Miller. What the hell happened yesterday afternoon? Where were you?'

Wada said nothing.

'Are you going to talk to me, Martin? You said you wanted to. So, what's the big silence all about?'

Still Wada said nothing.

'I'm going to hang up, OK?'

'Don't,' Wada said instinctively. She couldn't let slip the chance of learning something of value from the caller.

'Who's that?'

'Tell me—' A noise somewhere else in the flat distracted her in that instant, but she decided to press on with the call. 'Tell me who you are first.'

'I've already given you my name.'

'How do you know Martin Caldwell?'

'He's an old friend of my late mother. Hold on, though. Are you Japanese? You sound as if you might be.'

'You're right,' she replied hesitantly. 'I might be.'

'Are you the Japanese woman Martin's supposed to be meeting in London this week?'

'Yesterday. He was supposed to meet me yesterday.'

'Me too. What's your name?'

The pretence had to be maintained if Wada was to make any progress. 'Mimori Takenaga,' she said softly.

'So you're the woman who's trying to identify the English guy your late father employed in London back in 1977?'

'Yes. Peter Evans.'

'Or maybe Peter Ellery. What are you doing answering Martin's—'

The line was suddenly dead. There was no dialling tone. There was nothing. It was as if—

A shadow fell across Wada as she turned towards the door. A tall man was standing there, remarkably tall given that he looked Japanese. He was thin to the point of gauntness, with skin stretched tight over his jaw and brow. His eyes were so dark they could have been black, like his crew-cut hair. He was dressed in black as well: jeans and sweatshirt. In his right hand he held the telephone cable. He tossed it on to the floor as he stared at Wada and stamped on the jackplug, shattering it.

'Who are you?' Wada asked. There was a slight tremor in her voice, which she could only hope the man wouldn't notice. 'How did you get in?'

'Who are *you*?'

'Mimori Take—'

'No. You are Wada. Kodaka's errand-runner.'

The game was up. He knew who she was. He probably knew why she was there. And he was blocking her only exit. As she watched him, his gaze slid past her to the box in the middle of the floor. With the word *sarin* written on it, in Japanese.

He looked back at her. 'Tell me what you know about Martin Caldwell.'

'I know nothing.'

'That would be good for you. If it was true.'

'It is true.'

He took a step towards her. She dodged round to the far side of the desk. He moved right. She moved left. Right. Left. Suddenly, he grasped the rim of the desk and heaved it bodily to one side.

The desk landed upside down on the floor with a crash, sending up a cloud of dust from the boards. There was nothing between them now. She stooped and grabbed the desk lamp, which had fallen at her feet. But as she rose, brandishing the lamp as a weapon, he was on her, closing his hand round her throat and shoving her back against the wall. With his other hand, he batted away the lamp.

'Where is Kodaka's Nishizaki file?' the man rasped, glaring into Wada's eyes as if he'd find the answer there.

'I . . . don't know . . . any . . . Nishizaki file.'

'Where is it?'

She still had the lamp in her hand. In pushing it away the first time, the man had apparently dismissed it – and her – as a threat. But she wasn't as weak as he seemed to think. She swung the lamp up fast and hard, striking him on the side of the head with the metal base.

He cried out. His eyes flared in pain and anger. His grip loosened just enough for her to squirm free. She made a dash for the door, but he grabbed her by one ankle, pulling her off her feet as she ran.

She fell. One of the upturned desk's legs was directly in front of her. As she plunged towards it, she knew her head was going to hit it.

The blow was sharp and stunning. She went down into a pool of darkness.

Oblivion didn't last long. Wada regained a woozy form of consciousness to find herself lying across the underside of the upturned desk, with her back against one of the legs, her shoulder bag pinned beneath her. The man was in front of her, but looking away, rummaging through the sarin box, searching for . . . whatever he was searching for.

At that moment there was a banging on the front door. She heard a male voice shouting on the other side of it. Wally Stapleton was her guess. *'Open this door. I know you're in there. You took the key. Open up right now.'*

The man stopped rummaging and glanced towards the door. Perhaps he was regretting hurling the desk out of his way so noisily now. It had alerted the Stapletons to Wada's presence in the flat – and inadvertently to his.

'I'll call the police if you don't open up. I've got my phone in my hand and I'm going to dial 999 if you don't open the door right now.'

The man grunted in irritation. This was evidently a complication he hadn't anticipated. He pulled a black plastic bag out of the pocket of his jeans and flapped it open. He emptied the box into the bag, then grasped the computer that was lying screen down on the floor and stuffed that into the bag as well. Wada lay quite still, hoping he'd assume she was still unconscious. The banging on the door continued.

'All right. That's it. I'm hitting the buttons now. Nine, nine, nine.'

The bag split as soon as the man picked it up. Some of the documents, including the wallet of photographs, spilt out on to the floor. He gave another grunt of irritation. Cradling the split bag under one arm, he stooped and retrieved the photographs, but ignored the rest and hurried out of the room without even glancing at Wada. She saw him take a turn into the kitchen and guessed he must have broken in via the fire escape.

Wally Stapleton was still talking on the other side of the door, but more quietly. Wada pushed herself upright and felt a lancing pain in her head. When she touched the spot, it was tender and there was blood on her fingers. Her head swam as she staggered to her feet and started moving.

She stumbled several times and had to steady herself against the wall as she headed along the hall. But Wally was still talking when she reached the front door and pulled it open.

At the sight of her, however, he suddenly fell silent.

'I came as fast as I could,' she said hoarsely.

'Hold on,' said Wally into his phone. He was a burly, balding, grey-haired man with a pugnacious set to him. He frowned at Wada. 'What the hell's going on? How'd you get that cut on your head?'

'I was attacked.'

Wally peered past her. 'Is someone else in there?'

'No. He left. Fire escape.'

'Bloody hell.' Wally put the phone back to his ear. 'There's been a break-in *and* an assault. I *think*. It's all a bit— Can you just get over here?'

Wada's wooziness suddenly worsened. She felt herself falling.

Then Wally's arm was round her. She was leaning heavily against him, aware that he was the only reason she was still on her feet. 'I think we might need an ambulance as well,' she heard him say into his phone.

EIGHT

CONCUSSION DIDN'T MAKE IT EASY FOR WADA TO DOUBLE-THINK HER way out of trouble with the Devon and Cornwall Police. But the young officer who took a note of her account looked as if he believed her, and whatever technical offence she'd committed by taking the key from the Stapletons' flat and letting herself into Caldwell's seemed to take a back seat to questions about the intruder who'd injured her. Fortunately for Wada, Joan had seen the man making off with a large black bag under his arm, so clearly she hadn't dreamt him up, and signs of a forced entry from the fire escape into Caldwell's kitchen along with the mayhem in the rest of the flat told their own story.

Wada claimed, truthfully enough, that she had no idea who he was, but she didn't add she had little doubt who he was working for. She stuck with the name she'd given the Stapletons and luckily the policeman never asked to see her passport. Luckily also, she remembered the name of the hotel in South Kensington where she and Hiko had stayed during their honeymoon holiday back in 1994 and claimed that was where she was staying now. She calculated the police were unlikely to check. They were much more interested in circulating her description of the intruder and leaving Wada to rest in hospital.

She improvised a story about contacting Caldwell on the internet as a result of their shared interest in the history of sarin production, hers based on the death of her husband in the 1995 Tokyo subway attack, his on personal knowledge which he'd promised to impart when they met. As far as she could tell, the policeman swallowed this story whole. But, then, why wouldn't he? Wada could play the winsome innocent when she had to and the gash on her forehead only made that easier. He ended up apologizing to her for being attacked in such a normally peaceful neighbourhood, which she thought was, ironically, very Japanese of him.

The doctor who examined her at the hospital diagnosed concussion, which explained her dizziness and the strange sensation whenever she moved that her brain was lagging a fraction of a second behind her body. She was given an MRI scan, her wound was dressed, painkillers were prescribed and she was told she'd be kept in overnight for observation. By the morning, the police might have more questions for her, but the doctor saw no reason, barring a sudden deterioration in her condition, why she shouldn't be discharged at that point.

The Stapletons' outrage at her abuse of their hospitality had given way to sympathy. She was a stranger in a strange land; she'd lost her husband in awful circumstances; she'd meant no harm by taking the key: what had happened wasn't her fault. They assured her they'd encourage the police to go gently on her. And if there was anything they could do to help when she left hospital . . .

'That's too kind of you,' she told them. And, really, she knew it *was* too kind. She'd lied to them. And she was still lying. Sadly, she didn't see any way she could tell them – far less the police

75

– the truth. That, after all, would require her to mention the *facetrail* memory stick which could so easily have ended up in her attacker's hands. Maybe it was that he'd principally been looking for. As it was, she had it. And she was keeping it. If there were clues to follow, she meant to be the one following them. She couldn't trust anyone except herself to get the job done.

Lying in bed in a sparsely populated ward late that afternoon, she did her best between unpredictable bouts of sleep to plan her next move. To read what was on the stick, she needed her laptop, which she'd left in London. The phone number on Caldwell's jotter pad was a different matter, however. Fishing her phone out of the bedside locker, she tried the number.

'Hotel Arnarson.' It was a man's voice, speaking English with a non-English accent.

'You are . . . a hotel?' Wada asked in an undertone.

'Pardon me?'

She raised her voice slightly. 'You are . . . a hotel?'

'Yes. Of course.'

'Where . . . are you?'

'Reykjavík.'

'Reykjavík . . . Iceland?'

'Of course.' He was beginning to sound tetchy now.

Wada thought as quickly as she could, which she sensed wasn't as quickly as usual. 'Ah, I think a friend of mine is staying there. Martin Caldwell.'

'Mr Caldwell? From the UK?'

'Yes.'

'He *was* staying here. But he left . . . two days ago.' What? Why was Caldwell in Iceland the day before he was due to meet her – and Nick Miller, apparently – in London? Wada couldn't imagine what that signified.

'Did he say . . . where he was travelling on to?'

'I wasn't on duty when he left. Back to the UK, maybe?'

Maybe. Yes. *Maybe*. 'Did he—' Wada broke off. A man had appeared at the foot of her bed. He wasn't a doctor. There was no white coat. It was hard to tell exactly what he was. A plain clothes police officer? Too old, surely. He was a thin, rumpled, slightly stooping man of seventy or more, bald, bespectacled, but keen-eyed and alert. His tweed jacket and corduroy trousers hung off him as if he'd lost quite a bit of weight since buying them, although that didn't look to be recently. 'I will phone again,' she said, ending the call.

'Didn't mean to interrupt,' the man said. 'Mind if I come in? The nurse seemed to think it'd be all right. They know me here, you see. I'm what you might call a regular.'

'A regular what?' Wada asked suspiciously.

'Visitor. Patients who don't have family or friends dropping in like a chat with someone from time to time. I do my best to oblige. Glad to see you're well enough to, er . . . be making calls.'

'I don't want a "chat", thank you, Mr . . .'

He smiled ambiguously. 'Holgate. Barry Holgate.' He studied her reaction for a moment, then added, 'I think you might recognize the name.'

She did. He was the reporter who'd written most of the newspaper articles kept by Caldwell. 'You are a journalist, Mr Holgate.'

'Retired journalist, actually, though I still do a bit of free-lancing, when I'm not hospital visiting. I'll clear off if you say the word. Or you can get me frogmarched out of here by pulling that red cord behind your bed. But you don't want to do that, do you? Mind if I sit down?' Without waiting for an answer, he perched himself on a chair beside her. 'I've still got contacts on the Force. They told me about the to-do at eighteen Barnfield Hill. So I thought I'd come and see you.'

'Why?'

'Because Caldwell's collection of cuttings dated from the late seventies, according to your statement, and that means my name was on most of them. Correct?'

'Yes.'

'That whole episode is unfinished business as far as I'm concerned. So, Mrs Takenaga . . . I was rather hoping you could fill me in on what Caldwell's been up to.'

'I do not know what he has been . . . "up to".'

'That can't really be true. You came a long way to meet him.'

'But I have not met him.'

Holgate sighed and leant forward, rubbing his large hands together. 'Maybe we could help each other.'

'How?'

'You tell me what you know in return for . . . background information from me.'

'Information about what?'

'You're not making this very easy, Mrs Takenaga. They tell me . . . you lost your husband in the sarin attack on the Tokyo subway in 1995.'

She looked straight at him. 'Yes. I did.'

'My condolences.'

'Thank you.'

'That must have been a terrible experience.'

'It was. And the journalists who came to see me then said they could help me. But I learnt they were only helping themselves. I was just . . . something to fill a column.'

'Ouch.' Holgate visibly winced. 'Well, I can't deny my profession doesn't have the highest of reputations.'

'You could do *your* reputation some good, Mr Holgate.'

'How?'

'Tell me about Nancekuke. And the people who lived at eighteen Barnfield Hill in 1977.'

'You've never heard of Nancekuke?'

'Never. Until today.'

'Well, it was a wartime airfield on the Cornish coast converted after the war into a nerve gas production plant. It's about a hundred miles west of here. Nothing much to see there now. It's all been cleaned up. The site was chosen because of its remoteness: no nearby large centres of population at risk in the event of an accident, and any gas that leaked likely to be blown out to sea. They produced sarin there throughout the nineteen fifties. It continued as a research station, producing smaller amounts of chemical agents, until the late seventies. It actually closed in 1980. None of what I've just said was officially available information when it was up and running, you understand. That's all come out since. So, when I was writing those articles and people like Martin Caldwell and his activist friends were handing out leaflets to holidaymakers stuck in summer traffic jams on the A30 – that's the main road into Cornwall – protesting about what was going on at Nancekuke, what *was* going on was basically just rumour and conjecture. I suppose you could say it was rumour and conjecture that got two of his friends killed there in June of seventy-seven.'

'How so?'

'Several workers at Nancekuke had died under . . . well, medically unexplained circumstances. Quite a few more had been laid off with long-term nervous disorders. It was pretty obvious something sinister was going on inside that chain-link fence. I started sniffing around. Maybe I was partly to blame, for planting ideas in idealistic young minds. But it was a genuine story. It needed following up. There was one aggrieved ex-Nancekuke worker who fed me some fairly alarming stuff, most of which I was never allowed to put in the paper. I discovered later he was also in touch with Peter Ellery and Alison Parker, housemates of Caldwell's at eighteen Barnfield Hill – the two who died. I think that's what got them started.'

'Started on what?'

'Hard to be certain. But something that involved trying to break into Nancekuke. Alison Parker's body was washed up at Porthtowan, barely a mile from the base. Peter Ellery's body was never found. They were seen, with Caldwell, in a pub at Towan Cross, a mile or so inland, on the evening they went missing. That ex-Nancekuke worker I mentioned – Tom Noy? He lived at Mount Hawke, a stone's throw from Towan Cross. None of that's a coincidence. What exactly happened – how they died – I don't know. Accidental drowning? Or a fatal encounter with base security? I can't say. Whether Caldwell can say I've never been sure. But he's never left the mystery alone, has he? Your journey from Japan confirms that. So are you going to tell me what you were hoping to learn from him? Or what you think *he* was hoping to learn from *you*?'

'He said he had information about who'd given Shoko Asahara, leader of Aum Shinrikyo, details of how to manufacture sarin.' Wada wondered if Holgate would query this, but she was guessing he knew very little of how the cult had functioned. 'I hoped he'd give me evidence about other people who might have been responsible for my husband's death.'

'I'm surprised Caldwell saw any connection between Nancekuke and the Tokyo attack.'

'Sarin is the connection, Mr Holgate.'

'Even so . . . it's a stretch, isn't it? Although . . .' Holgate frowned and kneaded his hands. 'Caldwell's missing. And the man you told the police stole his computer was Japanese, wasn't he?'

'He appeared to be.'

'So, there clearly is a Japanese angle to this. What else can you tell me?'

'Nothing. But you could tell me more about the other residents of eighteen Barnfield Hill. Was one of them called Miranda?'

Holgate's eyebrows shot up. 'Yes. That would be Miranda Cushing. Baroness Cushing, as she is now. If I'd known she was going to make a name for herself in politics and end up in the House of Lords, I'd have paid her more attention. But how—'

'There was a message from her on Caldwell's phone.'

'I'm surprised they're still in touch. What did the message say?'

'That Caldwell had not turned up – in London, I guess – to meet someone called Nick Miller. Miranda wanted to know why.'

'Miller? One of the other residents was called Miller, I think. A girl. I can't remember her first name.'

'It sounds like a man to me.' Wada didn't propose to explain how she knew for a fact Nick Miller was a man.

'You can't judge someone's sex by their name these days, Mrs Takenaga. Not in this country, anyway. But . . . it could be her husband, I suppose.' Or her son. But Wada had no intention of saying that. 'It all suggests something's going on that's stirred up memories from forty years ago. I wish I knew what.'

'So do I.'

Holgate looked narrowly at her. 'I reckon you've got a better idea than me of what it might be, Mrs Takenaga.'

'I do not understand why you think so.'

'Instinct.'

'A journalist's instinct?'

'If you like.' Holgate sighed. 'What are you going to do now?'

'Go back to Japan, I suppose. If Caldwell does not . . . reappear.'

'Really? Give up? Just like that?'

'What choice do I have?'

'I might be able to help you, Mrs Takenaga. But I need you to be more . . . open with me. More . . . forthcoming.'

'I am not generally . . . forthcoming . . . with people I hardly know, Mr Holgate.'

'Particularly not when they're journalists?'

'Well . . .' She smiled at him. 'You are one. You said so.'

He sighed again, then took out his wallet, removed a card from it and laid it on the bedside cabinet. 'Sorry it's a bit grubby. I haven't had a batch printed for a long time. But it tells you how to contact me. And I hope you *will* contact me. When you're ready.'

'Why would I do that?'

'To discuss where you go from here. Because I seriously doubt it's back to Japan.'

'I am feeling tired. I think I would like you to leave.'

'Then I'll go.' He rose from the chair. 'Thanks for the chat. Especially since you didn't actually want to have one.'

It had been another frustrating day for Nick. He'd made no progress with his landscape after foolishly deciding to make one last effort to contact Caldwell. All he'd got for his pains was a fleeting telephone conversation with Mimori Takenaga, the Japanese woman Caldwell had supposedly been meeting in London. But she was answering Caldwell's phone in Exeter, which made no sense to him. And she was giving away very little. Until the line had suddenly gone dead. Which it had stayed ever since. What the hell was going on?

That evening he was meeting Mike Bennett, an old university friend, now a barrister, for one of their monthly get-togethers over a drink. The venue was, as usual, a smart pub overlooking Blackheath Common. Nick tried to put Caldwell out of his mind and concentrate on Mike's account of an entertainingly convoluted libel case he'd handled recently, but his thoughts kept drifting back to Caldwell. This didn't escape Mike's attention. Eventually, Nick ended up telling him all about the mystery that had recently seeped into his life.

'You're not going to be able to let go of this, are you?' said Mike when he'd finished.

'Can't see I've got much choice in the matter.'

'You could always do what this Takenaga woman seems to have done.'

'What do you mean?'

'Run the guy to earth. After all, you do know where he lives, don't you?'

'Yeah, but . . .' Nick's words drizzled into silence.

'Exactly.' Mike raised a satirical eyebrow at him. 'But what?'

Wada felt exhausted by her verbal fencing match with Holgate. There was more she'd have liked to ask him, but that would only have made it obvious to him that she was holding something back. Her entrenched suspicion of journalists made it unlikely she'd ever confide in him. But . . . 'You never know' – one of Kodaka's favourite sayings – came into her head and made her smile at the memory of how he would say it. She could still hardly believe she was never going to hear his voice again. But so it was. She acknowledged his posthumous advice with a little nod and slipped Holgate's card into her bag.

The *facetrail* computer stick was safely stored in there as well. She was eager to know what was on it, but couldn't find out without returning to London, or using somebody else's computer, which she couldn't imagine being able to arrange safely.

For the moment, all she could do was use her phone to look up *facetrail* on the internet. She got a hit straight away. According to its website, Facetrail offered a search service for missing persons. It used an existing photograph or likeness of the missing person to trawl through millions of online images, seeking a match. It claimed its finely tuned algorithms put it way ahead of any similar service. It claimed, indeed, to be foolproof. *If they're out there somewhere and there's an image of them, we will find them for you.*

Had Caldwell been trying to find someone? It certainly looked like it. But who? Maybe the answer was on the stick. And maybe that answer was why he'd gone to Iceland.

So many questions. They whirled in Wada's head. She couldn't corral them into order. A trip to the toilet revealed she was still light-headed and unsteady on her feet. Her head ached dully despite the painkillers. She was irritated by her own weakness. But she couldn't will it away, try as she might.

She was asleep when they brought her supper. And asleep again soon after eating it. Her body had won out in the struggle with her mind. She was going to rest, whether she wanted to or not.

NINE

WADA WOKE FEELING MUCH MORE LIKE HER NORMAL SELF. SHE'D always been quick to recover from injuries or illnesses. Haha claimed Wada had inherited this resilience from her, although there might have been another explanation. 'Why is Umiko up and about so soon?' she'd once heard her father ask following a bout of glandular fever. 'Because I haven't made the mistake of fussing over her,' her mother had replied.

It was early morning, the ward was quiet and Wada's mind was clear. She got out of bed and walked around experimentally. There was less pain and much less wooziness, although sudden movements still needed to be avoided. She dressed and left the ward, telling the nurse on duty she was going out to get some fresh air. The nurse didn't seem to notice Wada was carrying her bag under her arm. In fact, she barely noticed her at all. Which wasn't unusual in Wada's experience.

Outside, there were several people standing at a bus stop. They paid Wada no attention as she joined them. It was a cold morning and most of them were concentrating on keeping as warm as they could.

The bus arrived and, conveniently for Wada, its destination was St David's station. She clambered aboard with the others and bought a ticket. 'All the way, please,' she told the driver.

At the station, she found herself with half an hour to wait for the next train to London. The business day would be drawing to a close in Japan, but it wasn't too late to call Dobachi. His secretary answered and said Dobachi was out of the office, but she confirmed the despatch of a package to Wada by express international post on Tuesday. 'It should arrive today, Wada-san.' But that wasn't all she had to report.

'Dobachi-san asked me to tell you if you called that he has made enquiries about Kodaka-san's client, Mimori Takenaga. She has been admitted to a psychiatric clinic; no visitors allowed. That is all he has been able to establish.'

'Thank you.' Wada's heart sank as she rang off. Kodaka was dead, Caldwell might well be dead too and Mrs Takenaga was now under close control. That left Wada alone, vulnerable and poorly equipped to anticipate her enemies' next move. Her best hope was that they thought her so poorly equipped she wasn't worth bothering about.

She made another phone call then, to the Hotel Arnarson in Reykjavík. The man who answered sounded slightly friendlier than the man she'd spoken to the night before. She repeated her enquiry about Martin Caldwell without mentioning she'd already been told he'd left.

'Ah, Mr Caldwell. So many people are asking about Mr Caldwell.'

'They are?'

'Yes. We have heard from the police also about him.'

'Has he done something wrong?'

'I cannot say.'

'Do you think he's still in Iceland?'

'I guess he must be. The police said there was no record of him leaving the country. But . . . can I have your name?'

'I am just a friend.'

'Yes, but, excuse me, you sound . . . well, are you Japanese?'

'Why do you ask?'

'One of the people who came looking for Mr Caldwell was a Japanese gentleman.'

'What was his name?'

'He didn't give a name. Like you.'

'Was he . . . tall?'

'Yes. He was. Taller than me. And I am not short.'

'Thank you for the information.'

'Can I—'

She ended the call there and stared for a moment into the distance. Building work was underway on the land beside the station, as it seemed to be underway everywhere in Exeter. But Wada's gaze was fixed on the hilly horizon. The tall Japanese man looking for Caldwell in Reykjavík had to be the same tall Japanese man who'd come to Caldwell's home in Exeter. Something he'd found on the computer he'd taken must have told him where Caldwell had gone. But what was Caldwell *doing* in Iceland?

By the time she boarded the train, she was exhausted all over again. The effort of leaving the hospital and travelling to the station had taken a lot out of her. Or maybe it was the phone calls that had done it. There was just so much she didn't know. But she was determined to learn more. And determination had carried her through before. Maybe it would again.

Nick woke early as well. Over breakfast, he debated with himself whether he should do as Mike had suggested. The clincher was the question of what else he could do. It seemed, in the end, there was no other way to get Caldwell out of his head. He'd have to go to Exeter and see what he could find out.

The morning was cold but fine. As soon as the rush hour was over, he set off. There and back in the day was his aim. There and back with the Caldwell issue settled.

It felt good to be on the move. What he was going to learn in Exeter he didn't know. Maybe nothing. But at least then he'd know there was nothing to learn. That would be an end in itself.

Wada was confident she hadn't been followed from the hospital. The intruder at Caldwell's flat had seemed more interested in Caldwell's computer – and his photographs – than in Wada. But she was aware she had something – the *facetrail* stick – that the man might also have been looking for, so she couldn't afford to be complacent. It was time to use some of the tactics Kodaka had taught her. From Paddington she went by taxi to the National Gallery, left shortly after entering and by a different door, then took the Tube to Russell Square. Access to the street was by lift and she was pretty confident none of the other occupants of the lift were anything but ordinary travellers.

At the Envoy, she asked if there'd been any parcels delivered for her. The answer was no. Not yet, anyway.

No matter. While she awaited the parcel's arrival, she was free to investigate the contents of the *facetrail* stick. She hurried up to her room. Where a shock greeted her.

The small safe in the wardrobe, where she'd stowed her laptop, was not as she'd left it. The door was open. And the laptop was gone.

Nick reached Exeter around lunchtime. He stopped at the motorway service station on the outskirts for a sandwich, then drove into the centre, following his satnav to 18 Barnfield Hill.

It was a large, detached Victorian villa, bay-windowed and red-bricked. The house next door had become a doctors' surgery, but number 18 had been converted into flats. And there was Caldwell's name, against the bell-push for flat 6. Nick rang it. As expected, there was no response. His plan was to find someone living there who *would* answer, then press them for information about Caldwell and his Japanese visitor.

It never came to that. Before he could try any of the other bells, the door opened. A bald, stooping man who was probably in his seventies, dressed in a tweed jacket and corduroy trousers, took half a step out of the door, then stopped. He peered curiously at Nick. 'Looking for someone?'

'Martin Caldwell.'

'Join the club. He's a man in demand.'

'You know him?'

'Slightly. I've just been talking to his neighbours about him. He's, er, gone missing, it appears. I'm a journalist. Well, was. I'm retired now. I first met Martin Caldwell when he was living here as a student back in the seventies. My name's Barry Holgate.'

'Nick Miller.' They shook hands.

'*Miller?*' Holgate's eyes gleamed behind his glasses. 'You're the fellow Caldwell was supposed to meet in London a couple of days ago.'

'How did you know that?'

'Mrs Takenaga told me. She listened to a message on Marty's phone yesterday, apparently. From Baroness Cushing, no less.'

'Really? Is Mrs Takenaga here?'

'Fraid not. She's gone missing as well, actually. Discharged herself from the hospital early this morning. Well, walked out, more accurately.'

'*Hospital?* Why was she in hospital?'

'Long story.'

'I've got time to hear it.'

'And I've got time to tell it. It's a strange thing, but . . .' Holgate peered at Nick. 'You remind me of someone.'

'My mother, maybe. She lived here as well back then. Caroline Miller.'

Holgate shook his head. 'No, not her. It's . . . What year were you born?'

'1978.'

'Ahah.'

'Maybe it's my father I remind you of. Geoff Nolan.' Nick had never seen much of a resemblance in the photograph he had of his father, but maybe there was something he'd missed.

'Geoff Nolan?' Holgate rubbed his chin thoughtfully. 'That's interesting.'

'Not very.' But the expression on Holgate's face suggested otherwise. 'What?'

'Nothing. Look, why don't you come inside? I'll take you up to the Stapletons' flat. They can explain better than me what happened here yesterday. And maybe you can do a bit of explaining yourself. There's a lot to take in.'

'There is?'

Holgate nodded emphatically. 'Oh yes. A hell of a lot.'

The hotel manager was summoned to deal with Wada's report that her room safe had been opened in her absence. He expended a lot of charm and effort in trying to persuade her that she must somehow be mistaken. Perhaps she'd programmed it wrongly. Perhaps she hadn't programmed it at all. He then reminded her of the notice in the room denying responsibility for the loss of valuables not deposited in the hotel's own safe at reception. Finally, he put it to her plainly. Did she wish to contact the police and report a theft?

Wada pondered the question for several seconds and decided against it. 'Perhaps I was mistaken,' she said through gritted teeth. Which pleased the manager. But left her in several quandaries. The contents of the laptop would actually tell whoever had taken it nothing about Wada's current activities. It was, nevertheless, clear they knew where she was staying, which she'd hoped they didn't. She was more vulnerable than ever. And in greater danger than ever. Somehow, she had to protect herself.

Her first inclination was to book out of the hotel straight away. But she couldn't do that before the parcel arrived from Dobachi. Her head was swimming as she left the manager's office.

She took a couple of paracetamols and sat in one of the oversized leather armchairs in the hotel's gleamingly marbled lobby. Time passed. But her anxiety didn't. She picked up a copy of the *Financial Times* that was lying on the table in front of her and turned to the shares page. Nishizaki were one of the FT500, priced at ¥10574, up slightly on the week, the only Japanese stock listed that had gone up rather than down.

Who was Wada kidding? Nishizaki was unchallengeable, certainly by the likes of her. She might as well—

That was when the reception clerk materialized beside her, smiling broadly, and announced that a package had just arrived for her.

They went to the desk, where the clerk handed her the parcel. 'Thank you,' she said. 'Could you prepare my bill, please? I'm going up to clear my room, then I'll be checking out.' The decision, now she'd taken it, seemed inevitable, even though her plan for what to do next was still barely half formed in her mind.

'You're leaving us today?'

'Yes. I am.'

As Holgate had said, there was a hell of a lot for Nick to take in. The Stapletons sympathized with him in that respect, having learnt more about Martin Caldwell in the previous twenty-four hours than they had in all the years of being his close neighbours. They described the events following Mimori Takenaga's arrival on their doorstep the day before and Barry Holgate recounted how he'd followed up the deaths of Peter Ellery and Alison Parker as a reporter in June 1977. If Nick now understood why Mrs Takenaga had answered Caldwell's phone, there was much he still didn't understand, but he wasn't alone in that either.

The Stapletons had heard nothing from the police. According to Holgate's contact on the Force, however, the search for the intruder – described by Mrs Takenaga as an unusually tall Japanese man – was continuing, despite no reported sightings of him after leaving the house. As for Mrs Takenaga herself, it was assumed she'd gone back to London. 'I don't think this case is being given much priority,' Wally Stapleton complained. 'These days, a burglar has to murder you in your bed for the boys in blue to take much notice.'

'It's complicated but not serious.' Holgate treated them to a cynical smile. 'So I'm afraid it probably won't get much attention.'

'They won't even be looking for Martin, as far as I can tell,' lamented Joan Stapleton. 'Not missing, they say. Just away from home.'

'The answer to all this,' said Holgate with a degree of relish he couldn't quite disguise, 'goes back forty-two years. I'm certain of that.'

'And what is the answer?' asked Nick.

'Ah, well, there you've got me. But I reckon it must be something to do with you.'

'Me?'

'You said Caldwell had information he wanted to give you about your father. Because of something that happened recently.'

'That's certainly what he said.'

'Why don't we pop up to his flat and see if there's anything we can spot that might give us a clue?'

'Not sure about that,' objected Wally. 'The police put crime scene tape across the door and told us to keep out.'

'But you've got the key?'

'Yeah. Mrs Takenaga gave it back to me. But . . .'

'We won't disturb anything. You can come with us if you like and make sure we tread carefully.'

'Can't see as it can do any harm,' said Joan.

Her approval seemed to swing it for Wally. 'All right, then. Let's go.'

Stooping under the blue and white police tape was easier for Nick than his two companions. Holgate, who was about as nimble as an ironing board, needed a helping hand to manage it. Once inside Caldwell's flat, they found few signs of the previous day's events. The desk in the study had been put back the right way up, with the telephone standing on it, apparently undamaged, although close inspection of the flex wound round it revealed the broken jackplug. The lamp Mrs Takenaga had hit the intruder with and the documents that had fallen out of the plastic bag Mrs Stapleton had seen him carrying had been taken away by the police as evidence, along with the empty box.

This was a big disappointment to Holgate, who'd hoped to find the cuttings of his old newspaper articles waiting for him. But they'd gone. And the remaining boxes didn't appear to hold anything of interest. The locked filing cabinet promised to be a different matter, but, without the key, they could make no progress there. Otherwise, the flat contained Caldwell's furniture, books, videos, DVDs, records and CDs. There were no pictures on the walls. There were no framed photographs standing around. The bookcase was filled with crime fiction paperbacks.

The record cabinet revealed his musical taste was frozen in the 1970s.

'Seen enough?' asked Wally when they'd run out of rooms to prowl around.

'Guess so,' Holgate agreed.

'Haven't you got a collection of your old cuttings, Barry?' Nick asked as they left the flat.

'Not as comprehensive a collection as it sounds like Caldwell had.'

'Why did he keep them, do you think?'

'Ah, but were they *his*? There was Japanese writing on the box, according to Mrs Takenaga. And who do we know who lived here in 1977 who understood Japanese?'

'Peter Ellery.'

'Exactly. Mrs Takenaga never had the chance to study the exact dates of the cuttings. And Caldwell might have added some on his own account. But my bet is most of the contents of that box – the cuttings and all the other documents, whatever they were – belonged originally to Ellery.'

'What's my father got to do with any of this? He didn't go on the trip to Nancekuke. Did you actually ever meet him?'

'Geoff Nolan? No. I don't think so. But maybe you're asking the wrong question.'

They'd reached the door of the Stapletons' flat on the floor below. Nick looked at Holgate in puzzlement. 'What's the right question, then?'

'Could you give me a lift back to my house? There's something there you ought to see. I expected to find another . . . example of it . . . upstairs, but . . .'

'An example of what?'

'Just come and see, Nick. I think you'll find it very . . . revealing.'

*

94

Wada's thoughts were only slightly better organized when she arrived at the internet café north of Oxford Street than they had been when she checked out of the Envoy. She had the parcel from Dobachi, unopened, in her bag, having decided to give immediate priority to Caldwell's *facetrail* computer stick. Beyond that her mind was racing to assess what her best and safest options were. Her head still ached. And her brain's strange tendency to lag a few fractions of a second behind her movements was still troubling her.

She slid the stick into the computer and opened it. There were lots of email communications over the course of a couple of months between Caldwell and someone called Kirk Mosley at Facetrail. Many of the emails had attachments. Caldwell had engaged the company's services to trace a man, referred to only as the Subject, missing, so far as Caldwell was concerned, since 1977. He had supplied Facetrail with a photograph and some biographical information. *Born 1953. Educated Sherborne and Cambridge. Fluent in Japanese.* It sounded as if the Subject could be Peter Evans. And it sounded as if Caldwell knew him well.

Facetrail applied staged facial ageing processes to the photograph, producing plausible likenesses of the Subject at five-yearly intervals since his disappearance. At the same time they trawled a vast range of pictorial images available on the internet in search of men of the right age, appearance and qualifications. Within weeks, they had begun supplying Caldwell with candidates, noting the degree of likelihood in each case, which was never high. Caldwell ruled out each one with a stock response. *Not him.*

Then, just a few weeks previously, the breakthrough came.

Peter Driscoll. Right first name. Right age. Photographically a good match to the computer modelling. His background was vague, but that was actually an argument in his favour. His career was veiled in a certain amount of mystery as well. He was currently chairman and CEO of Quartizon, a company specializing in facilitating complex negotiations between organizations that preferred it not to be known they were negotiating at all. They had offices in Brussels, New York, Tokyo and London. The London office was described as being in a 'discreet location' in Mayfair.

Caldwell responded differently this time. *Could be him.* Facetrail probed further and turned up a Japanese connection beyond the mere existence of a branch office in Tokyo. Quartizon was fifty per cent owned by . . . the Nishizaki Corporation.

It *was* him. It had to be. And finally . . .

Caldwell had given Facetrail the names of four friends of the Subject: Miranda Cushing, Vinod Hardekar, Caroline Miller, April Vyse. And Facetrail had scored a hit with one of those names.

It was the woman who'd left a message on Caldwell's phone: Miranda Cushing – Baroness Cushing as she now was – who had shared a house with Peter Ellery in 1977. She was paid by Quartizon as an occasional consultant, though what they consulted her about was unclear. Facetrail speculated it was for access to decision-making circles at Westminster.

Whatever her exact role, Wada reckoned it made her a good choice for indirect communication with whoever had sent the man she'd encountered in Caldwell's flat: Nishizaki, Driscoll, maybe both. And Caldwell had helpfully included her home address in the background information he'd supplied to Facetrail.

Wada studied Baroness Cushing's face in the photograph adorning her website. It was a very English face and she looked good for her age. Born 1956. Graduate of Exeter University. But there was nothing about her brush with activism while she was a student there.

That was only to be expected. Wada saw . . . what was it: wariness, caution, cynicism? . . . behind the baroness's relaxed smile. She always put her own best interests first. And yet she wasn't wholly unreasonable. That was Wada's conclusion. And it was one she proposed to take advantage of.

She copied the contents of the stick on to another stick she'd bought on arrival at the internet café. Then she made an airline booking she could cancel if she needed to. And then she prised open the parcel from Dobachi.

It held the *kage-boshi* file, as promised. It was dog-eared, which suggested Kodaka had consulted it frequently. The papers comprised notes in his recognizable scrawled hand, along with copies of emails and letters too, dating back years in some cases. Wada was going to have to give them her close attention. And she didn't have time to do that now. She stowed them in her bag and set off.

Barry Holgate lived in a semi-detached house in one of the eastern suburbs of Exeter. It was obvious from the street he was no gardener. And once indoors it was equally obvious to Nick he didn't devote much time to housekeeping either. The photograph on the drawing room mantelpiece of a warm-eyed woman who might easily have been Mrs Holgate, combined with the sensed certainty she no longer lived there, suggested he was probably a widower. But Nick didn't ask and Holgate didn't say. They weren't there to swap life stories.

Holgate led the way upstairs to the spare bedroom he used as a study. It was lined with crammed-full bookcases and was clearly where he did the small amount of journalistic work he still engaged in. He pulled open a green steel-doored cabinet and heaved down off the top shelf one of a set of box files. The tattered label on its spine read *Nancekuke*.

97

'I expect most of the cuttings I've got here were replicated in Caldwell's collection – or Ellery's, as I'm inclined to think of it,' Holgate said as he laid the box file on the desk and opened it. 'You can browse through them if you like. But you'll be particularly interested in the article I had in the paper on . . .' He slid his glasses to the end of his nose and flicked through yellowed clippings from the *Western Morning News*. 'Here we are. Wednesday the eighth of June, 1977.'

Nick took the cutting from him. The headline was *Female student found drowned at Porthtowan – fears for life of male student also*. He scanned the column below.

The body of Alison Parker, 21, a student at Exeter University, was discovered on the beach at Porthtowan early yesterday morning by a woman walking her dog. A post mortem is being performed, but she is believed to have drowned. Fears have also been expressed for the life of another Exeter University student, Peter Ellery, 24, reported missing along with Miss Parker.

A spokesman for Devon and Cornwall Police said a third Exeter University student, Martin Caldwell, 21, had been with them on the beach late on Sunday night, but had lost contact with them after falling asleep. He told police they had expressed the intention of 'going for a swim'. All three had driven down from Exeter earlier in the day and had been seen drinking during the evening at the Victory Inn, Towan Cross. Tidal conditions along the coast west of Porthtowan are known to be hazardous for inexperienced swimmers. The spokesman added it was thought highly likely that Mr Ellery had also drowned.

'Doesn't sound particularly sinister, does it?' said Holgate. 'Drunken students getting into trouble late at night on a Cornish beach with tragic consequences. The editor wouldn't let me add that Ellery and Parker had both been arrested and cautioned for staging protests at Nancekuke, which is just a mile or so from Porthtowan. Caldwell was too frightened to say much at the time, but I never believed for a moment they'd gone all the way to Porthtowan for a midnight dip. There was more to it than that, starting with the police impounding Ellery's camper van. But . . . there was nothing definite to go on.'

'So you left it there?'

'No. I spoke to Tom Noy, who'd been seen in the pub with them, though I didn't mention that in the paper. Tight-lipped bugger, unless you wanted to hear about his lawsuit against the MoD. I got nothing out of him except the distinct impression he'd put Ellery and Parker up to something but wasn't about to say what it was because they'd wound up dead and he'd land himself in a whole load of trouble by spilling the beans. Then I heard from one of my colleagues in our Plymouth office that a contact he had on the Nancekuke staff claimed a guard had suffered a supposedly accidental bullet wound while on duty at the base over the bank holiday weekend. Coincidence? I doubt it, don't you?'

'A guard was *shot*?'

'That's right. Accidentally. Officially.'

'What are you suggesting?'

'I'm suggesting Ellery and Parker broke into the base to follow up some lead Noy had given them and then . . . God knows exactly what happened, but it ended badly for them. There was serious stuff going on at Nancekuke at the time. You messed with it at your peril.'

'You're saying they were killed by guards at the base and one of the guards got shot in the process?'

'How can I say that? Alison Parker drowned. She had serious head injuries according to the post mortem, but they weren't inconsistent with being thrown against rocks after drowning. As for Peter Ellery, the police concluded he'd drowned too, but his body was never recovered. Washed out to sea, or trapped in a cave. That was the verdict. Which you knew nothing about until recently, because your mother never told you. I've got that right, haven't I?'

'Yes. You have.'

'And according to her, Geoff Nolan was your father.'

'Yes. What about it?'

'This photograph.' Holgate delved further in the box file and pulled out a large black-and-white print. 'I didn't keep the article it appeared with. But the date's on the back.' He turned it over. 'Ninth of April, 1977. Easter Saturday. They set themselves up by the side of the Redruth to Portreath road.' He handed the picture to Nick.

He recognized Caro and April at once from other pictures he'd seen of them in their early twenties. He recognized Martin Caldwell as well. And he took a guess the other two in the group of five were Peter Ellery and Alison Parker. They were standing on a grass verge beside a busy road, thick with seemingly stationary traffic. Caro and April were holding a banner mounted on two poles. The lettering on the banner was big and angry. *YOU ARE ENTERING A CHEMICAL WARFARE ZONE.* Alison – a blonde-haired, attractive young woman in jeans and a sweater – was handing out leaflets for passing motorists to take if they wanted to. Martin was next to her, doing the same.

The fifth member of the group, who had to be Peter Ellery, had a camera looped round his neck. He was gazing across the road, straight at the photographer. He looked calm but committed. His expression was somehow challenging and passive at the same time.

But it wasn't his expression that caught Nick's attention and held it fast. It was his face – the set of his features, the flop of his hair across his brow, the angle of his chin. It was instantly familiar.

'I saw the resemblance the minute I opened the door to you at Barnfield Hill,' said Holgate. 'I'd call it pretty striking, wouldn't you?'

'This is Peter Ellery?' Nick asked numbly.

'Oh yes. That's him.'

That was him. Peter Ellery, presumed drowned at twenty-four, in June 1977, eight months before Nick's birth. Peter Ellery. His father. Not Geoff Nolan. But this man. Peter Ellery. Unmistakably.

TEN

BARONESS CUSHING LIVED IN A LARGE WHITE-FRONTED HOUSE IN AN expensively quiet street in Chelsea. Wada asked the taxi to wait while she rang the doorbell. The result was as she'd feared: no response. That left her with no choice but to try the phone number Cushing had used to call Caldwell's flat. Wada would much have preferred to seize whatever advantage she could from an unannounced face-to-face encounter, but there was nothing else for it now. Time was short.

Rather to her surprise, the call was answered with a brisk, 'Hello?'

'Baroness Cushing?'

'Yes. Who's this?'

'I am the Japanese woman your friend Martin Caldwell was supposed to meet in London two days ago.'

'I don't know what you're talking about.'

'I think you do. Please don't hang up. I have a proposal.'

'A proposal?'

'To solve our problem.'

'*We* don't have a problem.'

'Yes we do. Martin Caldwell. Peter Ellery. Nancekuke. Shitaro Masafumi. I have . . . material . . . I am willing to surrender.'

Silence ruled at the other end of the phone for several stretched moments. Whatever Cushing was thinking, it was clear she was thinking hard.

'Can we meet?'

'I'm at Westminster. I'm very busy.'

'It won't take long.'

There was another long pause. Then she said, 'Parliament Square. Half an hour. OK?'

Wada had barely got her own 'OK' out when the call was ended.

The pavement outside the Houses of Parliament was crowded with campaigners waving flags and banners. They were a loud and colourful symbol of the Brexit controversy Wada had read about in the newspapers. She supposed Baroness Cushing, as a member of the House of Lords, was playing some part in the continuing debate. But the taxi driver's discontented muttering as he dropped her off didn't suggest he'd be impressed if he knew what it was. 'More crooks in there than Wormwood Scrubs,' he growled.

Cushing hadn't said where in Parliament Square they were to meet, but Wada crossed over to the green in the centre of the square, where it was slightly quieter and there were only tourists and passers-by to contend with.

She'd walked along one side of the green in the direction of Westminster Abbey and turned to retrace her steps when she saw a woman heading purposefully towards her who she guessed was Cushing even before she recognized her face. She was

103

wearing a light wrap-coat and a colourful scarf. And the uptilt of her chin somehow combined dismissiveness with suspicion.

'You must be Mimori Takenaga,' she said as she approached.

'You must know I am not.'

'Do I? Marty said that was the name of the woman he was meeting.'

'My name is Wada.'

'Really? So what was Takenaga? A nom de plume?'

'You said you were busy.'

'I am.'

'Me also. I have a plane to catch.'

'Where are you flying to?'

'New York. To visit my brother.'

'How nice for him.'

Wada took the *facetrail* stick out of her pocket and handed it to Cushing. 'Give that to Mr Driscoll.'

'Who?'

'Just pass it on. Please.'

'I don't know anyone called Driscoll.'

'The stick belongs to Martin Caldwell.'

'You stole it?'

'I took it. Now . . . I want you to have it. For Mr Driscoll.'

'No doubt you've kept a copy.'

'I want Mr Driscoll to understand I am no threat to him. I am going to New York. For some time. I am . . . no longer doing any work on the Takenaga case. I am . . . out.'

'Out?'

'If he leaves me alone, I will leave him alone.'

'That's your offer?'

'Yes.'

'You do understand I've no idea what you're talking about, Miss Wada, don't you?'

'Will you pass on my message?'

Cushing opened her handbag and dropped the stick into it. She gave Wada a strange little half-smile. 'I hope you enjoy New York.'

'So do I.'

'Goodbye, then.'

Baroness Cushing turned and walked away. Wada watched her go. There was no glance back over her shoulder. If a deal had truly been done, it wasn't one she wished to acknowledge.

And it wasn't one, come to that, that Wada had any intention of honouring.

Wada walked slowly towards St James's Park. She hailed the first free taxi she saw and asked to be taken to Heathrow airport. In the back of the cab, as it headed west through the city, she opened the *kage-boshi* file again and began to inspect the contents, this time in detail.

She was out over the Atlantic on a flight bound for New York before she'd got the measure of the information Kodaka had amassed about Hiroji Nishizaki and his business operations. Some of it was culled from cases he'd handled over the years: sokaiya operations, commercial espionage, missing persons; some appeared to be his own conclusions and speculations about Nishizaki's activities based on an overview of those cases.

There wasn't much doubt Kodaka thought Nishizaki had often engaged in illegal activities: bribery, blackmail, rigging of share prices, corrupt use of inside information. And there were suggestions of worse than this as well. Several missing person cases involving executives in companies Nishizaki had had dealings with had ended with the discovery of bodies floating in Tokyo Bay.

It looked to Wada as if Kodaka had started amassing information about Nishizaki after sensing his hand in a number of cases, and then, perhaps to his surprise, he'd found him everywhere, in reports and documents and obituaries and court rulings and police files, even though his name hadn't actually appeared in any of them. Initially, it had only been by constant cross-reference that Kodaka had been able to make the connections. Then, at some ill-defined point, those connections had acquired a critical mass of their own.

Nishizaki's success appeared to be based on *not* being what the authorities instinctively looked for in commercially related crime. No known sokaiya groups were associated with him. He had nothing to do with yakuza. As far as they were to know, he was just a phenomenally accomplished entrepreneur.

But they hadn't looked hard enough. They had no reason to. There was always something else to move on to.

Kodaka was a different matter. When Wada thought about him, as she did through that long flight into the night, she remembered both his stubbornness and his patience. He'd never give up. And he'd take as much time as it took. The *kage-boshi* file was a testament to that. The detail. The precision. The accuracy. Dates; times; names; places; links; associations; conclusions hinted at but never spelt out. Was it really Nishizaki's shadow the file was named after? Or was Kodaka the one casting a shadow – a shadow over his prey?

If so, his prey had eventually noticed. And Kodaka had paid for that with his life. Wada knew what he'd say to her if he could. 'Don't make the same mistake.' And she knew what she'd say to him. 'I won't.' Yet here she was, reading the file, preparing, in all likelihood, to ignore his advice.

And there, contained in its own clear plastic wallet at the end of the file, was the clinching piece of information: the reason why, as Kodaka must have anticipated, she was bound to make the same mistake. *Exactly* the same mistake.

Yozo Sasada. The Aum Shinrikyo member who'd released sarin in the subway carriage her husband Hiko had been travelling in on the morning of 20 March 1995. Sasada had also been accused, but not convicted, of participating in the murder eight months previously of the Chijimatsu family, carried out by feeding sarin into the ducting of their air-conditioning system. The court hadn't been able to identify any motive for Aum Shinrikyo to go after the Chijimatsus and had eventually dropped the charge.

Kodaka had decided to delve into Sasada's background. As well as the background of Mitsugi Chijimatsu, head of the family. And there he'd found . . . Nishizaki.

Mitsugi Chijimatsu was a corporate lawyer who'd advised the targeted company in several failed takeover bids by the Nishizaki Corporation over the years. There was no hard and fast evidence on the point, but Kodaka clearly suspected this had made him a thorn in Nishizaki's flesh.

As for Yozo Sasada, Kodaka's researches established that before joining Aum Shinrikyo he'd worked in some junior capacity at a company part-owned by Nishizaki: Quartizon.

The circle was complete, a circle Kodaka had only ever seen part of but was now clear and stark in Wada's mind. Peter Ellery; Peter Evans; Shitaro Masafumi; Hiroji Nishizaki; Yozo Sasada; Peter Driscoll. And in the middle of the circle: sarin.

Many of Wada's fellow passengers were asleep by now. But she was alert in every fibre of her being. There was a connection. There was a thread woven over forty years. And her own husband's death was part of the fabric.

She didn't know what it all meant. She could see the shape of the secret, but not its pattern. Somehow Martin Caldwell had seen it too. He'd reasoned his way to the answer, or something close to it. And now he was at best a fugitive from Nishizaki, at worst another of his victims.

Wada could risk joining the list of those victims. Or she could run and hide and hope to be forgotten. But what would that achieve, for a solitary, newly unemployed forty-seven-year-old woman? Survival, obviously. But a survival full of regrets. She didn't want that.

And she wasn't going to have it.

The plane was late landing at JFK and it took Wada more than two hours to clear immigration and retrieve her suitcase. A cab carried her through the skyscraper canyons of Manhattan she was familiar with from the imported American TV shows her father had loved to watch, and delivered her to the apartment block facing the Hudson river where her brother lived. It was an expensive address, suggesting he'd done well at Nomura, even though the apartment itself was small by American standards and would have looked smaller still if there'd been anything to fill it with. But Haruto didn't appear to have accumulated many possessions since moving to New York, apart from a wardrobe's worth of suits.

He greeted her affectionately but wearily. It was past midnight and he generally started early at the bank. There was little in the way of conversation, though he must have been puzzled by her arrival at such short notice. This didn't surprise Wada. The key to their relationship had always been minimal inquisitiveness about each other's lives – the secret of harmonious co-existence in the tiny house they'd grown up in. He didn't even ask how long she planned to stay. If he had, his puzzlement would only have grown.

Realizing he'd never make it to Porthtowan before nightfall, Nick booked himself into a cheapish hotel on the outskirts of Newquay and did his best to ignore the holidaying families around him. He wandered into the town centre, ate something inauthentically Italian, and wandered back again. His mind was fixed on the mystery surrounding the man he knew now he had to think of as his father: Peter Ellery. There was going to come a time – and it was going to come soon – when April would have to explain the lie she and Caro had peddled to him. Meanwhile, Nick felt compelled to see the place where the official record of Peter Ellery's life had ended, along with that of Alison Parker, forty-two years before.

There was no doubt, of course, that Alison Parker had drowned off Porthtowan beach that June night in 1977, though there was considerable doubt about *how* she'd drowned. But Peter Ellery's death was just an assumption, a likelihood, a *probability*. It was hard not to believe Martin Caldwell thought he could prove Peter Ellery was posing as Peter Evans in London three months after his supposed death in Cornwall. And it was surely a betting certainty he'd planned to tell Nick Peter Ellery was still alive to this day, posing as someone else.

Nick was disorientated by what he'd learnt in the space of a few hours: that his father wasn't who he thought he was; that his father might not be dead after all. He'd grown accustomed to the absence of such a figure in his life. But that absence hinged on his death when Nick was a toddler, somehow excusing his neglect of his son up to that point. That had all changed now. Nick's mother had deceived him. His real father had probably never known he had a son at all.

Was he alive, though? Was Caldwell really on to something? The answer wasn't waiting for Nick at Nancekuke tomorrow, with the nerve gas factory long since demolished and the site cleared of all traces of what it had once been used for. It was just an RAF radar station now. Officially, anyway. Holgate had said there were still rumours of strange goings-on there. But rumours were always popular. Generally, people couldn't get enough of them.

Nick had no use for rumours. He wanted facts. He wanted the truth that had for far too long been denied him. And he meant to get it.

But, first, he needed to see where the mystery had begun.

*

Wada was a light sleeper, especially when she wasn't sleeping in her own home. It was still dark when she heard Haruto moving around in the kitchen in a manner that suggested he was trying hard not to wake her.

His first words to her when she walked into the room were an apology for disturbing her. She brushed that off and asked for a cup of the tea he was preparing.

They sat with their cups either side of a marble-topped table. The spot-lighting gleamed on the whorls in its surface.

'I have to be in early this morning,' Haruto explained. Given that it was not yet five thirty, the explanation wasn't strictly necessary.

'They work you hard?'

'There are just things to be done.' The reply was evasive, but she wasn't inclined to press.

'I will not be staying long.'

'But for the weekend at least?'

'No. I'm leaving tonight, actually.'

'*Tonight?*'

'Sorry.'

'Where are you going?'

'It's better for you not to know.'

Haruto frowned. 'Now you're worrying me.'

'We could have lunch before I go.'

'I do not believe you came all the way to New York just to have lunch with me.'

'No. I did not.'

'Then why?'

'I will explain at lunch. Just one thing, though.'

'What?'

'Please do not mention my visit to any of your colleagues.'

'Why not?' Haruto gave her a knowing look. 'You'll explain at lunch, I suppose?'

'Yes.'

'I don't get long.'

'We'll make the most of it.'

He held his gaze. 'I guess we will.'

Nick left the hotel early and was at Porthtowan by nine o'clock. The village seemed deserted, though the morning was bright, the sunlight skittering over the rolling breakers. But there was a cold wind driving the tide in. Tiny granules of sand pecked at his face as he made his way through the dunes that fronted on to the beach.

According to the account Caldwell had given the police back in June 1977, he and his two companions had brought some bottles of beer and wine down to the beach after leaving the Victory Inn, up above the village. They'd sat in the shelter of the dunes, drinking and smoking, as darkness fell. Caldwell had fallen asleep. The deepening chill had woken him some time after midnight. He was alone, his companions gone.

Eventually, he'd travelled back to Exeter by bus and train, although the presence of Peter's camper van in the car park had left him baffled as to what he and Alison were doing. He'd hammered on the door but got no response. Were they playing some kind of bizarre trick on him?

When they hadn't shown up or phoned by the following morning, he and the other residents of 18 Barnfield Hill had agreed the time had come to raise the alarm, little knowing Alison Parker's body had already been found on the beach where Caldwell had last seen her.

Nick cut back up the beach to the footbridge across the stream that ran through Porthtowan to the sea, then climbed the long slope to the clifftops south-west of the village. With the tide coming in, there wasn't much to be seen of the shore below the cliffs, or of any of the caves into which Peter Ellery's body might have been washed and somehow become trapped. There was no sign either of the pipe that had fed effluent from the nerve gas factory out to sea. According to one of Holgate's clippings, there were claims by bathers to have suffered mysterious neurological complaints after swimming in the area of the pipe when the factory was active, and long after as well.

The factory had vanished many years ago, of course, along with numerous outbuildings. The photographs Holgate had shown Nick revealed what amounted to a small industrial estate on the site in the 1950s and 60s. All he could see in the distance now was a couple of low structures and a radar dome.

He followed the line of the chain-link perimeter fence as it rose and dipped with the level of the cliffs, wondering where and how Peter and Alison had entered the site. He wasn't in any serious doubt they *had* gone in, though for what purpose exactly he wasn't sure. Neither was Holgate. Whatever Tom Noy had told them he'd kept quiet about in the aftermath of the drowning. So had Martin Caldwell. The shock of Alison's death – and Peter's presumed death – had effectively silenced them, perhaps because it had frightened them. And with good reason.

Tom Noy had taken the secret to his grave in 1982, killed by liver cancer at the age of fifty-seven. 'There was never any danger of the MoD overspending on pensions for Nancekuke workers,' Holgate had wryly remarked.

As for Caldwell, at some point he'd obviously stopped being frightened. Or perhaps the discovery that Peter Ellery probably hadn't died that night had finally driven him to act. But still, it seemed, there was good reason to be frightened. Even forty-two years later.

Half an hour's stiff walking showed Nick all of the little there was to be seen of Nancekuke – or RAF Portreath as it had officially been renamed. An old airfield with a few buildings on a wind-scoured plateau on the edge of the land high above the Atlantic Ocean. Its death-dealing past had been erased, its buildings demolished, its materials buried, its land decontaminated. All gone. And best forgotten. If you believed what you read in the newspaper.

The signs on the fence remained, however, as uncompromising echoes of that past. *MINISTRY OF DEFENCE PROPERTY – KEEP OUT.* Keep out; stay away; pretend it never happened. That was the message. Whatever it was that had happened . . . officially hadn't. There was no story. There was no secret. Nothing.

Except the clean, cold wind blowing in.

And the question, lodged in Nick's mind, sharpened by the belief – the growing certainty – that Peter Ellery was his father. What happened that night? What *really* happened?

Haruto admitted to Wada he'd never eaten at the restaurant where they met at twelve thirty that day. But it wasn't far from his office, its sushi came highly recommended and he'd engineered a full hour's break to spend with his sister, so she stifled her objections to the tastelessly large 'Hello Kitty' figurine waggling its paw at her from the corner of the bar.

It transpired Haruto hadn't spoken to their mother for several weeks. 'Every time I think of calling her I think of how she'll cross-question me about my social life, and decide it can wait,' he admitted. Wada sympathized. 'Are you still working for that private detective?' he asked.

'Sort of,' she replied. Well, that was true enough. Kodaka was dead and technically she was no longer his employee, but she was carrying on his work.

'So, is this a holiday or a business trip?'

'What would you say if I told you I was trying to track down one of the men responsible for Hiko's death?'

'I'd say they hanged Asahara and that other guy, Sasada, last year. I'd say that pretty well settles it.' He gave her a sideways look. 'But it's not settled for you, I'm guessing.'

'There's someone else. Behind Sasada. A shadow of someone else, you could say.'

'I don't know what that means.'

'If anyone asks where I've gone, tell them . . . California . . . or Alaska.'

'Where are you really going?'

'Where the shadow leads.'

'You realize that sounds totally mad, right?'

'You think I'm mad?'

'No. I've never met anyone less mad than you, Umiko. You are the sanest person in the world. I mean, with what happened to Hiko, you could have . . . lost it. But you didn't. You just . . . went on.'

'The private detective, Kodaka?' She hadn't decided until this moment to tell Haruto about Kodaka. But now she felt she had to. 'Maybe you should know. He's dead.'

Haruto started with surprise. 'How?'

'Hit-and-run.'

'Does this have anything to do with—'

'Oh yes. Of course.' She turned towards Haruto. 'The investigation involves taking a few risks.'

'A few *risks*? You've just told me your boss has been . . . murdered.'

'I think so, yes. It looks like it.'

'Then . . . drop the investigation. While you still can. Hiko's dead. The guy who actually released the gas is dead too. And it all happened more than twenty years ago.'

'It's only a few days since they killed Kodaka.'

'Who are "they"?'

'I am not going to tell you. That would endanger you. And I am the one taking the risks, not you. Big sister talking, OK? Better you know nothing.'

His expression knotted faintly, a sign of exasperation. 'Then why tell me anything at all?'

'Because I need you to understand this is serious.'

'I get that, Umiko. What I don't get is why you've come to New York.'

'To lay a false trail. To make them think I've done what they want me to do. Give up. But I am not going to give up.'

'No.' Haruto shook his head dolefully. 'Of course you're not.'

'So, you will help, won't you? By telling anyone who asks that I'm touring the United States?'

'Sure.' He didn't look happy about it. But he looked as if he meant it, which counted for more. 'What else would I do?'

'And don't worry about me. I'm tougher than I look.'

'I know. But are you tough *enough*?'

She smiled at him. 'Well, we'll find out, won't we?'

After walking back to Porthtowan, Nick drove round to RAF Portreath's main entrance on the inland side of the site. From there he had a closer view of the buildings he'd already seen at a distance. There was a guard post and a camera-monitored gate as well. That was all. Nancekuke's present wasn't much like its past.

If only he could go back in time to that June evening in 1977 and follow Peter Ellery and Alison Parker after they left Martin Caldwell on Porthtowan beach and climbed the path he'd climbed himself that morning, he'd know. He'd understand. Barring that, there was only one way to find out what had happened.

He had to find the man who knew. His father. And ask him.

*

Half an hour later, he was on the A30, heading east, towards London, and the start of his search.

Haruto returned to work after his sushi lunch with Wada. She'd be gone from his apartment by the time he returned there that evening, so there was an unspoken poignancy to their goodbyes as they parted outside Nomura's Worldwide Plaza HQ.

From there Wada walked out on to Fifth Avenue and wandered slowly north, towards Central Park. She sensed, amidst the tumult of traffic and bustling pedestrians, the security of utter inconspicuousness. One small, solitary, middle-aged Japanese woman making her way along the streets of New York. No one would have thought she was in a hurry. No one would have thought she had any bold or hazardous intentions. No one would have thought anything about her at all.

And that was how she liked it.

ELEVEN

IT WAS A LONG AND WEARYING DRIVE TO LONDON FROM CORNWALL through the Friday afternoon traffic. Nick reached Catford as a chill dusk was setting in. He'd worried April might be out, but there were lights on in the house, so it looked as if he was in luck. Which was *un*lucky for April. She had questions to answer. And Nick meant to ask them.

'Nicky,' she almost sang as she opened the door to him. 'You should have let me know you were coming.'

'I'm not interrupting anything, am I?'

'No.' She frowned slightly. 'But I'm going out soon.'

'Got a date?'

'Since you ask, yes.'

'Nan?'

'Yeah.'

'That's nice for you.'

'But there's time for a quick drink. Do you want a beer? Or a glass of wine?'

'No thanks.'

They were in the kitchen by now. April swung the door of the fridge open, lifted out a bottle of white wine and poured herself a glass. She waggled the bottle invitingly at Nick. 'Sure?'

117

'Nothing for me, thanks.'

'OK.' She put the bottle back in the fridge and took a sip of wine. 'How are things?'

'Things?'

'You don't seem quite your normal self, Nicky. What's wrong?'

'Quite a lot, April, actually. Quite a fucking lot.'

'So . . . tell me what's up.'

He showed her the photograph Holgate had lent him, then. The photograph of five young protesters standing by the Redruth to Portreath road on Easter Saturday, 1977. He didn't say anything. He just let her hold it and look at the black-and-white images of the younger versions of herself and her friends: of Caro and her holding the *YOU ARE ENTERING A CHEMICAL WARFARE ZONE* banner; of Martin Caldwell and Alison Parker forcing leaflets on passing motorists; and of Peter Ellery gazing across the road into the camera.

'Christ,' she said, taking a big swallow of wine. 'This is memory lane stuff.' She was trying to sound unfazed, trying desperately to pretend there was no lie staring back at her from the photograph.

'Why did you and Caro switch fathers on me, April?'

'We didn't . . .' The words died in her throat. 'Where'd you get this, Nicky?'

'Barry Holgate. Retired *Western Morning News* reporter. If it matters.'

'Have you been down to Exeter?'

'I have. To eighteen Barnfield Hill, as a matter of fact.'

'You can't believe anything Marty says. He's . . .'

'Missing, actually. Whereabouts unknown. I haven't seen him. But Holgate told me most of what I needed to know.'

'You can't believe anything he says either. Holgate? I remember him. Typical journalist. Anything for a story. He didn't like any of us. We weren't his type. Well, not his readers' type I—'

Nick grabbed the photograph out of her hand so forcefully some wine splashed out of her glass on to the floor. They looked at each other in silence for a moment. In her face Nick saw guilt and regret and something very like fear. 'Could we just drop all that crap, please, April? It's beside the point, isn't it? I don't know what's going on with Martin. A lot, that's for sure. But what I do know – what's glaringly obvious – is that the guy in this photograph, the one who isn't Martin, looks just like me when I was that age. I mean, it's clear, isn't it?' He held the picture in front of her. 'Well, isn't it?'

She didn't reply. He could hear her breathing, shallowly and rapidly. He was distressing her and he hated doing it on account of all the love she'd given him for as long as he could remember. But he didn't hate it enough to stop. She didn't owe him much. But she did owe him the truth about his father.

'Peter Ellery was my father, not Geoff Nolan. You're not going to deny that, are you?'

Her silence continued, growing heavier all the time. Eventually, she said, 'I need to sit down.'

She walked over to the table and lowered herself very slowly into a chair. She took another gulp of wine. The glass was nearly empty. 'Pass me the bottle, would you, Nicky?'

He took it out of the fridge, poured some into her glass and sat down opposite her.

'For what it's worth,' she said, forming her words with evident care, 'I told Caro I thought it was a mistake to pass Geoff off as your father. I lived with it, though. I backed her up in the . . . little white lie.'

'Was it so little?'

'Well, Peter was dead. Everyone was sure of that. And you were approaching an age when you had to be told something. Then Geoff died. Providentially. Conveniently. So . . .'

'What would have been so bad about the truth?'

119

'Caro predicted – and the way you're behaving now goes to show she was probably right – that if you knew your father's death was just a legal presumption, that nobody could be sure, beyond a shadow of a doubt, that he *was* dead, then you'd never stop wondering if he was actually alive and well and out there, somewhere in the world. She worried it would become an obsession, something that would . . . distort your life. And she wanted the best for you, Nicky. We both did. A phantom father to chase didn't sound like the best to us. Whereas Geoff, dead and definitely buried, was . . . preferable. A whole lot preferable.'

'But the others – Martin, Miranda – must have realized I was actually Peter's son.'

'Caro never told them who the father was. And the resemblance wasn't obvious until you were older, by which time they didn't often see you and there was no reason for them to challenge the Geoff Nolan version of your paternity. I guess they decided to let sleeping dogs lie.'

'I suppose they did. But then, of course, there were a lot of sleeping dogs to choose from, weren't there, April? I mean, taking Peter Ellery out of my life was one thing. Taking out everything about how Alison Parker died and he supposedly died with her . . . well, that was quite another.'

'Telling you about all that might have made you curious about Peter. And if you ever saw a photograph of him . . .'

'The game was up.'

She swallowed some more wine and looked at him, honestly and openly. 'We did what we thought was best for you, Nicky, we really did. What difference does it make which of two dead men was actually your biological father?'

'None at all, I suppose. Unless the one who was isn't dead after all. You wouldn't have done your best for me then, would you?'

'But he *is* dead. There's absolutely no reason to think otherwise.'

'Really? Are you sure Martin Caldwell hasn't found a reason?'

'Marty's always wanted to believe Peter's alive. To assuage some of the guilt he feels about what happened that night, I suppose. He wants to believe it so badly he'll twist the facts into any shape that suits him.'

'Did you know what they were going down to Nancekuke to do?'

'Not at the time. Caro and I didn't trust Peter's informant.'

'Tom Noy?'

'That's right. We just didn't think he was reliable. He was so embittered about how the MoD had treated him, you couldn't believe a word he said. Peter and Alison thought otherwise. We agreed to disagree. They obviously decided it was better not to tell us what they were planning. Marty went along basically because he was so gone on Alison he'd have done anything she suggested. And she was . . . made of warrior stuff. Handing out leaflets and waving a banner was too tame for her. She wanted . . . engagement. Marty told us later they'd intended to break into Nancekuke to film stocks of sarin and something even more sinister Noy claimed had been produced there. He didn't tell the police that and neither did we. We were all scared stiff we'd be arrested as their accessories. It was a terrible time. Alison dead; Peter presumed dead; Marty in full meltdown mode; Miranda blaming us for letting them go down there in the first place; Geoff obsessed with the idea the police would find his drugs stash; and Vinod hardly saying a word. We didn't go to Alison's funeral, you know. We couldn't face her family. It was way up in Lincolnshire, but . . . I've always felt ashamed about that.'

'The police must have known you were holding out on them.'

'That depends on how much the MoD told them. They wouldn't have wanted any information leaking out about what went on at Nancekuke. Or what measures they took against intruders. Maybe they were happy for the police inquiry to go nowhere.'

'And so were you?'

'There was nothing we could do to bring Alison or Peter back, so in the end we . . . tried to put it behind us.'

'Where it stayed. Until now.'

April sighed. 'I'm sorry, Nicky. Truly I am.'

'I know you and Caro thought you were protecting me, April. But it seems to me you were protecting yourselves as well.'

She looked at him without evasiveness. One of April's most endearing features was her willingness to confront her own failings when she had to. There were tears welling in her eyes as she spoke. 'It's true.'

'And what you said about Martin persuading himself to believe Peter was alive? Didn't you and Caro persuade yourselves to believe the exact opposite?'

'I suppose we did.'

'I had a right to know.'

'Yes. And we denied you that. We just never . . . thought of what we were doing in those terms. What a bloody mess.' She drained her glass. 'Do you have any idea where Marty's gone, Nicky?'

'None at all. But I'm not the only one looking for him. There was a break-in at his flat.'

'A *break-in*?'

'Two, if you count the Japanese woman who helped herself to a spare key. Which didn't turn out well for her. She got hit over the head by the man who stole Martin's computer. He was Japanese as well, apparently.'

April's mouth had fallen open. She stared at him in astonishment. 'They were both *Japanese*?'

'Yeah. Does that mean something to you?'

'Did you meet the woman?'

'No. She'd discharged herself from the hospital and taken off by the time I arrived. But Holgate met her.'

'Do you know her name?'

'Mimori Takenaga.'

'Takenaga?' April's expression suggested this wasn't the first time she'd heard that name. 'What do you know about her?'

'Well, she told Holgate she'd arranged to meet Martin in London because he claimed to have information about how Aum Shinrikyo – you remember them? – got hold of the manufacturing method for the sarin they used in their attack on the Tokyo subway in 1995. Her husband was one of their victims. Martin didn't show up for the meeting. So she'd headed down to Exeter.'

'Why would Marty have information about Aum Shinrikyo?'

'God knows. But sarin was manufactured at Nancekuke, wasn't it? That has to be the connection.'

'It can't be. That doesn't make any sense.'

'It might, if you told me what *you* know about Mimori Takenaga. Because it's obvious you know something.'

April frowned and rubbed her forehead. 'Was she saying Marty had contacted her? Or was it the other way round?'

'No. *He* contacted *her.*'

'Christ. How did he . . .' Her thoughts seemed frozen. Something was troubling her. Deeply.

'How did he what?'

'Wait here.' She jumped up and hurried out into the hall. Then he heard her pounding up the stairs.

He didn't wait, as instructed, but got up and followed, as far as the foot of the stairs. He looked up and saw her shadow moving on the wall. He could hear her panting as she struggled with something in the cupboard at the end of the landing. 'April?' he called.

'I won't be long,' she called back breathlessly.

'What are you looking for?' He started up the stairs.

By the time he reached the landing, he saw she'd removed several bags and boxes from the cupboard and had pulled up the square of carpet beneath them. 'Fuck,' she said dismally beneath her breath.

'What's wrong?'

She sat slowly down and leant back against the banister. Tears were visible on her cheeks as she looked towards him. 'Your mother,' she said in an uneven voice. 'So sentimental. She wouldn't hurt a fly. Literally.'

'I know.'

'I loved her because of her gentleness. Because of her . . . humanity.'

'I know that too.'

'She must have taken pity on him at the end. Or near the end. No surprise, really. She took pity on everyone. Except herself'

'Who did she take pity on?'

'A few days before Christmas, about a week before she died, I came home and realized from the state she was in that she'd . . . exerted herself somehow. She said she'd gone for a walk, which was crazy. She was in no state to leave the house unaided. I thought maybe it was . . . an imaginary walk. But now I think she did go. And my guess is she went to the post box. And posted a letter to Marty.'

Nick moved to where she was sitting and knelt down beside her. 'Containing what?'

'An advert that appeared in the *Evening Standard* in May 1992.'

'Placed by Mimori Takenaga.'

She seemed shocked by the realization that he already knew about the advert. She thumbed away her tears. 'Who told you?'

'Miranda. Martin showed it to her. He didn't say how he'd got hold of it.'

'Why did he show it to *her*?'

'I suppose he hoped she'd agree with him that Peter Evans was Peter Ellery. She didn't. Even though she admitted to me there was a resemblance. But I think she's worried about Martin.'

'Miranda only worries about herself.'

Nick patted April's hand and felt the moisture of her tears on her thumb. 'Don't you think you're a bit hard on her?'

'Maybe. But she has no principles. You can't trust someone who has no principles.'

'Caro had principles.'

'Oh yeah. By the bucketload. More than I could handle sometimes.'

'But she didn't tell me about the advert, which was evidence – not clinching, but still evidence – that my father didn't die that night at Nancekuke.'

'She wanted to tell you. I talked her out of it. You were going through a difficult phase around then. How old would you have been? Fourteen? Fourteen-year-old boys are quite a handful, let me tell you. Fortunately, though, they don't tend to leaf through the pages of the *Evening Standard* when they come home from school every day.'

'Did you think it was Peter in the photograph?'

'We weren't sure. That's the honest truth. And to tell you *he* was your father rather than Geoff Nolan? That's quite a deception to unravel when you don't have to. If he was alive, he obviously didn't want any of us to know. So, we . . . said nothing . . . and prayed none of the others had seen the advert . . . or, if they had, that they'd say nothing either. Marty didn't live in London, of course, so we reckoned he wouldn't have seen it. The same went for Vinod. That only left Miranda. And she was in the middle of running for Parliament at the time. We were confident she'd do nothing that drew attention to her connection with Peter.'

'But you kept the advert?'

'Caro insisted. She said the day might eventually come when you needed to be told about it. Instead, it looks like the day came when she decided Marty needed to be told. The advert gave the name and address of a woman in Japan who was offering a thousand pound reward for information identifying Peter Evans, who'd worked for her father in London in September 1977. I guess Marty took the hint. He wrote to her.'

'And eventually got a reply. Suggesting they meet in London. Earlier this week. He was planning to meet me as well. To tell me what he'd unearthed about my father. But his contact with Mimori Takenaga seems to have attracted some hostile attention. Now Martin's missing. And Takenaga might as well be missing, because I've no idea where she went from Exeter.'

'It sounds like someone doesn't want Marty or anyone else following up the Peter Evans connection.'

'Peter himself, perhaps?'

'It's possible. There was always a hidden side to his nature. He never let you in on what he was really thinking. Unknowable is what he was. Which made him attractive on one level. And he had, well, I suppose you'd call it charisma. Caro couldn't stop herself being fascinated by him, though she was over that by the time he . . . well, did or didn't die. If he's alive, then he must have deliberately turned his back on his old life and remade himself as someone else. Maybe he can't afford to have his previous identity dragged into the light. I wouldn't want to go up against Peter. I think he could be . . . ruthless . . . if he felt he needed to be.'

'And dangerous?'

'Who knows what forty years might have done to him? I knew Peter Ellery, Nicky. This other man he's become – if he *has* become him – is an unknown quantity.'

'But he's my father.'

April leant her head against his shoulder. 'Is that really so important?'

'Maybe it shouldn't be, but . . . it feels as if it is.'

The phone started to ring in the kitchen downstairs. 'That'll be Nan,' said April. 'Wondering where I am. Actually, I'm wondering that myself. When's Kate due back?'

'Tomorrow.'

'You should talk this through with her. Before you do anything about it, I mean. Marty's not your responsibility. Nor is this Japanese woman. And Peter, if he's alive, clearly doesn't think you're his responsibility either.'

'He probably doesn't even know I exist.'

'It might be better for you to leave it that way.' The phone stopped ringing. 'But you're not going to, are you?'

'I may have no option. If I can't find Martin. Or Mimori Takenaga.'

'I wish I could believe that would stop you. But you've inherited Caro's stubbornness. There were things she just wouldn't give up on. That goes for you too. And this is one of those things. Maybe she sent Marty the advert because she knew he'd end up telling you about Peter. And then . . .'

'The truth would come out?'

'Yeah.' April nodded glumly. 'Whatever the truth is.'

TWELVE

A SECOND LONG FLIGHT IN TWENTY-FOUR HOURS WASN'T A PROSPECT Wada had been relishing, but she reckoned the effort was worth it. If anyone had been paying attention – and she suspected someone had – she'd done all she could to give them the impression she was baling out of Kodaka's enquiries into Nishizaki's business affairs. She'd even used her personal credit card to pay for this leg of the journey rather than the company card.

She had little clear idea of what was awaiting her in Iceland and tried to prevent herself brooding on the point by returning to her comfort reading, *The Makioka Sisters*, as soon as the plane took off from JFK. It proved a futile effort, not because she wasn't in the mood to enjoy Tanizaki's playful storytelling, but because the man sitting next to her, a paunchy, shock-haired American in a business suit he'd obviously bought when he was about ten kilograms lighter, insisted on conversing with her.

Wada's prejudices about Americans – particularly American men – were confirmed by almost everything George Guptill said. He volunteered his name and a handshake she found difficult to refuse, then alternated unsought disclosures about himself (married, childless, resident in New Jersey, en route to

Iceland to try to establish a franchise arrangement for his boss's East Coast burger chain) with unwelcome curiosity about Wada. She thought her responses were cool if not curt enough to persuade him to give up, but he seemed to regard her reticence as a challenge and started making wild guesses about her which she ended up correcting, thereby giving him the satisfaction of finding out more about her than she'd intended.

It wasn't much, of course. But George was undaunted. 'There's nothing more attractive in a woman than an air of mystery, Miss Wada.' (She'd dodged giving him more than her surname.) 'That's something my wife's never understood.'

By the time George had embarked on his third in-flight drink, he was quizzing Wada about the writings of Tanizaki and the intricacies of the Japanese language. Slowly, to her own astonishment, she was drawn in. She even found herself illustrating a linguistic point to him by explaining that the Toyoda family were thought to have changed their corporate name to Toyota because it could be written with the numerologically auspicious eight strokes foretelling prosperity. For some reason, this amused him enormously. What *was* she thinking, she later wondered.

George fell asleep shortly afterwards, for which she was grateful.

Falling asleep herself took rather longer.

It was as the plane began its descent to Keflavík airport through thick cloud and drizzle on Saturday morning that Wada realized why she'd succumbed to George's attempts to engage with her. He had nothing to do with Kodaka or Nishizaki or any of the many mysteries set in train by the death of Shitaro Masafumi. He was completely and reassuringly uninvolved. He was safe. And in talking to him she'd succeeded in forgetting, at least for a short while, the problems she was going to have to confront.

George didn't wake until the plane had actually landed. Bleary-eyed and dishevelled, he was still hunting for his bag in the overhead locker when Wada disembarked. And that, she assumed, was the last they were going to see of each other.

But she'd underestimated him. Hiring a car was out of the question, for the simple reason that Wada couldn't drive. Like many residents of Tokyo, she'd never seen any reason to learn. Accordingly, she joined the queue to buy a ticket for the bus into Reykjavík. Within minutes, George appeared beside her. 'Why don't we share a cab, Miss Wada? I don't know about you, but personally I hate waiting for buses.' There was something in his rumpled smile that made it impossible to refuse.

Instructing the taxi driver meant they both knew which hotel the other was staying in. The Hilton, in George's case, while Wada had booked herself into the Sol, which had the advantage of being quite close to the Hotel Arnarson, where Caldwell had last been heard of.

They drove away from the airport through blackened and desolate lavafields across which the low cloud rolled like smoke. 'This for sure is nothing like New Jersey,' was George's reaction.

It was for sure nothing like anywhere, in fact, that Wada could think of.

Reykjavík was a sprawl of mostly modern buildings, the Hilton a big glass and steel block beside a busy highway just outside the centre. George gave Wada his card and urged her to contact him if she found herself with time on her hands in the evening. 'You can rely on me to show a girl a good time.' Wada wasn't sure when she'd last been called a girl, but the novelty wasn't enough to make her give him her phone number. A good time, in the evening or at any other stage of the day, simply wasn't on her agenda.

*

The Sol was in a quieter location, neither new nor old, middle-ranking, with modest facilities, all of which suited Wada just fine. She went to her room, unpacked, showered and gave in to the mild jet lag the flight had left her with by taking what she thought would be a short nap.

Nick hadn't slept well in Greenwich. Crossing time zones wasn't the problem in his case. But travelling into other people's pasts had taken a similar kind of toll in its way. He felt disorientated and half removed from his normal life. Only a few days ago, he'd been looking forward to Kate's return home that afternoon. Now he found himself wishing she was away for longer, freeing him to delve further into the mystery surrounding his father without having to explain to her what he was doing and, fundamentally, why he was doing it.

He got up early, aware that Kate would expect him to do some food shopping before she arrived. But the idea of checking what he needed to buy and then going out to buy it, as if this was an ordinary weekend and nothing had changed in his world, wasn't so much absurd as ungraspable. He needed answers to the many questions April's admission had left him with, answers she'd been unable to supply.

At the moment, he could only think of one person who might be able to tell him more. He reckoned the earlier he called on her the better his chances of catching her unawares, so he hurried through breakfast, threw on some clothes and headed out.

The residential streets of Chelsea, lined with stuccoed town-houses and colourfully prinked front gardens, were quiet so early on a Saturday morning. The weather was cool, shower-clouds blocking the sun at fitful intervals. Parking was at a premium and Nick was left with a five-minute walk to Miranda's door.

As he approached, he was surprised to see a tall dark-haired man emerge into view from behind a swag of wisteria blossom and step out on to the pavement.

Nick's surprise was heightened when he realized the man was Asian and could easily be Japanese, though unusually tall if he was. The intruder at Caldwell's flat in Exeter had been an unusually tall Japanese man, according to the description Mrs Takenaga had given the police. Was this him again?

The man turned smartly left and walked away from Nick, but gave him a fleeting yet piercing glance over his shoulder as he did so. The effect was chilling. Nick pulled up, then started moving again, more slowly, waiting for the man to reach the end of the street and turn out of sight. It was a relief when he did.

The response to Nick's knock on the door was much quicker than he'd anticipated. Miranda yanked the door open and glared out at him. Then her expression softened. It was obvious she hadn't been expecting to see Nick on her doorstep. She was wearing a tracksuit and looked markedly less well groomed than when they'd met for lunch. Less relaxed, as well. Much less.

'Nick,' she said. 'This is a surprise.'

'Did you think he'd come back?'

'Who?'

'Your last visitor. I saw him leaving.'

She gazed past him and along the street. 'You mean the Irishman.' There was something wary but also dismissive in her tone. Nick couldn't quite get the measure of her mood.

'He didn't look Irish to me.'

'I didn't say he was.'

'Well, if he's not Irish, why—'

'Are you coming in?'

'Can I?'

'Of course.' A little of her jauntiness had been restored.

She led the way along a high-ceilinged, corniced hall to the kitchen – large and well equipped in a stripped-down style. They were at the back of the house now, overlooking a well-kept garden, vibrant with spring blooms. Birdsong was audible through a half-open window, though the house itself felt silent and empty.

'You want a cup of coffee? I just made some.'

'Thanks. That'd be great.'

She picked up her cup and drank from it, then grabbed the cafetière and poured a cup for him. He noticed a whisky bottle standing open-topped near her cup. His guess was she'd added some to her coffee. His further guess was that this wasn't something she generally did on a Saturday morning.

'Sorry if I've, er . . .'

'It doesn't matter. What's brought you here, Nick?'

'My father.'

'I think I said everything I had to say about Geoff over lunch.'

'I'm not talking about Geoff Nolan.'

'But you just said—'

'Peter Ellery. My father. My *real* father.'

'Ah . . . Right.' She sat down at the kitchen table and waved for him to do the same. 'So, Marty went ahead and told you.'

'No. He didn't.'

'But you met him?'

'He never showed up.'

'Well, that's Marty for you. One hundred per cent unreliable. So, who did tell you? Not April, surely.'

'Barry Holgate.'

'Who?'

'Retired journalist. Used to work for the *Western Morning News*. Down in Exeter.'

'You've been to Exeter?'

'Yes, Miranda, I have. I've been to eighteen Barnfield Hill, as a matter of fact. Looking for Martin Caldwell. But he wasn't there. No one knows where he's gone. But lots of people are looking for him apart from me. Including you, if the message you left on his phone is anything to go by.'

'You heard that? How?'

'I didn't – Holgate told me. The neighbours let us into Martin's flat. There was a break-in. His computer was stolen. The Japanese woman Martin was supposed to meet got injured by the thief, though she's vanished since as well, so I can't ask her what the hell's going on. As for Peter Ellery, Holgate showed me a photograph dating from 1977 in which he appears, along with Caro, April, Martin and Alison Parker. The resemblance to me is obvious. As it must have been obvious to you and everyone else all my life.'

'Christ. I need a cigarette. Wait here.' Miranda went off in search of a smoke, calling back to Nick from the adjoining room. 'None of this is down to me, Nick. Caro decided you were better off not knowing Peter was your father. I can't say I blame her.' She returned, lit cigarette and pack in hand. She offered him one. He shook his head. 'Well, now you know.' She sat back down. 'Feel better for it, do you?'

'I'm coming to terms with it.'

'Not sure I can help you do that.'

'Peter Ellery's still alive, isn't he?'

'Marty believes he is.'

'And so do you.'

'Do I?'

'Why did you phone Martin?'

'I was worried about him.'

'With good reason, apparently.'

'I meant I was worried about his state of mind.'

'Any idea where he's gone?'

'None at all. Listen, Nick, I'm sorry you had to wait so long to find out the truth about your paternity, but that's down to Caro and April. It wasn't my decision. It was nothing to do with me. So I really don't know what I can say. Maybe Peter drowned with Alison. Maybe he didn't.'

'Why would someone steal Martin's computer, Miranda? I mean, let's consider the possibilities. Breaking and entering is fairly heavy-duty stuff. And this particular bit of breaking and entering was for a specific purpose. What does Martin know that's so important – so damaging – that the people he knows it about go to such lengths to cover it up?'

Miranda took a long drag on her cigarette and shook her head. 'I simply can't imagine.'

'Really? Didn't your earlier visitor fill you in?'

'How could he? He has nothing to do with this.' She hesitated, floundering to find some faintly plausible explanation for her association with such a man. 'What he was doing here is none of your business.'

'You'd be right about that but for the fact that before she vanished Mrs Takenaga – the woman who came all the way from Japan to talk to Martin – gave the police a description of the intruder at his flat. It matched your . . . Irishman . . . to a tee.'

Miranda stubbed out her cigarette and gazed at Nick long and hard.

'Who is he really?' Nick pressed. 'Who does he work for?'

'Not me. Since you ask.'

'Then who?'

Miranda's gaze faltered slightly. Something seemed to give way inside her. 'If Peter didn't drown with Alison – if he's still alive to this day – he's obviously decided, for reasons of his own, to turn his back on his old life, his old identity, on everything Peter Ellery was until June 1977. It takes a lot to do that. There needs to be a good reason to make the effort, I'd say. To write off everything about yourself. To start again. To rebuild your life. With a new name, a new personality, a new *you*.'

'Do you know why he might go to all that trouble, Miranda?'

'No.'

'I reckon it has to be about what happened at Nancekuke that night. Peter and Alison broke into the base looking for secrets about the nerve gas being produced there. Alison ended up drowned. One of the guards was shot. And Peter . . . disappeared.'

'I don't know anything about a guard being shot. Where'd you get that from?'

'Holgate.'

'He's just an old hack peddling conspiracy theories.'

'Maybe. But you said yourself there had to be a good reason – a compelling need – for Peter to run away from his former life.'

'Yes. And I'm suggesting that means you should think twice about looking for him. If he's alive, he either doesn't know you exist or he knows and doesn't want to have anything to do with you. It's hard, I know, but maybe you should . . . let it go.'

'Are you trying to warn me off?'

'I'm trying to give you some good advice, Nick, that's all. Think about taking it.'

'Do you know where he is?'

'I'm sorry.' She lit another cigarette. 'I can't help you.'

'I think you can.'

'I'm going to have to ask you to leave if you go on like this.'

'If I tell the Exeter police I saw the man they're looking for in connection with the break-in at Martin's flat and the assault on Mrs Takenaga here, at your house, they'll want to ask you some questions. He was seen by one of the neighbours as well as Mrs Takenaga, by the way. And he does have a pretty distinctive appearance. Do you want me to do that?'

She looked straight at him. 'I'd certainly rather you didn't.'

'Then tell me who he is. Tell me who he works for. Tell me what you know. Because you know *something*, Miranda. That's as clear as day.'

'I know you'd be better off forgetting all about this.'

'But I'm not going to. I don't think I can.'

'That's a pity. For both of us.' She studied him closely as she drew on the cigarette. 'You know, Nick, you never think, when you're young, that the things you do – the crazy things, the unwise things, the downright wrong things – are going to catch up with you when you're older. You think they're over and done with. And they can seem like they are. For years. For decades. For the greater part of your entire life. And then . . .'

'How can I find my father?'

'I'm thinking of going away for Easter. I reckon I deserve a break. Maybe you should give yourself a break too.'

'That doesn't sound like an answer to my question.'

'Well, some questions can't be answered, can they? But . . . if you do want to go somewhere . . . I could suggest a destination. In return for being . . . left in peace.' She caught his eye. She was offering him some kind of deal. That was what it had come down to between them.

'Where?'

'I need to fetch something. Wait here.'

She left the kitchen and he heard her climbing the stairs. There was a creak from the floorboards of the room above him. He couldn't tell what she was doing. He picked up her coffee cup and sniffed it. There was a definite aroma of whisky cutting through the coffee. She was hiding it well, but she was under a lot of strain. And Nick wasn't the cause of most of it. What kind of message had the Irishman delivered to Baroness Cushing? And who was the message from?

He heard her coming back down the stairs. She walked into the kitchen, empty-handed. She crossed to the French windows leading out into the garden and signalled for him to follow.

A few seconds later, they were standing on the patio, with birdsong and breeze around them. There was a wrought-iron table and a pair of chairs close by.

'Any particular reason we've come out here?' Nick asked.

Miranda didn't answer. From her tracksuit pocket she took a small slim grey metal case and laid it on the table. Perhaps, he thought, that *was* her answer.

'What's this?'

'The case is shielded against all forms of scanning,' she replied, hardly speaking above a whisper. 'It's the sort of shielding some people are using for their credit cards these days, but this one's at the triple X end of the scale. Open it.'

Nick eased the case open. Inside, nestling in a frame, was a black card with a single word printed in the top left corner in white capitals. *EMERGENCE*. He took the card out of the case and turned it over. There was nothing on the back. The material felt odd. He couldn't have said with certainty whether it was plastic or metal.

'I need a clear understanding with you, Nick,' Miranda went on. 'After this, I don't hear from you again, OK? And I especially don't hear from the police.'

'That depends what you're giving me.'

'Admission to an auction. To be held next Wednesday at six p.m.'

'What kind of auction?'

'You'll have to go and find out.'

'Where's it being held?'

'Do we have an understanding? Date, time, place, admission. That's all I can give you. Anything else is . . . not mine to reveal. So, are we agreed?'

Nick looked down at the card in his hand. *Emergence*. What did it mean? What was being auctioned? 'This will lead me to my father?'

'*Are we agreed?*'

Her expression gave nothing away. Nick had to make a choice. But he sensed that in the final analysis there was really only one. He nodded. 'We're agreed.'

'Good. Laugavegur three, Reykjavík, Iceland. That's the address.'

'And—'

'And nothing.' She took the card gently from his hand, replaced it in the case and clicked the case shut. 'Don't show that to anyone until you use it at the auction.'

'But—'

'Goodbye, Nick.'

It was nearly noon when Wada woke. Annoyed with herself for sleeping so long, she hurried out and followed the free map she took from the lobby to the nearby Hotel Arnarson, which looked a few degrees smarter than the Sol, but still a long way from swanky. She was pretty sure she recognized the reception guy by his voice as the more helpful of the two men she'd spoken to on the phone. According to his lapel badge, he was called Bjarni. And it soon transpired he recognized her voice as well. After offering Wada his personal apologies for the weather – 'Horrible, but that's spring in Iceland' – he frowned slightly at her and said, 'Did we speak on the phone recently? I feel I know your voice.'

'I called to ask about my friend Martin Caldwell.'

'Ah. Of course. Yes. You did not leave your name.'

'I am Wada.'

'Have you heard from Mr Caldwell, Miss Wada?'

'No. That is why I have come to Iceland.'

'Well, maybe the police have news of him. I can give you the name and phone number of the officer dealing with the matter.'

'That would be kind. Thank you.'

Bjarni looked at his computer and jotted the information down on a hotel card. 'I can contact the officer for you if you wish.'

'There is no need to do that.' Wada was hoping to avoid all contact with the police if she possibly could. They were likely to have more questions for her than she had for them. 'On the phone, you mentioned other people have been seeking information about Mr Caldwell.'

'Quite a few, Miss Wada. We have had several calls, in fact. It is strange. Most of the callers did not leave their name. Except one. I guess you may want to speak to that person, yes?'

'I do.'

'Well . . .' He consulted some kind of day-book. A second hotel card was handed to her. 'Here you are.'

'Thank you.' Wada looked down at what he'd written. An Icelandic-sounding name – Erla Torfadóttir – and a phone number. 'Do you expect to hear from the police again?'

'Possibly. You wish me to tell them where you are staying?'

'I would prefer you . . .'

'Not to?'

'For now, yes. Until I have . . .'

'Spoken to Erla, maybe?'

'Yes.' Wada smiled gratefully. 'Exactly. Until I have spoken to Erla Torfadóttir. And then . . .'

Bjarni smiled back at her. 'And then you let me know.'

THIRTEEN

AS SOON AS HE ARRIVED HOME, NICK BOOKED A FLIGHT TO ICELAND for Monday and a four-night stay at a hotel in Reykjavík. It was all ridiculously expensive at such short notice, with Easter pending, but he no longer cared about such considerations. Nor had he decided exactly what he was going to tell Kate, but he had the rest of the weekend to persuade her he hadn't lost his mind. He didn't want her worrying about him, so there could be no question of revealing everything he'd discovered.

Kate's family was a model of middle-class English normality. It was obvious her parents loved each other and neither of them had ever been married to anyone else. There were no children of a previous relationship, just level-headed Kate and her two level-headed sisters. Nick's background was outrageously unconventional by comparison.

Around the time Kate's flight was due to land at Gatwick, Nick settled on a version of events he thought she'd find it possible, if not necessarily easy, to understand. Martin Caldwell had decided the time had come to tell Nick who his real father was and that the man in question was going to be present at an

141

auction in Reykjavík on Wednesday. Nick had decided to meet Caldwell in Reykjavík, attend the auction, introduce himself to his father and see what came of it.

He phoned April, who promised to tell Kate nothing, if she pressed her for information, beyond confirmation that she and Caro had misled Nick about the identity of his father.

'I'm going to be away for a few days,' he explained. 'I don't want Kate fretting on my account.'

'Where are you going, Nicky?'

'To find him.'

'You're going to come back safe, aren't you?'

'Of course I am. Why shouldn't I?'

'I don't know. But—'

'I'll be fine, April. This is something I have to do. Once I've done it . . .'

'Everything will be like it was before?'

'Of course. Just make sure Kate doesn't have any cause to be anxious about me.'

'I'll give her none, Nicky. You can rely on me.'

'I know I can.'

'Just tell me you'll be careful.'

'I'll be careful.'

He heard her sigh gently. 'I suppose that'll have to do.'

Wada sat in a coffee shop in the centre of Reykjavík, waiting for a response to the phone message she'd left for Erla Torfadóttir. The weather was cold and drizzly, the clouds hanging low over the grey city and the silvery arm of the sea it faced.

The city was certainly popular with tourists. There were swarms of Americans, Chinese and assorted Europeans on the streets – even some Japanese. As Wada huddled over her bowl of soup, she wondered what had drawn so many people here. Glacier-trekking, geysers, hot springs, volcanoes and the Northern Lights, according to the adverts on the back of her map. They wouldn't have drawn her.

But then travel for its own sake had never attracted Wada. She didn't like breaks in routine. They discomposed her. And she was certainly discomposed now. Though that wasn't going to stop her doing what she needed to do.

When her phone rang, she answered it even before she saw the caller was Erla Torfadóttir.

'Hello?'

'Umiko Wada?'

'Yes. Erla?'

'Yes. I'm Erla. I got your message.' She sounded young, but not exactly carefree. There was a ragged edge of anxiety to her voice. 'About Martin Caldwell.'

'Do you know him?'

'We met last week. We were supposed to meet again.'

'I was supposed to meet him also. In London. He did not turn up.'

'And you've come to Iceland looking for him?'

'Yes. Can you help me?'

'You're Japanese, Umiko?'

'Yes. I travelled to London from Tokyo to meet him.'

'You must have had a good reason to make such a long journey.'

'I did. Can we discuss this face to face, Erla?'

'Maybe. But . . . I need to know . . . do you work for a Japanese company?'

'No. I do not.'

'We have to be careful.'

'I am always careful. Can we meet?'

There was a long pause, then Erla said, 'Reykjavík Roasters, Brautarholt, one hour from now. It's a coffee shop. OK for you?'

'OK.'

*

143

Wada was tempted to call Dobachi before she met Erla, to see if there was any news of the police investigation into Kodaka's killing. But she reminded herself, as she marched along the waterfront promenade with the drizzle thickening around her, that she wasn't supposed to be in Iceland and she wasn't supposed to be pursuing the mystery of her boss's death at all. She was on her own. And it had to stay that way.

Reykjavík Roasters was crowded with students tapping at laptops and iPhones and gaggles of young mothers with toddlers in pushchairs. Wada took her coffee to the bench by the window and gazed out as she sipped it, eyeing the passers-by and trying to guess which one might be Erla. Numerous candidates walked past in the form of willowy young blonde-haired Icelandic women, but none of those who entered the coffee shop approached her, though as the sole Asian on the premises she was easy to spot.

Then her phone rang.

'Hello?'

'This is Erla. You can see a Euromarket across the street, yes?'

There was a convenience store on the other side of the road. From where she was Wada couldn't be sure of the name, but she reckoned that was the place Erla meant. 'I see it.'

'I'm just coming out.'

As Wada watched, a young woman stepped into view from inside the shop. She was, as Wada had expected, tall, young, slim and blonde. She was wearing jeans and a yellow anorak. She looked in Wada's direction and started walking.

'Follow me.'

Erla ended the call there and put her phone in her pocket. Wada abandoned her coffee, shrugged on her coat and set off after her.

Erla kept up a steady pace and didn't look back. Wada closed the gap between them, then slowed slightly. She thought it best not to catch up.

They crossed a side street and arrived outside a large, modern three-storey building decorated in garish shades of red, blue and yellow. It was the Stúdentagarðar, according to a large sign on the wall. Wada's guess was that it was a student hall of residence, which explained why there'd been so many students in Reykjavík Roasters.

Erla entered a central courtyard and climbed the stairs to the second floor, then followed the open walkway along to the door of flat 240. She still didn't look back, though she must have been aware Wada was following her. She let herself in, but left the door ajar.

Wada pushed the door open just far enough to slip inside, glancing along the walkway as she did so. There was no one in sight.

The flat wasn't small by Japanese standards, but Wada suspected that to an Icelander it was tiny. There was a vestibule area, a kitchen no more than one person could comfortably enter at a time, a closed door that presumably led to the bathroom and one other room that appeared to serve as lounge, study and bedroom all rolled into one. Dark blue paint on the walls didn't make it seem any larger.

Erla had taken off her anorak and hung it on a hook. She was standing in the doorway of the lounge. Wada could see herself over Erla's shoulder, reflected in a high, narrow wall-mirror.

'Welcome,' said Erla.

'Hæ,' came another, male voice. A man, even taller and thinner than Erla, swung his legs off the bed, where he'd evidently been lying, and stood up, the top of his head coming close to brushing the ceiling. He was clearly older than Erla, maybe by ten years, but he had the loose-limbed casual look of the perpetual student about him.

'This is Kristjan Einarsson,' said Erla. 'Kristjan, this is Umiko.'

Kristjan had light brown hair tied back in a ponytail and a wispy beard that accentuated the narrowness of his face. He fixed Wada with a sapphire gaze. 'You're Japanese, right?' he asked, with no hint of politeness.

'Right,' said Wada. 'And you're Icelandic.'

'Sure. For every generation backwards.'

'Do you both know Martin Caldwell?'

'Yeah. We both know him. How do *you* know him?'

'We were supposed to meet. In London. He didn't show up.'

'And you came all the way here to find him?'

'It was an important meeting.'

Erla murmured something in Icelandic. Kristjan nodded. 'Martin said he was going back to England to meet a Japanese woman. That's you, I guess. Though he never gave us your name.' The glance he exchanged with Erla then left Wada questioning whether that was true.

'Can you help me find Martin Caldwell?'

'Can *you* help *us* find him?'

'Maybe. Maybe we can help each other.'

'Yeah. But that means we have to trust each other first. And I don't trust you . . . Umiko.'

'My friends just call me Wada.'

'Was Martin your friend?'

'No. I have never met him.'

'We're ahead of you there. But we don't know where he is. It seems he hasn't left Iceland. Beyond that . . .' Kristjan shrugged.

'What was your business with him?'

'Why should we tell you?' Erla cut in. 'Give us a reason.'

Wada weighed her options. The pair were clearly suspicious, maybe with good reason. She'd come to Iceland to learn whatever she could. She wasn't going to learn much without taking a few chances. It was time to take one of those chances. 'Martin Caldwell was expecting to meet a woman called Mimori Takenaga. But she could not leave Japan. She sent me instead. I work for a private detective. Mr Caldwell told Mrs Takenaga he could give her information about an Englishman who worked for her father at the time of his death – supposedly by suicide – in London in 1977. As far as I have discovered, the man was a student with Mr Caldwell named Peter Ellery. But Mrs Takenaga knew him as Peter Evans. And now it seems he's known as Peter Driscoll.'

'Who's the private detective you work for?' asked Kristjan.

'Kazuto Kodaka. I must tell you he was killed – hit-and-run – after I left Tokyo. And Mrs Takenaga has been placed in a psychiatric clinic by her family.'

'And Martin's disappeared.' Kristjan shook his head. 'That's a shitload of bad news, Wada.'

'Yes. It is.'

'What do you know about Peter Driscoll?'

'He runs a deal-brokering company called Quartizon, part-owned by the Nishizaki Corporation.'

'What sort of deals does he broker?'

'I am not sure. Maybe you know.'

'Maybe we do.' Kristjan said something to Erla in Icelandic. She opened a drawer in a cabinet by the bed, took out some cigarette papers and a sachet of what Wada assumed wasn't tobacco and started rolling a couple of spliffs. Kristjan sat down on the edge of the bed and frowned at Wada. 'If your boss is dead and your client's been put away, why haven't you given up the case?'

'I liked my boss. And I am not sure I really have a choice. I am not sure I would be *allowed* to give up.'

'You're in big trouble, Wada.'

'Yes.'

'Bigger than us.' Erla handed Kristjan his spliff. They both lit up. 'You want one?'

'No.'

'A drink, maybe? There's vodka.'

'Nothing for me. Except answers.'

Kristjan exchanged another look with Erla, which seemed to settle something. 'OK,' he said, waving away a cloud of cannabis-scented smoke. 'I write a blog about foreign ownership of land in Iceland. Under-the-radar buyouts of farms and estates. There's a lot of it going on and some of us don't like it. I named Quartizon as broker for many of the transactions. There are rumours they have options on hundreds, maybe thousands, of parcels of land. They've been on my case ever since. Threats, injunctions, the full legal heavy stuff. Plus some non-legal threats to my personal safety. Erla's also.'

'Quartizon are frightening,' said Erla quietly. 'I wish I'd never heard of them.'

'Some of my blogs were in Icelandic, some in English. Martin had read one of the English ones. He contacted me. I told him I was getting serious aggravation from Quartizon. He offered to help. He said he had information about Peter Driscoll that might get them off our backs. But he wanted our help too. To find out what exactly Quartizon's plan was. The big picture, he called it. There's no reason their land-buying operations should be limited to Iceland. And Quartizon's strings are being pulled by Nishizaki in Japan. So, what's really going on?'

'I believe the Nishizaki Corporation has criminal connections,' said Wada. 'I believe investigating them is what got Kodaka killed.'

'We should leave this alone,' said Erla. She looked appealingly at Kristjan. 'It's too dangerous.'

Kristjan scowled. 'Let them get away with it? Fuck no. We're Icelanders, Erla. This is *our* land. They have no right to do any of this.'

'But we can't stop them.'

'Maybe we can. With Wada's help. She's *Japanese*.'

'Why is that important?' Wada asked.

'Quartizon opened an office in Reykjavík last year. Very small, very low key. I know someone who works there. He doesn't like what they're doing – even the things he actually knows about – but they pay well, so . . . he just does his job. But he likes to drink. And when he drinks . . . he tells me things.'

'What kind of things?'

'Recently, Quartizon have leased bigger premises right in the centre of the city. It's opened as some kind of art gallery, but according to my friend it's a front for something big that's in the pipeline. The company's running a hush-hush project he's frozen out of called Emergence. He's no idea what it's about. He's not approved for access to the files. Only the Japanese staff – and there are only a few of them – are in the know. Plus Driscoll, obviously.'

'Is Driscoll here, in Reykjavík?'

'We think so. Preparing for the launch of whatever the fuck Emergence is. If we could find out what it's about . . .'

Erla grabbed his arm and began talking rapidly in Icelandic. Wada caught the names Quartizon, Driscoll and Caldwell as Erla went on. The expression on Kristjan's face suggested he wasn't really listening to her. When she'd finished, he rolled his eyes.

'We either do something or we do nothing,' he said after a moment. 'And I'm not going to do nothing while Driscoll sells bits of my country off like fillets of fish. From what my friend's told me, Wada, you might be the person we need. The Emergence files are all in Japanese, so he couldn't understand them even if he opened them. But you could, couldn't you?'

'You said he did not have access.'

'He's not *approved* for access. But I'm pretty sure he could get in if he wanted to. That would be some kind of breach of company rules. It could mean dismissal. And it's not worth the risk if he can't read what's in the files. But with you it *is* worth the risk. He knows what they're doing at Quartizon is bad for Iceland. I think he'll cooperate. We just have to persuade him. What do you say?'

Wada didn't have to think long. 'Yes. I say yes.'

'Great. I'll call him now. Try to set up a meeting.'

Kristjan grabbed his phone. Wada watched Erla rubbing her hands together nervously. She didn't like what they were doing. Maybe she knew Kristjan's friend only too well. A few moments passed.

'He's not picking up,' said Kristjan. 'I'll text him.'

'Have you met this man, Erla?' Wada asked as Kristjan thumbed out his message.

Erla nodded. When she spoke, it was in an undertone. It seemed to Wada she was hoping Kristjan wouldn't listen to what she said. 'Ragnar's like the stool in my kitchen.'

'And what is that like?'

'It wobbles.'

'Yeah,' said Kristjan, finishing the text and grinning thinly at Wada. 'Ragnar's a wobbly stool. But he's *our* wobbly stool.'

'What did you tell him?' asked Erla.

'I told him we have someone he's absolutely got to meet. As soon as possible. For his sake, our sake, everyone's sake.'

A brief silence fell. It was as if they were all waiting for Ragnar to respond. But Wada hadn't stopped thinking about what they were up against. 'Where does Driscoll stay when he's in Iceland?'

'The Borg, I expect,' said Kristjan. 'It's our classiest hotel. But I don't actually know.'

'You've seen him, though?'

'No. Not with my own eyes. He comes. He goes. Some guy in a suit in a limo with tinted windows and a private jet waiting at Reykjavík airport. Our lines don't cross, Wada. He's part of the international capitalist set. I'm . . . one of the little people.' There was a beep from his phone. 'Hold on.' He looked down. 'Ragnar's come back.'

'What does he say?' asked Erla anxiously.

'We're on. Jarðfræðingur, ten o'clock.' Kristjan looked at Wada. 'It's a bar. It'll be noisy. But that's good. No one will hear what we say.'

'He'll be drunk by ten,' said Erla dolefully.

'That's not so bad,' said Kristjan. 'We need him a bit drunk to agree to do this.'

'Maybe he'll be more than a *bit* drunk.'

'Give the guy a chance. Give *us* a chance. And you don't need to come anyway. But you'll come, won't you, Wada?'

Wada nodded. They had to try this. There wasn't a doubt in her mind. Though as to the result . . . there was nothing *but* doubts wreathed around that. 'I will come.'

Perhaps because she was feeling completely relaxed after her Tuscan holiday, Kate took the news of Nick's imminent departure for Iceland with greater equanimity than he'd expected and even failed to query his logic that he'd assumed she wouldn't want to go with him because she'd only just got back from a trip herself. She went on to surprise him by saying she'd never been entirely convinced the conveniently dead Geoff Nolan was his father. This sounded to Nick like one of her characteristic pieces of wisdom after the event, but he let it ride, grateful she wasn't more curious than she was about the identity of his real father.

'This is obviously something you have to do,' she declared, as if that explained everything, although . . . 'Whatever you find out about him, you will be back by the end of the week, won't you? Don't forget Mummy's invited us to Easter lunch.'

So, there it was. He had to be back in time for Easter lunch. Nothing else mattered, apparently. And between then and that cosy lunch party . . . some kind of truth would be uncovered. Nick was determined to make sure of that.

Wada had arranged to meet Kristjan at nine forty-five, at the west front of Hallgrímskirkja, the vast concrete Gothic church that dominated Reykjavík's skyline. The drizzle had persisted, blurring the floodlights that bathed the church, but there were still a few tourists admiring its imposing architecture. Wada tried to do some admiring herself, but her heart wasn't in it. She was early for the rendezvous, having fretted away the early part of the evening at her hotel. Now she paced around, trying to keep warm in the deepening chill, hoping Kristjan would be early as well.

He wasn't. But someone else, it transpired, had guessed Wada might show up before she strictly needed to. Wada's phone rang and the caller – Erla – asked her to walk across to the shadowy southern side of the square surrounding the church.

She set off. And Erla stepped out of a deep shadow to greet her.

'Nervous?' Erla asked, pulling on a cigarette with every appearance of nervousness herself.

'I thought you were not coming with us,' said Wada.

'I'm not. I'm here to warn you.'

'You do not think Ragnar is reliable. I know.'

'He could be worse than unreliable.'

'How?'

'He works for Quartizon. Maybe he's just pretending to have doubts about them. Maybe this is a trap.'

152

'But *we* asked to meet *him*. How can it be a trap?'

'If Driscoll knows we've been asking questions, then he could be ready for you.'

'Kristjan thinks Ragnar is on our side.'

'He *wants* to think that.'

'He knows him better than you do.'

'And I know Kristjan better than he knows himself. This is a bad idea.'

'You have a better one?'

Erla had no answer to that beyond several fretful puffs on her cigarette.

'Well then . . .'

'Don't believe everything Ragnar says, that's all. Shit.' She glanced past Wada. 'I think I see Kristjan coming. Don't tell him I was here.'

Wada looked over her shoulder and spotted a tall, rangy figure on the far side of the square wearing a long, flapping coat. When she looked back, Erla was gone, with only the scent of her cigarette smoke hanging in the air to prove she'd ever been there.

Wada shrugged and started walking back towards the church. Erla might be right to have her doubts about Ragnar. But Kristjan might be right about him too. And Wada already knew she wasn't going to make much progress without taking some risks.

'You look even smaller out here than in Erla's apartment,' was Kristjan's bemusing greeting.

'Is my size important?'

'No. I just— Forget it.'

'Are we far from the bar?'

'No. Ten minutes tops.'

'Let's go, then.'

'OK.'

153

Kristjan led the way, setting a stiff pace thanks to his long, loping stride. Wada had to hurry to keep up with him.

'You ought to know Ragnar doesn't like the Japanese guys he works with,' Kristjan went on. 'So, you might not be his . . . cup of tea.'

'It is not necessary for him to like me.'

'I guess not, but, just to play safe, don't give him your real name.'

'Why not?'

'Less for him to follow up if he gets twitchy later. Or talkative.'

'Very well. I will be . . . Abe.'

'Like your prime minister?'

'It is a common name.'

'OK. Abe it is.'

Jarðfræðingur was loud and dark and very busy. It favoured some kind of Icelandic heavy metal music. Wada possessed excellent hearing, which she'd often found as much a disadvantage as an advantage. She also had no ear for music, to which she was either indifferent or, as in this case, profoundly averse.

Not that it mattered. Kristjan insisted on buying her a bottle of the same lager he was drinking, then grabbed her hand – either to imply to other customers they were together or simply to make sure she didn't get lost – and piloted her through a couple of crammed side rooms with rough-hewn walls, where stray darts of strobe lighting revealed a ruck of mostly leather-clad drinkers. The men sported large beards and tattoos, the women long hair and tattoos of their own.

The last room they came to was marginally less crowded and slightly less noisy on account of its distance from the sound system. It also featured some low leather couches, on one of which a fat, pale-skinned young man was almost lying flat, supporting a bottle and an iPhone on the dome of his stomach. He had dark, receding hair and an incipient double chin, but no beard, which made him conspicuous in these surroundings, as did his choice of denims and T-shirt. He and Kristjan exchanged a glance and several phrases of Icelandic.

'This is Ragnar,' said Kristjan. 'Ragnar, this is Abe.'

'*Hæ*,' growled Ragnar. He didn't smile as he looked up at Wada. '*Konnichi wa.*'

'I was told you did not speak Japanese,' said Wada. 'Was I misinformed?'

Kristjan laughed. Ragnar didn't. He went on looking at Wada, with no sign that what he saw impressed him. 'Thanks for meeting us,' said Kristjan brightly.

'No problem,' said Ragnar slowly.

Kristjan followed up with something in Icelandic. He sat down beside Ragnar and signalled for Wada to sit down on the other side of him. As she did so, the depression in the couch caused by Ragnar's weight threatened to pull her down against him. She had to anchor herself to the arm to prevent that happening.

Ragnar took a swig from his bottle and looked at them each in turn. 'Why am I meeting some middle-aged Japanese woman on a Saturday night in Reykjavík, Kristjan?' he asked. 'I get enough of her kind all week in the office.'

Kristjan leant in close to answer. He spoke at what would have been normal pitch anywhere else, but counted as a whisper in the booming confines of Jarðfræðingur. 'You said yourself you'd need to be able to read Japanese to make sense of those files, Ragnar. So I've brought you someone who can read Japanese. Because she is Japanese. But she doesn't work for Quartizon.'

'How can you be sure of that?'

'She's the woman Caldwell was planning to meet in London.'

'The one who was supposed to give him some dirt on Driscoll?'

'I have information about Driscoll's past that could be damaging,' Wada cut in. 'But I think we should concentrate for the present on what his company is doing in Iceland. Can you help us find that out?'

'Why should I?'

'Because you care. According to Kristjan.'

'Well?' Kristjan grasped Ragnar's shoulder. 'Don't you?'

Ragnar gave the question some thought, aided by a deep swallow of lager. Then he said, 'You want me to get you in?'

'*Já*. All the way.'

Ragnar shook his head. 'It's too risky.'

'You let us worry about that.'

Ragnar snorted. 'It's *me* I'm worried about.'

'We're not asking you to come with us. Just tell us how to do it. We'll share what we get with you, Ragnar. Abe will be able to tell you exactly what Driscoll's plan is.'

'Maybe I don't want to know what his plan is.'

'Yes you do. It's eating you up.'

Ragnar nodded slowly. 'It's true. Those bastards laugh at me. Not because I'm funny. But because they know more than I do.'

'Then . . .'

'I can get you in. And on to the system. Sure, I can do that. You'll be on your own, though. You understand? I can't help you after that.'

Kristjan squeezed his shoulder. 'We understand.'

There was another lengthy pause, then Ragnar said, 'How soon do you want to do this?'

'Before the launch.'

'That could be any day this week. Something's brewing.'

'Very soon, then.'

'You'd have to go in at night.'

'Of course.'

'Tomorrow?'

'Why wait until tomorrow?' asked Wada.

Ragnar gave her a scornful glance. 'I thought you people were famous for your patience. You know. Tea ceremony. All that painstaking shit.'

'I do not like being called "you people",' she said levelly.

'*Sumimasen*, I'm sure.'

'And you have not answered my question. Why wait until tomorrow?'

'Because I'll be prime fucking suspect if it's discovered the files have been accessed without authority, as it will be sooner or later, probably sooner. So I'll need an alibi. Tomorrow night I'll stay over with my parents in Akranes. I can give you the entry codes to the building and Quartizon's office and the password for one of the terminals. You'll have to memorize them. I don't want anything written down or recorded.'

'That all sounds good, Ragnar,' said Kristjan.

'Yeah? Well, what sounds good can end bad. You remember that, Kristjan.'

'I will. So . . . do we get the entry codes and the password? Or do I have to buy you another beer first?'

FOURTEEN

SUNDAY IN REYKJAVÍK WAS NO LESS BLEAK THAN SATURDAY, WITH drizzle, sometimes intensifying into rain, drifting across the grey city. Wada could do little but wait for the day to pass. She wasn't due to meet Kristjan until midnight. Until then she was on her own. Kristjan himself was meeting Ragnar at some point, before his departure for Akranes, which lay twenty kilometres or so north along the coast. That was when the entry code and password were to be disclosed. Ragnar had refused to reveal them the night before, perhaps fearing they wouldn't wait until Sunday to use them. Or perhaps, as Erla no doubt suspected, he needed time to set the trap they were going to walk into. Wada conceded this possibility to herself, but she'd decided to trust Kristjan's judgement of Ragnar and there was no turning back now, because to turn back would be to admit defeat. And it probably wouldn't stop there. If she didn't go after Nishizaki, he'd ultimately come after her.

She did the small amount of reconnaissance she could in the morning, by tracking down the address of Quartizon's Reykjavík offices. They occupied the upper floor of an unremarkable building in Hafnarstræti, one street north of the main shopping street,

Austurstræti. The physical evidence of the company's presence amounted to no more than the embossed letter Q on a brushed steel plaque. There were no cameras trained on the entrance or any other sign of overt security, but the windows on Quartizon's floor were made of reflective glass. Wada looked up at them and saw nothing but a mirrored image of gulls in flight across the sky.

The location wasn't far from the Hotel Borg, an elegant Art Deco building standing on the eastern side of Austurvöllur Square. On the southern side was the Icelandic parliament. The proximity caused Wada to wonder if Driscoll had dealings with Icelandic politicians in the course of whatever his business was. There was a pattern to everything he did, she sensed, but as yet she couldn't see what the pattern was.

She was tempted to go into the Borg and ask if Driscoll was a guest, but reckoned it was safer to sit in the pleasantly Parisian Café Paris on the northern side of the square, sip coffee and monitor the comings and goings at the Borg from there. No limousine drew up outside. No one resembling the Peter Driscoll she'd seen in the Facetrail report strolled obligingly into view. If Driscoll was in residence, he was keeping a low profile.

She kept up her vigil for the better part of an hour, then left, deciding the only sensible course of action now was to lie low at her hotel and wait out the hours.

It was going to be a long day.

Nick and Kate went out for Sunday lunch and strolled home afterwards through Greenwich Park. Nick encouraged Kate to talk about what she and her friends had got up to in Tuscany, but that didn't distract her for long from the subject she was finding increasingly fascinating: the identity of Nick's father. 'I'll want to know everything that happens in Reykjavík as it happens,' she told him. And he assured her she would. In the circumstances, it was an assurance he felt he had to give. Even though he had no idea what was actually going to happen when he presented the card Miranda had given him at the auction. From that point on, all bets were off. Which was something Kate definitely didn't need to know.

Night came to Reykjavík at last. Wada ate a room service supper, then sat through a couple of hours of Icelandic Sunday night television before heading out for her rendezvous with Kristjan. It had stopped raining, but a chill mist clung to the streets. There were few people about. Even so, Kristjan wasn't easy to spot in his black jeans, baseball cap and hoodie, one vertical shadow amongst many in the gulf of darkness between the city centre and the Harpa opera house.

'Ready?' was all he said before leading the way by an indirect route to the deserted stretch of Hafnarstræti where Quartizon's Reykjavík branch office was located.

They walked slowly past the door, then doubled back when they were sure no one was following them or just wandering along the street behind them. They appeared to have this quarter of the city entirely to themselves.

Not that there would have been anything dramatic to be seen by anyone who'd happened along. Kristjan keyed in a six-figure number, the door unlocked itself with an obliging buzz and they entered the foyer. Motion-sensitive lighting revealed a space of marbled nothing. From there they took the lift two floors up, emerging into a featureless hallway. The lighting was motion-sensitive here as well. Double doors ahead had the distinctive and faintly mysterious Q inscribed on a plate beside them. They opened when Kristjan keyed in a second six-figure number.

And low lights came up as they entered Quartizon's office.

It had the look of standard administrative premises: pastel carpeting and walls, with offices and conference rooms opening off a central reception area. The silence and the emptiness were eerie, but no more so than was to be expected from a workplace out of hours. 'Third office along on the left,' whispered Kristjan. 'That's where the terminal is that Ragnar says we can use.'

'Not *his* terminal, I suppose,' murmured Wada.

'Definitely not. I guess it belongs to some colleague he's happy to land in the shit. Come on.'

Kristjan loped ahead and Wada followed.

He turned in through an open doorway. There were Venetian blinds at the window. He adjusted them to blank out the glass and the night beyond, then turned his attention to the computer. He pulled a small roll of insulating tape out of his pocket, tore a piece off and placed it over the camera above the computer screen. 'Can't be too careful,' he said, catching Wada's eye. Then he switched the computer on. 'Leaving machines on standby is *verboten*, according to Ragnar,' he added. 'We'd better hope the code he's given me works.'

'Why shouldn't it?' asked Wada.

'No reason, I guess. Just . . . you know.' The screen lit up. 'Well, here goes.' He carefully tapped in eleven digits. A moment passed. 'Yes. We're in.'

Wada sat down beside him. A crowded desktop appeared, with file names in Japanese. Scanning the names, she spotted what she was looking for almost immediately. *Emergence.* She pointed to it and whispered into Kristjan's ear, 'There.'

He clicked on it. A forest of sub-files appeared, again with titles in Japanese. *Emergence parcel 1, 2, 3* and so on. She translated for Kristjan.

'I don't see any numbers,' he objected.

'They have used kanji instead of Arabic numbers,' Wada explained. 'Unusual, I would say, in an administrative system.'

'Harder for a non-Japanese speaker to understand.'

'This is true.'

'Lucky I've got you.' He stood up and ushered her into the seat.

She opened *parcel 1*. More numbers appeared in kanji form, in groups of four. Each group appeared to be linked to a set of notes elsewhere in the document. This was all she could glean at a glance. It would clearly take time to understand what it all amounted to.

'Well?' asked Kristjan.

'Not sure what to make of this. It's . . . complex.'

'But you can read it?'

'Sure.'

'Then let's load the whole fucking lot on to a memory stick and get out of here.'

He slipped a stick out of his pocket and plugged it into the back of the computer. Wada looked at the groups of numbers as they waited for the machine to recognize the stick. At that point, she noticed the kanji for north and west imbedded amongst the numbers. North and west? Appended to groups of six numbers? They had to be geographical coordinates, surely, with the kanji for degrees, minutes and seconds omitted.

The machine's recognition of the stick distracted her in that moment. She triggered the download. And . . . nothing. The download didn't happen. The message *Invalid procedure* flashed on to the screen.

'It's not working.'

'Why the fuck not?' Kristjan almost pulled Wada out of the chair and started whirling the mouse and clicking. It didn't go any better for him, though. *Invalid procedure.* 'They've blocked downloading.'

'Then I'll just have to sit here and read it all.'

Kristjan grimaced. 'The longer we're here the more exposed we are. That's a bad idea.'

'You have a better one?'

'Maybe.' More clicks of the mouse followed. 'It looks like we might be able to print the file even if we can't download it. Which is good enough, right?'

'Sure. But I see no printer.'

'It must be in another room. Let's see what happens if I . . .'

A few seconds later, the sound of a printer operating carried to them along the corridor.

'Check it out,' said Kristjan. 'It looks like I'll have to move it on from one sub-file to the next, so I'll stay here.'

Wada followed the chunking sound down the corridor and into a windowless room where several PCs faced each other across a large table, cabled up to hard drives that hummed away gently behind louvred steel cabinet doors. There was a heavy-duty printer as well, currently flicking pages into a tray. She lifted the latest page out. *Yes.* It was what she'd seen in *Emergence parcel 1.*

She was about to head back to give Kristjan the good news when the printer suddenly died. Silence fell. And a red light blinked on the machine's control panel. It was out of paper. Wada began opening cupboard doors in search of more. And then—

She heard a voice that wasn't Kristjan's, raised in what sounded like a command. A man, speaking in Icelandic. Another man, equally insistent.

Then Kristjan said, loudly and clearly, in English, 'You're police officers. Why are you here?'

'Why are *you* here?'

'I don't have to explain myself to you.'

'Are you alone?'

'Yes. There's no one else here.'

Wada's mind raced. Kristjan was covering for her as best he could. He was speaking English so she'd know what was happening. And he'd pointed out that the men talking to him were police officers for the same reason.

Had they triggered some kind of silent alarm when they entered the office? Or had Ragnar betrayed them? The answer didn't really matter for the moment. Wada scooped the twenty or so pages that had already been printed out of the tray and rolled them up. She grabbed a rubber band from a stationery basket as she headed towards the door and sheathed it on to the roll.

Peering out carefully, she could see the uniformed back of one of the policemen blocking the doorway of the room Kristjan was in. 'What are you doing?' was the next question she heard them fire at him.

'I'm working late. Catching up with a project.'

'Our information is you don't work here.'

'Who told you that?'

Wada looked along the corridor to the reception area. She might be able to make it to the exit before they intercepted her. But the lift was the only way down from there and another police officer could easily be waiting in the foyer. Looking the other way, she saw a door at the far end with the green fire escape symbol on a sign above it. She glanced back. The policeman hadn't moved.

'Stop operating that computer.'

'Why?'

The response came in Icelandic. The policeman moved suddenly into the room. Shadows of some kind of struggle spilt into the corridor. Wada heard several grunts, followed by the crash of something toppling over. 'Let go of me,' came a muffled shout from Kristjan.

He'd done the best he could for her and now was her chance. She stepped into the corridor and began running towards the fire escape, shoving the roll of pages inside the waistband of her trousers as she went.

She reached the door, glanced over her shoulder to check she still hadn't been spotted, then turned the handle, bracing herself for some kind of alarm to sound.

None did. She stepped through on to a narrow landing above flights of plain concrete stairs. The lighting was low but adequate. She closed the door gently behind her, then started down the stairs, making as little noise as possible.

There were doors on each landing and by Wada's calculation she'd gone down into the basement by the time she reached the bottom of the stairs. She eased the door open and found herself in a small underground car park, occupied by exactly one car. A ramp took her up into a yard at the rear of the building from which an access alley led round to the street.

Wada moved cautiously, following the alley. As she rounded the corner of the building, she saw a steel gate ahead. It was too high to climb and she began to worry that she was trapped, but, as she approached, she saw there was a narrow pedestrian gate to one side. She could only hope it opened from the inside.

It did, though there was an initial squeak from the hinge that made her stop. Then she went on pulling it open, much more slowly. There were no more squeaks.

She held the gate open and peered out along the street. There was a police car parked outside the entrance to the building. An officer was standing beside it, leaning against the roof of the car as he spoke into a microphone from which a cable snaked back into the vehicle.

She was going to have to close the gate and walk away along the street. The policeman might turn round at any moment and see her, of course. Or his colleagues might emerge with Kristjan and spot her.

Or they mightn't spot her. As was often the case in her life. This was the only chance of escape she had. The odds were probably a little better than fifty-fifty, though probably not a lot better.

But they were the best odds she was going to get. She eased the gate shut and started walking.

She didn't look back. She didn't break into a run.

And no one shouted after her.

FIFTEEN

ONCE SHE WAS A SAFE DISTANCE FROM QUARTIZON'S OFFICES, WADA phoned Erla. Calling her was a risk, but she had to be told what had happened. And she had to be told without delay.

'*Halló.*' The speed of Erla's response suggested she hadn't been asleep.

'It's me.'

'It went wrong, didn't it?' She had feared it would, of course. And it had.

'The police arrived. I don't know why.'

'Ragnar.'

'Maybe.'

'Where's Kristjan?'

'They took him in.'

'But you got away?'

'They didn't see me. I got out by the fire escape.'

'Kristjan's got a record. He did time in prison for throwing a petrol-bomb at a banker's house after the crash in '08. This'll go badly for him. It would've been better if they'd got you.' The words came out like an accusation.

'I am sorry.'

'Did you get anything?'

'Possibly.'

'What does that mean?'

'It means I have to look at it.'

'Look at what?'

'We should not talk about this on a phone.'

'But we shouldn't meet either if they're holding Kristjan. So, what do we do?'

'I will contact you. When it's safe.'

'Kristjan will tell them nothing about you. You know that, don't you?'

'Yes. I do.' She was actually surprised by her confidence on the point.

'And I'll say nothing either.'

'Thank you.'

'But Ragnar . . .'

'He doesn't know enough for them to find me.'

'Are you sure?'

'I cannot talk any longer now. You will hear from me. Thank you again. And I'm sorry again also. About Kristjan. Now I must go.' She ended the call.

A direct route back to the Sol took Wada along largely deserted streets. She felt certain Erla was right about Kristjan: he wouldn't breathe a word about her to the police. Ragnar didn't even know her real name. And none of them knew where she was staying. But if Ragnar had betrayed them, the police would be aware Kristjan had a Japanese accomplice. Whether they launched any kind of search for her depended on just how seriously they regarded what had happened. Trespass on business premises, with no evidence of an actual robbery, didn't sound like something that justified a huge expenditure of effort on their part. They mightn't even keep Kristjan in custody for long, despite his previous conviction.

But that assumed they'd handle the case in a routine fashion. If Driscoll wielded a lot of influence with the Icelandic authorities – a possibility she couldn't dismiss – the police might be required to devote more resources than usual to the inquiry. The speed with which they'd arrived at the scene suggested this was disturbingly likely.

What was the best thing to do? Make a run for the airport? That would feel like betraying Kristjan and Erla – *and* Kodaka. If there was a route to the truth, it surely led through the tangled workings of Quartizon, *here*, in Iceland. On balance, she reckoned the Sol was as safe as anywhere else. And she certainly needed to be somewhere where she could study what was on the pages she'd hidden inside her coat.

The night porter at the Sol paid her little attention. Once again, her inconspicuousness – the cloak of obscurity she seemed to walk around wearing, even in Iceland – was in her favour. She headed up to her room and made herself some tea. The first time she'd used one of the sachets of green tea the hotel supplied the results had been uninspiring, which was only to be expected considering it was of Chinese origin, but any tea was better than no tea when she needed to concentrate. And she *did* need to concentrate.

Looking through the document confirmed her first impression. The grouped sets of six numbers, each followed by *north* or *west*, had to be geographical locations by latitude and longitude. And with latitudes in the sixties it stood to reason many of them were in Iceland.

She downloaded an app on to her phone that offered mapped locations for specific coordinates and looked several up. They were, as she'd suspected, in Iceland – mostly remote, hilly parts of the interior. Some actually impinged on the vast Vatnajökull glacier in the south-east of the country. She checked those three times and there was no mistake.

Based on the lengths supplied by the app for longitudinal and latitudinal degrees, minutes and seconds, each group of four appeared to cover about the same area, amounting more or less to half-kilometre squares. According to Kristjan, Quartizon had been buying up any Icelandic landholdings they could get their hands on. If the list she was looking at was anything to go by, their acquisitions exceeded his worst fears. And she was only looking at a fraction of the whole. There were all the other parcels they hadn't got the chance to print out to be taken into account.

She picked her way through the notes appended to the list for clues to what was really going on. Kodaka had taught her that details were often more revealing than overall appearances. Details contained unfiltered information. And unfiltered information was exactly what she needed now.

Mostly the notes detailed how and when the land they referred to had been purchased, although what had actually been purchased was an *option* to buy, within varying timeframes, none less than twenty-five years, some fifty years, some seventy-five. The amounts paid out weren't specified. They fell into different categories – *lower, middle, higher, premium* – of what were called *disbursement levels*. Nor were the sellers of the land named. They were described as *accredited vendors*. Dates and conveyancing lawyers' names were recorded, though. And in almost every case the concluding phrase in the note was the same. *Available for final stage with full title on exercise of option subject only to company lien.*

Exactly what that meant Wada wasn't sure. Final stage? Company lien? This was all part of some overarching plan, but the nature of the plan itself wasn't referred to, probably as a security precaution.

In the hope of enlightenment, she delved into the few cases where the concluding phrase was different. Generally, the note indicated that some small legal snag was still being resolved but that the operative responsible was confident of early resolution, in any event no later than – and this was a date several times mentioned – Wednesday 17 April.

That was in just two days. It had to be the launch date for Emergence. Something was brewing, as Ragnar had said. But exactly what?

Wada found herself wondering if the answer was to be found in the single note that ended differently from all the rest. It referred to a piece of land about ten kilometres square about a hundred kilometres east of Reykjavík. There were no legal details and no indication of availability, just the curt phrase *Refer to CEO*. Presumably it wasn't going to play a part in the launch on Wednesday. And the only person who seemed to know why was the CEO of Quartizon: Peter Driscoll.

Wada studied the satellite map of the plot of land. There were rivers, tracks, lakes and hillsides of densely bunched contour lines. And a habitation of some kind. A farmhouse, maybe. The map gave it a name. Stóri-Asgarbær.

Even at maximum magnification, though, the image was only that: an image. There was no way to tell from it what was going on there or who, if anyone, lived there. There was no inference she could draw that might explain Driscoll's particular interest in the place. *Refer to CEO*. That was all she knew.

Wada must have fallen asleep at some point. She woke to find herself propped up on the bed, still fully dressed, with the phone lying beside her and daylight shafting through the window. She took a shower and tried to order her thoughts.

Order them how she pleased, however, the way ahead remained unclear. It was just gone seven and she decided to go down to breakfast in the hope that eating something might sharpen her reasoning.

The breakfast room was deserted, apart from a zombie-like waiter. The buffet was well stocked, however. And seeing all the food on display reminded her just how hungry she was. She retreated to a table with a plate of fruit, a bowl of muesli and a mug of black coffee.

She'd eaten the fruit and most of the muesli – and been joined by two other guests, a quietly spoken Swedish couple dressed for hiking – when another man entered the room. Wada glanced in his direction. And her heart sank.

'Hi there,' said George Guptill, waving cheerily to her as he approached her table. 'Mind if I join you?'

'What are you doing here?'

'Found myself passing your hotel and thought I'd look in. I had you down as an early bird, Miss Wada, and it seems I was right. The guy on reception said I'd find you in here, so I signed myself on for breakfast as well.' George sat down opposite her and looked around, grinning at the Swedish couple, who failed to reciprocate.

'Is breakfast not served at the Hilton?' Wada asked.

'Oh, sure. Quite a spread. But I needed to get out of there. I needed some . . . fresh air. So I drove out to the headland west of here. My hire car was dropped off at the Hilton yesterday and I reckoned I should give it a run. They've got a golf course out there, would you believe? Kinda windy, you'd think. And you'd be right. You wouldn't want to loft your tee-shots on that course, let me tell you. Anyhow, I decided to drive back a different way and then I saw the sign for this hotel and . . . well, I thought of you.'

'That was . . . nice of you.'

'Glad you think so. I'll just go grab a bite to eat. Can I get you a refill?' He nodded at Wada's empty coffee mug.

'Er, thank you. Yes.'

With a parting grin and the mug clasped in his large hand, George bounced up and headed for the buffet.

He returned with a heavily loaded plate and two mugs of coffee. Wada tried to tune out his good-humoured ramblings and concentrate on the problem of what she should do for the best, but it proved impossible.

'Truth is, Miss Wada, I needed to see a friendly face this morning, I truly did, which is why I came here in hopes of catching you. Bad news caught up with me yesterday. Some boardroom head-to-head went the wrong way for my boss. He's out. And so, it seems, am I.'

'I am sorry to hear that, George.'

'Thank you.'

'But a man like you will surely be able to find another job quite easily.'

'Dunno about that. I'm not getting any younger. But I'll give it my best shot.'

'When are you returning to New York?'

'Switching to an earlier return flight than planned would be a personal expense for me. So, since my new and soon to be ex-bosses have already paid for the hotel *and* the hire car, I plan to see out the trip. But as a tourist, obviously. I'm off the clock.'

'Well, I hope you enjoy . . . seeing the sights.'

'All on my lonesome doesn't sound like a riot. I wondered if you'd care to join me. They reckon Thingveller is the place to go. Birthplace of Icelandic democracy plus some spectacular canyon where the island's literally but very slowly tearing itself apart. Teutonic plates or some such. We could maybe go on to Gullfoss after: Iceland's answer to Niagara Falls. Make a—'

Wada held up her hand. 'I am sorry, but I have other plans.'

'Really? That's too bad. But you don't have a car, do you? And these coach tours are kinda take it or leave it, not to mention pricey. So, I'm probably your best bet. Let me show you where we'd be going.'

George took a slurp of coffee and spread out a tourist office map of Iceland on the table, swivelling it so that it was at right angles to both of them. His podgy forefinger traced a route east out of Reykjavík to what he'd called Thingveller but was spelt on the map Þingvellir, and on beyond that to Gullfoss.

Wada looked at where George's forefinger had ended up, lingering somewhere in the emptiness east of Gullfoss. An idea formed suddenly in her mind. 'Excuse me a moment,' she said. 'I must check something.'

She called up the satellite map showing the location of Stóri-Asgarbær on her phone. Þingvellir was only thirty or so kilometres away. She doubted talking George into taking her there would be difficult. And the chance was too good to miss.

'Could we maybe . . . take a diversion . . . after Thingveller?'

George smiled. 'Sure we could. As many diversions as you like.'

'There is a property in that area . . . I need to visit.'

'Sounds intriguing.'

'Not really. It is simply, er . . .'

'A matter of business?'

'Something like that.'

'But what business, hey? No, don't tell me. I said you were a woman of mystery and I like that, so you'll just have to let me guess . . . as the day goes by.'

Nick had to set off at dawn to be sure of making it to Heathrow in plenty of time for the eight fifty flight to Iceland. Kate was barely awake when he left. He'd felt ever guiltier about holding out on her as the weekend had progressed. He was relieved to be on his way now.

The plane took off into a benign spring morning, but, as the three-hour flight proceeded, ever more disheartening reports of conditions at the other end were passed on by the co-pilot. Rain. Three degrees. Snow flurries.

By the time the plane landed at Keflavík, it was snowing quite steadily. Nick knew Iceland from a half-term trip to see the Northern Lights five years previously, so the bleakness of the landscape was no surprise, nor the fickleness of the weather. He and Kate hadn't seen any lights in the sky beyond the street lamps of Reykjavík, although she'd fallen in love with the Blue Lagoon and Nick had enjoyed exploring Icelandic art.

They'd hired a car on that trip, but Nick didn't anticipate needing to leave Reykjavík, so he took the transfer bus into the city. He'd stayed with Kate in some luxury at the Borg, but he'd settled this time for a cheaper hotel, the Foss, at the eastern end of the city centre.

The snow hadn't settled in Reykjavík, but still it was much more like winter than spring when he left the Foss shortly after checking in and headed along Laugavegur for a first look at the building where the Emergence auction was to be held on Wednesday.

It covered a wide street frontage and had probably once been a large shop. The high windows had been tricked out with modish tinting since then. There were three floors and a basement, with little sign of activity beyond the ground floor, which proclaimed itself to be an art gallery called Aldrei Aður – helpfully translated on the door as the Never Before Gallery.

Nick went in, passing a broad staircase leading to the upper floors across which a velvet rope had been strung bearing a bilingual *STAFF ONLY* sign. He was greeted in the gallery itself by a willowy young Icelandic blonde who'd have fitted right in as a gallerina in London's West End. She handed him a catalogue for the exhibition. The artist had a Spanish name: Elena Herrera. Nick had never heard of her.

'You're not a showcase for homegrown talent, then?' he remarked casually.

'Our mission is to promote Reykjavík as a showcase for *world* talent,' came the cool reply.

'Who owns the gallery?'

'The Quartizon Foundation.'

'And who owns them?'

'This will explain the foundation's work.' She handed him a pamphlet printed on expensively milled paper. 'Enjoy the paintings.'

'Thank you.'

He moved on past her and did his best impression of someone earnestly studying the pictures and the biographical notes on the artist. The paintings were small but luminous. Despite their modest size, they were best appreciated from a distance. To his surprise, Nick liked them rather a lot. Perhaps the Quartizon Foundation was a good judge of artistic ability.

If so, it seemed their judgement also inclined towards the benefits of reticence. Three paragraphs of well-turned phrases, supplied in English, Icelandic and either Chinese or Japanese – he wasn't sure which it was – told him more or less nothing about the Quartizon Foundation apart from its *commitment to bringing inspiring and transformative new figures in the art world to an ever more cosmopolitan Icelandic audience*. As to who ran the Quartizon Foundation or where it was based or what else it did, the document was silent.

And of that cosmopolitan Icelandic audience there was currently no sign. Nick was the only browser. What he knew of the art world suggested the cost of running the Never Before Gallery was likely to outstrip the proceeds – Elena Herrera's paintings

176

were optimistically priced, to put it mildly – by a long way. Which suggested it might exist to serve some purpose not declared in the blurb.

Nick was tempted to tease the gallerina with an oblique reference to Emergence. But he left without doing so. Like the Quartizon Foundation, he could see the value of reticence.

For now.

The rain that started shortly after George and Wada set off on their drive soon turned to sleet and, as the road took them ever higher into the Icelandic moorlands, snow. According to the car's thermometer, the outside temperature was creeping towards zero. The car was a large and well-appointed four-wheel-drive, which, according to George, virtually drove itself. This show of modesty on his part rather surprised Wada. When she commented on the conditions, he merely said, 'It snows in New Jersey too.'

They hadn't been on the road long before he wheedled her first name out of her and brushed aside her pleadings that everybody simply called her Wada. 'Umiko's a beautiful name. You can't expect me not to use it.' It wasn't much longer after that before he established how and when she'd been widowed. 'A thing like that can make or break someone, Umiko. It's pretty obvious you're a fighter.' This was all blatant flattery, of course. And Wada was dismayed by how pleasant it was to be on the receiving end of it.

The windchill and slanting snow that greeted them at the Þingvellir visitor centre came as a shock after their cosseted journey. Wada wasn't dressed for such weather and, after George had prevailed on her to borrow his coat, which enveloped her like a duvet, *he* wasn't dressed for it, so their exploration of the rift valley carved out by the tearing apart of the North American and Eurasian continental plates was short-lived.

Cutting short their visit suited Wada, since it meant they could head on to Stóri-Asgarbær, but George argued lunch had to be factored in. There was said to be a good restaurant on the road to Gullfoss that served steaks from a local farm . . . and he was driving.

It was mid-afternoon when they left the restaurant. George argued they really should see Gullfoss now they were so close and there'd still be time to take in Wada's detour on the way back to Reykjavík. Wada didn't have much choice but to agree.

According to George's bellowed enthusings, the falls were an awesome sight, but she had to pull the hood on her borrowed anorak so low to keep out the wind-driven snow that she couldn't really tell where the spray ended and the snow-bearing clouds began. Warming up over hot chocolate in the visitor centre would have been welcome in other circumstances, but she only wanted to get to Stóri Asgarbær and eventually George registered her impatience.

'It's OK, Umiko. It's your business opportunity in the boondocks next, I promise. Don't worry. There's hours of daylight left.'

And so, with Wada navigating now, they set off.

The version of events Nick had supplied to Kate had him meeting Martin Caldwell that evening. Inventing a message from Martin saying his arrival in Reykjavík had been delayed by twenty-four hours got him off that hook and he planned to report Martin had been further delayed later.

The real question remained, though: was Caldwell in Iceland? Was this where he'd fled after leaving Exeter? Nick got hold of a list of hotels and guesthouses in Reykjavík from the tourist office and started phoning round, asking if Martin Caldwell

was staying with them. No was the consistent answer, until . . .
the Hotel Arnarson. Caldwell wasn't a guest of theirs. But he
had been. Until the previous Monday.

'Are you a relative of Mr Caldwell, or a friend?'

'A friend. My name's Miller. Nick Miller. I can't seem to contact Martin and I'm becoming concerned for his safety.'

'We have had several enquiries about Mr Caldwell. Actually,
the police have been looking for him.'

'The police? Why?'

'They did not tell us, sir. But it seems Mr Caldwell has not left
Iceland, so . . .'

'Who are these other people who've been asking after him?'

'Well . . .'

'I'm really very worried. It would be a great help if you could
at least put me in touch with some of them.'

There was a pause. 'To be frank, sir, only two of those who've
enquired about Mr Caldwell have left names and phone
numbers.'

'Could you give me them?'

'Mmm. I will have to check with a colleague.'

'Look, you're not far from where I am now, so I'll come and
see you and hope your colleague's given you permission in the
meantime. How does that sound?'

'As you wish, sir.'

The weather closed in around them as they approached Stóri-
Asgarbær. The road became a track, with plenty of bumps and
dips. The landscape lost all its features and merged with the sky.
It was no surprise when George suggested they turn back.

'I'll gladly bring you out here another day, Umiko,' he said,
slowing to a crawl. 'Otherwise we're gonna have the makings of
a Jack London novel here.'

'I do not know the novels of Jack London.'

'Well trust me, the endings of some of 'em wouldn't be any comfort in this situation.'

'But we are only a few kilometres from our destination.'

'Yeah. And this track leads to it. So we can probably get there. But can we get back?'

He'd come to a halt by now. The wipers were batting away great clods of snow. But for the posts dotted along the side of the track, they could easily have gone into a snow-filled gully. The journey had become hazardous at some point they'd already passed. And she knew going on would only make it more hazardous still.

'Can you actually turn round here?'

'Not sure. But there was a swing-round sheltered by some damn great rock a few hundred yards back. I can reverse as far as that.'

'I really need to get to Stóri-Asgarbær today, George.'

'You realize we could be trapped there overnight? My phone doesn't work out here and I'm taking it yours doesn't either.'

Wada checked. 'No signal,' she reported dismally.

'Right. So, we'd be kinda counting on finding some hospitality at this place. You know? Roaring fire, roasted reindeer, that kinda thing. You said you had business there.'

'I did say that, yes.'

'With whoever lives there?'

Wada sensed it was time to drop the pretence. 'I do not know if anyone lives there, George.'

'You don't?'

'No.'

'So, this business of yours . . .'

'Is complicated to explain.'

George sighed. 'I can't complain, I suppose, when a woman of mystery turns out to have a lot of secrets.'

She sighed too. 'We will go back if you think we should.'

'I think we should. Sorry, Umiko. As soon as the weather clears, we'll take another crack at this, I promise.'

He engaged reverse, slung one large arm across the back of her seat, swivelled his neck to see where they were going and began to steer a careful course back they way they'd come.

And all Wada could do was stifle her disappointment.

Nick was greeted at the Arnarson by the man he'd spoken to on the phone. His name, according to his lapel badge, was Bjarni.

'Hello, Mr Miller,' he said, smiling amiably. 'I am sorry if I was . . . unhelpful . . . when you called.'

'That's OK. I guess you have confidentiality issues to consider.'

'Indeed. One of the people who asked about Mr Caldwell and left a name said she was happy to hear from anyone else asking about him. The other . . . I am not so sure about.'

'I understand.'

'So.' Bjarni handed Nick a hotel card. 'This I can give you.'

Nick looked at the note. It gave a name – Erla Torfadóttir – and a phone number. 'Thanks.'

'And for the other . . . I could call her and ask if she was willing to speak to you.' *Her*, Nick noted. 'Would you like me to do that?'

'Yes, please.'

'OK.' Bjarni stepped back into the small office behind the reception desk and put a call through on the hotel phone. A few seconds passed. He frowned, then put the phone down and returned to the desk. 'There is a fault on her number.'

'That's unfortunate.'

'I will try again later and let you know the outcome. I have your number.'

'Is this woman Japanese, by any chance?'

The look of surprise on Bjarni's face was an answer in itself. But he was still determined to stonewall on her behalf. 'I can't say, Mr Miller.'

'That's OK, Bjarni. You don't really need to.'

They'd covered perhaps a hundred metres in slow reverse when George exclaimed, 'Son of a bitch,' and came to a juddering halt.

'What is wrong?' Wada asked.

'See for yourself.'

Wada turned and peered through the rear window. Behind them, to her astonishment, she saw the slowly approaching headlamps of another vehicle.

'It seems we're not alone out here after all,' said George

Wada's heart missed a beat. Another vehicle? It was a chunky four-wheel-drive, dark bodywork showing through layers of snow, its headlamps glaring at them through the slashing flakes like the eyes of some living creature.

'Maybe this guy lives at Story Asperger.' George hadn't yet mastered the pronunciation of Stóri-Asgarbær.

'Maybe,' said Wada. But somehow she doubted it.

'Well, we sure can't get past him, specially not in reverse.'

'Perhaps we should go forward.'

'Hell, no. We just agreed not to do that.'

'What, then?'

'I'll go have a word with him. He's probably local. He'll likely know what's best.'

'Is that wise?'

'Why not? Someone's got to make the first move.' George yanked on the handbrake, dragged his anorak off the back seat and went to open the door.

'George—'

'It's OK, Umiko.' He grinned at her. 'I've got this.' He pushed the door open and struggled out. A flurry of snow and freezing air buffeted in. Then the door was slammed shut.

Wada adjusted the rear-view mirror and watched George stump along the track to the other car. He tapped on the driver's window. Some kind of conversation ensued. George flung up his arms in a gesture of bemusement. The conversation didn't seem to be going as he'd hoped. Wada craned over her shoulder for a clearer view of what was happening.

Something appeared through the open driver's window of the other car. At first, Wada couldn't work out what it was. But suddenly, to her horror, she realized it was a gun.

She didn't hear the shot. But she saw George's head jerk back. He went straight down, like a tree falling, and lay motionless in the snow at the edge of the track.

The driver's door opened. The driver got out. And started walking towards her.

Something in the man's stature and the way he held himself told Wada who he was, even though his face was buried in the hood of a parka.

He was the tall Japanese man who'd attacked her in Caldwell's flat in Exeter. She was certain it was him.

And she was certain in that moment that he meant to kill her.

SIXTEEN

WADA COULDN'T DRIVE. THAT IS, SHE WASN'T QUALIFIED TO DRIVE. But she was nothing if not observant. She'd driven around with Haruto often enough in his tiny old Nissan to have some grasp of the basics. And George's hire car was an automatic, which made things easier. Besides, it wasn't a matter of choice. It was a matter of survival.

She released the seatbelt and half slid, half jumped over into the driver's seat, praying to all the gods she didn't believe in – there being none she *did* believe in – that she wouldn't stall the engine. She released the handbrake, then shoved the stick into drive.

She was about to press her foot down hard on the accelerator when a movement reflected in the wing mirror caught her eye. George's killer was closing on her fast. There he was, only a few metres from the rear of the car.

The decision was made in an instant. She moved the stick to reverse and stamped on the accelerator pedal, pulling the steering wheel down with her left hand as the car skidded back, slewing towards the side of the track.

There was a thump and the sound of a shot and then another thump as she hit one of the trackside posts. She pressed down on the footbrake and peered round. She saw the man lying in the snow beside the post. He wasn't moving.

She knew what she should do. Drive forwards, then reverse over him – make sure she finished him. But she wasn't confident she could control the car well enough to do that. And she wasn't certain the tyres would grip if she left the track.

Maybe he was dead, though she doubted it. Maybe he was at least too badly injured to come after her. She had her doubts about that too. But she had to make a choice. And she had to make it now.

She put the stick into drive and pushed her foot down on the accelerator. The car surged forward. It began jolting and skidding as she moved her foot too violently on the pedal. It took her a few seconds to gain proper control. Then she accelerated smoothly along the track, steering a middle course between the posts.

She glanced in the rear-view mirror as she picked up speed. She could see George's body lying where he'd fallen. And she thought she could see blood on the snow around him. Her eyes filled with tears.

The snow she'd ploughed up reversing against the post obscured her view of his killer, and the pitch of the track meant she couldn't be sure whether he'd moved or not. Or maybe her uncertainty was caused by the tears blurring her vision.

For the moment, it didn't matter. She was alive. And she was moving, even if no one else was.

Nick phoned Erla Torfadóttir as soon as he left the Arnarson. She didn't answer, so he left a message explaining he was anxious, as apparently she was too, to track down Martin

Caldwell. Could they perhaps help each other? He didn't mention Mimori Takenaga, though he suspected she must have been in touch with Erla. Who Erla was, of course, and what her connection with Caldwell might be, he had no idea. That went for a whole lot else as well. He was beginning to wonder if he'd ever come close to understanding what was going on in the secret world of Peter Ellery, into which Caldwell had lately vanished.

Within an hour, however, he had heard from Erla Torfadóttir, in the form of a text message. *Can we meet at Reykjavík Roasters Brautarholt 0930 tomorrow?*

There could be only one answer to that, which he texted back straight away.

Yes.

Wada drove on towards Stóri-Asgarbær with no definite plan as to what to do when she arrived. It was Quartizon property, so going there was crazy on one level. But she couldn't go back. That much was certain. So she had to go on.

Keeping the car on the track and judging the route ahead by reference to the wayside posts required all her concentration. And the less she thought about what she'd left behind her the better able she'd be to cope with whatever lay ahead. She should never have persuaded George to drive her here, of course. She should have bided her time and chosen some safer method to prise open Quartizon's secrets. Her impetuosity had cost George Guptill his life. And it might yet cost her hers.

Which was ironic in its own tragic way. Because no one would ever have called Umiko Wada impetuous.

What looked like an unusually tall wayside post at first sight revealed itself to be a signpost as she drew closer. But the snow had blotted out whatever was on the sign and she couldn't stop to investigate. She wasn't confident of starting again if she did. She pressed on.

Then she saw something that gave her no choice *but* to stop: a gate across the track, with a low snow-capped wall stretching away on either side.

She came to a halt, took the stick carefully out of drive and gently lifted her foot from the accelerator, fearful for some reason that the engine might cut out. It didn't.

She glanced about before climbing out of the car, but there was no one anywhere around, just wind and snow. It seemed colder than ever when she emerged into the open air. She didn't have George's anorak to shield her from the weather now.

She hurried round to the fastened side of the gate and felt a wave of relief when she saw it wasn't padlocked. Shifting the bolt took all her strength, though. The steel felt as if it was freezing itself to her skin. She had to raise the gate slightly with one hand and pull at the bolt with the other before it slid across. And it did so with a jolt that carried her off her feet.

She scrambled up and walked the gate open. There was a chain that had to be looped over a post to hold it in place. That done, she slithered back to the car.

She'd driven only a short distance beyond the gate when, looking ahead, she saw a building.

Three gables sprouted from a long, low-roofed structure, hummocked with snow. The gables were wood, but the other walls appeared to be rough stone. There was another, squarer-roofed building that looked as if it might be a barn away to the right.

One end of the main building was in a poor state of repair, but the part around the front door looked well maintained. Wada had thought initially a light was shining in one of the adjacent windows, but there was no sign of it as she drew closer and she concluded it was probably a reflection from the

187

car's headlamps. She braked to a halt near the main door and studied the windows one by one. Nothing moved. Nothing glimmered.

The place might be empty, of course. But Wada's options were few and none of them was ideal. She needed to take shelter and phone for assistance. Her own phone didn't work. She recalled the man in the convenience store who'd sold her an Iceland-compatible SIM card telling her it would be useless in remote areas. At the time, she hadn't anticipated going to a remote area. But she was in one now.

That at least meant there was a chance the house was fitted with some reliable means of communication. She couldn't find out whether it was or not without going in. She had to leave the car and try her luck. She didn't really want to. Leaving the car meant giving up the small amount of control over her situation that she still had. But it had to be done.

She turned off the engine and at once heard the wind howling like some kind of demon in the gable eaves. That, she told herself, was simply what wind did. It couldn't hurt her. As to what *could* hurt her . . . she would gain nothing by thinking about that.

She pulled her woolly hat down low over her eyes, took the key out of the ignition and slipped it into her pocket, then clambered out of the car and headed for the main door of the house.

She rapped hard on the door six or seven times with the heavy knocker, enough, she reckoned, to alert anyone inside to her presence. She was actually relieved when there was no response, even though she knew that wasn't necessarily good news. She tried the handle, but it wouldn't turn.

She peered through the nearest window and could dimly see a wood-framed interior, fitted out with wooden bedsteads. The room didn't appear to be in use. She tried another few raps at the knocker, but still nothing stirred. And wrench at the handle as much as she liked, the door wasn't going to open.

There was nothing for it but to see if she could gain access at the rear. She headed for the dilapidated end of the building, sheltering under the eaves as she went as best she could.

She came to what might once have been stables and a back door, sheltered by the overhang of the stable roof. Through the narrow window next to it she could see a stone-flagged passage leading into the house, with doorways off into other rooms. She tried the door handle. It turned, but the door was locked shut.

The window appeared to be her only chance of entry. There were loose stones lying in the snow at the foot of the stable wall. She picked one up and punched a hole in the pane of glass closest to the window latch, then knocked out the remaining shards, reached in and lifted the latch.

The window opened with a squeal of swollen wood and she clambered in over the sill. But the sill was so wide, because of the thickness of the wall, that she ended up falling into the passage.

As she scrambled to her feet, a figure stepped into the passage from one of the rooms ahead: a tall, thin man dressed in corduroy trousers and a bulky sweater. He had lank grey hair and a narrow, bony face. His sunken eyes peered at her from behind black-framed glasses.

Wada took all that in at once, but somehow failed to notice the double-barrelled shotgun he was holding in his hands until he raised it to chest height and pointed it straight at her.

'Who are you?' The voice was gruff, as if from lack of use. The accent was that of a well-educated Englishman.

She stared at him, unable for the moment even to speak.

'*Who are you?*' he repeated.

She had to say something. But the truth might be as fatal as a lie. Who was *he* became the vital question.

And the answer came to her as she looked into his raw-rimmed blue-grey eyes. He was Martin Caldwell. In the end, there was no one else he could be. 'I am the woman you were supposed to meet in London,' she said quietly.

'No you're not. She never left Tokyo.'

'If you mean Mimori Takenaga, then, yes, you are correct. My boss sent me to see you posing as her because her family would not let her leave the country. My name is Wada.'

'And your boss's name?'

'Kodaka.'

'Who met with a fatal accident last week.'

'That is also correct.'

'Why didn't you give up then, with Kodaka dead and his client, as I understand it, confined to a psychiatric hospital?'

'Why did you not meet me as planned in the British Museum?'

'I got held up here.'

'Will you lower the gun, Mr Caldwell? You are making me nervous.'

'You don't look nervous.'

'But I am.'

'How did you know I was here?'

'I did not know you were here.'

'Then why did you come?'

'Please lower the gun, Mr Caldwell.'

'First tell me what brought you here.'

'The Emergence files in Quartizon's offices. Kristjan and I found out what was in them.'

'And what is?'

'Grid references for parcels of land all over Iceland, apparently owned by Quartizon. Including *this* parcel of land. But

Stóri-Asgarbær seems to be different from the others. It's not part of whatever's planned for Wednesday.'

'Where's Kristjan now?'

'Under arrest.'

'How did you get away?'

'I was lucky.'

'Well, maybe your good luck is my bad luck.'

'I am not a threat to you, Mr Caldwell. I am not your enemy. Please lower the gun.'

Something softened in his expression. He turned the gun away. 'I'd never have fired, Miss Wada. I'm not a killer.'

'I never thought you were.'

'Follow me.'

He led her a little further along the passage and turned into a large, low-ceilinged kitchen. It looked out to the rear of the house, across climbing, snow-covered ground. The sink, the range, the dresser and the table and stools belonged to a bygone age, maybe a century past. There was nothing modern or labour-saving to be seen. The light was thin, falling on well-worn flagstones and dust-laden surfaces.

Caldwell propped the shotgun in the corner. 'Does anyone know you're here?' he asked. It seemed to her she could read fear in his eyes as he posed the question.

'I came with a friend.'

'Where's this friend now?'

Wada took a deep breath. Should she tell him what had happened? There was no way of predicting how he might react. But if she *didn't* tell him . . . 'He's dead. Shot.'

'*What?*'

'We were followed.'

Caldwell stiffened apprehensively. 'Who by?'

'I do not know his name. But he is Japanese, I think.'

191

'Where's *he* now?'

'I reversed the car into him.'

'You killed him?'

'I think so. I hope so.'

'But maybe not?'

'I do not know for certain. I could not take the risk of stopping to check.'

'Do you know anything about him?'

'He was at your flat in Exeter last week. I suspect he works for Hiroji Nishizaki.'

Caldwell closed his eyes for an instant. 'You've led the Irishman straight to me,' he said dolefully.

'He is not Irish, Mr Caldwell.'

'It's what they call him.'

'And if he is dead—'

'But what if he isn't?' Caldwell's eyes were open again. He was glaring accusingly at her 'I was supposed to be safe here.'

'Do you have a phone that works?'

'No.'

'It was heavy contact. At speed. Even if he is not dead, he will be seriously injured, I think.'

'You *think*?'

'And therefore unable to—'

They both heard it at the same time: a car, engine roaring, approaching fast. They looked at each other in horror. It could only be the Irishman. Not dead. And not giving up.

'Mr Caldwell, I—'

'We're as good as dead. You understand that, don't you?' Caldwell glared at her. 'If only you hadn't interfered.'

There was a final roar of the engine, then silence. Caldwell made no move towards the gun. He slumped back against the rail of the range. It was as if he'd lost all hope.

Wada didn't wait for him to rediscover any. She grabbed the gun. As she did so, a car door slammed outside.

The weapon was surprisingly heavy and she couldn't really imagine using it. But she was going to have to start imagining. And soon. She looked at Caldwell, but he was simply staring into space. Whatever she was going to do, she was going to have to do it alone. She hurried out into the passage.

She moved towards the front door, but as she passed the open door of one of the bedrooms she saw the Irishman through the window, heading in the opposite direction. He was following the footsteps she'd left in the snow, leading to the back door. He was limping, but still he was moving fast.

She turned round and headed back past the kitchen, glimpsing Caldwell, still leaning against the range. As she approached the back door and the broken window beside it, a shadow fell across the smashed pane. She couldn't see the Irishman, but she felt sure he was there. Then she saw the door handle turn and the woodwork strain against the lock.

She raised the shotgun, wondering if she should fire now, hoping to hit her target on the other side of the door. But she had no spare cartridges. There'd be no chance to reload if she missed. She had to wait until she had a clear shot.

Suddenly, there were several deafening cracks. The Irishman was firing into the door. The wood splintered around the lock. Then the whole lock mechanism was blasted off, crashing to the floor as the door sagged open.

Wada heaved the gun up against her shoulder, aware the barrel was shaking as she held it. Her fingers trembled around the triggers. She heard the Irishman kick the door. It flew wide open. She saw his face, twisted with fury. And she saw the gun in his hand, the gun he'd used to kill George Guptill.

She fired, both barrels.

But all she hit was wood. The door had struck the wall behind it so violently it had bounced back across her line of fire.

Then he was in and on her. The shotgun was wrenched from her grasp and flung aside. He shoved her against the wall and clapped the barrel of his gun to her temple. 'Where is Caldwell?' he demanded in Japanese.

She couldn't speak at first. All she could register was the brutality in his eyes and the cold, heavy pressure of the gun barrel against her skin.

'Where is Caldwell?'

She mustered her thoughts and forced out an answer, in English, so that Caldwell would understand. 'Caldwell is not here.'

'You are lying. You came here because you knew this was where he was hiding.'

'There is no one else in the house.' It was strange to confront her own stubbornness. It was the only weapon she had at her disposal.

'Tell me where he is.'

'I do not know where he is.'

Keeping the gun to her head, he grabbed her by the hair with his other hand and began dragging her along the passage, looking into each room as they went. She had to go with him, or be pulled off her feet. His right leg was stiff, she saw, with a length of wood strapped to the side of his knee as some kind of splint. He was probably in a lot of pain. And she was responsible for it. But he wasn't ready to kill her quite yet.

They reached the kitchen. Caldwell wasn't there. When he'd left and where he'd gone Wada couldn't guess. He might never have heard their exchanges for all she knew.

The door of the next room was closed. The Irishman kicked it open with his uninjured leg. It was a bathroom, fitted with a cupboard, hand-basin, loo and claw-footed bath that all looked about as old as the kitchen furnishings. The Irishman let go of Wada's hair for a second, pulled a set of handcuffs out of the pocket of his parka and closed one cuff round her right wrist. Then he forced her to the floor, bent over her and snapped the other cuff round the downpipe under the basin.

'When I have found Caldwell and killed him,' he rasped into her ear, 'I will come back to question you, Wada. And you will answer my questions, I promise you. You will answer every one of them.'

As he stood upright, he winced and steadied himself against the rim of the basin. Seeing her chance, Wada drew back her legs and aimed a kick at his splinted knee, using all the force she could summon. Something cracked under the impact. The Irishman cried out and fell. The gun went off as he toppled. There was an explosion of plaster from the ceiling above the basin.

Then there was another crack, as the Irishman's head struck the curved rim of the bath. He thumped to the floor, his head taking a second heavy blow. The gun was jolted from his hand. It slid across the tiles and came to rest against the wall beneath the window.

The Irishman's eyes stared sightlessly at Wada. He didn't move. A pool of blood appeared beneath his head, slowly widening. Wada scrambled to her feet, sliding the handcuff up the pipe. But she was unable to stand fully upright because it snagged against the underside of the basin. And from that position the gun was out of her reach.

'Mr Caldwell,' she called out. 'Come here. To the bathroom. It is safe. I need your help.'

The house was enveloped in silence, magnified and muffled by the snow outside. Nothing moved. There was no answer from Caldwell.

'*Mr Caldwell!*'

Still nothing. Wada knelt and stretched out her free hand to where the Irishman lay, his face flattened against the floor, his eyes gaping like those of a giant tuna on the slab at Tsukiji Fish Market. He had to have the key to the handcuffs somewhere about him, but, even lying down, she couldn't reach beyond the left sleeve of his parka.

He didn't seem to be breathing. It came to her then that he might be dead. She wasn't certain. He might just be unconscious. And how long he'd remain unconscious she didn't know. But while he was, they had to act.

'*Mr Caldwell!*'

No response. He was hiding somewhere. He had to be. Perhaps he feared she was trying to lure him into a trap at the Irishman's bidding.

'I tripped him up and he has knocked himself out,' she called. 'We have to take this chance. But I am handcuffed to the basin. I cannot reach him. Or the gun. Please come. Now.'

At last, there was a sound, faint and ambiguous. But it was something. And soon it became a succession of sounds that were surely footsteps in the passage, drawing slowly closer.

'Mr Caldwell?'

And then there he was, in the doorway, looking in at her and the Irishman. He was trembling. His breathing was fast but shallow.

She rattled the chain of the handcuffs. 'You see?'

'What . . . what happened?' he asked in a voice hoarsened by stress.

'I told you. Please search his pockets, Mr Caldwell. We need to find the key for these handcuffs.'

'Is he dead?'

'I think he may be.'

Caldwell moved cautiously into the room and stooped over the body on the floor. He pressed his fingers to the side of the Irishman's neck. 'I can't feel a pulse,' he said. 'Hold on.'

There was a round metal-framed mirror hanging on the wall above the basin. He took it off its hook and, kneeling carefully clear of the pool of blood, held the glass close to the Irishman's mouth and nose. Several slow moments passed. Then he glanced at the mirror and turned it round for Wada to see. The glass was clear. The Irishman wasn't breathing.

'It seems you've killed him, Miss Wada. What do you think we should do with him now?'

'Just find the key.'

Caldwell nodded and began working his way through the Irishman's pockets. He pulled out a passport and a wallet from one. Opening the passport, he grimaced, then laughed oddly.

'What is wrong?'

'His name. Ohara. That's why they call him the Irishman. I suppose they think it's funny.'

Wada wanted to ask who *they* were, but decided that could wait. 'The key, Mr Caldwell.'

He nodded again and went on searching. He pulled a phone from a zipped side-pocket of the parka and a car key from Ohara's jeans. But not the key to the handcuffs. He stopped and shrugged his shoulders. 'It doesn't seem to be here.'

'It must be.'

'Maybe he left it in his car. I'll go and take a look. But before I do . . .' He stood up and hurried out of the room, returning a few moments later wearing rubber gloves. He stepped over to the window and picked up the gun, holding it carefully by the handle and barrel. 'I'll put this somewhere safe. And I'll be back as soon as I can.'

*

By Wada's watch twelve long minutes of silence elapsed, during which she could only wonder what Caldwell was doing. Then she heard several thumps and grunts from the direction of the back door, as if he was carrying something heavy and unwieldy into the house.

A moment later, he was back in the doorway of the bathroom. 'I couldn't find the key,' he announced. 'Sorry.'

'It has to be somewhere.'

He smiled oddly. 'True enough.'

'What was that noise I heard just now?'

'There are tools in the barn,' he said, seeming not to hear her question. 'Given this is a farm, they probably include a pair of bolt-cutters. I'll check. Meanwhile . . .'

He grasped Ohara by the ankles and began dragging him towards the door, leaving a gleaming smear of blood on the tiles. 'Where are you taking him?' Wada asked.

'I'll explain . . . when I come back.'

Wada sat down and waited. At least she no longer had to look at Ohara. What Caldwell was planning for him she had no idea. As far as she could tell from the sounds that reached her, he dragged Ohara as far as the kitchen. There were muffled scrapes and bumps and thumps after that that she couldn't interpret. And several more grunts of effort from Caldwell.

Then he was back, breathing more heavily than ever. And sweating, despite the chill that hung everywhere in the house beyond the range-warmed kitchen. He leant against the doorpost and looked down at her apologetically. 'I've had to . . . improvise,' he said.

'What do you mean?'

'There's a chest freezer in the scullery, at the back of the kitchen. I've put him in there. Along with your friend, whose body I found under a tarpaulin in the back of Ohara's car. In the circumstances, it seemed the best thing to do. The only thing, really. They'll keep there until Thursday.'

'What happens on Thursday?'

'I'm going to be collected. We can sort everything out then.'

'Who is collecting you?'

'You have to stay until Thursday as well.' Caldwell rubbed his eyes behind his glasses. 'Sorry.'

'That is three days from now. I cannot stay here for three days.'

'You have to. If you left, you'd go back to Reykjavík and do your best to interfere with Emergence. You know you would. More importantly, *I* know you would. And that would . . . upset the arrangements.'

'What arrangements?'

'Everything will be sorted out, I promise. On Thursday. You'll come to no harm. All you have to do is . . . remain here. With me.' He shrugged. 'I'm sorry, but there it is.'

The truth suddenly dawned on Wada. 'You have the key to the handcuffs, don't you?'

Caldwell nodded. He took his hand out of his pocket and there it was, nestled in his palm. Wada made a move towards him and he took an apprehensive half-step back, though she could never have reached him.

'Let me go,' she said, firmly but calmly. 'You have no right to hold me prisoner.'

'I agree.' He looked genuinely regretful. 'But I notice you've made no attempt to deny that you'd try to obstruct Emergence if I allowed you to leave here before Thursday. Which unfortunately leaves me with no choice in the matter.'

'You have a choice, Mr Caldwell. It is absurd to try to blame what you are doing on me.'

'Not from my point of view it isn't.'

'Let me go. Now.'

'I can't.'

'You must.'

'But I'm not going to, Miss Wada. My mind's made up, I'm afraid. It's force majeure. You're going to be spending the next three days here. And there's absolutely nothing you can do about it.'

SEVENTEEN

THE SNOW THAT HAD FALLEN THE PREVIOUS EVENING WAS THAWING slowly by Tuesday morning. Nick made his way to Reykjavík Roasters along slushy pavements under a pale blue sky. The coffee shop was busy but not crammed, the customers comprising a predictable mix of laptop-tapping student types and mothers with tiny children and enormous buggies.

No one paid Nick any attention as he settled in a corner, so he assumed Erla Torfadóttir wasn't there yet. He was early anyway, so that was no surprise. By the time Erla herself was late, it became more of a cause for concern.

That was when he noticed a tall, slim, blonde-haired young woman loitering on the other side of the street. She was wearing jeans and a yellow anorak and appeared to be studying him with greater interest than young women normally displayed for men of his age. He gave her a cautious smile.

A few minutes later, she was seated at his table, cradling a mug of hot chocolate. 'I am Erla,' she announced.

'Hi. Nick Miller.'

'Can I see your passport?'

'My passport?'

'You have it with you, don't you?'

'Er, yes.' He pulled it out and showed her the page with his name, date of birth and photograph on it. 'Happy?'

'No. I'm not happy. I'm worried. As you should be, Mr Miller.'

'Call me Nick.'

'OK. Nick.' She looked around, perhaps to confirm that all the nearby customers were absorbed in their own affairs, as they certainly appeared to be. 'You're the guy Martin Caldwell was going to meet in London, right?'

'You know about that?'

'Martin told us.'

'Us?'

'My boyfriend Kristjan and I. Before Martin went . . . missing.'

'How did you and . . . Kristjan . . . come to know Martin?'

'Not sure I want to trust you with that yet, Nick.'

It was then Nick noticed Erla's hands were trembling slightly. There were hollows under her eyes as well. Her youth and prettiness were hiding a lot of anxiety. 'You said you were worried, Erla. Just about Martin? Or is there something else?'

'There's a lot else.'

'Maybe I can help.'

'Maybe. But you're not the only person looking for Martin. And trusting the last one didn't work out well for Kristjan.'

'In what way?'

'In the police way. He was arrested Sunday night.'

'How did that come about?'

'It came about because someone betrayed him.'

'Do you know who?'

'Not for sure. But it could be the other person who was looking for Martin.'

'Would that be a Japanese woman called Mimori Takenaga? Also supposed to meet Martin in London?'

'That's not her name. She told us she was only posing as Mimori Takenaga. Her real name's Umiko Wada. She works for a private detective hired by the Takenaga woman. So she said, anyway.'

'What happened Sunday night?'

Erla put down her mug and looked intently at him, searching his face, it seemed, for some sign she could be sure he wasn't trying to set her up. 'I wasn't there. I don't know exactly what happened. What Kristjan and Wada were doing went wrong somehow. Now the police are holding Kristjan and they won't tell me what they're charging him with. But I don't believe they *can* charge him with anything that would justify keeping him in custody, so there's obviously a lot of sinister stuff going on behind the scenes. Wada wasn't arrested and she promised to contact me, but she hasn't. Her phone's off. Has been for the past twenty-four hours. I don't know what that means. But Kristjan went up against some powerful people, I know that. I'm frightened and maybe you should be frightened too.' She took a breath. 'Tell me everything about why you've come all this way looking for Martin Caldwell, Nick, and . . . maybe I'll tell you everything from my side too.'

'Only *maybe*?'

'Yeah. No promises. I have to be certain about you. Which means you have to convince me you're on the level. Think you can do that?'

Wada had given up trying to persuade Caldwell to release her. He was a stubborn as well as infuriatingly polite jailer. Considerate too, in his way, supplying her with a duvet to keep warm and a pillow to help her sleep. She could reach the loo from where she was chained and he brought her food and drink whenever she wanted it, although the food he gave her was either tinned or frozen. The house had been provisioned for a long but scarcely luxurious stay.

Employees of Quartizon – which meant employees of Peter Driscoll – had done the provisioning. Caldwell didn't try to deny it. Nor did he deny Peter Driscoll was his friend of student days, Peter Ellery, aka Peter Evans. Caldwell had traced him to Iceland, where he'd evidently met him and been instantly recruited to whatever exactly Emergence was. He never pre-cisely said as much, but Wada couldn't otherwise make sense of what he was doing. His earlier promises to help Mimori Takenaga identify and track down the man she blamed for her father's death clearly no longer held good.

He was tight-lipped about Driscoll's present whereabouts and intentions. He insisted Driscoll wasn't to blame for Kodaka's murder – or Shitaro Masafumi's death back in 1977, come to that. Hiroji Nishizaki was responsible for everything, appar-ently. And Ohara answered directly to him. When Wada pointed out that Driscoll ultimately answered to Nishizaki as well and had loyally done his bidding for the past forty years, all Caldwell said was, 'You don't understand, Miss Wada.' And evidently he didn't think it was for him to make her understand.

Caldwell moved Ohara's car to the barn. He nailed a board over the broken window at the end of the passage and mopped up the blood in the bathroom, passage and kitchen. As for the bodies in the chest freezer, Caldwell seemed blithely confident Driscoll's representatives would deal with the problem in due course. Out of sight was, as far as Caldwell was concerned, out of mind.

His assurances about Driscoll cut no ice with Wada. She didn't believe he was blameless in the matter of Kodaka's murder. And therefore she didn't believe she could simply wait for Thursday to roll round, confident that whoever Driscoll sent to Stóri-Asgarbær would release her and allow her to leave. That didn't seem to her a remotely likely outcome. The longer she stayed where she was, the greater the danger she was in.

But Caldwell had the key to the handcuffs, hidden she knew not where. And he'd made it clear he was determined to see she went nowhere until Thursday, when, in his words, 'Everything will be sorted out.'

'Maybe it won't be sorted out the way you imagine,' she'd countered.

But that approach had taken her nowhere. 'You won't succeed in sowing doubt in my mind, Miss Wada. I'm acting for the best. As you'll appreciate yourself in the fullness of time.'

Quizzing him about Emergence had proved equally fruitless. 'If I have to stay here until Thursday, you can surely tell me what is going to happen in the meantime.'

'No, Miss Wada, I can't. I'm not obliged to explain anything to you. Remember, I didn't ask you to come here.'

'In a sense, you did, by agreeing to meet me in London and then failing to turn up.'

'I agreed to meet Mimori Takenaga, not you.'

'So, you are saying it would be different if I really was Mimori Takenaga.'

He'd bridled at that. 'No, I'm not saying that, dammit. You're trying to bamboozle me, but it won't work.'

She'd left it there. Angering him didn't strike her as a good idea.

As to what might constitute a good idea . . .

The snow had evidently stopped. A slow thaw had set in. Wada could hear a steady drip-drip from the eaves, though she could see nothing of the outside world, because Caldwell had shuttered the bathroom window and refused to *un*shutter it. Eighteen hours into her captivity, she'd brought her fear and frustration under control and was now thinking, coolly and logically, about how to escape.

Caldwell, she reluctantly concluded, was the answer. He would have to be induced to set her free. He would have to be made to trust her.

She would have to make him trust her.

Nick decided to tell Erla everything because he could see she was genuinely frightened and only complete sincerity was going to persuade her to open up to him. He showed her pictures on his iPhone of his paintings and the paintings of some of his students. They seemed to convince her he really was the person he claimed to be. And then, of course, there was the famous *Western Morning News* photograph of Peter Ellery, Martin Caldwell, April Vyse, Caroline Miller and Alison Parker waving their protest banners by the Redruth to Portreath road on Easter Saturday, 1977. Erla recognized Caldwell. And she recognized Nick in his father's younger self. She recognized the truth.

It wasn't long before she was telling him the truth from her side as well. She wanted to confide in someone. She needed help and advice. She needed to know what to do.

She'd heard nothing from Umiko Wada since one brief phone call on Sunday night, reporting that the raid on Quartizon's offices had gone wrong and Kristjan had been arrested, but she'd got away – with something. What that something was she hadn't said.

'I phoned round the hotels until I found the one she's staying in. The Sol, in Oðinsgata. But she's never there when I call. Late last night. Early this morning. Same story. I get the feeling she's left the place.'

'Surely they'd tell you if she'd checked out,' said Nick.

'She hasn't. But she's never there. And she hasn't called me, as she promised she would. So, either she's run out on me . . . or she's in trouble.'

'I don't see what you can do in either event.'

'I can't do nothing, Nick. You understand?'

He nodded. Yes. That he *did* understand.

The day passed slowly at Stóri-Asgarbær. Initially, Caldwell was reluctant to be drawn into conversation with Wada, fearing she'd try to talk him round. Eventually, though, he was worn down by the sheer lack of anything else to do. His strategy, as he'd several times made clear, was to wait until Thursday. But a waiting game was a wearing game. So, why not respond when Wada pressed him to say something – anything – about himself?

She began by persuading him to describe his working life in the insurance business. He must have thought this was safe ground. And so it was. But the object of the exercise was to accustom him to confiding in her. If that meant hearing about the intricacies of annuities, endorsements, endowments, moral hazard and mortality tables, as it turned out it did, she wasn't about to object.

Because, inevitably, Martin Caldwell revealed more and more of Martin Caldwell as he went on.

'I was never much of a salesman, Miss Wada. I didn't have the gift for instant rapport. Still don't, I suppose. I was more at home in the back office, calculating the balance of risk. Many people dismiss insurers as leeches, happy to take their premiums but ready with an excuse not to pay out when the worst happens. That's really not how it is. When I did go out in the field, it was as a loss adjuster. And I never tried to exploit the fine print of a policy to reject a claim. It was a matter of principle. And principles are important to me. That's not to say I never took a firm line. Fairness cuts both ways. I'm afraid there are lots of people out there in the world willing to make false or exaggerated claims. Naturally, I had to make sure they weren't rewarded for their dishonesty, however entertainingly ingenious their methods sometimes were.

'Let me give you an example. It must have been, oh, some time in the late nineteen eighties when this happened. I'd better explain the background to the case. Then you'll appreciate the irony of the situation as it developed. It does have its funny side.

'So . . .'

'It's incredible to think you're Peter Driscoll's son,' said Erla, gazing at Nick over the rim of her coffee mug. They were at her flat in Stúdentagarđar now, not far from Reykjavík Roasters. An eerie sense of emptiness prevailed in the corridors and along the walkways, most of the other students having left for the Easter vacation.

'I'm having some trouble believing it myself,' said Nick. 'But there doesn't seem to be any doubt about it.'

'A father you've never met. I mean, I don't see much of mine. He split from my mother when I was just a baby. But *never*? That's something else.'

'Is that Kristjan in the picture behind you?' Nick felt uncomfortable having the strangeness of his paternity pointed out to him by a woman twenty years his junior and seized on one of the photographs drawing-pinned to a cork board on the kitchen wall as a way of changing the subject.

The photograph showed Erla and a tall, thin, wispily bearded man who looked a few years older than her. Both were swathed in hiking clothes: parkas, scarves, gloves and woolly hats. They were grinning into the camera in some wilderness location of lichened rocks and gushing streams.

'Yeah,' said Erla, swivelling round to look at it. 'That was when we walked the Laugavegur trail last June. Freezing, even at that time of the year. But beautiful.'

'How long have you known him?'

'Since a few months before we did that hike. He loves the country. I mean, the *land*. He has a connection with it. So do I, but not like Kristjan.' She looked back at Nick. 'Quartizon are trying to take the land from us. But it doesn't belong to them. It belongs to us.'

'Not my father?'

'Absolutely not your father. But I wouldn't want to be held responsible for some of the things *my* father does, so . . .' She shrugged.

'Kristjan and Wada were going after proof of what Quartizon are doing. Proof only Wada would be able to understand. Right?'

Erla nodded. 'Right.'

'And she got something, but we don't know what.'

'No. Because since that one brief phone call I've heard nothing from her.'

'Have you been to her hotel – or just phoned? I mean, are you sure she's really never there? She could have instructed the front desk to say she was always out.'

'I guess she could. But why would she do that? She knows I'm anxious to speak to her.'

'I don't know. But maybe we should go there late tonight – or early tomorrow morning – and see if there's any sign of her. Does that sound like a good idea?'

'Yeah.' Erla nodded. 'It does.' She looked relieved.

'And this guy Ragnar. Do you know where he lives?'

'Yeah. I know.'

'So, why don't we drop in on him and see how he explains what happened?'

'He'll deny ratting on Kristjan.'

'But when he denies it, will we know whether he's lying or not?'

'Maybe. Probably.'

'I'll settle for that.'

'OK, then. We'll go. But, Nick . . .' She hesitated.

'What?'

'You're looking for your father, right? Are you sure you're ready to find out he's a scumbag?'

'I'm ready for the truth, Erla. Whatever it is.'

'I let my job become my life, Miss Wada,' Caldwell said ruefully as his reminiscences about the insurance business wound back on themselves. 'It was only when I retired that I realized how empty my existence was. My fault, of course. No one else's. You think there's time to put right your mistakes, to alter the way you present yourself to the world. Then, suddenly, time runs out. And you find yourself facing a dismal old age.' He was talking to himself as much as to Wada now.

'Moving back into the house that holds so many memories of when I was young and my friends were young probably wasn't a good idea. The past is always there, despite how much the building's been altered. It's always waiting to tap me on the shoulder. And it doesn't stop at Barnfield Hill. There was an army surplus store round the corner, in Magdalen Road. It's long gone. But whenever I walk past where it was I remember the brass-buttoned greatcoat I bought there that I thought made me look so cool. If I go into the Mount Radford, the pub at the end of the road, I'll remember the gang sitting round the table with me, though I'm not sure all eight of us were ever actually there at the same time.

'Alison in particular is never far away. I adored her. I loved her as I've never loved anyone else. I've probably idealized her, of course. It's easy to do that with the dead, especially those who died young. But her energy, her passion, her determination, were . . . intoxicating. I'd have done anything for her. For the nine months we lived under the same roof I was a completely different person from what I was before or have been since. I know it was me, but sometimes I can't quite convince myself of that. I believed in the things she believed in. I was committed to the causes she was committed to.

'So were the others. Well, Caro and April anyway. And Peter, of course. He was older than us. And wiser, as we thought. He enjoyed planning our campaigns and seeing them carried through. He was adrift, after Cambridge and his parents' deaths. He needed a purpose, a mission. We helped him find one.

'Looking back, I can't really say whether he or Alison was the driving force behind the things we did. Perhaps they fed off each other. Together, they were unstoppable. Which meant we all were. Or felt as if we were. It was a good feeling. The best, in fact.

'The world seemed old and stale to us. It needed changing. Protesting outside the nuclear submarine base at Devonport or sitting in front of bulldozers destroying ancient woodland on the route of a new dual carriageway? That made us feel as if we were making a difference, as if we were actually altering the way society was run. Nonsense, of course, in the greater scheme of things. We weren't altering anything. And we were never going to. But we hadn't lived long enough to understand that.

'There's no point pretending we were always thinking straight. The pot-smoking didn't amount to much, but Geoff was a source of some seriously mind-bending stuff as well. I steered clear of it as far as I could, but that wasn't quite as far as it should have been, especially not when Alison was the one encouraging me to try something new. It probably made us . . . over-confident at the very least, so I suppose it was inevitable that, sooner or later, we'd overreach ourselves.

'The end of term was approaching – the end of our time together. I was worried I'd never see Alison again. My attempts to tell her I loved her had all misfired. She didn't take them seriously. What she really took seriously was our latest cause: exposing what was going on at Nancekuke. No one outside the base knew sarin was being produced there until long after production had ceased in the late fifties, although there were rumours it hadn't really ceased at all. What *was* known, when we started to take an interest, was that Nancekuke was manufacturing CS gas on a large scale. We staged a roadside protest at the start of the Easter holidays and got our pictures in the paper. Well, the local paper. "You are entering a chemical warfare zone." That line on the banner was Alison's idea. She always had the best ideas.

'The picture in the paper caught the attention of Tom Noy, who'd worked at Nancekuke, and, like quite a few others employed there, had gone down with a series of mysterious neurological disorders. He got our address from the university office and, one day, showed up on the doorstep. Thin as a lath, ferret-eyed and twitchy from the nerve damage, he wasn't someone you'd feel inclined to socialize with, but Alison and Peter wanted to hear what he had to say. We were the only ones at home at the time. We took him down to the Mount Radford and plied him with beer while he coughed his way through half a dozen cigarettes and told us his story.

'He said several large condensers had been removed from a German nerve gas factory at the end of the war and put into long-term underground storage at Nancekuke while the scientists tried to figure out exactly what they contained. The tanks were labelled *Rasierklinge* – razor blade in German. Samples were taken of the contents under strictly controlled conditions for analysis.

'The tanks deteriorated over time. They should have been safely destroyed, but no one was too sure how to do that. So

212

they were simply patched up to prevent leaks whenever they looked worryingly rusty. Noy claimed his illness dated from when he was sent down into the bunker where they were stored to do a repair job on one of the tanks. He claimed the scientists had eventually come up with the chemical formula for the contents and had manufactured some of it. Super Sarin, it was nicknamed. Super deadly, by implication. They were still producing small trial batches, according to him.

'Alison and Peter wanted to prove Noy was telling the truth. If he was, the authorities were lying about what was going on at Nancekuke and were putting local residents and holidaymakers at risk with their irresponsible experiments. Noy said he could show them how to get into the base without being detected. He had some keys he was supposed to have handed back when he was laid off but had hung on to. They'd open the doors that gave access to the bunker. Security was slapdash, according to him. There was nothing to prevent us photographing the condensers and their *Rasierklinge* labels and then going to the press with the evidence.

'I didn't like it. Was security really as lax as Noy claimed? And if the condensers were in such a poor state of repair, was it safe to go into the bunker? They'd been down there for more than thirty years by then. Alison and Peter dismissed my concerns. A few risks were worth taking for the sake of exposing Nancekuke's dirty secret. We had a responsibility to tell the world what was happening behind that chain-link fence. And they were excited by the idea of getting away with it. I could see that was a big part of the appeal to them.

'They were excited, while I was scared stiff. But Alison was determined to go, and that meant I was determined to go too. The others cried off. Too dangerous, they reckoned. And I reckoned they were right. But Alison and Peter were going whatever anyone else said. If I cried off too, my last chance with Alison was blown. That's how I saw it, anyway.

'A plan was hatched. We'd go in during the extra long Silver Jubilee weekend, when everybody's attention was fixed on the celebrations: the night of Sunday the fifth of June. We were to meet Noy in the Victory Inn near Porthtowan, where he'd hand over the keys and a sketch plan showing the best route to the bunker from the seaward side. We'd need wire-cutters for the fence, a torch and a good camera with a flash unit to take the photographs. Beyond that, all we really needed was nerve – and luck. I didn't have enough of the former and I wasn't convinced we'd get enough of the latter. But my reservations didn't stop me going. I sensed Alison was testing me – she kept saying, "You don't have to come if you don't want to." And I couldn't face failing the test. I had to go. I couldn't bear not to.

'We'd been down to Porthtowan a week before to reconnoitre the site. Getting through the fence from the coast path didn't look difficult. Beyond that, we'd have to rely on the accuracy of Noy's sketch plan – and his confident prediction that none of the locks were likely to have been changed since he'd left.

'It was a long drive in Peter's camper van that evening of the fifth. The sun was in our faces most of the way. Alison's skin looked golden in the light. She glanced at me quite often during the journey, for no apparent reason. I couldn't see her eyes behind her sunglasses. I couldn't guess what she was thinking.

'Now I can. She was thinking she shouldn't let me go in with them. I was too frightened to be careful. I'd mess up somehow, alert base security to our presence, blow our chance. *That's* what she was thinking.

'She must have got hold of some knockout drug from Geoff. He denied it later, but his denials weren't worth much, especially with the police breathing down our necks. We took some wine and some bottles of beer down to Porthtowan beach after leaving the pub, lit a fire and did our best impressions of idle students watching the sunset. My guess is, once night had fallen and there was only the firelight to see by, she put the drug in my bottle of beer. I remember at some point, when it was too dark to make much out, feeling her hair brush against my cheek. Maybe that was the moment, though at the time . . . I can still recapture the sensation, if I try hard enough. You could say it was her farewell to me. Because soon after that, I was out for the count, and they were free to go ahead without me.

'I never saw Alison again. Or Peter. Until a week ago.'

EIGHTEEN

THE APARTMENT BUILDING WAS ON HRINGBRAUT, A MAIN ROAD south-west of the centre. It was a big five-storey block with several entrances. There was no answer when they pressed the bell for Ragnar's apartment. It was six o'clock, the road was busy and people were returning home from work. But not Ragnar. Not yet.

They followed a mother and child in, helping her manoeuvre her buggy through the doorway, then left her waiting for the lift and climbed the stairs to apartment 42 on the top floor.

They knocked, but there was no reply and no sound from within. It seemed he really was out. They sat on the step at the top of the stairs. And waited.

'You know, don't you, Nick,' Erla began carefully, 'this guy Driscoll – your father – well, he isn't a good person? You get that, don't you?'

'My mother was a good person,' Nick said thoughtfully. 'Maybe one out of two isn't so bad.'

'Was?'

'She died a few months ago.'

'Shit. Sorry.'

'You could say that's what set all this going. You could say *she* set it going. Well, the Caldwell side of things anyway. Which is how I found out Driscoll is my father.'

'It's not too late to forget all about him and go home.'

'I'm not going to do that. I don't think I could. Forget, I mean. Besides . . .' There was a rumble at that moment from the lift shaft. Someone was coming up. 'If this is Ragnar, it's already too late.'

And it was.

Ragnar didn't cut an imposing figure: young, pale and paunchy, with receding hair and a slight unsteadiness that suggested he'd come from work via a bar. He wore a three-piece suit, but no tie, under a light parka. A heavy shoulder bag was dragging him down on one side.

He greeted Erla unsmilingly in Icelandic. She replied in English. 'This is my friend Nick Miller. Nick, this is Ragnar Reynisson.'

There were no handshakes. Ragnar's expression suggested he wished he'd stayed in the bar. 'What do you want?'

'To talk,' said Erla. 'About Kristjan.'

'I've got nothing to say.'

'Why don't we step into your apartment?' Nick said in his most reasonable tone. 'You can say nothing there in greater comfort.'

Ragnar glared at Erla and said something in Icelandic. She rolled her eyes at Nick. 'He says we should basically fuck off.'

'Nice,' said Nick. He took half a step towards Ragnar, who took a full pace back. 'Listen, Ragnar. Erla's put me in the picture. I know you helped Kristjan and Wada get into Quartizon's computer system on Sunday night. After what happened, I imagine Quartizon would like to be able to identify which member of their staff leaked the access codes. You want me to point them in your direction?'

Ragnar looked at Nick for quite a while, weighing up the problem. Then he said, 'Who's Wada?'

'Kristjan's Japanese friend. Erla hasn't heard from her since Sunday.'

'She told me her name was Abe.'

'OK. Abe.' Evidently – and perhaps wisely – Wada had used a pseudonym. 'We want to know why the police turned up so quickly, Ragnar. The obvious explanation is . . . you tipped them off.'

'I didn't tell anyone anything.'

'Someone did.'

'Not necessarily.' Ragnar glanced over his shoulder, as if afraid they might be overheard, though they were alone on the landing. 'All right. We'll talk. This way.'

He led them to the door of his apartment and went in.

It was immediately obvious Ragnar lived as slobbishly as he dressed. Clothes were strewn everywhere and, as they passed the kitchen, Nick glimpsed a stack of unwashed dishes and a teetering tower of crushed pizza boxes.

They followed him into the lounge, which appeared to be the centre of the general chaos. He didn't offer them a seat as he unloaded his shoulder bag on to a table and took off his parka. The bag brushed against a trio of empty lager bottles, causing them to topple over and roll noisily around, one of them falling to the floor. Ragnar paid no attention.

'Who is this guy, Erla?' he asked, nodding towards Nick.

'I told you.'

'You told me his name, yeah, but . . . who is he?'

'A friend.'

'Of Martin Caldwell's,' Nick cut in.

Ragnar gawked at him. 'So you're English, right?'

'Right.'

'You remind me of someone. Who is it?'

'How should I know?'

Ragnar frowned. 'It'll come to me.'

'While it does, why don't you explain why things went wrong on Sunday night?'

Ragnar looked at Erla. 'Does Kristjan know you've involved this guy?'

'Just answer his question.'

'I didn't rat on Kristjan, OK? Why would I? As the person who got him and Abe into the building, I had more to lose than anyone from them being caught.'

'So,' said Nick, 'what went wrong?'

'My guess? Some booby trap built into the system. Any attempt to access the files out of hours triggers an alarm. This Emergence shit is even more sensitive than I thought. The office has been like a North Korean interrogation camp these past two days. Real heavy stuff.'

'What are they worried about? Didn't the booby trap work properly?'

'You tell me. The police only caught Kristjan, right? So, did Abe get away with anything?'

'What's the consensus among your colleagues?'

'My *Japanese* colleagues, you mean? They don't tell me anything. I'm not in the loop. The launch is still on for tomorrow, so obviously Driscoll isn't too bothered. But then he's never much bothered. On top of Kristjan breaking into the Emergence files, some guy Nishizaki HQ sent over here has gone missing, though I'd seen nothing of him even before he dropped off the radar, and now they're sending some other guy to investigate, but none of that seems to— Hold on.' Ragnar stared at Nick for a moment, then snapped his fingers. 'That's it. That's who you remind me of. You look a bit like a . . . younger version of Driscoll.'

219

'Do you see much of Driscoll?'

'No. But he comes and goes at the office when he's in Reykjavík. I see him then.' Ragnar was peering at Nick intently now. 'Are you . . . related to him?'

'You'd need to ask him.'

'What does that mean?'

'Who is the missing man from Nishizaki HQ, Ragnar?' asked Erla, adroitly changing the subject.

'His name's Ohara. Met him, have you? Unusually tall for a Jap, so they tell me.'

'Ohara?' queried Nick.

'Yeah. O-H-A-R-A.'

Of course. A Japanese name that sounded like an Irish one. It was some kind of joke, though not a very funny one. Ohara was the Irishman. But he wasn't Irish. 'Missing, you say?'

'Evidently.'

'Since when?'

'Since I'm not fucking sure exactly when, because, like I said, I never met the guy anyway. But it's got them spooked in Tokyo. Ohara answers direct to Nishizaki himself, according to one of the few rumours my honourable co-workers shared with me. And the same goes for Zayala, the second-in-line shark they're sending to find him, so it's quite a big deal.'

'Why did Nishizaki send Ohara here in the first place?'

'Dunno. Maybe I should text him and ask.'

'Come on, Ragnar. You're not really the dope you pretend to be. What's going on?'

Ragnar snarled something to Erla in Icelandic. 'Apparently, he doesn't appreciate your sarcasm, Nick,' she explained.

Ragnar gave a grumpy harrumph and leant back against the table. He folded his arms. 'I don't get what your interest is in all this . . . Nicholas.'

'I'm a friend of Martin Caldwell. He's missing too.'

'I know. Kristjan told me. Missing's getting to be contagious.'

'Why do you think Nishizaki sent Ohara here? You must have some idea.'

'Maybe to check up on Driscoll. It'd be kind of nice to think those two don't trust each other.'

'Any real evidence for that?'

'The evidence is Ohara coming over and going missing and Zayala coming after him. First signs I've ever seen that anyone at Nishizaki HQ could find Iceland on a map of the world.'

'How has Driscoll reacted?'

'He hasn't. But then he wouldn't. Cool as ice, that guy.'

'Where does he stay when he's in town?'

'The company owns a house in Fjólugata. Number nineteen. Low-key but smart. I hear he stays there.'

'And he's in town now?'

Ragnar nodded. 'Naturally. The launch is tomorrow.'

'What will that involve?'

'I don't know. I'm not *allowed* to know. But it's a sure bet it's to do with all this land that's been acquired in Quartizon's name. Well, the land I *think* we've acquired. Like I told Kristjan and Abe, I'm kept out of that side of things. Japanese staff only. I work on deal-brokering business, which has been pretty quiet lately, like it's just . . . a sideshow.'

'Or window-dressing?'

'And they dress a shop window with dummies, right? I'm ahead of you, Nicholas. Funny guy, aren't you?'

'How could I attend the launch?'

'You'd need an invitation. Without one . . . you won't get past security.'

'And these invitations are . . . hard to come by, are they?'

'For you, impossible to come by.'

Nick stopped himself from smiling. 'That's a pity.'

'Yeah. With Kristjan in a police cell, Abe, Caldwell *and* Ohara all missing and the little I can tell you still being way short of enough, I'd say you were out of options, Nicholas, wouldn't you?'

Now Nick did smile – faintly. 'We'll see.'

Fjólugata 19 was an elegant whitewashed villa, boasting more of a garden than Nick had seen elsewhere in the city. The low boundary walls were topped with railings and the wrought-iron entrance gates were firmly closed. There was a bell and an intercom on the left-hand gate pillar, suggesting simply walking in wasn't an option. A Bentley coupé stood on the sloping drive. Lights burned in several windows, but the blinds were closed.

The house was next door to the Norwegian embassy in what passed for Reykjavík's diplomatic quarter. A gentle night had fallen and the last of the snow and ice was streaming away along pavements and gutters. From the far side of the road Nick gazed across and slightly up at what all the evidence suggested was his father's Icelandic home from home.

'Are you thinking of going across and ringing the bell?' asked Erla. They were standing in the shade of a tree, well away from the nearest street lamp. It seemed unlikely anyone inside the house would be aware of their presence. But if Nick crossed the road and rang the bell, all that would change. And much else might change with it.

'No,' he answered quietly. 'He's here for the launch and that's where I plan to meet him.'

'What about the small problem of an invitation?'

'I have that sorted.'

'You do?'

'I didn't want Ragnar to know, but, yes, I have an invitation.'

'How did you wangle that?'

'Somebody gave me one to make me go away.'

'I guess it's best if I don't ask who.'

'Probably.'

'So, if you're going to wait until tomorrow, why are we here?'

'Not sure. It's just a house, after all. But the idea that he might be . . . in there . . . doing whatever he does . . . while we're out here . . . so close and yet so distant . . .' Nick sighed. 'It's a strange feeling.'

'It must be.'

'Perhaps, in fact, the strangest feeling I've ever had.'

They went to a restaurant Erla recommended on the grounds that she couldn't afford to eat there but Nick could. They were in no hurry, reckoning the later they arrived at the Sol the better their chances of finding Wada in her room. Nick had hidden from Erla the reason why he hadn't rung the bell at Fjólugata 19. Now it had come to the point, he'd started wondering whether he really should take the final step. He *was* going to take it, no question. But, afterwards, would he be happy he had? Would the day come when he regarded this journey to Iceland as the biggest mistake he'd ever made?

The Sol was quiet, the reception area enveloped in shadows. The baby-faced young man behind the desk was fiddling idly with his phone. But he was all attention when Nick and Erla approached him.

'Umiko Wada?' He consulted a computer screen. 'I'm sorry, she isn't here at the moment.'

'But she does have a room here?'

'Oh yes. But . . . she's not here at present.'

'Can you tell me when she was last here?'

'Er, I'm not sure. I'm not on duty all the time.'

Erla asked something in Icelandic, smiling and making encouraging eye contact with the young man. He smiled back and said a lot more than he had to Nick, though, judging by Erla's expression, it wasn't much more helpful. She pressed on. He began to look flustered.

'Are you friends of Miss Wada?' he asked at last, breaking out of Icelandic.

'Yes,' said Nick. 'We are. And we're worried about her. We haven't been able to contact her since Sunday night.'

'You haven't?'

'Has she actually been here since then?'

'As I say . . .'

Erla chipped in with more Icelandic and more smiling.

The young man gave a little exasperated smile of his own. He leant forward across the counter and lowered his voice. 'Look, I never told you this, OK?'

Nick nodded. 'OK.'

'Miss Wada hasn't been here since Monday morning. That is, the bed in her room hasn't been slept in since Sunday night, according to housekeeping. She's booked in for the rest of the week, but, er . . . we haven't heard from her either.'

'Have you done anything about that?'

'Such as what? If she wants to rent a room here but not use it . . .' He shrugged.

'You are absolutely sure she's not here, aren't you, Johann?' Nick asked, reading the young man's name on his lapel badge.

'I'm sorry?' Johann looked bemused.

'Well, one of the things we're concerned about is her state of mind. She might be . . . hiding in her room.'

'Not according to housekeeping.'

'Could you just call her room? On the off chance she's up there.'

'But her key's here, you see.' Johann pushed his chair back on its castors and pulled open a drawer in a tall cabinet. Bemusement returned to his face. 'That's strange.'

'What is?'

'The key . . . actually . . . isn't here.'

'Meaning she's in her room after all?'

'No, no. That can't be right. I'm certain . . .' But he didn't look certain of anything. 'I'll phone her room.' He grabbed the house phone and dialled. A deep frown crossed his face. 'That's . . . weird,' he said. 'The line's out of order.'

'There's a fault?'

'No. There shouldn't be. But . . .'

'If you gave us her room number, Johann, we could go up and check.'

'No.' Johann thought for a moment. Then he burrowed in a cabinet and pulled out a key with a tattered cardboard tag on it bearing the number 22. 'I will go.'

'Actually,' said Nick, 'why don't we all go?'

Johann might have argued with Nick's suggestion if he'd been less distracted. As it was, he seemed so baffled by the missing key and the dead phone line that he gave little thought to Nick and Erla as they joined him in the lift.

A few minutes later, they were all at the door of room 22 on the second floor. There was no sound from within. Johann knocked, then knocked again more loudly. There was no response. He made a third attempt, then put the key in the lock, called 'Housekeeping' and opened the door.

Wada wasn't there. Nobody was there. But someone clearly had been there since the last chambermaid's visit.

The room was in chaos, with every drawer open and clothes strewn across the bed. The door of the safe in the wardrobe was wide open. It, like the wardrobe itself, was empty. The bedside cabinets had been pulled away from the wall, disconnecting the phone that stood on one of them in the process. A suitcase was lying open and upside down on the floor. Its contents, like those of the drawers and wardrobe, appeared to have ended up on the bed. Glancing into the bathroom, Nick saw that the panels under the bath and basin had been unscrewed and removed. No hiding-place had been overlooked.

The room had obviously been thoroughly searched, though whether the search had been successful was another matter. The removal of the panels in the bathroom smacked to Nick's mind of desperation. Maybe they hadn't found what they'd been looking for. Maybe Wada had taken it with her.

A shocked Johann herded them back down to reception and said he would have to phone his manager to decide their next course of action. Nick persuaded him first to check security camera coverage of the reception area. Johann seized on that as a 'Good idea' and commenced scrolling back through the footage on his computer. Only to discover, to his amazement, that the camera hadn't been working since 8.41 that evening, which he reckoned coincided with him leaving the desk to help an elderly guest into a taxi.

'That's when they came in, isn't it?' murmured Erla as Johann scurried into the back office to phone his boss.

'Looks like it,' said Nick. 'We only missed them by a few hours.'

'I think the hotel manager will say call the police.'

'Maybe. Or maybe he won't want to admit there's been a breach of security. Either way, we shouldn't hang around to answer questions. Let's clear out while Johann's busy.'

'This means they're on her trail, doesn't it?' said Erla as they exited the hotel and hurried away along the street.

'Yes,' said Nick. 'But it also means they haven't caught up with her yet. And that they have no more idea than us about what her next move will be.'

'Maybe they don't care about her any more. Maybe they got what they wanted this evening.'

'I doubt it. I think what they wanted is still out there. With Wada. Wherever she is.'

NINETEEN

WEDNESDAY MORNING AT STÓRI-ASGARBÆR. WADA ATE THE PORRIDGE Caldwell cooked for her and drank the tea he brewed. She thanked him for both. She showed no anger or resentment. And he responded with courtesy and kindness – up to a point. But she was still his prisoner.

If her strategy was to work, she had to start altering the bal ance of their exchanges. Caldwell had been happy to recount past events from his point of view – a tiresomely self-pitying one in her unspoken opinion. She'd allowed that to run its course. He'd talked himself to a standstill, as he tacitly acknowledged that morning. 'Sorry if I bored you last night with my tragic tale, Miss Wada.' It was as if they agreed: the time had come for her to do some talking.

'Did you always believe Peter Ellery had survived?'

'Hoped. Suspected. Wondered. All of those things. But I didn't believe it until . . . Caro sent me the *Evening Standard* advert from 1992. That clinched it.'

'But you did not contact Mimori Takenaga straight away?'

'No. I debated whether to act for a long time. Eventually, I realized I had to. Otherwise the doubt would never go away.'

'The doubt about whether Peter Ellery was alive? Or how Alison Parker had died?'

'Very perceptive of you, Miss Wada. Yes, of course, it was as much as anything about Alison that I wanted to know. She was the centre of my thoughts. Only Peter could tell me what had really happened to her. *If* he was alive.'

'Why do you think Caroline Miller sent you the advertisement?'

'Because she knew I'd been torturing myself over what had happened for more than forty years and, with death approaching, felt she should do what she could to lighten my burden.'

'You mean she thought you deserved to know the truth?'

'Yes. That's what it comes down to.'

'And she was right to think that?'

Caldwell frowned at her. 'Obviously. It was a truth that profoundly involved me. I had a stake in those events that I'd argue entitled me to a proper understanding of them.'

'I agree. And . . . do you have a proper understanding of them now?'

He nodded solemnly. 'Yes. I do. Peter has told me everything that occurred.'

'Everything that occurred that night?'

He nodded again, a little impatiently this time. 'Yes.'

'And everything that occurred later that summer, between him and Shitaro Masafumi?'

'He gave me the gist of that as well. Likewise the circumstances that led him into business partnership with Hiroji Nishizaki. But if you think I'm going to share any of those details with you, then I'm afraid you're going to be disappointed. Matters are unfolding that I'm not free to speak of. They require discretion on my part – and inaction on yours. Hence the regrettable necessity of holding you here, Miss Wada.'

'Actually, you may be interested to know that *Miss* Wada is not strictly the correct way to address me. I am a widow.'

'Oh. Sorry. You should have mentioned it sooner.'

'I did not quite know how to. It involves a strange coincidence. My husband was killed in the sarin gas attack on the Tokyo subway in 1995. You have heard of it?'

'Yes. Of course.' Caldwell looked genuinely sympathetic. 'I'm very sorry to hear that.' His expression grew cloudy. 'Sarin again. Such a terrible thing.'

It might be more terrible than Caldwell knew, of course, since Yozo Sasada, the man who'd released the gas, had worked for Quartizon. But now wasn't the moment to allege a connection between Quartizon and the Aum Shinrikyo cult. Now was the moment to capitalize on the sympathy she'd just generated. 'This handcuff is beginning to chafe my wrist, Mr Caldwell.' She raised her arm so he could see the rash the ring had caused on her flesh. 'It will only get worse, I fear.'

'There's nothing I can do about that, I'm afraid.'

'You can release me.'

He sighed. 'As I've already explained, I can't trust you not to go back to Reykjavík and try to interfere in Peter's plans.'

'I cannot drive, Mr Caldwell. I drove George's car the short distance from where Ohara killed him, it is true, and I was lucky to keep it under control. There is no way I could drive it to Reykjavík. And obviously I cannot walk there. Nor can I telephone for assistance. So, what do you lose by releasing me? I would become your ally.'

'My ally in what?'

'Who sent Ohara to find you?'

'I can't—'

'Nishizaki. It has to have been. Nishizaki, not Peter Driscoll. So, there is no longer unity between them. They do not trust each other. That is why you are in danger. That is why we are both in danger.'

'Not while we lie low here.'

'People will be coming here tomorrow. This you have told me. Who will they be working for? Driscoll? Or Nishizaki? Or both?'

'Peter has assured me—'

'It does not matter what he has assured you, Mr Caldwell. What matters is who these people are actually working for. How will you know you can trust them? How will you know that for certain, with your life at stake?'

Caldwell looked stumped by the question. He frowned deeply.

'We should not stay here, Mr Caldwell. The weather has cleared. We should go. Not to Reykjavík. But to somewhere less isolated than this farm. There is a hikers' hostel on the road from Þingvellir to Gullfoss. I saw the sign when George and I drove past. No one would know that was where we had gone. You could call Driscoll from there on Thursday – your phone would work there, I think, or, if not, there would surely be a payphone – to make whatever arrangements with him you think are best. But staying here . . . is not wise. It is not wise at all.'

Caldwell looked searchingly at her, then stood up and walked out into the passage. He moved out of her sight, though she could still see his shadow on the wall, cast by low sun shining through the windows and doorway of the next room. He appeared to put his hands on his head and stoop forward slightly. And he stayed like that for close to a minute.

Then he came back into the bathroom.

'I have your word you'd make no effort to contact anyone . . . if we did . . . go to this hostel?'

'You could keep my phone, Mr Caldwell. But I would not try to contact anyone, I promise.'

'You would have to do exactly what I told you to do.'

'I would. I am certain lying low, as you call it, is the sensible course of action. But not lying low *here*.'

'Perhaps . . . you're right.'

231

He licked his lips nervously. He knew, just as Wada knew, that he could only release her once. From that moment on, he'd have to trust her to keep her word. And she knew, just as he didn't, that she hadn't decided yet whether she would.

She said nothing. She waited, her instinct for patience winning out over the temptation to press him further. He stood, looking down at her. He dried his lips with the side of his hand. He adjusted his glasses. Then he reached into the pocket of his trousers and took out the key to the handcuffs.

She didn't move as he knelt awkwardly beside her. She had to let him do this of his own volition. It had to be his decision.

He grasped the cuff attached to her right wrist and twisted it towards him to reach the keyhole. Then . . . he hesitated. 'I . . . I'm not sure,' he muttered. 'Perhaps . . . it's safer . . . to leave things as they are.'

Wada saw the change in his eyes and knew at once. He wasn't going to let her go. She'd brought him to the brink. But now he was edging back.

The key was close. The chance was there. And it wouldn't last longer than a few more seconds.

She plucked the key from his fingers. '*No*,' he shouted. She rolled under the basin, twisting the cuff round the downpipe to evade his grasp. He lunged after her. But already she'd slid the key into the keyhole. One turn. And she was free.

Caldwell tried to pin her against the wall. He grabbed at the cuff that was still in her hand, banging his head against the underside of the basin as he did so. He was dazed for an instant. It would have been enough for Wada to escape. But there was a way to make her escape more certain and she took it. She closed the cuff round Caldwell's wrist and snapped it shut, then scrambled away from him across the floor.

Caldwell tried to go after her, but the handcuff chain clanged taut and he fell on to his elbow with a grunt of pain, then rolled on to his side. 'Stop, stop,' he cried. 'I'm sorry. I shouldn't have done that.'

She wasn't listening. She slipped the key into her pocket and dodged past his flailing feet to the door.

'I'm sorry, I'm sorry,' he mewled on. 'That wasn't meant to happen.'

She ignored him and headed for the back door. However bad a driver she might be, she was going to drive away from Stóri-Asgarbær now. She was going to drive far away. And while she was on the road, she was going to decide what to do next. As for Caldwell, he would have to take his chances. If he'd let her go, it would be different. But his change of mind had made her mind up. He deserved nothing from her.

He was still calling after her as she left the house and hurried round to the front, where George's car was parked. Soon, mercifully, she could no longer hear him.

She reached the car and opened the tailgate to confirm her shoulder bag was where she'd left it, complete with the *kageboshi* file and the printed extract from the Emergence files. They were all in Japanese, of course, so, even if Caldwell had looked at them, he wouldn't have understood what they meant.

She closed the tailgate, went round to the driver's door and climbed in. She slid the key into the ignition and turned it. Lights glowed on the dashboard. But the engine did no more than sputter and die. She tried again. There wasn't even a sputter this time. Then she saw the red light on the fuel gauge. *Empty.*

She stared at the red light in disbelief. How could that be? There'd been no warning of low fuel when she'd driven the car. George had filled up as they left Reykjavík on Monday morning. This made no sense.

Then she remembered the shot Ohara had fired when she reversed into him. She'd heard a metallic crack as well as the shot itself. Could it be . . .

She jumped out of the car and ran round to the rear wing that had impacted with the roadside post. There was the flap over the filler-cap. And, below and to the left of it, a bullet-hole in the bodywork. She sighed and leant against the car, cursing her luck. The gasoline must have been leaking out while she fought for her life with Ohara – and later, while she made her first futile attempts to persuade Caldwell to release her. Leaking out – until it was all gone.

She took a breath and stood upright. This wasn't going to stop her. There was a second car – Ohara's – in the barn. She collected her shoulder bag and hurried across the yard.

The barn doors weren't fully closed. Maybe the wood had swelled in the snow, preventing Caldwell from securing them properly. The snow had melted since, exposing wheel-rutted mud. Wada pulled the doors open. Ohara's car was a tight fit inside. Caldwell had collided with a pile of paint pots while driving it in. The pots were jumbled and jammed between the car and the wall. There was a big pool of white paint extending beneath the vehicle. Wada had to hop over it to reach the driver's door.

The first question to answer was whether Caldwell had left the key in the ignition, or taken it into the house. It was dark inside the barn and even darker inside the car, but stretching in, Wada located the key, still plugged into the ignition. She clambered into the seat and slammed the door behind her.

She turned the key. There was a different sound from the sputter of the engine in George's car. It was more of a whimper, a mechanical moan. There was no burst of ignition. The engine was dead. She knew that even without trying again, though she did try again, of course.

234

Her second attempt told her what the problem was. Caldwell hadn't turned the key all the way off. She saw then that the stalk beside the steering wheel was adjusted to the headlights-on position. They weren't on now, though they probably had been for most of the past two days, draining the battery.

An empty fuel tank and a dead battery. She sat staring into the darkness at the back of the barn, trying very hard not to be overwhelmed by her situation. She had the use of two cars, neither of which was going anywhere. Unless . . .

She jumped out of the car and hurried round to the rear. She raised the tailgate and peered into the storage compartment, hoping Ohara might have been carrying a set of jump leads. She had no experience whatever of using such things to start a flat battery, but she'd give it her best shot.

Nothing. It was a hire car, supplied with the bare minimum of tools: a jack, a pump, a tyre lever. No jump leads.

She let the tailgate fall shut under its own momentum, turned round and leant back against it. All she could see around her, beyond the roofline of the farmhouse, was a bleak and empty landscape. She had no means of navigating her way across it. Following the road out on foot was a daunting prospect. She wasn't sure she had the stamina to walk as far as she might need to. She couldn't actually remember how far along the road the last habitation was that they'd passed.

Was it worth checking *inside* the car for jump leads? She had nothing to lose. She went back round to the driver's door and climbed in. The door pockets contained an owner's manual and a road map of Iceland. She pulled open the glove box.

No jump leads. But there was a phone. Wada wondered whether Ohara might have taken care to ensure he could use it wherever he went in the country. She picked it up and pressed a few buttons experimentally. The screen lit – at least it hadn't lost all its charge – but there also were the dreaded words *NO SIGNAL*.

She tossed the phone back into the glove box. Then a frail hope flickered. Was there no signal because, like her phone, Ohara's didn't work this far into the interior? Or simply because she was inside a car inside a barn with thick stone walls?

She picked the phone up again, climbed from the car and headed out into the daylight.

She was ten metres or so from the barn when a service provider's name popped up in place of *NO SIGNAL*. And she smiled for the first time in days.

She hurried over to George's car and took her phone from where she'd left it on a shelf beneath the dashboard. She wasn't going to call the police. There would just be too much to explain, and if they linked her to the break-in at Quartizon's offices in Reykjavík she might simply be swapping one kind of imprisonment for another. No. She needed to get away from Stóri-Ásgarbær. So, she needed someone to come and fetch her.

She called up Erla's number on her phone, then rang it on Ohara's, hoping Erla would answer, even though she wouldn't recognize the number.

She didn't. No matter. Wada started recording a message. 'Erla, this is Wada. It's very—'

Then Erla interrupted. 'That's you, Wada?'

'Yes.'

'Where are you?'

'A place called Stóri-Asgarbær. It is a farm. A long way from Reykjavík.'

'Why are you there?'

'There is no time to explain. Erla, I am in serious trouble. I have to get away from here. But I have no car I can use. I am stranded. Can you help me?'

'You want me to come and get you?'

'Yes. Yes please. As soon as you can.'

'I've got no car. But . . . I could hire one.'

'Do that.'

'OK. OK, I'll hire one and come to you. But where is . . .'

'Stóri-Asgarbær.'

'Where is that . . . exactly?'

'I can give you the coordinates.'

'The coordinates?'

'Precise latitude and longitude.'

'OK. I guess that would work.'

'Hold on.' Wada moved to the tailgate and swung it open. She slipped the Emergence document out of her bag and read off the coordinates for Stóri-Asgarbær. 'You have that?'

Erla read them back.

'Yes. Correct. You can find me with those?'

'Sure. No problem.'

'And you will leave straight away?'

'I'll fix up a car and set off as soon as I can. I'll text you when I leave the city.'

'OK. Good. I am relying on you, Erla. You understand? I have to leave here.'

'I'm on it.'

'Thank you.'

Nick was lingering over coffee after a late breakfast at his hotel. He'd just sent an anodyne and largely fictitious text to Kate when his phone rang. It was Erla.

'I've heard from Wada.'

'You have? Where is she?'

'A farm several hours from here. She wants me to come and get her. She's got no transport for some reason. She sounded . . . well, as though she needed to get out of there.'

'You said you'd go?'

'Of course. But I've got no car, so I'll have to hire one.'

'I can do that.'

'I was hoping you'd say that. There's a car hire place under the opera house. Can you meet me there in . . . twenty minutes?'

'I'll be there in fifteen.'

'OK. Great. See you soon.'

Nick put his phone down and drained his coffee cup. So, Wada had broken cover. And the likelihood was that she still had whatever she'd taken from Quartizon's offices, which the raid on her hotel room suggested somebody wanted back – badly.

Suddenly, the truth seemed almost close enough to touch. He pushed back his chair and stood up. It was time to go.

The morning passed with agonizing slowness for Wada. She walked as far as the gate on the track at the farm boundary and back to the house twice. Then the text she was waiting for came in. *Leaving city now.*

She went indoors and made some tea. She gave Caldwell a cup and dealt with his attempts to persuade her to let him go by not speaking at all. She said nothing about the empty fuel tank in George's car or the dead battery in Ohara's. She made no mention of the fact that she now had a functioning phone. She gave no hint rescue was on the way.

'I don't know what your intentions are,' Caldwell said, 'but I can assure you I'll fall in with whatever you decide. I'm sure you realize I pose no threat to you. Our misunderstanding earlier – my . . . hesitation over releasing you – was just a . . . fleeting loss of nerve. There's absolutely no reason why we can't cooperate with each other. I think we should do exactly what you proposed: head for that hostel you spotted. You have my solemn word I won't try to stop you doing whatever you judge best in the circumstances. It's not for me to criticize your decisions. You've had a lot to contend with and you've coped admirably. If we can just discuss the situation rationally, then I'm confident . . .'

But his confidence was misplaced. They weren't going to discuss the situation, rationally or *ir*rationally. They weren't going to discuss anything. Wada had heard enough from him. She collected his empty teacup, washed it and hers in the kitchen, then went back outside and checked for messages on Ohara's phone.

There were none. That didn't matter. Erla was on her way. There were no messages for Ohara either. She couldn't decide whether that was good news or bad before concluding it was probably neither.

Eventually, she went back indoors and sat by the range in the kitchen, ignoring Caldwell's calls from the bathroom until he finally gave up and fell silent.

And the silence sounded good.

Until it was broken. She couldn't have said by what. The sound was distant and indistinct: a rumble of some kind. The view from the kitchen window hadn't altered. Nor the one from the bedroom window on the other side of the passage. Wada walked to the front door, opened it and stepped outside. The wind stirred her hair and whispered in the eaves. There was nothing else, just the blank surrounding moorland. Nothing had changed.

She went back into the house. As she passed the bathroom, Caldwell asked her why she'd gone outside. She ignored him.

Back in the kitchen, she checked the time. Whatever the noise, it was too early to be the sound of Erla's car approaching.

A few minutes passed. Normality resumed. The waiting began again.

*

Then sounds came in a rush. Running footsteps approaching the house. A loud crash from the direction of the front door. The sound of wood splintering. Wada jumped up from her chair. There were more footsteps now – *inside* the house.

Then she heard Caldwell's tremulous voice.

'My God. Who . . . who are you?'

'Where is Ohara?' The man spoke English with a Japanese accent.

'Who?'

'Stupid to play games with a gun pointing at you.'

'Maybe . . . if it wasn't . . . I could think more clearly.' Caldwell sounded frightened. But he was doing his stubborn best to hold himself together.

'Ohara left you like this?'

'Er . . . yes.'

'You are Martin Caldwell?' The man's Japanese accent was strong enough for Caldwell's name to sound like Cordwell when he pronounced it.

'Yes. Yes, that's . . . that's me.'

'So, where is Ohara?'

'Who are you?' Caldwell countered.

'That does not matter.'

'Still, I should like to know.'

'Zayala. My name is Zayala.'

'You . . . work for Ohara?'

'Who else is here, Caldwell?'

'No one.'

'I know that is a lie. Where is Wada?'

Don't tell him, Wada silently urged Caldwell, though in truth he might as well, since she was only a few rooms away with no means of escape. If she stepped into the passage, Zayala would surely see her. If she climbed out of one of the windows, he would surely hear her. And he had a gun.

How had he found them? A sickening answer came to her as she cast around the kitchen, looking for some way out. Ohara's phone. Perhaps, as soon as she removed it from the barn and re-established a connection, Zayala was able to track it. And to arrive where the signal led him long before Erla.

'Ohara and Wada have gone,' Caldwell lied, none too convincingly to Wada's ear. 'I don't know where.'

'They left together?'

'Er . . . yes. Together.'

The last part of the room Wada looked at was the ceiling. And there, directly above the chair she'd been sitting on, she saw a loft hatch. It was maybe the only chance she had of escaping.

She stood on the chair, moving with enormous care to avoid any scrapes or creaks, stretched her arms above her head and waited for some sound from the bathroom that would camouflage whatever noise the hatch made. There was a clank of the chain on Caldwell's handcuffs that gave her what she needed. She pushed the hatch upwards and slid it to one side.

'What was that?' Zayala immediately demanded.

'I . . . didn't hear anything,' said Caldwell.

Wada knew she had to act fast. She was surely only seconds away from detection. She jumped up, grasped the frame of the hatchway and pulled herself bodily up, her muscles straining but adrenalin driving her on.

Then she was in the loft, scrambling on to a surface of planking laid across the joists. As she replaced the hatch, she glimpsed a movement down in the kitchen: the shadow of Zayala entering the room. But the hatch had slid back into place before she saw the man himself.

Silence. Wada crouched where she was. Did Zayala know she was there? Had he seen or heard the hatch being moved? She barely breathed as she waited. Maybe, she thought, just maybe—

241

Then a gunshot tore a hole in the hatch and pinged against one of the rafters. Wada shrank back.

No further shots followed. A tense silence fell. Maybe Zayala was trying to judge exactly where in the loft she was. Glancing around in the thin light seeping in beneath the soffits, she saw it ran the length of the house, planked for maybe half that, with several brace-beams breaking up the space.

Wada eased herself up on to the nearest brace-beam and waited, wondering what Zayala's next move would be. Her heart was hammering inside her chest. She was drawing fast, shallow breaths. There was sweat on her forehead, despite the chill hanging around her in the dusty air.

She could hear voices below, but she couldn't make out what was being said. She couldn't even distinguish between Zayala and Caldwell, although one raised and piercing note was surely Caldwell crying out – in pain, maybe, or panic.

Then the voices stopped. A minute or so passed. She heard a thump from the direction of the kitchen, followed by another. Another minute of silence. Then one brief scream – and a gunshot.

Wada didn't doubt what had happened. Caldwell was dead, executed by Zayala, who would surely now do the same to her. She lowered herself off the brace-beam and began to move along the loft, away from the hatch. She had no clear plan of escape. Was there another hatch at the other end of the house? Was there any kind of way out? She could only hope against hope.

She heard the hatch being pushed up behind her and immediately shrank down in the shelter of the large water tank she'd just passed. The light in the loft changed as the hatch opened. She saw Zayala's bird-like shadow cast across the underside of the roof.

'Show yourself, Wada,' he called, speaking in Japanese. 'I will not kill you.'

She didn't answer. He was obviously lying. He had no intention of letting her leave the loft, let alone the house, alive. Her shoulder bag was hanging on a chair in the kitchen. She assumed he'd already inspected it and satisfied himself that it contained the *kage-boshi* file and the stolen Emergence documents. With that established, there was no reason to refrain from killing her.

'Come out now from wherever you are hiding.' His voice was too harsh for his words to be at all persuasive. She wondered if he realized that. Perhaps he didn't care. 'This is your only chance.'

In Wada's mind there was no only chance. There was in truth no chance at all. She could think of no way out of the situation she was in. She was trapped. She was helpless. Death was coming for her.

'Stay where you are, then. And take the consequences.'

The shadow vanished. But the hatch stayed open. Then she heard a click. And a second later a bottle with a flaming cloth stuffed in its neck was tossed up into the loft, followed by two more. They smashed against the rafters and fell to the floor. The gasoline inside them burst into flame and spread in a blue-yellow tide across the planks, which crackled and smoked and began to burn.

Wada retreated along the loft as smoke billowed towards her. The speed with which the fire had caught was frightening. She was in a tinderbox of old, dry wood. The roof was covered outside in turf, and though that might burn more slowly than wood, it would surely only produce more smoke for Wada to choke in as it did so. She had to get out. But there *was* no way out.

Then she saw a chimney breast ahead. The mad idea entered her mind that maybe this could be her escape route. Hurrying towards it, she failed to register that she'd reached the end of the planked section of flooring. Her foot suddenly plunged into the gap between two beams and her leg disappeared through the lath and plaster ceiling of the room below.

She grasped the beams on either side of the gap to haul herself back up, but to her horror she felt her foot seized and yanked downwards. She cried out and heard Zayala grunt with the effort of pulling her down. She fell sideways into the gap and lost her hold on the beams. In an avalanche of wood and plaster, she descended through the ceiling.

Zayala let go and allowed her to crash to the floor. Her shoulder took most of the impact. She felt the fluffy surface of a rug beneath her cheek. Then he pushed her on to her back with his foot and she saw the jagged hole in the ceiling above her.

In the next instant, Zayala appeared in her field of vision. His face was bony and sheened with sweat. His eyes were narrow, his mouth a hard gash beneath a flat nose. He stepped over her, so that his feet were planted either side of her chest. In his right hand he held a gun, which he trained on her head.

'Was it you or Caldwell who killed Ohara?' he demanded.

He must have forced Caldwell to tell him where Ohara's body was, though telling him hadn't helped Caldwell in the end. Wada realized full well what that meant for her. 'It makes . . . no difference,' she gasped.

'It was you, I think.'

'I will not tell you . . . how Ohara died.' Her refusal to answer was the only way she could defy him. And she was grimly content for those to be the last words she spoke.

TWENTY

THE FIRST SIGNS NICK AND ERLA HAD THAT SOMETHING WAS WRONG were the helicopters: one police, one fire service, buzzing low overhead and heading in the same direction as them. Erla rang the number Wada had given her but got no answer. 'The number doesn't even ring,' she reported. 'There's nothing.' She tried Wada's own phone. 'The same. Nothing. A dead line.'

'Let's not jump to conclusions,' said Nick. 'Those helicopters could be going anywhere.'

'But they're not, are they? They're going to Stóri-Asgarbær.'

'We don't know that.'

'Don't we?'

Nick could find nothing to say in reply. He just kept driving.

The smoke on the horizon, first seen several kilometres back, had already prepared them for the sight that greeted them when they arrived. That and the fire engine and the police car that had overtaken them on the road.

They'd never seen Stóri-Asgarbær intact. Now it was a smouldering ruin, fragments of gable and the stumps of chimneystacks standing like the ribs of some animal reduced to a carcass.

There was a burnt-out car standing in front of the house and another in a gutted outbuilding.

They pulled up on the far side of the yard. Two firemen were hosing down the remains of the walls while a couple of boiler-suited forensics officers picked their way through the accessible areas. A policewoman noticed their presence and started walking towards them.

'Don't tell her why we're here, Erla,' cautioned Nick. 'We can't afford to get caught up in their investigation. Remember, I have to be back in Reykjavík by six.'

'OK. But it doesn't look good, does it?'

'No.' There was nothing else to say.

Erla got out of the car and greeted the policewoman in Icelandic. Nick watched from the driver's seat as they talked, glancing towards the house at intervals.

Then Erla came back and the policewoman headed off to rejoin her colleagues. 'Well?' Nick asked apprehensively as Erla got into the car.

'I explained we seemed to have taken the wrong road. She told me we should leave. I asked what started the fire. She didn't say, but it was obvious from the way she spoke about it that it wasn't an accident. And when I asked if anyone had been injured, she said . . .'

'What?'

Erla drew a deep breath. 'Four fatalities.'

'Four?'

'It's what she said, Nick. No details. And I couldn't ask for any, could I?'

'No.' He sighed. 'Christ. What happened here?'

'Not a clue. Not sure the police have yet. But four people are dead. How they died? Who they were? Whether one of them was a middle-aged Japanese woman? There's no way we're going to find out today.'

'I thought we were going to find Wada – and all the answers.'

'So did I.'

'Instead . . .'

'Everything's fucked.'

Nick looked at the policewoman who'd spoken to Erla. She'd turned and was eyeing them. 'We're going to have to leave, Erla,' he said glumly.

'And then? What are we going to do?'

'At the moment . . . I have no idea.'

There was nothing for it but to drive back to Reykjavík. Initially, they were too shocked to say much. And when they did speak there was nothing good to say.

The route took them past Þingvellir. Coachloads of tourists were milling about and swarming over the rocks at the top of the walk down through the rift valley. Nick and Erla huddled over coffees in the visitor centre café and looked solemnly at each other.

'We don't know Wada is one of the four fatalities,' Nick reasoned half-heartedly.

'She asked for help,' said Erla. 'She said she was in serious trouble and had to get away from Stóri-Asgarbær. She didn't get away. And the serious trouble arrived before we did. Are you going to tell me I'm wrong about that?'

'No. Just that you can't be . . . certain.'

'The phone she called me on isn't working any more. Nor's the phone she used in Reykjavík. Why? Because they were both destroyed in the fire. Along with . . .' Erla took a moment to compose herself. 'I need a cigarette. Can we go outside?'

They stood in the car park, Erla smoking her way through one cigarette, then another. She was shivering, though it wasn't particularly cold. Nick felt a little unsteady himself. The fire – and the reported fatalities – had forced him to acknowledge that the stakes were far higher than he'd ever supposed. Violent deaths forty years ago were one thing. But these deaths were in the present – the here and now.

'Maybe you shouldn't go to the Emergence thing this evening,' said Erla.

'Chicken out, you mean?'

'It's too late to help Wada. As for Kristjan, the police will release him eventually. He might have to do a few months in prison. But he'll be OK. And we can all get on with our lives. I'll settle for that.'

Thinking seriously about dropping his pursuit of the man who was his father and the secrets he harboured made Nick realize how important the truth had become for him. He'd come too far in his search to turn back now. Go home, tell Kate Caldwell hadn't shown up and he'd got nowhere, then sit down to Easter lunch with her parents and make small talk about nothing very much? There was simply no way he could do it.

'I know Driscoll's your father, Nick, but you've lived this long without knowing him. Maybe that's how it should stay.'

'No.' He shook his head and looked Erla in the eye. 'I'm going on.'

Nick dropped Erla at Stúdentagarđar, then drove back to his hotel for a shower and a change of clothes. He was aiming for a sophisticated look, his best guess as to what would help him blend in at the auction. He didn't feel sophisticated. There was a knot of tension in his stomach that only tightened as he made his way to the Never Before Gallery, arriving a little after the event's scheduled start time.

The evening was soft and windless, a stark contrast with the snow and slush of two days before. Invitees were arriving: middle-aged men in dark suits and open-neck shirts with expensive tans and chunky wristwatches – and a few middle-aged women, also dressed in dark clothes and favouring luxury brand handbags. The gallery itself was closed. Those entering were directed upstairs, after their credentials had been verified. Nick saw cards like the one Miranda had given him being discreetly scanned and returned with a smile – and an iPad.

His own card survived scrutiny. The tablet he was given was evidently something more specific than a standard iPad. 'For your use this evening, sir,' he was told, which sounded both enticing and limiting at the same time.

He went up the curving stairs into a long, softly lit room, where glamorous young waiters and waitresses were circulating with champagne and canapés. There were almost as many of them as there were guests. There was no crush, no deafening clamour. The air was cool, the mood restrained but expectant. Above the melange of expensive perfumes and colognes there was some strange energizing quality in the atmosphere.

The first-floor windows overlooking the street were curtained off. The walls had become giant screens, displaying pictures that split and split again into a carousel of images: mountains, streams, forests, moors; open skies, wide horizons. When Nick activated his tablet, it established interactivity with the nearest screened image, which he could toggle round to different perspectives. The tablet then informed him that he was seeing a *future-enhanced representation of local conditions* for a particular lot number. It seemed that what was for sale at this auction really was the land that Erla and Kristjan believed should never be for sale.

'You look like a discerning man.' The words were spoken by a tall, dark-skinned, good-looking fellow guest who'd appeared at Nick's elbow. 'Independent too, I would say.' There was an accent Nick would have guessed was Middle Eastern. 'Perhaps not a proxy.'

'Perhaps not,' Nick replied, smiling coolly.

'Very good,' said his new friend with a flash of dazzlingly white teeth. '*Perhaps* not. So, discreet as well as discerning.'

'Are you a proxy?'

'Of course. The kind of people who can play this game are also the kind of people who can send someone else to make the actual moves. This you know, though.'

'I don't have anyone to send to something like this.'

'That must make your life . . . full.'

Nick smiled. 'I guess so.'

'Yet you have found time to be here. Why?'

'Curiosity.'

'Ah. I see. You are a spectator. Perhaps an official observer.'

'Definitely not official.'

'How did you obtain an invitation?'

'By knowing the right people.'

The man nodded. 'The true division of mankind. Not male and female. Not black and white. Not even rich and poor. But the right people . . . and the wrong people.'

'Will you be bidding this evening?'

'That is what I have been sent here to do. And you?'

'Not sure.'

'Are you limitlessly wealthy?'

'Is anyone?'

'Surprisingly, yes. More than you might imagine. Many of them are represented here. Because this is a unique opportunity: to buy something that properly speaking cannot be bought.'

'Which is?'

The man looked at the image of a sparkling waterfall on the screen nearest to them. 'The future,' he murmured. 'Nothing less.'

Further conversations of a more humdrum nature ensued as Nick wandered through the gathering. Everyone was polite but guarded. No one was really willing to tell him anything, about themselves, about the people who'd sent them, about what exactly they thought they were buying. Champagne was sipped, canapés were nibbled, tablets consulted. The screens continued to display their seductive visions of idyllic landscapes, in ever greater abundance as more and more of the guests manipulated their particular favourites. The atmosphere in the room seemed to absorb the freshness and clarity of the images on the screens. Suspicious as he was of everything and everyone there, Nick nevertheless felt a strange elation growing within him.

An hour had passed with deceptive speed when the tablets informed their holders that bidding would begin in five minutes. No auctioneer appeared. This clearly wasn't going to be an auction on traditional lines. To this point no one had stepped forward to identify themselves as a spokesperson for Quartizon. No one had taken charge of the event. It was obvious to Nick the other guests knew something he didn't. There'd been preliminaries to the event he hadn't been party to.

'Feel excited?' asked the man he'd had the elliptical conversation with earlier, reappearing next to him.

'Yes, I do.' And it was true. Nick did feel excited – and apprehensive.

'That will be the extra-oxygenated atmosphere.'

'Are you serious?'

'Oh yes. Nothing has been left to chance. Even though no one who really matters is physically present here this evening.' He cast a glance round the room. 'I know. It is hard to believe we are all so . . . inconsequential.'

The five minutes were up. Silence descended. Lot numbers began to spring up on Nick's tablet, followed almost instantly by notifications of bids that appeared and disappeared with bewildering rapidity. Nick caught tantalizing glimpses of numbers accompanied by the repeated message *subject to standard multiplier*. The process was almost subliminal in its speed. He wasn't sure what currency was being used in the bids. He had no idea what the multiplier was. He wondered if individuals were actually doing the bidding or if computers were handling the whole process algorithmically.

Then, on his tablet, the numbers suddenly faded to grey, overlaid by a message. *Authorization fault. Please contact a member of staff immediately.*

Nick looked around, wondering if anyone else had received such a message. There was no obvious sign they had. They appeared rapt in their concentration on their tablets.

Except for the man moving between them and heading in Nick's direction. He was short and rotund, of Asian appearance, Indian maybe, aged sixty or seventy, with steely grey hair and sad, spaniel-like eyes behind gold-framed glasses. His dark suit wasn't quite as elegantly cut as those of most of the other men in the room and, unusually in this gathering, he was wearing a tie. He looked slightly out of place. But he also looked as if that didn't bother him.

He smiled as he reached Nick. 'I'm sorry to interrupt,' he said quietly, almost deferentially.

Nick tried hard to look blasé. 'Is there a problem?'

'My name is Vardekar.'

'Yes?'

'Yours, I think, is Miller.'

'Have we met?'

'Not until now.'

'Look, Mr Vardekar, I . . .'

'Would you mind accompanying me to an adjoining room? We need to discuss a delicate issue. And we need a little privacy to do it in.'

'I prefer to stay out here.'

'That would be unwise. We do have security personnel here, though they masquerade as waiters very effectively. Technically speaking, Baroness Cushing failed to register you as her proxy. Removing you forcibly would be within our rights as set out in the terms and conditions of participation.'

'Bullshit.'

'Well, that's one view of the small print in our contracts. But, legally speaking, we are in the right, so I'd advise compliance with my request.' He gave Nick an avuncular grin. 'There's nothing to be afraid of.'

Nick was far from sure he believed him. The two waiters threading a path towards them looked to be carrying a lot of muscle under their well-cut shirts and their expressions suggested they took their duties – whatever they were – quite seriously.

'Nobody here will spring to your defence, Nick. They're not the kind of people who do that, as I'm sure you realize. So, just come with me. And we can have a quiet word together. That's all I'm asking you to do.'

'I have a lot of questions, Mr Vardekar.'

'I'll try to answer them.'

'Really?'

'Yes. Really. Shall we go?' He gestured with his hand. 'This way please.'

The close company of the two muscular waiters persuaded Nick he had little choice but to go. A curtain was drawn back near the entrance to the room, revealing a door through which Vardekar led the way into a long, comfortably furnished lounge. One wall of the room comprised the reverse sides of the screens, which functioned like two-way mirrors. Nick could see Emergence's guests flicking at their tablets as the auction

253

proceeded, overlaid by the ghostly, transparent images of the pictures projected on the screens, drained of colour.

Glancing behind him, he saw that the two waiters hadn't come into the room with them. It was just him and Vardekar – plus comfortable couches and an extensive drinks cabinet.

'Would you like something stronger than champagne, Nick?' Vardekar asked with a smile. 'Whisky? Brandy?'

'Just those answers you promised.'

Vardekar poured himself a whisky. 'Sure you won't keep me company?'

'I'm fine, thanks.'

'So . . .' Vardekar sat down and gestured for Nick to sit down too, but he remained standing. He didn't want there to be anything remotely cosy about their conversation. 'What do you want to know?'

'What is Emergence?'

'A commercial initiative of Quartizon, acting in partnership with the Nishizaki Corporation.'

'But what is it – *exactly*?'

'The confidentiality Quartizon guarantees its clients means I can't be specific.'

'So much for answering my questions.'

'I only said I'd try.' Vardekar's smile was becoming annoying.

'Where is Peter Driscoll?'

'Detained elsewhere, to his regret.'

'But you represent him?'

'In a personal rather than a commercial capacity, yes.'

'What are you – his lawyer?'

'No. I'm an accountant by profession. Did I tell you my name is Vardekar?'

'Yes, you did.' Nick's impatience was growing.

'Well, it's not, actually. It's Hardekar. Vinod Hardekar.'

*

254

Vinod Hardekar. The Indian student from the house in Exeter. Forgotten by his former friends – except one. 'You're . . . Hardekar?'

'Yes. Why don't you sit down, Nick? You look as if you've had a shock.'

Nick lowered himself slowly on to the couch and stared at Hardekar, not even trying to disguise his astonishment. 'What the hell is going on here?'

'Two things I've been tasked with keeping apart. Emergence, currently proceeding with well-oiled efficiency. And your search for your natural father, Peter Ellery, now known as Peter Driscoll, chairman and chief executive of Quartizon.'

'How long have you known he didn't die in 1977?'

'That's really unimportant. I'm afraid we don't have infinite amounts of time to play with. I needn't tell you Marty Caldwell's recent dealings with you and Mimori Takenaga have caused a great deal of trouble, beginning with Kazuto Kodaka's enquiries – and those of his assistant, Umiko Wada – on behalf of Mrs Takenaga regarding her father Shitaro Masafumi's death forty-two years ago. This persuaded Mr Nishizaki that drastic action had to be taken to cover his tracks in the matter – and in other matters concerning his business activities and practices. This action has culminated in a . . .' Hardekar looked upset for a moment. He raised a hand in apology and took a sip of whisky. 'I'm sorry. The news that reached us today . . . has rather knocked me.'

'What news?'

'You accompanied Erla Torfadóttir to Stóri-Asgarbær earlier today. What you found . . . is the news I refer to.'

'How do you know I went there?'

'That hardly matters.'

'Who died at Stóri-Asgarbær?'

'The police are still trying to determine the identities of the deceased. But it's certain Marty Caldwell was one of them.'

'Martin? What was he doing there?'

'Hiding, with Peter's help, from Nishizaki's wrath. Sadly, Wada managed to lead Nishizaki's agents straight to him.'

'Was Wada also killed?'

Hardekar nodded. 'So I've been informed.'

'And the other two? Who were they?'

'An irrelevant question at this stage. Peter's concern – and mine – is to avoid any more deaths. Especially . . . yours.'

Nick couldn't quite credit the directness of the threat to his life that Hardekar was suggesting. 'Why should Nishizaki want to kill me?'

'Because your attempts to discover the truth of your paternity threaten to expose some of his secrets. And because his traditional response to any kind of threat is to neutralize it.'

'Does he . . . know I'm in Iceland?'

'Does he *personally* know? I'm not presently sure. But we need to ensure you stop doing anything that could be construed as interference in his affairs.'

'Including trying to contact my father?'

'Indeed.' Hardekar sighed. 'I am sorry. Peter is clear this is how it has to be. It's in your own best interests, which he's naturally anxious to safeguard. Nishizaki will leave you alone if you leave him – and those associated with him – alone. It really is as simple as that. And the death toll at Stóri-Ásgarbær should tell you how foolish it would be to go up against him. That was Kodaka's mistake. And Wada's. And Marty's too, though he never knew that was what his actions amounted to. Peter wants to protect you, Nick. As a father would.'

'But he won't see me?'

'It's too big a risk. At present. But . . .'

'But what?'

'We've booked you on the first Icelandair flight to London tomorrow morning. Be on it. Go home. Enjoy Easter. Relax.

Forget all this . . . unpleasantness. Let a little time pass. Then . . . Peter will contact you. He's asked me to give you his word on that. He will be in touch. You will meet your father.'

'When?'

'When it's safe. For you. And for him.'

'Which could be . . . months from now?'

'Nothing like so long, I'm sure. But haste, at this stage, could be fatal.'

'How do I know he's not just fobbing me off?'

Hardekar frowned. 'I understand how difficult this is for you. You've never met him, so you've no way of judging whether you can trust him. And some of the things you've learnt recently must make you doubt it. But *I* know him. You *can* trust him.'

'Like Alison Parker trusted him?'

'Staying here, at this time, in this situation, puts your life in danger. You must leave. But you *will* hear from him. And when you meet him . . . he'll answer all your questions.' Hardekar leant back in his chair and spread his hands. 'There's nothing else I can tell you.'

TWENTY-ONE

'I WILL NOT TELL YOU . . . HOW OHARA DIED.'

Wada's refusal to answer was the only way she could defy Zayala. And she was grimly content for those to be the last words she spoke.

Then a shadow moved behind Zayala. His right arm was wrenched upwards just as he fired. The shot went through the hole in the ceiling. And the blade of a knife gleamed in reflected flame. In the next instant, his throat was opened in a tide of blood.

His assailant was a bulky, darkly clad figure. He lowered Zayala gently to the floor, where the blood went on flowing and the man who'd been about to kill Wada died beside her in a spasm of twitches.

His killer strode past her and on along the passage. She rolled clear of the blood and began struggling to her feet. She was still half stunned by her fall through the ceiling and her brain couldn't for the moment compute what had happened.

Before she was fully upright, Zayala's killer was back, scooping her up as if she weighed no more than a child and carrying her out of the burning house into the yard. He propped her against the wing of George's car and held her by the shoulders.

He had bright blue eyes and a lined, serious, faintly Asiatic face with a few days' growth of grey-brown beard. He was wearing a woolly hat, windcheater and jeans. The knife he'd used on Zayala was back in a holster at his waist.

'Who . . . are you?' she managed to ask.

'Espersen.' The name – and his accent – suggested he was Icelandic. 'Can you stand?'

'Y – yes.'

'Good.' He let go of her, at which point she realized she was visibly trembling. 'Caldwell is dead. Shot through the head. By Zayala, yes?'

She nodded. 'Yes.'

'Where is Ohara?'

'There's a . . . freezer in the room behind the kitchen. His body's . . . in there.'

'Who killed him? You?'

'Yes. It was . . . partly an accident.'

'A lucky accident for you, I would say.'

'There is another body in the freezer. A friend of mine. Ohara shot him.'

'Did Ohara also handcuff Caldwell to the wash-basin pipe?'

Wada didn't know how to shape an answer to that. 'It is . . . difficult to explain.'

'If I search you, will I find the key to the handcuffs?'

Wada tried to think what was the best thing to do. But thinking didn't seem to take her very far. She took the key out of her pocket and handed it to Espersen.

'Wait here,' he said. 'I won't be long.'

He turned and ran back into the house. The fire had spread the whole length of the roof by now. The ground floor was still intact, but filling fast with smoke.

Wada watched numbly as the flames rose. Roof timbers were cracking in the heat like gunshots. She wondered who

259

Espersen worked for. There was a white pick-up truck in the yard she hadn't seen before, but whether it belonged to Zayala or Espersen she had no way of knowing. Maybe she should try to run away. But she felt too weak to consider the idea seriously.

Then Espersen was back, coughing and blinking. She noticed he was carrying her shoulder bag, which he must have found in the kitchen. He grasped her by the elbow and moved her further away from the house. Without the car to lean on, she tottered and might have fallen but for his support. She sensed an ox-like strength in him.

'I took the handcuffs off Caldwell and checked the freezer,' he said, his voice hoarsened by smoke. 'If I were you, I wouldn't mention the handcuffs again.'

'Who wouldn't I . . . mention them to?'

'I can't read Japanese, but I'm guessing the papers in this bag are Kodaka's *kage-boshi* file and the stuff you printed out from the Emergence files. Correct?'

She nodded.

'We'll take those with us. My car is down by the gate. Think you can walk that far?'

She nodded again. 'Yes. If you . . . give me a moment.'

'Where's Ohara's car?'

She pointed towards the barn. 'In there.'

'Right. So, Zayala came in the pick-up. And this car's yours?'

'It was George's.'

'The dead friend. OK. The vehicles have to burn with the house. Fire cleanses. Fingerprints. DNA. You understand?'

'Who do you work for?'

'Who do you think I work for?'

'Not Nishizaki . . . obviously.'

'No. Not Nishizaki. Listen to me, Wada. We don't have long. I'll deal with the cars and the truck. You start walking as soon as you think you can make it to the gate. I'll catch up. Don't try to run away. You wouldn't make it far and having to waste time catching up with you would seriously piss me off. OK?'

She nodded. 'OK.'

'Good. Go when you're ready.'

He let go of her then and strode purposefully towards the barn, her bag still slung over his shoulder.

She took a few gingerly steps, which went steadily enough, then started walking. She didn't look back.

It must have taken her five or six minutes to cover the distance to Espersen's SUV, pulled up in the gateway and facing away from the house. She was feeling less shaky by then, which left her with more attention to spare for the spattered patches of Zayala's blood on her clothes. There was quite a lot on her hands as well and, to her horror, in her hair.

She heard a couple of muffled detonations behind her as she neared the car, deeper sounds than the continuing snap and crackle of the fire. Then she looked back and saw Espersen loping towards her along the track.

He passed her without a word, releasing the door locks on the car as he went. He opened the tailgate, tossed the bag inside and removed a sheet, which he spread over the passenger seat.

'You can get in now,' he said, gesturing to the covered seat.

She hesitated. 'Who sent you here?'

'I work on contract for Quartizon.'

'Driscoll, then.'

'Ohara followed you here, yes? And you managed to kill him. What brought Zayala here?'

'I made a phone call this morning.'

'You made more than a phone call. You made a big mistake. Whose phone did you use?'

'Ohara's. Mine did not work.'

'And Caldwell didn't have one. Just in case he was stupid enough to use it. Zayala was monitoring Ohara's phone. Standard practice. Once it was activated, it became a homing beacon. Luckily for you, I was monitoring it as well.'

'Are you taking me to Driscoll?'

'Yes. You may have to explain to him why his friend Martin Caldwell died here today. But the alternative's worse. After we've left, I'll make an anonymous call to the emergency services reporting the fire. When they sift through the wreckage, they'll find four bodies. Eventually, they'll work out none of them actually died in the fire, so they'll start looking for the person who murdered them. And the only way you don't end up being that person is to come with me. Right now.'

In the final analysis, it wasn't a difficult decision. Wada wasn't remotely equipped to make a run for it across the Icelandic interior. She was fortunate still to be alive, well aware Espersen could have killed her along with Zayala if he'd wanted to. What would happen at the end of their journey – how Driscoll would react to her account of all that had happened at Stóri-Asgarbær – she couldn't predict. There were plenty of ways it could go badly. But she was tired and out of options. And Espersen seemed to radiate the certainty that defying him was a very bad idea.

Beyond that, though, Wada had a certainty of her own to steady her nerves. Somehow, against the odds, she'd emerged from Stóri-Asgarbær alive. She'd survived. Since leaving Tokyo, she'd become more cunning, more resourceful. And the discovery of what she was capable of had made her stronger.

After they'd been on the road for half an hour or so, Espersen pulled over and phoned in the fire report. By then, Stóri-Asgarbær was likely to have been reduced to embers and ashes. Identifying the bodies was going to be a complicated exercise.

The launch of a quadruple murder inquiry was still a long way off. Just so long as no one pointed the police in the right direction. That, apart from anything else, was the hold Espersen had over her.

There was nothing to stop her questioning him, however. 'Do you know what is in the Emergence file I printed, Mr Espersen?' she asked as they set off again.

'Pretty much. Some vendors needed a special kind of persuasion to sell an option on their land.'

'And you are fine with Quartizon buying and selling chunks of your own country?'

'It's not my country. I'm Danish.'

'But even so . . .'

'You're a clever woman, Wada. You wouldn't have gotten this far otherwise. But you keep making mistakes. Hard to avoid when you don't know what's really going on, I suppose.'

'What is really going on?'

'A big play. In a long game.'

'What does that mean?'

'It means if you don't shut up I'll have to turn on the radio. And, believe me, you don't want to have to listen to an Icelandic phone-in the rest of the way to Reykjavík. So, shall we drop the subject?'

It was late afternoon when they reached Reykjavík. Espersen told Wada to wrap the sheet round herself as they headed into the centre. 'We don't want anyone seeing all that blood on you.' He drove to a quietly affluent residential area which Wada calculated couldn't be far from her hotel. She was surprised when he pulled in through the open gate of a big house right next to an embassy. She wasn't sure which embassy it was. Danish or Norwegian was her guess, based on the flag. She could have asked Espersen, but something deterred her.

263

The door of a large double garage opened ahead of them. Espersen drove in and stopped. The door closed behind them. He got out, fetched Wada's bag and signalled through the passenger window for her to get out as well.

Nothing was said as she followed him through a door at the rear of the garage into some kind of annexe detached from the house. There was a kitchenette and, beyond that, a small plainly furnished bedroom, with en-suite bathroom.

'You need to take a shower,' he said. 'Wash all the blood off. Leave your clothes in the tub. They'll have to be burnt. I'll put some clean clothes for you to wear on the bed.'

'And then?'

'That'll be up to Mr Driscoll. But no one's going to hurt you, Wada. Not while you're here.'

'I have your word on that?'

He nodded. 'You do.'

It was good to peel off her bloodstained clothes – some of the stains had even penetrated to her underwear – and wash away the visible evidence of what had happened at Stóri-Asgarbær. For some reason she couldn't properly analyse, she believed she could rely on Espersen's guarantee of her safety. She still had no idea what Driscoll was going to say to her. But part of her was perversely looking forward to facing him at last.

The clothes Espersen had left for her were a reasonable fit, though she would never have chosen them herself. Jeans and a chunky sweater divided into bands of orange and red were about as far from her natural look as it was possible to get.

The annexe seemed to be deserted, which surprised her. Was there actually anything to prevent her leaving through the garage? She certainly had no sense of imprisonment or confinement. Meeting Driscoll felt more like an invitation than an obligation.

Lured by this sensation, she followed a short corridor leading into the main part of the house, then another passage at the end of which double doors stood open to a large, minimally furnished lounge. The room looked out on to the garden. There was something Japanese about the atmosphere. Wada thought she could detect, at the very edges of her hearing, koto music being played somewhere.

There were more double doors on the far side of the lounge, leading into a dining room. As Wada crossed the parqueted floor, a figure appeared in the doorway ahead of her: quite tall, though hunched slightly at the shoulders, white-haired and square-jawed with a frowning, far-seeing gaze. There wasn't a lot of spare flesh on him. He was wearing a well-cut dark blue suit and a white open-necked shirt. He looked rather as Wada might have expected Peter Driscoll to look: like a successful if unconventional businessman whose success hadn't given him as much satisfaction as he'd once anticipated.

'Wada-san,' he said. 'Where on earth did Kodaka find you?' His voice was husky, his accent educated English with a subdued stress of individual syllables that hinted at long exposure to Japanese pronunciation.

'He put an advertisement for a secretary in *Asahi Shimbun*.'

'But it seems he got rather more than a secretary for his money.'

'I became his general assistant.'

'And proved yourself invaluable in that role, I have no doubt.'

'You are Peter Driscoll, formerly Peter Evans, formerly Peter Ellery?'

'I'm Peter Driscoll, yes. For the rest, they're lives I no longer lead.'

'I must thank you for sending Espersen to Stóri-Asgarbær. He saved my life.'

'But he didn't save the life I sent him there to save, did he?'

'I suppose you think that was my fault.'

'Fault? Well, there's a lot of that to share round.'

He invited her with a gesture of his hand to sit down on one of the low soft-leather armchairs and sat down himself on the sofa facing her. He looked at her with a frown that was part bafflement, part disappointment.

'If Marty hadn't contacted Mimori Takenaga . . .' he began, 'if she hadn't hired Kodaka . . . if he hadn't kept a file full of dirt on Nishizaki . . . if you hadn't insisted on continuing with the case after Kodaka was killed . . . and if you'd stayed off the phone, as I expressly told Marty to . . .' He sounded sad rather than angry as he itemized the chain of events that had led to Caldwell's death. 'Then, amongst other things, we wouldn't need to be having this conversation.'

'I am sorry Caldwell-san died.'

'Me too. You realize, I trust, that I had nothing to do with your employer's murder?'

'Who killed him?'

'It would have been set up by Ohara. Acting on Nishizaki's orders.'

'Do you not act also on Nishizaki's orders?'

'Ostensibly, yes. But I'm sure you've worked out that he and I aren't . . . serving the same agenda, shall we say?'

'What is your agenda?'

'To put it simply, none of your business.' He smiled thinly. 'Why did you go on with the case after Kodaka was killed? You weren't working for him any more. He wasn't paying you. You owed him nothing. And you must have known you were taking a big risk by continuing. Why didn't you just give up?'

'Have you read the *kage-boshi* file?'

'I cast an eye over it while you were in the shower. None of the contents came as a surprise to me. But for a private detective to have amassed so much damaging information about Nishizaki?

That *was* a surprise. I fear Kodaka may have been skating on thin ice for a long time. His intervention in the affairs of Shitaro Masafumi's family wasn't something Nishizaki was ever likely to tolerate.'

'Did Nishizaki have Masafumi killed?'

'I suspect so, though I can't be absolutely sure. It could genuinely have been suicide. But back to you, Wada-san. Why didn't you give up when it was obviously the best and safest course of action?'

'Because of what's in the *kage-boshi* file.'

'Nishizaki isn't the only villain operating in the Japanese business world. He isn't even the biggest. I can't believe you were shocked by what you read. It didn't affect you personally in any way.'

'But it did.'

'How?'

'Yozo Sasada.'

'*Sasada?* What was he to you?'

'My husband's killer. That is what he was to me.'

'Ah.' Driscoll slid back on the sofa and looked at Wada with greater attention than before. 'Your husband died in the sarin subway attack. I didn't know that. I should have known, of course. Sarin.' He sighed. 'Thus the whirligig of time brings in his revenges.'

'Sasada worked for your company.'

'But he was always Nishizaki's man. He'd been given a secret mission: to penetrate Aum Shinrikyo and use their people to carry out elimination operations against Nishizaki's enemies in exchange for know-how and funding. The plan had to be abandoned after Nishizaki realized the organization was becoming dangerously unstable. By then, Sasada had succumbed to their crazed philosophy.'

'Did Aum Shinrikyo use sarin of their own accord? Or did Sasada suggest it to them?'

'You're going to blame me, aren't you? You're going to say my past, which I didn't – couldn't – hide from Nishizaki, was the germ of the idea – the cause of the whole mad murderous mess.'

'Was it?'

'There's no yes or no answer. Not one I've ever found, anyway.'

'Have you looked?'

'I could tell you I have and be lying. I could claim I've lain awake at night wondering what measure of responsibility I bear and you wouldn't know any better. What difference does it make what I say? The dead will stay dead.'

'What will you do with the *kage-boshi* file?'

'I'll destroy it.' The ghost of a disingenuous smile hovered at the corner of his mouth. 'Obviously.'

'What is Emergence?'

'Something I can't allow you to imperil.'

'How do you intend to stop me?'

'I'm not going to threaten you. I'm not going to say Kristjan Einarsson will rot in jail – or whoever replaces Zayala will be pointed in Erla Torfadóttir's direction – if you don't leave well alone. But you must understand. I'm fully committed to this project. *Fully committed.*'

'Why? What is so important about it?'

Driscoll glanced over his shoulder. 'Nanoq,' he called.

Espersen appeared in the dining room doorway. Wada momentarily failed to recognize him without his woolly hat. He too was wearing a suit.

'What arrangements have you made for Wada-san?' Driscoll asked.

'MS *Horisont* sails from Þorlákshöfn tomorrow morning, bound for Rotterdam.'

'Journey time?'

'Three days. Depending on the weather.'

Driscoll nodded in apparent satisfaction. 'Good enough.'

'There'll be no record of her passage. The skipper's someone I've worked with before.'

'What if I refuse to go?' Wada asked, cutting into their cosy discussion of her removal from Iceland.

Driscoll gave her a pained smile. 'Your consent isn't strictly essential, though I'd urge you to cooperate. The deaths of Ohara and Zayala will trigger a vigorous response by Nishizaki. You wouldn't want to be here when whoever he sends next starts looking for answers. I'm offering you an undetectable escape route. Take it. You won't get a better offer.'

'That is certain,' murmured Espersen.

And, despite herself, Wada believed him.

Driscoll spared her no more time. He left shortly afterwards, instructing Espersen to transport her to Þorlákshöfn that evening. After he'd gone, Espersen said they'd set off as soon as it got dark. He cooked her a meal, which was surprisingly good. He did nothing to prevent her leaving the house, but he didn't really need to. She had nothing to leave with. Espersen had her passport, not to mention her phone. Driscoll had the *kage-boshi* file and the Emergence print-out. Her hard-won gains had all been taken from her.

'But you're alive, Wada,' said Espersen as he served her salmon fishcakes and a glass of white wine. 'Unlike the two people Nishizaki sent to kill you. That puts you ahead of the game.'

'He did not send them to kill me,' Wada objected. 'Caldwell was the target. And he is dead. Thanks to me, some would say.'

'We all have to take our chances.'

'You did not tell Driscoll about the handcuffs?'

'No.'

'Why not?'

'It would have upset him. I know how difficult Caldwell was to handle. So, I'm not making any judgements. He's dead. You're alive. How are the fishcakes?'

'Delicious.'

'Good. Drink your wine. There'll be no alcohol on the *Horisont.*'

'What does Driscoll expect me to do when I reach Rotterdam?'

'Stay out of his way. And out of Nishizaki's. That really would be the smart thing to do. Think you can manage that?'

Wada looked at Espersen across the table. And said nothing.

The evening drive to Þorlákshöfn took them south from Reykjavík along empty roads. Little was said, there being little to say. Wada was leaving Iceland. The investigation Kodaka had begun and which she'd foolishly tried to continue was over. Kodaka was dead. So was Martin Caldwell. And Mimori Takenaga was beyond her help. She should count herself lucky to be alive. And she should concentrate on staying that way. As Espersen had said, it was the smart thing to do.

Þorlákshöfn wasn't much of a place. They seemed to arrive at the entrance to the docks almost as soon as they'd passed the sign welcoming them to the village. Wada could see a large cargo vessel at the quayside: the *Horisont*, obviously.

She expected Espersen to drive straight to the quay, but he pulled up just short of the dock gates and out of range of the nearest street lamp. He turned off the engine and wound down his window to let in the chill night air. There was the sound of a crane operating ahead of them and occasional shouted exchanges between deck hands and dock workers.

'The *Horisont* is a Danish-owned vessel,' Espersen said quietly, handing her her passport. 'But the skipper and the first mate are the only Danes on board. The crew don't speak much English. And you shouldn't try to speak to them anyway. You'll be allowed out of your cabin when they're at sea. But until the ship sails tomorrow and during a stopover in the Faroe Islands, you'll be kept below decks. Understood?'

'I understand.'

'The only ship-to-shore communications are on the bridge. Stay away. OK?'

'I will not try to use their radio, I promise. And since you have my phone, I will be completely out of touch with the world until the ship docks in Rotterdam. That is as you want it, I assume.'

'Correct.'

'Are you taking me any further? Or do I have to walk the rest of the way?'

'No. I'll take you aboard. In a moment.'

A moment passed. Then several more.

'What are we waiting for?' Wada asked.

'This.' He took a computer memory stick out of his pocket and handed it to her.

'What is this?'

'The Emergence files. The whole lot. Everything.'

'How did you get it? When Kristjan and I tried to download those files, we were blocked.'

'I found the stick in Zayala's truck. He must have come to Iceland with some way of harvesting the information from Quartizon's records. My guess is he's already sent it back to Nishizaki HQ in Tokyo. Who knows what they'll make of it there. Driscoll probably has some plan to deal with the fallout, but the whole thing sits wrong with me. It's all in Japanese, of course. I only know what it is because I've seen Emergence written in Japanese so often I recognize the word.'

'Why does it "sit wrong" with you?'

271

'As I told you, I'm Danish. I was born in Copenhagen. But my mother's a Greenlander. You probably heard Driscoll call me Nanoq. It's a nickname. My real name's Uffe. Nanoq is the Greenlandic word for a bear. I know the country. And a bit of the language. I closed land purchase option deals for Quartizon there as well as here in Iceland. In Canada too. When some . . . persuasion was needed.'

'And this troubles you?'

'There's something about Emergence that just doesn't smell right. Like the fact that all the records are in Japanese. There's a secret buried inside it. A secret no one's allowed to know. That bothers me. Has done for quite a while. I can't do anything about it, though. I wouldn't know where to start. But you?' He turned his head to look at her. '*You* can do something.'

'How?'

'Quartizon used a climatologist at Cambridge University to research background details for the Emergence project. The whole operation was supposed to be based on her work. But some of the locations I went to . . .' He paused. 'It didn't add up.'

'How did it not "add up"?'

'I can't explain. If she won't talk to you, it's better you don't know any more. Try to get her to look at the files. You'll have to translate the contents for her. See if she thinks her findings have been properly followed.'

'Is there some reason why they might not have been?'

'Just listen to what she says.'

'What's her name?'

'Dr Michaela Morrisette.'

'Where can I find her?'

'Cambridge University climatology department should do it.'

'It is the Easter vacation. Nobody will be there.'

'She's a workaholic. Probably looks on Easter as a good opportunity for quality time in the lab.'

'And if not?'

'Her home address is forty-four Alford Street, Cambridge. Speak to her face to face or not at all.'

'But I won't be able to speak to anyone for at least three days.'

'More like four, by the time you've travelled from Rotterdam to Cambridge. There's nothing I can do about that. As for the travelling, go by train and ferry. Avoid airports.'

'What do you expect me to do about whatever Dr Morrisette says – if she says anything?'

'I don't know, Wada, because I don't know what she's going to say. You'll just have to work it out for yourself.'

'You said the smart thing to do was to stay out of Driscoll's way.'

'It still is. But sometimes there's the smart thing . . . and the right thing. And I get the feeling you know the difference. Sorry to dump it on you. There's no one else I can ask.'

Wada didn't know what to say to that. She held the memory stick in her palm and considered the possibility of handing it back. But she didn't.

'Ready to go aboard now?' Espersen asked eventually.

'Yes,' she replied. 'Ready.'

TWENTY-TWO

NICK WATCHED THE RUNWAY FADE FROM VIEW AS THE ICELANDAIR morning flight to London took off from Keflavík airport. He felt a keen sense of frustration about his failure to accomplish what he'd specifically gone to Iceland for: a meeting with Peter Driscoll. It was tempered by relief that he'd avoided straying into the intrigues that had swallowed Caldwell and Wada. He was alive and well and free to carry on with his comfortable existence. He knew he should be grateful for that. It wasn't a small thing. Caldwell's death was a continuing reminder of that. Yet he knew the mystery of Peter Driscoll wouldn't leave him alone until he could see and speak to the man who was his father.

He'd been promised that would happen, as and when Driscoll judged it safe. But would it really? Would Driscoll ever judge it safe? There was no way for Nick to tell. He didn't know how the man's mind worked. Or what was needed to make their meeting safe.

He'd gone to Iceland with myriad questions. Some of them had been answered. But they'd only given rise to others. There was still so much he didn't understand. And in the short term there was the problem of what he was going to tell Kate.

He'd phoned her late the previous night and explained Driscoll had refused to meet him but had promised to be in touch eventually. Naturally, he'd said nothing about his dealings with Erla Torfadóttir, far less the death of Martin Caldwell. Telling her about such things would only alarm her. He didn't like deceiving her. In fact, he hated everything that doing so involved. But, for the moment, he couldn't see any way round it.

Perhaps, it occurred to him as the plane levelled off and the *FASTEN SEATBELTS* sign went out, it would be better if Driscoll never did contact him. He supposed he could find a way to live with that. Plenty of people got by without ever knowing their father. Maybe he ought to settle for being one of them.

The MS *Horisont* nosed out of Þorlákshöfn harbour into a grey swell. Wada watched the harbour wall fall away behind the ship through the porthole of her cabin, calculating it would soon be acceptable for her to show herself on the small portion of the deck she'd been given access to.

The skipper, a taciturn, grizzle-bearded man called Jakobsen, had made it clear Wada was aboard on sufferance. She had no doubt he'd been paid well to transport her, but that evidently didn't extend to treating her courteously. As soon as Espersen had gone back ashore, he told her bluntly that going on deck when the ship was in harbour, visiting the bridge without his permission or attempting to engage with the crew at any time would result in her being locked in her cabin. After her experiences at Stóri-Asgarbær, this wasn't something she wanted to risk, so she intended to follow his orders to the letter.

That was easier in principle than practice, however. She'd woken feeling sick, which she attributed to diesel fumes tainting the atmosphere in her cabin. She longed for some lungfuls of fresh air. But another cause of sickness – the rolling of the vessel – was already making itself felt. It promised to be a long three days to Rotterdam.

Eventually, though, the tedium and discomfort of the voyage would give way to the unpredictability of her next exploration of the secrets of Emergence. She had those secrets in her hand, on the memory stick Espersen had given her, but without a computer the stick was just a useless piece of plastic.

That would change once she was ashore. But for now all she could do was wait. Another look through the porthole showed the harbour wall as just a dark line on the horizon. Iceland was behind them.

With the memory stick wedged securely in her pocket, she headed for the door.

Nick found it hard to tell whether Kate was disappointed by his failure to meet his father in Iceland or not. She sympathized with him genuinely enough, but he nonetheless detected an unspoken relief that Peter Driscoll, man of mystery, hadn't entered their lives after all. She seemed to doubt whether Nick would ever in fact hear from him. Or was it that she hoped he never would?

Either way, a resumption of normality was clearly what suited her best. And Nick tried hard to behave as if it suited him too. The situation was out of his control anyway. Driscoll knew where he was. The next move was up to him.

On Good Friday, Nick called round at April's house, early enough to be confident of finding her in. He had to tell her something about what had happened.

'I haven't seen Peter,' he began. 'It turned out to be a wild goose chase. He covers his tracks well. I have to face it, April, he probably doesn't want to meet me and is making sure he doesn't. So, there it is, at least for now. I'm taking "don't want to know" for an answer.'

'Really?' April couldn't have concealed her relief even if she wanted to.

'What else can I do?'

There were a few things, of course, which he wasn't about to mention, such as pump Miranda for more information or track down Vinod Hardekar. But then he wasn't about to mention Hardekar at all. Nor the fact that April's old friend, Marty Caldwell, had died a gruesome death in Iceland. There was a lot he wasn't about to tell her. But his conscience was clear. April and Caro had kept the truth about his paternity from him all his life. He was entitled to do some keeping back of the truth now himself. And, really, what good would it do to tell her Marty was dead, anyway? He supposed she'd hear about it eventually. And, whatever she heard, whenever she heard it, it would be better for her to have no reason to think he knew anything about it.

'No point pretending I'm not pleased, Nicky,' she said, embracing him. 'I reckon it's better for you this way.'

'I know you do.'

And maybe, he thought, it truly was.

The deck of a freighter ploughing through the North Atlantic proved to be a hostile place to spend time, although Wada braved it as often as she could, since her seasickness tended to abate in the open air. Espersen had kept her phone, but not her copy of *The Makioka Sisters*. Unfortunately, reading only made her feel sicker, so there was little to distract her from the boredom and discomfort of the voyage. The crew kept their distance and all she got from Captain Jakobsen was a curt nod whenever they came within sight of each other.

The seasickness lifted during the ship's stopover in the Faroe Islands, but Wada saw nothing of their surroundings beyond a restricted view of Tórshavn harbour through the porthole of her cabin. Soon enough, the *Horisont* was back out on the grey, heaving ocean.

As the days at sea slowly passed, Rotterdam became an ever more alluring destination. No matter that it was probably just a featureless port city – Yokohama transplanted to the Netherlands – all she wanted was to arrive there. And then . . .

Easter Sunday came and, with it, the gathering of Kate's family at her parents' house in Virginia Water. Nick usually managed to throw himself into such events, entertaining Kate's nephew and niece and doing a good impression of being amused by her father's account of golf club politics. It was harder work than usual, however, and he suspected it showed. On more than one occasion he was accused, good-humouredly enough, of inattention – wool-gathering, as his mother-in-law called it. He did his best to laugh the accusations off and over-compensated by drinking more than he should have. He suspected Kate would be levelling a few complaints at him during the drive home.

All in all, he wasn't finding normality an easy place to go back to.

Terse and sour-mannered though he was, Captain Jakobsen was an expert in what he was paid to do. As the MS *Horisont* entered the vast complex of wharves and basins that was Rotterdam docks, Wada began to wonder just how easy it was going to be to leave the ship. But Jakobsen had arrangements for her well in hand. Within half an hour of the *Horisont* docking, she was able to disembark in the company of several Somali crew members under the cover of a group shore pass. It was Easter Sunday and harbour staff were thin on the ground. Within another half an hour, Wada was in a taxi heading for Rotterdam Centraal station.

At the station she made enquiries about ferry services to the UK. There was good news and bad. A ferry ran from Hoek van

Holland, less than an hour away, to Harwich, on the east coast of England. She reckoned getting from there to Cambridge couldn't be too difficult. The snag was that it was an eight-hour crossing and the next ferry was at ten o'clock.

Wada was going to have the pleasure of another night at sea.

Nick slept badly that night, partly because of a hangover after the lunch in Virginia Water. Kate hadn't reproached him for drinking too much. Perhaps she sensed the disappointment his trip to Iceland had left him with. He supposed that must have been clearer to her than he'd intended. He promised himself in the small hours of Easter Monday that he'd put the mystery of Peter Ellery/Evans/Driscoll out of his thoughts. The next move was his father's to take. Whether he took it or not was up to him. There was nothing more Nick could do.

And he was going to live with that.

TWENTY-THREE

WADA WAS THE FIRST PASSENGER OFF THE HOOK OF HOLLAND TO Harwich ferry on Monday morning. The seasickness had been even worse on the ferry than it had been on the *Horisont*. It was a relief to set foot on dry land.

The train journey from Harwich to Cambridge was complicated, involving two changes. But it was early on a bank holiday, so the trains were at least largely empty. Breakfast was a waxed paper cup of reheated porridge consumed at Ipswich station. The tea she bought to wash it down turned out to be undrinkable.

It wasn't yet nine o'clock when she reached Cambridge. She reckoned the chances were reasonable of finding Dr Morrisette at home. Without her phone to locate the address, she had to buy a street map of the city before leaving the station. Fortunately, Alford Street proved to be only a short walk away. She set off at a clip.

Dr Morrisette's home was in a narrow street of small terraced houses. Wada's guess was that she lived alone, or at any rate was childless. Espersen had described her as a workaholic, so it all fitted.

If she was a serious workaholic, she might already have left for the day, of course. Sure enough, there was no response when Wada tried the knocker. Tracking her down in whatever part of the university she might have gone to wasn't going to be easy. Wada stood where she was, trying to think how she could set about doing that. It wasn't clear it would be feasible on a bank holiday.

Then she saw a woman dressed in jogging kit and carrying a bottle of milk approaching along the pavement. She was short, honed and perspiring, her cropped dark hair plastered to her head. Morrisette? Wada could only hope so.

It *was* Morrisette. As she neared the door of number 44, she slowed and frowned at Wada. 'Can I help you?' she asked. There was quite a lot of muscle under her tight top and knee-length leggings. Her face was raw-boned and tanned. In her voice there was some kind of accent: Australian, maybe.

'Are you Dr Michaela Morrisette?'

'Yeah.'

'My name is Wada. It is extremely important I speak with you.'

'What about?'

'Emergence.'

Morrisette tensed. 'Are you from Quartizon?'

'No.'

'Well, in that case I probably shouldn't be talking to you. What did you say your name was?'

'Wada.'

'Right, Wada, well, I don't know what you're trying to pull by coming here this morning, but—'

'We have to discuss the situation, Dr Morrisette. There is something terribly wrong.' Wada took the memory stick out of

281

her pocket. 'Just look at what is on this. Then I think you will understand.'

'Have you been in touch with Quartizon?'

'The stick came to me from a Quartizon employee who told me you would know what was wrong.'

Morrisette put her hands on her hips, with the bottle of milk hooked on one finger, and stared at Wada. Her knotted expression suggested she was thinking. Hard and fast. 'OK. You can come in. I'll give you five minutes. Understood?'

Wada nodded. 'Understood.'

There was a knocked-through lounge to their right and a kitchen straight ahead beyond a narrow staircase. Wada brought up the rear as they headed into the smart but small kitchen, where Morrisette put the milk in the fridge and faced Wada across a bare table, arms akimbo.

'OK, Wada. Say your piece.'

'Emergence was launched last Wednesday. Did you know that?'

'I knew it was imminent.'

'It was a massive sale of options to buy parcels of land in Iceland, Greenland, Canada and maybe elsewhere too. Yes?'

'Sounds like you know all about it.'

'Quartizon used you to research the . . . what? The climate in the areas concerned?'

'There's a non-disclosure agreement attached to my contract with Quartizon. I can't answer a question like that.'

'Do you have a specialism . . . within climatology?'

'I do.'

'It cannot be a breach of your agreement to say what it is.'

'OK. I specialize in *future* climatology. The sort of weather we're all going to have to face down the line. You know? Fifty years from now. A hundred. Two hundred.'

The relevance of that was immediately obvious to Wada. 'You researched what the climate would – will – be like for the parcels of land in the period covered by the options.'

'Did I?'

'It seems to me . . . you must have done.'

'Well?' Morrisette grabbed a towel and mopped her face. 'Am I contradicting you?'

'Can we look at the contents of the stick on your computer?'

'Before we do that, I think I need to know where you're coming from. What's your interest in Emergence?'

'I work for a private detective in Tokyo who was hired to investigate the business methods of Hiroji Nishizaki, founder and chairman of the Nishizaki Corporation, which has a fifty per cent stake in—'

'Quartizon. Yeah, I know. Well, I didn't know the exact percentage, but there you go. Who hired your boss?'

'That truly does not matter. What matters is that Nishizaki is . . .'

'Yeah? What is he?'

'A crook, Dr Morrisette. That is what he is. A big-time crook.'

'Says who?'

'Just look at what is on the stick and see if there is something wrong with it. I can translate the contents for you. It is all in Japanese, of course.'

Morrisette smiled. 'No need. Quartizon supplied me with a Japanese translation program as soon as we started working together.'

'OK. Good.'

'So, there's zero chance of you stiffing me on the translation.'

'I am not trying to trick you.'

'Like you'd say if you were. Give me the stick.'

Wada handed it over. Morrisette stalked past her into the hall and took a smart left into the living room. There was a PC

283

set up on the dining table. She slipped a pair of circular-framed glasses on to her nose, clicked the mouse to restart the PC, loaded the stick and sat down in front of the screen.

'Since you're Japanese,' she said as she squinted at the screen and began clicking the mouse, 'you should be able to make a decent cup of green tea. Why don't you rustle some up while I look at this? Red and black caddy in the kitchen.'

'Is it Japanese tea?' Wada asked before she could stop herself.

Morrisette glanced up at her over the frames of her glasses. 'Rather than that Chinese crap, you mean? Yeah. Organic Sencha. From a tea garden near Kyoto. Good enough?'

'Good enough.'

Boiling water and brewing the tea took Wada about five minutes. During that time she heard several exclamations from the dining room. 'What the fuck?' seemed to be Morrisette's favourite.

She was still immersed in the Emergence files when Wada delivered the tea. Wada sat with her cup at one end of the table and watched Morrisette at the other, glaring and grimacing at the screen while she fiddled with the mouse and took occasional loud slurps of tea.

There was an overfilled bookcase behind her. Almost all of the titles Wada could see were scientific in nature, with a bias towards climatology. There were bound runs of various journals as well: *Proceedings of the National Academy of Sciences*; *Scientific American*; *International Journal of Climatology*.

Five minutes passed, then another five. Wada said nothing. And Morrisette spoke only to herself, in muttered expressions of disbelief. Her brow was set in a permanent frown. The glasses were so far down her nose they seemed perpetually about to slip off.

Then, at last, she sat back in her chair and looked down the table at Wada.

'You've read this?'

Wada shook her head. 'No. I have been travelling without a computer. And . . . you are the expert, not me.'

'Yeah. I'm the expert. Supposed to be.'

'There *is* something wrong?'

Morrisette exhaled explosively. 'You could say that. But tell me, this is all framed as a catalogue of lots to be auctioned on April seventeenth. That's five days ago. As far as you know, the auction went ahead?'

'As far as I know.'

'Yeah. Of course it did. The fuckers.'

'What is wrong, Dr Morrisette?'

'This isn't the list I signed off on. You get it, Wada? The doctor's list has been doctored.'

'How?'

'That NDA I mentioned probably prohibits me from saying.'

'Surely not, if this is not the list as you authorized it.'

'Interesting argument.' Morrisette fell silent for a moment. Then she jumped up and hurried out into the kitchen.

By the time Wada had caught up, Morrisette was punching a number into her phone. 'Who are you calling?' Wada asked, but only got a go-away-or-shut-up gesture in reply. She opted for shutting up.

A moment passed, then Morrisette started talking. Her tone was abrupt and demanding. 'It's me. Call me if something urgent crops up, you said. Well, it just has. Get back to me asap. Trust me, Vinod, you don't want to leave me hanging on this.'

She ended the call and slammed the phone back in the cradle, stood simmering for a few seconds, then looked at Wada as if she'd forgotten she was there.

'Where did you get the stick, Wada?'

285

'I told you. A Quartizon employee.'

'Name?'

'I have an informal non-disclosure agreement with him. Or her.'

'I bet you do.'

'The contents of the stick are genuine.'

'Like you'd know. But *I* know. It's genuine all right. How would you describe Nishizaki? I've never actually met him.'

'Neither have I.'

'But you've investigated him. So, give me some words. Ruthless?'

'Yes.'

'Treacherous?'

'I think so.'

'Greedy?'

'Probably.'

'Don't worry about probably. What they've done with Emergence clinches the point It's greed on a grand scale. With treachery and ruthlessness thrown in.'

'Please explain it to me, Dr Morrisette.'

'And break my NDA? It's tempting. It's very tempting.' Her phone began to ring at that moment. She looked down at it. 'That'll be Hardekar. Tell you what, Wada. Listen to this conversation and I reckon you'll get the gist. Take a seat, why don't you?'

As Wada sat down at the kitchen table, Morrisette pressed a button on the phone to answer the call, but left it in its cradle, triggering the loudspeaker function.

'That you, Vinod?' *Vinod.* There was something familiar about the name, but Wada couldn't place it.

'Yes, Michaela.' The voice was cultured and slightly Asian, probably Indian, as the name Vinod suggested. 'Is there a problem?'

'As number-crunching consultant on the Emergence project, I suspect you *know* there's a problem.'

'I'm not with you.'

'Probably lucky for you. How'd the auction go?'

'Very smoothly, thank you. If it's your bonus you're concerned about, there's likely to have been some delay because of the banking shutdown over Easter, but I can fairly say you'll be pleasantly surprised when—'

'I'm going to get a bigger pay-off than I was bargaining for. Is that what you're saying, Vinod?'

'In essence, yes. Much bigger.'

'A frenzy of competitive bidding, was there?'

'You could say so . . . without exaggerating.'

'I'll bet. And then, of course, there were more lots than there rightly should have been, weren't there?'

'I'm sorry?'

'I've got the catalogue file, Vinod. The *real* catalogue file. The *enhanced* catalogue file.'

'There was only one catalogue, Michaela.'

'Oh yeah? And who wrote it?'

'I'm not absolutely sure I—'

'Cut the crap, Vinod. Who do you work for? Who do I work for? Who does Driscoll work for?'

'Well, ultimately, we all answer to Mr Nishizaki.'

'So, he approved this, did he?'

'I assume so. I don't have direct dealings with him.'

'Is he a climatologist?'

'I think you know he isn't.'

'Are you?'

'No.'

'Or Driscoll?'

'No. Look, Michaela, where—'

'*I'm* the fucking climatologist, Vinod. Agreed?'

'Yes. Of course.'

'So, when I identified the areas that would be rendered culti-vable and/or habitable by rising temperatures, I did so based on a rigorous and painstaking analysis of all the available data. Everything. Altitude. Drainage. Geology. You understand?'

'You're the expert, Michaela. No one's ever disputed that. Your findings were invaluable in delivering the project. That's why your bonus is—'

'I don't want to hear any more about my fucking bonus. Listen to me very carefully. Someone at Quartizon added extra lots by extending the areas shown as viable in my report. Are you aware of that?'

'Could I ask how you are aware of it?'

'Someone sent me the catalogue file.'

'Who?'

'Someone who thought I ought to know you'd decided to make a shitload of extra money by shafting my professional reputation. Have you any idea what you've done?'

'If there's been some modest . . . extrapolation of your—'

'You can't *extrapolate* under an ice sheet, Vinod. Most of the bedrock in central Greenland is below sea level because of the weight of the ice on top of it. Below sea level means underwater when the ice melts. Add to that the marginal area that'll be flooded by rising sea levels and you have a tight limit on what can legitimately be projected as viable. You can't ignore topo-graphical facts. But that's what you've done. Not just in Greenland. Everywhere. As far as I can tell, you've *extrapolated* your way to about thirty per cent more land. And you've sold it, haven't you? Sold it for as much as you could get. But it doesn't exist. It's going to be under the fucking ocean. You've cheated whoever bought those lots. You've defrauded them.'

'I don't think you should throw a word like "defrauded" around, Michaela. People might misunderstand you.'

'There's no misunderstanding. It's what you've done. And you've put my name to it.'

'Perhaps I should ask Peter to call you.'

'Did he authorize this?'

'Obviously, as CEO of Quartizon, he saw and approved the final package.'

'And Nishizaki? Did he see and approve it?'

'He would have . . . set the parameters within which Quartizon . . . developed the business model for Emergence.'

'Spare me the corporate doublespeak, Vinod. What you're basically saying is that this fraud was planned at the highest level.'

'I do advise you to stop referring to fraud, Michaela. It's a highly emotive word.'

'OK. I'll make it simple for you. All sales that don't match areas categorized as viable by me have to be cancelled. Immediately. You understand?'

'That is quite impossible. There can be no cancellations. The consequences of acknowledging any kind of deficiency in the process would be . . . catastrophic.'

'Well, we'll see about that. I'm going to take this to the top.'

'You mean Nishizaki?'

'I do.'

'Drawing this to his attention would be . . . most unwise.'

'That's not how I see it, Vinod. How I see it is he'll have to make a choice. Either he fesses up to your clients or I do whatever I have to do to protect my reputation.'

'What might that be, Michaela?'

'I don't know. Media exposure, maybe.'

'Not a good idea. Not a good idea at all.'

'Exactly. Which is why I confidently expect Mr Nishizaki to see reason.'

'I'm really not sure—'

'Bye for now, Vinod.'

She ended the call and smiled grimly at Wada. 'Catch the drift of all that, did you?'

'I think so,' said Wada.

'Maybe you're going to tell me I should never have got into bed with people like Nishizaki and Driscoll. You'd be right. But I knew that anyway. The money was just too good to turn down. The research I can fund with it . . . will be transformative in my field. *Would* be transformative, that is. I can kiss goodbye to my academic career if it gets out that I've aided and abetted a scam like this.'

'What exactly did you believe you were doing for Quartizon?'

'Identifying areas of land within the North Circumpolar region that will become viable for cultivation and habitation as a result of climate change later this century. That's why the project was called Emergence in the first place. Because out of the carnage climate change will wreak elsewhere, some exciting opportunities will open up in the soon to be no longer frozen north. Quartizon's plan was to acquire options on as much of such land as possible and sell the options to the highest bidder. Who were those bidders? The sovereign wealth funds of rich countries likely to be hardest hit by global warming for starters, I imagine, like Middle Eastern oil-producing states awash with money but surveying a parched future and not liking the view. Plus stupendously wealthy individuals hoping to bequeath a high-latitude bolthole to their grandchildren. How Quartizon hoovered up the options was none of my concern, but, looking at many of the locations in the catalogue file, they must have bribed government officials to release state-owned land, unless the title legalities are fake, which I suppose is possible. Because a lot of the land's fake, after all. It doesn't exist in a viable condition and is never going to, for the reasons you heard me spell out to Hardekar. You get it, Wada? They grafted a great big con on to my closely reasoned projections.'

'Do you really intend to complain to Nishizaki?'

'Too right I do. I can't let them get away with this. I don't want anyone thinking I was their willing accomplice. Maybe Quartizon are banking on buying my silence with a humungous bonus. They'll probably argue no one will work out they've been sold a pup until it's too late to do anything about it. But that's not a risk I'm willing to take. The climatological verifications all lead back to me. And about a third of them are totally bogus. You don't seriously think I'm going to lie down under that, do you?'

Morrisette's righteous indignation was an impressive force. But Wada knew there was a stronger countervailing force. 'I think I ought to warn you, Dr Morrisette, that Nishizaki takes extreme measures against anyone who challenges him. My employer, for instance, Kazuto Kodaka.'

'What about him?'

'He was killed. Hit-and-run.'

'You're saying Nishizaki was responsible for that?'

'I believe he was, yes.'

'Even if you're right, that happened in . . . Tokyo?'

'Yes.'

'Well, there you are. Tokyo's a long way from Cambridge, Wada. Nishizaki's reach doesn't extend here. Besides, your boss was nosing into *all* his business affairs, wasn't he? My beef is much more specific. I just want him to set right the liberties Driscoll's taken on his behalf with my professional standing in this one case.'

'You really think he will agree?'

'I don't mean to leave him much choice in the matter. What time is it in Tokyo now?'

Wada looked up at the large clock on the wall. 'Approaching seven thirty in the evening.'

'OK. My contract's with Quartizon, but it was drafted by a lawyer at Nishizaki HQ. I had enough dealings with him putting the paperwork to bed to know he's pretty much always on call. I'll get my broadside off to him right now and he can dwell on it overnight before reporting to Nishizaki first thing tomorrow, which will be late tonight here. Sound good?'

'You must do what you think is best, Dr Morrisette.'

'My bet is I'll hear from Driscoll or Hardekar with a proposal of some kind before we ever get that far.'

'It is possible, I suppose.'

'Where are you going when you leave here?'

'To be honest, I am not sure.'

'Well, give me your phone number.'

'I do not . . . have a phone . . . presently.'

'Doesn't that make doing your job a smidge difficult?' She waved away the need for an answer 'Never mind. Go see the sights for a few hours, then come back. I might have some news for you by then.'

Wada felt certain Morrisette's confidence wouldn't survive first contact with a corporate lawyer at Nishizaki HQ. Maybe that would be the moment when Wada could persuade her to take more drastic action, such as implementing her threat to involve the media. As they'd talked, an idea had formed in Wada's mind about how to exploit Morrisette's outrage at what had been done to her. So, yes, she would be happy to come back later.

Morrisette went back into the dining room, retrieved the memory stick and handed it to her. 'Don't worry,' she said. 'I've downloaded everything and I'll back it up on a stick of my own. This evidence isn't going to disappear. I play for keeps.'

TWENTY-FOUR

MOST OF THE STUDENTS WERE AWAY FOR EASTER, BUT SWARMS OF tourists ensured Cambridge was far from quiet. Many were Japanese, so Wada blended in well. She had no interest in King's College Chapel or Trinity Great Court, but couldn't help envying those of her fellow countrymen and women who had nothing better to think about than smiling for the camera in front of yet another college.

The envy didn't cut deep, though. If Wada's experiences had taught her anything about herself, it was that sightseeing wasn't her thing. Rest and relaxation weren't for her. She thrived on purpose. And she had a purpose now.

She headed for the central shopping area and made a beeline for the nearest mobile phone outlet, where she bought a cheap pay-as-you-go model and put a call through to the numbers shown on the card Barry Holgate had insisted on giving her.

He didn't answer, either on his mobile or the landline. She left a message on both. 'This is Wada, Mr Holgate. I told you when we met that my name was Takenaga, but actually it is Wada. I have something I think you will find very interesting. Please call me back on this number as soon as possible.'

She sat in a coffee shop waiting for his response. After about half an hour, Holgate called. 'Mrs Wada, alias Takenaga.' She'd forgotten the irritating tone of his voice. It was somehow antagonistic and affable at the same time. 'Cast thy bread upon the waters: for thou shalt find it after many days.'

'Are you quoting Shakespeare, Mr Holgate?'

'No. The King James Bible. Ecclesiastes eleven. But forget my Sunday school education. What have you been up to? It's all gone quiet here since you left. Any news of Martin Caldwell?'

There was none Wada had any intention of imparting. Ignoring the question, she said, 'You told me you still worked freelance as a journalist. Is that true?'

'Of course. A true hack never retires.'

'I need to be able to offer someone coverage in a national newspaper.'

'Who's the someone?'

'The source of the story.'

'And what is the story?'

'The truth about Peter Ellery. Forty years ago and now. It is a big truth, Mr Holgate. It should be told.'

'This connects Nancekuke, Aum Shinrikyo and the people who are looking for Caldwell?'

'Yes. It is the whole thing.'

'And who's the source?'

'I cannot tell you that yet. I must be able to assure her the story will receive maximum publicity when the time is right.'

'When will the time be right?'

'Very soon, I think.'

There was a brief silence at the other end of the line. Holgate was thinking. 'All right,' he said at last. 'There's a bloke I know who writes feature stuff on this kind of thing for the *Guardian*.

I gave him a leg up when he was just a cub reporter. If what you're on to really is a big deal—'

'It is bigger than you can imagine, Mr Holgate.'

That seemed to impress him. Perhaps he already knew she wasn't prone to exaggeration. 'In that case, I'm sure I can get you the kind of coverage you have in mind.'

'Good.'

'But I need an inside track on this, Mrs Wada. Maybe we should meet. Where are you?'

'I could be in London tomorrow. Could you be there?'

'Yes. London's not much more than a couple of hours away on the train.'

'Very well. I will call you again soon. Thank you, Mr Holgate. Oh, and it is not *Mrs* Wada. Just Wada.'

'You told me you were married once. Sorry if I . . . misunderstood.'

'You did not misunderstand. But now I am just Wada. Goodbye, Mr Holgate.'

Wada anticipated Dr Morrisette would have got a cool response from the company lawyer and would therefore be open to the suggestion she planned to make. She returned to 44 Alford Street reckoning she'd soon be able to set something up with Holgate and his *Guardian* contact.

But Dr Morrisette wasn't in. She'd left a Post-it note stuck to her door referring Wada to a neighbour. The neighbour used her spare key to let Wada into the house. 'Michaela said to tell you to wait for her. She'll be back later.'

'Do you know how much later?' Wada asked.

'No idea. Michaela's not easy to pin down. Maybe you've noticed.'

Maybe she had.

*

Wada made herself some tea and sat in the lounge. Time passed. She felt grateful simply to be sitting somewhere with nothing to do. It had already been a long day.

She must have fallen asleep, because it was growing dark when she was roused by a key rattling in the front door. Dr Morrisette swept in with an armful of files and her laptop, plus a takeaway coffee and a supermarket shopping bag.

'Great news, Wada,' she announced. 'Lawyer Shimozuki reckons Nishizaki will be horrified when he hears what Driscoll's been up to. Quartizon shouldn't have gone it alone on this. The scam never had approval from Tokyo.'

'You believe him?'

'There's no reason for him to lie.'

'Is there not?'

'He's going to recommend cancelling the sales for the areas I didn't approve. All of them. Say there's been some error. He's confident Nishizaki will agree in order to avoid reputational damage to the company. Maybe he sails a bit close to the wind, but what businessman doesn't? Or maybe he started out a crook, like you say, and has gone respectable since. It's not unknown in that world, is it? Either way, he's as much an injured party as I am and he won't like it any more than I do.'

Wada hardly knew what to say. The lawyer had told Dr Morrisette what she wanted to be told. That everything would be made good. That her academic standing wouldn't suffer. But had he told her that because it was true? Or simply because he needed to shut her up?

'This explains why Hardekar was desperate to deter me from going to Nishizaki,' she continued. 'And why I've heard nothing from Driscoll. He hasn't got an answer. And pretty soon he won't have a leg to stand on either.'

'I am sorry, but I do not share your confidence,' said Wada cautiously.

'I'm promised definitive written assurances by tomorrow morning. So, we won't have to wait long to find out whether Nishizaki is going to deliver, will we? Where are you staying tonight?'

'I have nothing arranged.'

'No phone. No accommodation.' They were standing in the kitchen. Morrisette stepped closer and utterly astounded Wada by dapping her forefinger on the tip of Wada's nose. In the grey evening light Wada caught some look in Morrisette's eyes she hadn't expected to see. 'You're a bit of a waif, aren't you?'

'I meant to book something earlier. But . . .'

'Fat chance in Cambridge on a bank holiday. I can imagine. Never mind. Stay here. There's a spare bedroom. Then you can eat your words tomorrow morning when I get the email from Nishizaki. How does that sound?'

It sounded more than slightly worrying on several levels. But Wada didn't see that she had much choice. 'Thank you,' she managed to say.

'No.' Morrisette grinned at her. 'Thank *you*, Wada. It's possible you may have saved my life.' Her grin broadened. 'Professionally speaking, that is.'

Nick was still distracted by what had happened in Iceland. But the new term started on Wednesday. He was hoping the realities of daily teaching would set him back on an even keel.

He would have found it easier to cope if he hadn't received an unexpected phone call in the middle of Easter Monday afternoon from Barry Holgate. He didn't take the call and Holgate didn't leave a message, but, when he phoned again later, while Nick was alone, there seemed nothing for it but to answer.

'I was just calling to ask if you had any news,' Holgate explained. 'The Stapletons tell me there's still been no word from Martin Caldwell.'

Nick had no intention of revealing what he knew of Caldwell's fate. He assumed the Icelandic police were still trying to identify the bodies they'd found at Stóri-Asgarbær. For all he knew, they might never succeed. 'I've no news for you, I'm afraid.'

'What about your father – Peter Ellery?'

'I've given up trying to track him down.'

'Really?'

'He evidently doesn't want anything to do with me. So, I'm returning the compliment.'

'When we met, I had the feeling you were going to be more . . . persistent.'

"Fraid not.'

'What about the Takenaga woman? Heard anything from her?'

'Not a thing.'

'I see. Well, as it happens, I might be on to something halfway relevant. Do you want me to keep you posted?'

Nick thought about how to answer that question for so long Holgate had to prompt him.

'Are you still there?'

'Yes. I'm here.'

'So, do you want me to let you know what comes of it? If anything does.'

'Not sure.'

'Not sure?'

'That's right. I'm not sure at all.'

Wada navigated her evening with Dr Morrisette as if crossing a minefield. She thought it quite possible she was misinterpreting natural Australian friendliness. Michaela – as Dr Morrisette insisted she call her – was clearly a tactile and outgoing character. And the quantity of wine she drank with a rustled-up fish supper only made her more so.

Wada also considered the possibility that so long had passed since any hint of intimacy in her life she was simply out of practice at judging and handling such situations. She disliked talking about herself, which Morrisette urged her to do, but she hoped occasional mentions of her marriage to Hiko would at least persuade her hostess that nothing was likely to happen between them.

As early as she reasonably could, she complained of exhaustion after a taxing day – which was true enough – and said she really had to go to bed.

There were a few brushes of hand and hip in the dormer-windowed attic guest room while Morrisette gave her some towels. Wada decided to attribute these to the wine, although Morrisette's rueful smile as she left suggested there was more to it than that.

Left alone, which in many ways was her favourite state, Wada sank gratefully into bed. It seemed an age since she'd slept on her futon at home in Tokyo. She wondered when she might sleep on it again. She also thought about the likelihood – the certainty in her view – that Morrisette wouldn't receive the assurances from Nishizaki she was expecting. She rehearsed the arguments she'd use in favour of involving Holgate's *Guardian* contact. She speculated to herself about how best to handle the situation from that point on.

But before her speculations had progressed very far, she was asleep.

Tuesday morning came. For Kate that meant a return to work. But Nick had one more day of leisure ahead of him. After seeing her off and clearing up after breakfast, he walked up through

Greenwich Park to Blackheath, where he stopped for coffee and considered pressing on to Catford to see April. In the end, he thought better of it and wandered home.

As he headed along Greenwich Park Street, he saw there was a van parked outside their house, with a hose trailing out of the half-open rear doors. A man in a boiler-suit and baseball cap holding a brush attachment for the hose was gazing up at the windows.

He was a window-cleaner. But he wasn't *their* window-cleaner, who'd been less than a week before.

'Can I help you?' Nick asked as he came alongside the van.

The man turned towards him. 'Yeah, mate. I just rang your bell. But I'm beginning to think we've got the wrong address. Is this Greenwich Park Terrace?'

'No. Greenwich Park *Street*. I'm not sure there is a—'

A shadow darted across the pavement as the side door of the van slid open and a second man jumped out, colliding with Nick and grasping him by the shoulder.

'What the—'

Something was pressed against the side of his neck. He felt a sharp stabbing sensation.

And almost immediately he felt nothing at all.

When Wada woke, she was surprised by how late it was. Evidently she really had been exhausted. The house was silent. She packed her few belongings into her shoulder bag and went down to the kitchen, passing the open door of Morrisette's bedroom on the way. The room was empty.

Down in the kitchen there was a Post-it note waiting for Wada on a cupboard door. *Gone for a run. M.*

Wada decided to make some tea. As she waited for the kettle to come to the boil, she heard the front door open and close. Morrisette had returned.

'Lovely morning out there,' said Morrisette by way of greeting, as she entered the kitchen.

'Heard anything from Tokyo?'

'Not yet.'

This came as no surprise to Wada. She looked at the clock. 'It is past the end of the working day there.'

'I doubt Nishizaki works set hours. And I know lawyer Shimozuki doesn't. Have a little faith.'

'I have no faith in Nishizaki, Michaela.'

'I don't have a whole lot myself. I'm not being naïve about this. I've taken some appropriate precautions. But I—' She was cut short by a ring at the doorbell. She moved past Wada into the hall just as the kettle shut itself off with a discreet ping. Wada watched as she dodged into the lounge, then came back out just as the doorbell rang again. 'Window-cleaners touting for trade, would you credit it? Like I can't clean my own fucking windows.'

Something that would become apprehension within a few seconds stirred in Wada's mind as Morrisette headed on to the front door and flung it open. A tall man in a boiler-suit and a baseball cap was standing outside. 'Morning, luv,' he said with a smile.

'I'm not—' Morrisette began. But the man had already reached out and jabbed her in the neck with some object hidden in his fist. And Morrisette went down like an emptied sack. The man caught her and supported her in his arms. Then he noticed Wada.

'Company,' he called over his shoulder.

A second man, identically dressed, slipped past him and charged along the hall. Wada turned and started towards the back door, which led from the kitchen into a small rear courtyard, enclosed by high whitewashed walls. There was no obvious way out, but it was the only way she could go.

Then she swerved to her right, remembering that her phone and the memory stick holding the Emergence files were in her shoulder bag, looped over the back of a chair on the other side of the table. She grabbed the bag and lunged towards the door, but the man had cut her off, so she dodged round the other end of the table. He followed, then reversed course when he saw what she was trying to do and moved to block her path to the door.

There was a moment when they stood staring at each other. Then he advanced towards her. She saw the kettle to her left, grabbed it off its stand and hurled it at him. A faceful of kettle lid and nearly boiling water sent him recoiling against the table with a bellowed '*Fuck*'.

Wada dodged past him, yanked the door open and plunged out into the yard.

The walls running round all three sides were higher than she had any hope of scaling. But there was a small lean-to shed in the far corner, with a water-butt and a raised vegetable bed next to it. She scrambled up on to the butt and from there on to the corrugated iron roof of the shed. Beyond lay the rear courtyard of the house in the next street over. A little boy sitting on a blue and yellow toy pedal-bike stared up at her in wide-eyed wonderment. The door into the kitchen was open behind him, offering Wada the possibility of an escape route.

She heard heavy footfalls behind her. Looking round, she saw the man from the kitchen coming after her, despite the angry burn-marks on his neck and chin. He was breathing stertorously. His face was knotted in rage. 'Bitch,' he shouted as their eyes met.

Wada balanced on top of the wall, then slithered down the other side of it, clinging on as she tried to find a toehold. Her bag slipped from her shoulder and fell to the ground. Glancing up, she saw the man above her as he hauled himself up on to the roof of the shed. He was only a few feet away.

Then his greater weight told on the corrugated iron. It split and gave way under him. He crashed straight down into the shed – and out of Wada's sight.

She let go and dropped down into the rear neighbour's yard. She scooped up her bag, looked at the goggle-eyed but so far silent boy and raised her forefinger to her lips, then ran past him into the house.

There was a young woman working at the sink in the kitchen. As Wada rushed through the room, she whirled round and exclaimed, 'Oh my God.'

She had no time to do much more before Wada reached the front door, wrenched it open and ran out into the street.

All was quiet. There was a T-junction about fifty metres ahead. She headed down to it and turned right, away from Dr Morrisette's house and towards the city centre. She glanced over her shoulder every few metres. There was no sign of anyone coming after her, or of a van taking Morrisette away. But she knew it was stupid to believe they wouldn't come after her. It was just a matter of time – and chance.

Within minutes, she'd reached the main street into the historic centre. On the other side of the road was a hotel, in front of which a coach was parked, filled with tourists who looked to Wada as if they might well be Japanese. They were mostly gazing vacantly through the windows or chatting to their travelling companions. The last of their luggage was being loaded into the hold.

Instinct told Wada there was safety in a group. And there was no better group to lose herself in than a Japanese one. She dashed across the road between the traffic and peered round the front of the coach. The tour organizer was conferring with the driver about the loading of the luggage. Wada sprang up the steps into the coach, smiled blithely at the nearest passenger, who smiled blithely back, and made for the first empty seat she could see.

The elderly woman she plonked herself breathlessly next to looked at her placidly and asked what had delayed her, for all the world as if she recognized her as a legitimate member of the party. Wada said something unconvincing about losing a button, but the woman seemed entirely taken in and embarked on a monologue about working as a seamstress in Osaka back in the mid-Showa era. Wada didn't interrupt her and tried to give the impression of being utterly fascinated.

She heard the doors of the luggage hold clunk shut. A few minutes later, the tour organizer, a brisk young woman, came aboard, followed by the driver, who lumbered into his seat and started the engine.

'Next stop Ely,' the organizer announced through a microphone. 'Very beautiful cathedral.'

And the coach pulled away.

TWENTY-FIVE

NICK CAME TO HIS SENSES SLOWLY AND WAS CONSCIOUS FOR SEVERAL minutes before he remembered being attacked. The puncture-wound on his neck was sore to the touch. As for the journey, all he could dimly recollect was being jolted around in the back of a van. He had no clear idea how he'd arrived where he now was.

Eventually, he realized he was lying on a mattress on a concrete floor next to a breeze block wall. He sat up woozily and looked around.

He was in a wire cage at one end of a windowless steel-roofed shed illuminated by fluorescent strip lights. There was a closed roller door at the other end. The door to the cage was padlocked shut. Beside the mattress stood a plastic bucket and, on a shelf above it, several litre bottles of water and a pack of loo rolls.

As he turned, he suddenly became aware that his cage was one of three stretching across the rear wall of the shed. And one of the others, separated from him by an empty cage, was occupied.

A woman of about forty, with short dark hair, dressed in black running kit, was lying on the mattress in her cage. Her eyes were closed and Nick wondered if she was unconscious. 'Hello?' he called.

She wasn't unconscious. She raised her head and looked at him. 'You're back with us, then,' she said in a light Australian accent.

'Where am I?'

'Can't help you there.' She rose to her feet and advanced to the side of her cage. 'Did you run into some trouble with window-cleaners?'

'Yes. Did they . . . bring me here?'

'They brought both of us here, I have to assume. They injected me with a knockout drug. You too?'

'Yes.'

'I haven't seen anyone – apart from you – since I came to.'

'What in Christ's name is going on?'

'Never mind Christ. What's *your* name?'

'Nick Miller.'

'Means nothing to me. I'm Michaela Morrisette. You look like that means nothing to you either.'

'It doesn't.'

'But we're here for the same reason, aren't we? We must be. We're being held prisoner.' She rattled the padlocked hasp on the door of her cage. 'The question is who by? And why?'

'Any ideas?'

'Just one, Nick. And it's not good news if I'm right. Nishizaki.' She saw Nick's grimace of recognition at her mention of the name and nodded, as if her worst fears had been confirmed. 'I see you know him.'

'Know *of* him. You?'

'We've had dealings. What about Peter Driscoll? Ah. I see you know him too.'

'Why should having Nishizaki and Driscoll as . . . mutual acquaintances . . . land us here?'

'You really have no clue?'

Nick did have a clue, of course, though it wasn't any more than that. Michaela Morrisette, on the other hand, appeared to understand exactly why this had happened to her, if not to him. 'Look, if you know why we've been brought here, just tell me, will you?'

'OK. Well, I'm a climatologist at Cambridge University. I did some research work for Driscoll's company, Quartizon, and therefore, indirectly, for Nishizaki.'

'You worked on the Emergence project?'

She frowned. 'What do you know about that?'

'There was an auction in Reykjavík last week. Options on parcels of land were sold for huge sums of money.'

'Yeah. So I heard. Backed up by my research. Except many of those options *weren't* backed up by my research. A lot of fraud went down at that auction. When I found out about it, I raised hell with Driscoll and Nishizaki. Next thing I know . . . I'm here. So, why are *you* here?'

Yes. Why was he? There could only be one explanation. And as Michaela had said, it wasn't good news. 'Driscoll and Nishizaki used to be allies. I don't think they are any more.'

'And so? Which of them had us kidnapped?'

'It has to be Nishizaki.'

'Why?'

'Because I'm . . .'

'Yeah? What are you?'

Nick hesitated. But, in the end, there was nothing to be gained by holding out on his fellow captive. 'I'm Driscoll's son.'

'You're his *son*?'

'I only found out recently. I've never actually met him. But, yes, I'm his son.'

'And Nishizaki knows that?'

'I reckon he must.'

307

'Jesus.' Michaela aimed a kick at the bucket in her cage. It crashed against the wall and fell on its side. 'I guess I won't be doing that again if we're here any length of time.'

'You're here to shut you up about the fraud,' said Nick dolefully, 'and I'm here so pressure can be brought to bear on Driscoll.'

'That's about the size of it, I guess.' Michaela leant against the wire of her cage, stretching her fingers through the holes and bowing her head. Then she pushed herself upright and smiled – a tight, grim, fleeting smile. 'I should never have got involved with these fucking people,' she said, to herself as much as to Nick.

'What are we going to do?'

'What *can* we do?'

'Not much,' Nick admitted.

'There's only one sliver of sunshine that I can see.'

'What's that?'

'Well, there are just the two of us here. Which means, I reckon, that they didn't get Wada.' She paused and noted Nick's reaction. 'Ah. I see you know *her* too.'

Wada had disengaged herself from the Japanese tour party as soon as the coach reached Ely. None of the other disembarking passengers had seemed to notice her slip away, not even the Showa era seamstress she'd sat next to. But then they had the cathedral to concentrate on before the next leg of their tour. Wada was just an unremembered face.

Walking the genteel streets of Ely, while it was safer than remaining in Cambridge, didn't represent a solution to her problems. She had no doubt that what had happened was a direct response from Nishizaki to Morrisette's demand for cancellation of some of the sales made at the Emergence auction. It was likely the men who'd attacked Morrisette hadn't known Wada was there.

That wasn't much help now, though. Whoever had sent the men would soon work out who she was and assume she'd been acting as Morrisette's accomplice. They'd also assume she had a copy of the incriminating Emergence files. Which made her someone they'd badly want to find.

Wada had expected a blunt refusal to cancel the sales rather than a raid on the house. Her plan had been to persuade Morrisette to go to the media with her story at that point. Talking to Holgate's *Guardian* contact without Morrisette didn't strike her as a promising strategy. Where was the proof that what she said was true? Where was the first-hand climatological testimony? That kite wouldn't fly.

Wada's dismal conclusion was that on her own she couldn't accomplish much. And trying to accomplish anything risked drawing her pursuers to her. She had few resources and no allies.

Except Holgate. Maybe he could be induced to do some digging on her behalf. She put a call through to his landline number. No reply. Then she tried his mobile.

'Wada?' he answered promptly. 'About time.'

'About time for what, Mr Holgate?'

'For you to get in touch. I'm up in London, as per your request, staring down the barrel of spending some of my pitifully small pension on a hotel room. I'm not wasting my money, am I?'

'I did not ask you to travel to London.'

'You said we'd meet in London today.'

'I said I was hoping we could meet in London today.'

'And are we going to?'

'No.'

'So, I *am* wasting my money.'

'Listen to me, Mr Holgate. Things have become . . . difficult.'

'What's that supposed to mean?'

'I need you to make some enquiries . . . that I cannot make.'

'Such as?'

'Dr Michaela Morrisette is a climatologist at Cambridge University. There was an incident today at her house. Forty-four Alford Street, Cambridge. She was attacked by an intruder. I need you to find out what happened to her.'

'Why?'

'She is central to this matter. Without her . . .'

'Without her I don't have a story to flog? Is that what you're saying?'

'Yes. It is what I am saying.'

'What do you expect me to do? Go up to Cambridge? Ask the neighbours? I'm just a retired provincial reporter, Wada, not the Pinkerton Detective Agency.'

'I cannot do this, Mr Holgate. I am too exposed. We need to find out what has happened to her. Only then can we take the next step.'

'And where are you going to be while I'm gumshoeing around?'

'I have to stay out of sight.'

'Great.'

'Do you still want the truth, Mr Holgate?'

There was a long silence. Wada could hear Holgate's wheezy breathing at the other end. Then he said, 'Give me that name and address again.'

Nick and Michaela had no way of knowing what time it was or where they were. There were no windows in the shed. They had no phones. Nick had been abducted in Greenwich, Michaela in

Cambridge. Halfway between the two, maybe? It was impossible to say. They were in limbo.

Something would happen eventually. They wouldn't be left there indefinitely. But *what* would happen? If Nishizaki had had them kidnapped to put pressure on Driscoll, what would he demand as ransom? And would Driscoll pay it? Neither of them knew him well enough to say. Which left open a possibility that was chilling to contemplate. Nick didn't put it into words and neither did Michaela. But he had no doubt it was in her mind, gnawing away at her, just as it was gnawing away at him.

He was also anxious about Kate. What would she think had happened? What would she do? The only certainty was that she'd be worried. And all he could do was worry about just how worried she'd be.

The only way to distract themselves was to talk, as they did, slowly becoming ever more open with each other about how they'd got themselves, by such very different routes, into this situation.

'So what are we looking at here, Nick, with Driscoll and Nishizaki?' Morrisette asked after both their stories had wound their way to the bleak and threatening present. 'A falling-out among thieves? Or something more complicated?'

'More complicated is my guess. I think Driscoll's been planning this for a long time.'

'They've been confederates in crime for decades, right? Why would Driscoll betray his boss? Why take a monumental risk like that?'

'Not sure. Something to do with the death of Shitaro Masafumi?'

'But that's more than forty years ago.'

'I did say he'd been planning it for a long time.'

311

'Not that long, surely.'

'It's what got Wada involved in this.'

'We can be grateful for that. She's our best hope right now.'

'What do you think she'll do?'

'I don't know. She's hard to read.'

'I thought she'd died in the fire at Stóri-Asgarbær. I was certain of it. Will she go to the police, I wonder?'

'From what you tell me, she'd have a lot of explaining to do if she did. So, I suspect she won't. But maybe one of the neighbours – yours or mine – saw enough to call them.'

'Maybe.'

Michaela sighed. 'Or maybe not.'

'Exactly.'

'Which leaves us . . .'

'Stuck.'

Wada booked into the Lamb Hotel in the centre of Ely and waited as patiently as she could for word from Holgate. Once she'd found out what exactly had happened at Morrisette's house, she could decide what to do in response. Though what that might be . . .

The evening set in. Her room became claustrophobic. She left the hotel and walked to the cathedral, where she sat on a bench on the green and gazed up at its soaring spire and the blue sky it soared up into. The ancient stonework spoke of time and splendour – a history she knew little of. Everything in Ely was timelessly picturesque in a very English way, the grass a slightly different shade of green from what she was used to, the leaves on the trees marginally paler. She was far from home in all the ways that mattered.

She was about to leave the bench when her phone rang.

'Mr Holgate?'

'I'm at Cambridge railway station waiting for a train back to London. Are you in Cambridge, Wada?'

'No.'

'Sure?'

'Very sure, thank you.'

'Well, maybe that's best. I got a garbled tale from Dr Morrisette's neighbours after knocking on her door and getting no answer. It sounds to me, based on what you've said, as if she might have been taken away against her will. But there wasn't much for her neighbours to notice. A window-cleaning van no one recognized was outside her house for a while this morning, but that was about it. I talked the woman next door into using her spare key to go in and I tagged along. The house was empty. There was a kettle lying on the kitchen floor and the roof of the backyard shed had given way. There were no other signs of anything amiss. But the rear neighbour who I moved on to said a woman ran *through* her house this morning. That's right. Straight through from the backyard and out by the front door, then not seen for dust. And she saw some bloke – or thinks she did – in Dr Morrisette's backyard. She phoned the police, but they fobbed her off. Running through someone's house isn't actually a crime, apparently.'

'I suppose not.'

'That you, was it, Wada? It sounded like it might be.'

'I am very worried about Dr Morrisette,' she replied evasively.

'I think you should be, because it seems she may not be the only person these people took against their will.'

'What do you mean?'

'I called Nick Miller. You spoke to him once, I think. And maybe you've come across him since.'

Nick Miller. The son of one of Martin Caldwell's student friends. She'd spoken to him on the phone at Caldwell's flat in Exeter. 'No,' she said. 'I have not spoken to him since.'

'Well, it's a bit late to start now. I got his wife. She's worried sick. Nick hasn't been seen since this morning. He's not answering his phone. Nobody knows where he is. What do you make of that?'

'I am not sure . . . what to make of it.'

'Is this something we should take to the police, Wada? Are Nick Miller and Dr Morrisette in danger?'

'It is possible.'

'OK. So, what are we going to do about it? More specifically, since I don't know enough to do very much, what are *you* going to do about it?'

Michaela remarked at some point on the obstinacy of hunger. She had lots of grim contingencies to fill her mind with, but that didn't stop her stomach growling when long hours passed without food. Nick hadn't noticed until she said it how hungry he was himself. It was a kind of comfort in its way. They were alive and well, able to experience physical cravings. For the time being, at least.

Then, at last, something happened. They heard a vehicle pull up outside. A few minutes passed, then the roller door was raised. A black Transit van was parked in front of the shed. Night had fallen. The roof of the van was washed in a sickly amber light.

Three men, all wearing black boiler-suits and balaclavas, entered the shed, closing the door behind them. One of them, who appeared to be limping, stayed back. The other two walked towards Nick and Michaela. One was carrying a couple of pizza boxes and two plastic buckets looped over his arm. The other was carrying a baseball bat, swinging it loosely in his hand.

'Why are you holding us here?' Nick called to them as they advanced. They ignored him.

Pizza man stopped about six feet from the cages, lowered the buckets to the floor and stacked the boxes on top of them.

'Stand back against the wall,' said baseball bat man to Nick, speaking with a gruff cockney accent. Once Nick had retreated, he stepped up to the cage and unlocked the door.

His friend moved forward and tossed one of the pizza boxes into the cage. It landed flat on the floor with a thump. Then he threw the bucket in after it and moved back.

'Push the other bucket out,' said baseball bat man. Nick obeyed, painfully aware of the bat being raised as a precaution while he did so.

The door was closed and locked. Then they followed the same procedure with Michaela's cage. 'How long are you going to keep us here?' she demanded. She got no answer.

'The pizzas are cheese and tomato,' said baseball bat man after they'd finished. 'Thought we'd play safe in case you were vegetarians. Besides, they reckon shit stinks less if you don't eat meat, so it's win-win, ain't it?'

'You'll pay for this,' said Michaela with sudden sharpness.

'We'll *be* paid for this, luv. That I can guarantee. However it turns out for you.'

'Who are you working for?' asked Nick.

'Wouldn't know. It's all contract work. Know what I mean? Now, enjoy your supper. The lights are on a timer. They'll go out in about an hour. So, tuck in. And remember to eat your crusts like good little children.'

Wada had told Holgate she needed to sleep on the problem of what to do next. In truth, she didn't expect a night's sleep to make any difference. There was nothing she could do for Michaela Morrisette and Nick Miller. There wasn't much she could do for herself. She'd become Nishizaki's enemy and she knew what generally happened to them.

315

She went for a restless early-evening walk and ate a solitary supper back at the hotel, then took a long, cool bath, which she'd sometimes found led to a restful night.

It didn't this time.

*

It was utterly dark in the shed once the lights had gone out, apart from one tiny red gleam high in a distant corner, which Nick did his best not to look at. The effect, as he lay sleeplessly on his mattress, was similar, he imagined, to being in a flotation tank. Reality beyond the black void he was suspended in became ever harder to grasp. He thought Michaela was probably asleep. He was fairly certain he could hear her breathing. He tried to persuade himself not to think about what might happen when the lights came back on and a second day of captivity began. He tried not to run over and over in his mind all the times in recent weeks when he could have stepped away from the mystery of his paternity and allowed his world to continue moving in the safe and orderly way it always had – until now. He tried hard. On both counts.

It didn't work.

Wada lay awake deep into the night. Eventually, when she'd given up on the idea of sleep, oblivion finally came. And then, with seemingly no lapse of time, she was roused, with the morning already well advanced, by the ringing of the bedside telephone.

'Yes?'

'Reception here, Miss Wada. There's a man downstairs who'd like to speak to you.'

'Who is he?'

'His name's Driscoll. He says you know him. Shall I put him on the line?'

Driscoll. He was here. In Ely. He'd found her. How she couldn't imagine. But if he could, what was to stop Nishizaki? 'Put him on,' she said numbly.

'*O-hayo gozaimasu, Wada-san,*' came the smooth, by now familiar, voice. 'Shall I come up? Or will you come down?'

TWENTY-SIX

'WHY DON'T WE WALK ROUND TO THE CATHEDRAL GREEN AND TALK there?' Driscoll suggested as he greeted Wada at the foot of the hotel stairs with a smile. He was wearing a light suit, pale shirt and no tie. He looked businesslike but relaxed.

'Maybe I would prefer to talk here,' said Wada defensively.

'This isn't a trap,' he responded in an undertone. 'I've come alone. And we need to talk, you and I. Somewhere where we can't be overheard. The cathedral isn't far.'

Wada couldn't be sure what kind of risk she might be taking by going with him. But alternatives weren't thick on the ground. He'd found her. So hiding was no longer an option. 'Very well,' she murmured.

'Why did you come to Ely?' he asked as they walked out of the hotel.

'I needed to leave Cambridge urgently. There was an opportunity to come here. I took it. I did not think anyone would look for me in Ely.'

'*Anyone* probably won't. But you used your credit card when you booked into the Lamb, which was careless. We lifted the particulars from your phone. Lucky for you it's in our hands rather than Nishizaki's.'

'What is it that you want to talk to me about, Driscoll-san?'

'The past, the present . . . and the near future.'

'My future? Or yours?'

'Both, Wada. They're inextricably linked now, I'm afraid. For better . . . or worse.'

They sat on the same bench Wada had sat on for a while the previous day. The morning was bright but cool, the air clear, their words distinct.

Driscoll squinted up at the central tower of the cathedral. 'Ah,' he purred, 'the Lantern of the Fens. I used to come up here on the train from Cambridge when I was a student. Just to be somewhere that wasn't . . . part of the university world.'

'Is that the past you want to talk to me about?'

'No. We don't need to go back quite that far. Our raid on Nancekuke, in June of seventy-seven. That's where it begins. You know all about it from Marty, I imagine. I can't believe you spent two days immured with him at Stórí-Asgarbær without hearing the whole story. He never could move on from that night. The night Alison died.'

'How did she die? He did not reveal what you told him about that.'

Driscoll sighed. 'There were more guards than we antici-pated. I think they were expecting us. Maybe Noy had let something slip. He could be loose-lipped when he was drunk. And he was often drunk. We didn't know him well enough to trust him. And yet we *did* trust him. I suppose Alison and I were so eager to believe him we never stopped to consider whether we were wise to. But then wisdom and youth don't generally go together, do they?'

'Did you shoot one of the guards?'

319

'Not exactly. They were lying in wait for us in the underground corridor leading to the bunker where the condenser containing the Super Sarin was supposedly stored. There was a struggle when they tried to arrest us. I didn't actually realize the guard who was manhandling me was armed until his gun went off. In the mayhem after he was wounded, Alison and I tried to escape. But we were cornered and the only way out, according to the directions Noy had given us, was down a drainage chute that connected with a sea cave beneath the base. The tide was in, so the cave was flooded. We had to swim out. But something went wrong. When I reached the mouth of the cave, I realized Alison wasn't with me. I went back, but I couldn't find her. There was quite a long stretch where the water was up to the roof of the cave and it was so dark it would have been easy to swim into a flooded side-cave by mistake and drown before you'd found your way out. I think that's what must have happened to her. I've always regretted giving up looking for her that night, though I'm not sure I could have done much more without drowning along with her. That wasn't what I was thinking at the time, though. I was thinking about self-preservation. That's the truth of it. And the shame I felt on account of that was one of the reasons I ran away. Not just from Nancekuke, but from my life to that point. Plus the fear of being charged with attempted murder of a guard and sent to prison, of course.'

'So you became Peter Evans?'

'Yes. After swimming ashore, I left Marty out for the count on Porthtowan beach and walked through the night to Newquay. I caught a train there and dodged the ticket inspectors all the way to London. I could have got off at Exeter. When I stayed on, the die was cast. In London, I took a job serving behind a bar and set about turning myself into Peter Evans. It was a lot easier to pull off than it would be today, of course, with so much of ourselves on the Web. One asset I had was my fluency in

Japanese, though. That's how, later that summer, I found myself working as Shitaro Masafumi's translator. Which meant I came to know all about his and Nishizaki's sokaiya dealings back in Japan. Masafumi was under a lot of pressure, desperately trying to shore up his finances and failing at every turn. He drank a lot and often passed out, leaving incriminating paperwork lying around for anyone who understood Japanese to read.'

'Meaning you?' Why Driscoll was being so frank with her Wada still had no idea, but she didn't want to say anything to hold him back.

'Correct. I never imagined the effect learning Japanese would have on my life. It led me to Masafumi. And Masafumi led me to Nishizaki. I told you in Reykjavík I didn't know whether Masafumi killed himself or was murdered. Technically, that's true. But I have little doubt Nishizaki "arranged" his suicide. He was in London at the time. And Masafumi clearly lived in fear of him.'

'Yet this was the man you went into business with.'

'I didn't have much choice in the matter. Nishizaki and I ended up in something of a stand-off. I had evidence of his involvement in Masafumi's sokaiya dealings from the documents I'd helped myself to while Masafumi was in one of his drunken stupors. He had evidence I was actually Peter Ellery, wanted by the MoD police in connection with the shooting of a guard at Nancekuke. It was a nasty surprise when I discovered he'd been checking up on me and had managed to join up the dots that connected me to my previous identity. He was concerned I might know too much about his part in Masafumi's activities. And he was right to be concerned. As for how our stand-off was resolved, well, according to him, we had the basis for a good working relationship. I'd demonstrated my suitability to become his assistant as he took Masafumi's work forward in a more professional manner. He was willing to supply me

321

with a new identity that would bear more scrutiny than the Peter Evans persona. I could make a whole new life for myself – and become a wealthy man – by returning with him to Japan and throwing myself into helping him make a lot of money. And then a lot more after that.'

'And that is what you did.'

'Yes. For the next forty years I was his right-hand man. Not exactly his partner, because that implies equality, which isn't a principle Nishizaki believes in. But closer to him than anyone. He allowed me to start my own subsidiary, Quartizon, but only because I persuaded him it would be useful to have a channel for certain specialized operations that couldn't be officially tracked back to him.'

'You knew about all the murders that Nishizaki commissioned to dispose of people who stood in his way? And you knew all the details of his arrangements with Aum Shinrikyo?'

'I'm not about to insult your intelligence by pretending otherwise, Wada. I'm a living testament to what a man is prepared to overlook in order to live well. But Nishizaki has never trusted me. You must understand that. He has controlled and rewarded me. He retrieved the incriminating documents I had. But he retained the evidence that could prove I was Peter Ellery, wanted man, should he ever need to do so. We've grown old together. But old age is a problem in our line of work. Retirement is a delicate concept when so much is at stake. I asked myself, a few years ago, how it was likely to end between us. And I realized Nishizaki would be asking himself the same question. He's nothing if not ruthless. His success has been built on utter single-mindedness. There's no room for sentiment or loyalty in his world view. There was only one solution he was likely to arrive at to our shared old age problem: I wasn't going to retire. I was going to *be* retired. As in terminated, at a time of his choosing. It was a sobering moment when the certainty of that conclusion was borne in on me, and it was the moment I began planning a way to avoid that fate. I began planning, if you like, to get my solution in first.'

'And your plan involved . . . Emergence?'

'My plan *was* Emergence. But let's leave the details of that to one side for the moment. All would have gone smoothly, I believe, but for Marty's ill-judged communication with Mimori Takenaga, prompted, of course, by Caro's decision to tell him what she knew before she died. Once Nishizaki realized people were digging into the related questions of Masafumi's death and my buried identity, he became concerned that our many dealings over many years could unravel, including the extremely lucrative Emergence project. In the course of trying to neutralize the threat he perceived to his position, he had your employer killed and sent Ohara – the Irishman, as I dubbed him – to establish how much Marty knew. In the process, he discovered something about me that I'd hoped to keep from him at all costs, because I was well aware it would give him a hold over me just when I needed the greatest possible freedom of movement. He discovered I had a son.'

'Nicholas Miller?'

'Yes. He came across the information amongst the papers he stole from Marty's flat. And later he forced Miranda to confirm it. Caro was pregnant by me when I ran away, though I didn't know it at the time. If I had, I suppose I might have stayed and faced the music. Or maybe I wouldn't. It's hard to say. Anyway, it doesn't much matter now.'

'When did you find out?'

'When I began planning Emergence. I'm sure Dr Morrisette has told you the basis of the Emergence operation. I needed expert assistance from people I could rely on to set it up. I turned to two friends from Exeter days – Miranda Cushing and Vinod Hardekar. I offered them rich rewards if they helped me.

Miranda has expensive tastes and Vinod's career hadn't gone as well as he'd hoped. They both had good reasons to go in with me. I think they found it all rather exciting as well. Miranda pointed me in the direction of the right people to approach in several Middle Eastern oil states. She'd worked as a consultant for an international investment company that advised several of the biggest sovereign wealth funds in that part of the world. She did some of the initial sounding-out for me. Vinod's role was to prepare a financial network of offshore entities to channel the proceeds from the auction of the land options through Quartizon and out of Nishizaki's reach. It was Miranda who told me about Nick, passed off by Caro as Geoff Nolan's son, but actually mine. An obvious vulnerability, but one I thought I could disregard. Unfortunately, Marty proved more assiduous in his search for me than I'd anticipated, until, in the end, I had to rescue him from pursuit by the Irishman and hide him in Iceland. And when I became aware that Nick was also on my trail I realized to my surprise that having a son wasn't just the accidental outcome of a drunken tumble with Caro forty-two years ago . . . but an emotional connection I couldn't deny, even to myself.'

'You designed Emergence from the outset as a means of cheating Nishizaki?'

'It's how he'd probably see it. He's received none of the profits and Vinod's fixed things so he never will. But it goes beyond that. The money is only half the story, the half that was to supply me with a well-heeled and invisible retirement far from Nishizaki's clutches. The fraudulent element of Emergence is the crucial factor: the additional options Dr Morrisette has doubtless explained to you are essentially worthless. I always wanted her to expose the reality of the situation. It's why I instructed Nanoq to give you the memory stick detailing the whole thing and send you to her. Once the buyers of those options – all of them rich, powerful, dangerous people – realize they've been taken for a ride, they'll want more than their money back. They'll want revenge. More specifically, they'll want to show they can't be conned with impunity. And they'll blame Nishizaki for what's happened to them. He can protest all he likes that I'm the one who's done this to them, but they won't believe him, because he is – and always has been – the man ultimately in charge: the face of the Nishizaki Corporation. They'll never be convinced I would have dared to act against his wishes. They'll never be persuaded he hasn't tried to defraud them. And that can end only one way for him.'

'You mean . . .'

'It was him or me as I saw it. And I was determined it wasn't going to be me. It's not as if I was setting him up for a punishment he didn't richly deserve. I'm sure you'll agree with me about that, since your own husband was indirectly one of his victims.'

'Has he discovered yet what you have planned for him?'

'Oh, yes. Ohara's disappearance in Iceland while hunting for Marty was bound to alarm him. He sent Zayala to investigate. Zayala was considerably tech-savvier than Ohara. He demanded full access to the Emergence files. It was impossible to refuse him without openly challenging Nishizaki. I think Zayala smelt a rat and sent a worrying message back to his boss before he went the same way as Ohara. But it was too late to change the plan. We went ahead with the auction. The money changed hands. The fraud kicked in. And you tipped off Dr Morrisette. But Nishizaki was already on edge and he reacted to her complaints more quickly and more radically than I'd anticipated.'

'By kidnapping her?'

'Yes. And Nick Miller as well. They're being held somewhere in London by contract gangsters Nishizaki hired at short notice.

He's in London himself now as well. He's demanded I meet him to discuss the terms for their release.'

'Will you?'

'Ah. That's where we come to your role in all this, Wada. You must have been asking yourself why I've been willing to tell you so much I've kept secret for so long – why I've confided in you so completely this morning.'

'I have been asking myself that, yes.'

'The answer is that Nishizaki has agreed to let me send an authorized representative to meet him on my behalf. I'd hardly be safe in his company in the present circumstances, so he must have assumed I'd never agree to meet him face to face, knowing he'll be surrounded by his personal security staff. The venue is to be Quartizon's London offices, tomorrow morning at nine. Nishizaki's lawyers have scoured the terms of the sub-lease and obtained a court order seizing the property. I imagine they're ransacking the place and burrowing into all available records in search of the missing money even as we speak. I need hardly tell you they won't find it. As a result, Nishizaki isn't likely to be in the best of humours, I'm afraid.'

'And you expect me to agree to meet him?'

'It's actually in your own best interests that you do. Under stress, he tends to lash out in all directions. And he *is* under stress right now. More so than he's been in many years. When he finds a spare moment to consider the part you've played in bringing him to this pass, he won't just dismiss you as small fry and move on. That isn't the way he works. He'll come after you. And your mother. And your brother. Yes, I've done my home-work on you. Just as Nishizaki will have done. He'll spare no one.'

Wada didn't want to believe what Driscoll was saying. He might be exaggerating in order to obtain her agreement. But the ugly truth was that she didn't think he was exaggerating.

'How can I avert that outcome by meeting him as your representative?'

'It gives you the opportunity – which you shouldn't squander – to negotiate an amnesty for you and your family as part of the deal I hope to strike with him.'

'And what is the rest of the deal?'

'In return for the safe release of Nick and Dr Morrisette, I will surrender to Nishizaki the retirement package I put in place for myself. He can safely disappear and live well for the rest of his life, albeit not in Japan and not in continuing control of his criminal interests.'

'What about the fraud victims?'

'Well, in his absence, those of us left behind to answer for him . . . will just have to take our chances.'

'Surely you will become a target.'

'Very probably. But Nick will be safe. So will Dr Morrisette. And so will you, if you play your cards right.'

'Why should Nishizaki agree to speak to me as your agent? He must regard me as someone beneath his notice.'

'Oh, I think he's noticed you, Wada. In fact, I think he probably regrets not telling Ohara at the outset to kill you if he got the chance. You know too much for his liking. But that means you know enough to close this deal. Frankly, I can't think of anyone else who has a realistic chance of doing so.'

'You would trust me?'

A brief silence fell. Driscoll nodded. 'Yes. I would trust you.'

'Why? You do not know me.'

'I know you well enough. And however badly you think of me, it can hardly come close to how badly you think of Nishizaki. Your enemy's enemy truly is, in this case, your friend.'

'What if Nishizaki rejects your terms?'

'You'll simply have to negotiate as best you can.'

'And you will comply with whatever deal I strike?'

'If it spares my son's life, yes. I have no choice unless I'm to abandon him. And I've abandoned too much in my life to add my own child to the list.'

'What would you have said to Nishizaki if Dr Morrisette was his only hostage?'

Driscoll smiled faintly. 'I had an escape route ready to offer her after she'd exposed the fraud. She'd have come to no harm.'

'That is not an answer to my question.'

He looked at her directly. 'Perhaps the question can't be answered. We are where we are.'

'You are asking me to take a big risk.'

'Refusing to do this would be the bigger risk for you, Wada. Nishizaki *will* come for you.'

'And for you.'

'Yes. Which is why we find ourselves unexpectedly needing each other's help.'

'You've made the right decision,' said Driscoll as they walked away from the cathedral.

'It is too soon to say that.'

'No, it's not. Whatever happens – even if everything goes disastrously wrong – the alternatives are worse. Believe me. I thought them all through very carefully before coming to see you.'

Wada had tried to think some of them through herself as they'd talked. Maybe Driscoll was right: they were worse than whatever would come of seeking to prise a compromise out of Nishizaki. Or maybe he was wrong. There was no way to be certain. Wada would have to face the consequences of that uncertainty if she went through with this, as she'd just agreed to do.

There was another motive driving her on that she wasn't about to confess to Driscoll. By planting Yozo Sasada in Aum

Shinrikyo, Nishizaki was indirectly responsible for Hiko's death. Wada had only ever seen Sasada in a courtroom. She'd never actually spoken to him. But she could speak to Nishizaki. She could look into his eyes and see what kind of man he was. Driscoll had given her that chance.

'Nishizaki is a careful man, Wada. You'll be searched when you enter the building. So, just in case you see this meeting as an opportunity to take revenge for your husband's death . . .'

'I have said I will try to negotiate with him. That is what I will do.'

'Good. But be warned. He's quite capable of telling you one thing and intending to do another. He won't keep to an agreement simply because he's said he will. If he accepts my terms, you have to insist on the hostages being released at the same time as I deliver to him the means to access my retirement plan.'

'How will you make the delivery?'

'You call me when the deal's done and I'll provide the details then: where, when and how.'

'You will not tell me before?'

'The less you know of the arrangements I'm going to put in place the better.'

'In case Nishizaki forces the information out of me shortly before putting a bullet through my head?'

Driscoll pulled up and she stopped as well.

'You don't have to do this, Wada-san,' he said, softly and, she felt, sincerely. 'I may have exaggerated the risks of refusing to help me. If you run far and fast enough, it's possible he'll forget about you.'

'But I would have to live looking always over my shoulder.'

'Maybe you could cope with that.'

'Maybe I do not want such a life.'

'We can't always have what we want.'

'Do you think Nishizaki believes that?'

A few moments passed before Driscoll responded. Then he simply shook his head.

Wada met his gaze decisively. 'It is time he was made to believe it, I think.'

'I'll tell him you'll be there, then.'

'Yes. Tomorrow.'

TWENTY-SEVEN

TWENTY-FOUR HOURS TO PREPARE FOR THE MEETING WITH NISHIZAKI was about twenty-three too many, since Wada was already as prepared as she was ever going to be when Driscoll left her outside the entrance of the Lamb Hotel.

She read a couple of chapters of *The Makioka Sisters* on the train down to London that afternoon. More accurately, her eyes scanned the sentences without transmitting to her brain any of the calm the book normally gave her. Her phone logged several calls from Holgate, seeking news, but she didn't respond. There was nothing she could safely say to him. She was set on a course of action that was both dangerous and somehow inevitable. Beyond all the doubting and wondering, she sensed there was no alternative. This was the way it had to be.

Driscoll had booked her a room at Claridge's, where she spent the evening and night in conditions of disorientating luxury. The bath in her room was so big she found herself floating in it, the bed so vast she felt like a child when she laid her head on the enormous pillow.

Wada suspected she looked more like a maid than one of the guests, who clearly came from worlds very different from hers. Sitting in the Art Deco bar with a cocktail she regretted ordering because it was far too sweet, she tried to concentrate on the bubbling chatter around her as a distraction from why she was there and what she was going to do in the morning. But she remained undistracted.

To her surprise, she slept well and was woken by the beeping of the alarm on her phone. The day had come, cool and bright, with showers of rain that cast their shadows over the bathroom mirror as she looked at herself and wondered if the person she saw was equal to the task ahead. There was a gauntness to her features she was sure hadn't been there when she left Tokyo a couple of weeks ago. She wasn't the same Wada. But maybe, considering what lay ahead, that was a good thing.

Quartizon's offices were only a few minutes' walk from Claridge's. When she reached Berkeley Square, she called Driscoll, who answered instantly.

'I am about to go in,' she said simply.

'Very well. I'll await your report.'

'Are you close by, Driscoll-san?'

'That would be telling.'

'Do you have any last advice?'

'Be yourself. Putting on any kind of act for Nishizaki is a waste of effort. Fortunately, though . . .'

'What?'

'I don't think you can be anyone *but* yourself.'

The offices were at the Berkeley Square end of Bruton Place: a four-storey house converted into stylishly fashioned business premises. The brushed steel plaque by the door, featuring the embossed letter Q, was identical to the one at Quartizon's Reykjavík address.

The door opened as she approached. An impassive porter admitted her to a reception area that would have looked sleek and spacious but for the number of people trundling sack-trucks piled with documents away.

'Are you Wada?' the porter asked. He was Asian, but not, Wada suspected, Japanese. Korean, maybe.

'I am Wada.'

'Passport?'

She showed it to him. He nodded in satisfaction. 'I have to search you. I can call a female colleague if you wish.'

'That will not be necessary.'

He nodded again and picked his way meticulously through the contents of her shoulder bag, which did not include the Emergence memory stick, securely stowed in Claridge's safe. Then he patted her down, thoroughly but with cool detachment. 'You can go up,' he said. 'Floor two.'

The lift rose slowly through the building. The doors opened on to a short corridor that led to double dark-wood doors. A large shaven-headed Asian man so wide-shouldered it looked as if he had left the hanger in his jacket was standing in front of them, arms folded across his chest. He inclined his head and whispered into a lapel microphone, then pulled open one of the doors to let her proceed.

She entered what she took to be Quartizon's boardroom. There was a large table, glass-topped and steel-legged, with pale leather swivel chairs spaced around it. There was no other furniture. Decoration was confined to a number of maple-framed oil paintings of abstract colour washes.

There was a second broad-shouldered man standing just inside the door. He glanced round at Wada, then looked towards the figure sitting at the far end of the table.

Wada had seen Hiroji Nishizaki's photograph in photocopies of grainy newspaper articles stored by Kodaka in the *kage-boshi* file. They'd been taken when he was a younger man. She knew the year of his birth – 1945, Showa 20, the year of Japan's great humbling – and she therefore knew his age. His large, pugnacious face, with bags under the eyes like bruises, a nose that looked as if it had once been broken and sullen teak-brown eyes under a widow's peak of unnaturally dark hair, somehow suited him better at seventy-four than it had in middle age. He gazed at her expressionlessly, then gave a heavy-lidded nod to the man behind her, who left the room, closing the doors quietly behind him.

Nishizaki was wearing a pinstripe navy blue double-breasted suit, a crisp white shirt and a scarlet tie. However old he might be, he conveyed an impression of restrained power, of seething energy – or anger – barely held in check. He neither smiled nor scowled. He didn't get up and he didn't invite her to sit. She knew she must appear small and insignificant in such a room. But she didn't feel it.

She wondered if she should speak first, since Nishizaki showed no sign of saying anything. She decided not to. If silence was a test, she didn't intend to fail it.

At last, Nishizaki spoke. 'Why do you not use your husband's name?' he asked, forming the words slowly. 'It is expected of a widow as of a wife.'

'I am not here to discuss my husband,' she replied coolly.

'They tell me he took twelve years to die.'

'His killer took twenty-three years. If we are counting.'

'You are not a respectful woman, are you, Wada?'

'Are you a respectful man, Nishizaki-san?'

'Perhaps you can teach me to be.'

'I doubt I can teach you anything.'

'So do I.'

'I am here to—'

He held up a hand, interrupting her. 'I know why you are here. Driscoll – or perhaps we should call him Ellery – has chosen you as his . . . emissary. A strange choice. But he is a strange man. Loyal for more than forty years. Then . . . *dis*loyal.'

'Will you hear his offer?'

'Is it worth hearing?'

'I believe it is.'

He nodded. 'Then speak.'

'In exchange for the release of Dr Morrisette and Mr Miller, he will give you the use of the escape plan he prepared for himself. It will protect you against any victims of the Emergence fraud who come after you and will supply you with a safe and comfortable retirement.'

'He offers me the use of the rat-hole he planned to crawl into. Is that correct?'

'Since you know him well, you will appreciate that he would not have skimped on the arrangements he made for himself.'

'A luxurious rat-hole, then. Located where?'

'I do not know. Details will be supplied when the hostages are released.'

'It will not be in Japan, though, I assume.'

'No.'

'My father died before I was born, fighting to defend the fatherland against the Americans. You wish me to dishonour his memory by fleeing Japan in order to escape my enemies?'

'It is a way out for you, Nishizaki-san.'

'A way out of what? Dr Morrisette's claims about Emergence have not yet reached any of our clients.'

'But Driscoll-san will ensure they reach them if you do not release her and Mr Miller.'

335

'*Mr Miller.* Driscoll's son. The son he has never met. It is late for him to discover the ties of blood. Perhaps they bind tighter in such cases.' Nishizaki looked more intently at her than he had so far. 'You have no children, Wada?'

'I think you know I do not.'

'Because you were married to a twelve years dying husband.'

He was trying to rile her. He wasn't going to succeed. 'What Driscoll-san is offering you is what you need to survive, Nishizaki-san. That is the truth.'

'Is there to be money as well, to sweeten this pill you tell me I must swallow?'

'There can be.'

'And tell me, Wada, do you want anything for yourself?'

This was the moment to say what she wanted. But the words wouldn't come. She sensed he was merely awaiting her demands in order to reject them.

They looked at each other in silence down the reflective length of the table. It was raining outside now. The light had dulled in the room. Tears of rain streaked the windows.

'How did Ohara and Zayala die?' he asked suddenly.

'I am not here to speak of them.'

'How did they die – and you survive?'

'Some things cannot be accounted for.'

'But their deaths *can* be accounted for. By you.'

Wada considered her answer carefully. But, when it came, it felt instinctive. 'Chijimatsu. Enatsu. Agatsuma. Hirotsu. Oto—'

'Enough.' Nishizaki spat out the word.

'You remember them?' Wada remembered them. They were among the many victims of Nishizaki whose untimely deaths Kodaka had listed in the *kage-boshi* file.

'I remember everyone who has challenged or defied me.'

'Do you wish to account for their deaths?'

336

For the first time, Nishizaki came close to smiling, though in essence it was no more than an ironic twist of the lip. 'I see now why Driscoll chose you to represent him. He must have advised you to ask me for an assurance that I will not pursue you after this matter is settled. Yet you have not asked. Why?'

'Either you will pursue me. Or you will not. Whatever you say here today.'

'You are a perceptive woman, Wada.'

'Will you accept Driscoll-san's offer?'

Nishizaki sat back in his chair, then leant slowly forward again. He rested his elbows on the table and steepled his hands. 'No,' he said quietly. 'I will not.'

Wada said nothing. A few moments passed in silence.

'I will not be made a fugitive by Driscoll. How could I trust him not to reveal my whereabouts to my enemies? And, even if I did trust him, how could I be certain they would not force the information out of him?'

'Is that what you wish me to tell him?'

'Tell him his offer is not good enough.'

'What would be good enough?'

'I will release Dr Morrisette and Mr Miller if he surrenders himself to me in person. If not, they will die. He must do so within forty-eight hours' – Nishizaki consulted his gold-braceleted watch with an elaborate cock of his wrist – 'of now.' He sat back and gazed along the table at Wada. 'He can choose where and when in those forty-eight hours. I will give him that. But it is all I will give him. Is that clear?'

Wada nodded. She couldn't find the breath to speak.

'You should say it is clear, Wada.'

She summoned her voice. 'It is clear.'

'Good. Now you should call him and get his answer. There is a roof terrace. You can speak to him from there.' He glanced towards the windows. 'I think it has stopped raining. If not, there is shelter. So, I suggest you go and report to him. And then return with his answer.'

Wada took the lift up to the roof terrace, where, to her surprise, she found a Japanese tea garden, complete with a bamboo teahouse and an array of trimmed shrubs screening the part of the roof given over to air-conditioning units and ventilation ducts.

The rain hadn't in fact stopped, but the sun was out to the west and the clouds were moving fast. Wada took shelter under the eaves of the teahouse and called Driscoll's number.

As before, he answered instantly. 'Wada-san?'

'I am sorry, Driscoll-san. He has rejected your offer.'

'Ah. He has, has he? Well, it was to be expected.' Certainly, Driscoll sounded as if he had been expecting it. 'It was worth a try. Thank you for trying. What are his terms?'

'He will release Dr Morrisette and Mr Miller if you surrender to him in person within forty-eight hours. You may stipulate where and when you will surrender within those forty-eight hours.'

'That won't solve his problem with the victims of the Emergence fraud.'

'He said your offer would not solve his problems either. There would be nothing to stop you telling his enemies how to find him.'

'I would have given him my word. But that, I suppose, wasn't likely to be good enough for him.'

'He said his enemies could force the information from you even if you tried to withhold it.'

'Perhaps. But he would have had a head start. Still, he's made his choice. And I must make mine.'

'What answer do you wish me to give him?'

'Did you ask for an assurance that he would leave you and your family alone?'

338

'No.'

'Why not?'

'I did not think I would be able to believe any assurance he gave me. And I have no wish to be deluded by a false sense of security.'

'Logical, but . . . regrettable.'

'What answer do you wish me to give him?' she repeated.

The rain had almost stopped now. A faint rainbow had formed somewhere to the north. 'Tell him I agree,' said Driscoll.

'You realize—'

'Just tell him, Wada. I know what it means.'

He knew. And so did she. 'I will tell him.'

'As to where and when . . . six o'clock tomorrow morning, Porthtowan beach.'

'Porthtowan?'

'It began there forty-two years ago, when I crawled ashore after leaving Alison to drown in that cave under Nancekuke. So, it may as well end there. Tell him I'll wait at the western end of the beach, near the tideline. He should deliver Nick and Dr Morrisette to the eastern end. Nanoq will meet them and confirm they're OK. Then I'll be . . . at Nishizaki's disposal.'

'Is this the only way, Driscoll-san?'

'Yes. I rather think it is.'

'Then I will deliver the message.'

'Thank you. Will you be there too?'

'At Porthtowan?'

'I think you should be. I think you'll regret it later if you're not. Go up on to the western headland above the beach. You'll see it all from there.'

'Why—' Wada began.

But Driscoll had already rung off. Leaving her to watch the rainbow slowly dissolve and to wonder why he thought she needed to see what was going to happen at Porthtowan twenty hours in the future.

She went back down to the boardroom. She was puzzled, as she approached from the lift, by the absence of the guard. She knocked on the door and entered.

Nishizaki wasn't there. A slim, trouser-suited young Japanese woman with long and lustrous black hair rose from a chair at the table to greet her. They exchanged clipped but courteous bows. 'Wada-san,' the young woman said. 'My name is Nambu.'

'Where is Nishizaki-san?' Wada asked.

'Do you have an answer for him?' Nambu asked.

So. Nishizaki didn't intend to give Wada the benefit of any further discussion with him. He'd known what Driscoll would do. 'Driscoll-san accepts the terms,' she said.

'I am instructed to ask: where and when will he surrender?'

'Porthtowan beach, six o'clock tomorrow morning.'

'Porthtowan?' Nambu picked up her smartphone. 'Can you spell it for me?'

Wada spelt it out in English. Nambu tapped at her phone, which provided her with what she needed. She frowned quizzically at the screen. 'Porthtowan, Cornwall, is correct?'

'Yes.' Wada went on to detail the arrangements as Driscoll had specified them to her.

Nambu dutifully noted them on her phone, then read them back. 'Correct?'

Wada nodded. 'Yes.'

'Six tomorrow morning. Nishizaki-san will be there.'

'As will Driscoll-san.'

'Would you like me to show you out?' The question was a delicate way of indicating that their business was concluded.

'Not necessary. I know the way.'

'Before you go, Wada-san . . .'

'Yes?'

'Nishizaki-san asked me to give you this.'

Nambu flicked open a folder that was lying on the table and took out a sheet of paper which she handed to Wada.

The paper was so thick it was almost card. A statement was written on it in Japanese. Wada found herself admiring the penmanship. There was a fluid elegance to the characters.

Wada Umiko and her family have and will have nothing to fear from me. Nishizaki Hiroji. Heisei 31, fourth month, twenty-fifth day.

It was hard to know how to react. What Wada had asked for on Driscoll's behalf hadn't been granted. What she hadn't asked for on her own behalf had. She stared at the statement in silent incredulity.

'You should take good care of that, Wada-san,' said Nambu in a low, confidential tone. 'I have never seen anything like it before.'

TWENTY-EIGHT

THE STRAIN OF ISOLATION WAS BEGINNING TO TAKE ITS TOLL ON NICK. He'd moved through fear and anxiety into a state of nervous exhaustion, in which long hours passed unmarked while he and Michaela lay on their mattresses in their separate cages, staring into space. He no longer thought about what the future held for them. He simply didn't think.

All they could do was wait. Because the only certainty was that their imprisonment wasn't permanent. Nishizaki had a plan for them. And their captors would put his plan into effect. When the time came.

Wada sat in a coffee shop in Marylebone High Street, trying to decide whether she should act on Driscoll's recommendation and be at Porthtowan the following morning. Her room at Claridge's had been booked and paid for until the following week. She could stay there, cocooned in luxury, if she wanted. Or she could fly home to Tokyo. Or back to New York to spend more time with Haruto. They were all choices she was free to make.

But was Driscoll trying to tell her something? Was there some reason why he needed her to be at Porthtowan? Somewhere deep inside herself, she knew she'd already made her choice.

Michaela insisted, whenever she and Nick talked to each other, that they should remain optimistic. 'While there's hope, there's life, right?' Nick wasn't sure, but he didn't dispute the point. 'Your wife will be moving heaven and earth to find you, won't she?' There was no doubt Kate would be doing everything she could. And by now she was bound to have learnt from April – who'd be in a high state of panic – that Nick had misled her about his trip to Iceland. How much else she was likely to have uncovered he couldn't summon the concentration to imagine. When they met again, he would have a lot of ground to make up.

If they met again.

Wada sat on the train. She was following Peter Driscoll back to his beginning, to the place where he'd ceased to be Peter Ellery and become this other version of himself that had taken him so far – but not quite far enough. She was following. To see his beginning become his end.

Michaela was in the middle of one of her periodic exercise sessions. 'You've got to keep your strength up, Nick,' she reminded him breathlessly, as she went through the routine he was by now familiar with: press-ups, sit-ups, running on the spot, pulling herself up on the cage wire. Nick was tempted to ask why, but he didn't. Nothing would be gained by denting Michaela's spirit, which seemed to be stronger than his. Nothing, in truth, would be gained by saying or doing anything.

*

343

Six hours after leaving London, Wada reached Porthtowan, by taxi from Redruth station. A golden evening was stretching itself along the north Cornish coast, mellow light thrown up from lazily rolling surf. The beach looked a little like those of Okinawa she'd seen – as she'd seen so much of her homeland – only on television.

Wada had booked a room at Jubilee Villa B & B on the inland side of the village. It was a short walk to the shore. But Wada went straight to her room. She didn't know if Driscoll and Espersen were already in the area. Or Nishizaki, come to that. But she reckoned it was safer for her to lie low. Until morning.

The pizzas were delivered as usual. Michaela had devised nicknames for their captors, in an attempt to humanize them which she said would also diminish them as threats. This sounded like self-delusory nonsense to Nick, though he played along. Baseball bat man had become Chas, pizza man Dave and their limping accomplice Butch. Chas seemed to have run out of sarcastic remarks. He and Dave went about their business that evening in silence. Not that there was any need for them to speak. Nick and Michaela both knew the drill. Stand back against the wall. Take delivery of supper and a clean bucket. Push the used bucket out. Eat supper. Wait for the lights to go out.

As they did, an hour or so later.

And then, after an unmeasurable period of time, they came on again.

The roller door rattled up. Nick was so dazzled by the sudden glare that he never actually saw Chas and Dave crossing the floor towards him. He heard the jangle of the key in the padlock on his cage. He began to scramble to his feet, his vision still blurry. The door of the cage was flung open. Chas grabbed him and pushed him back against the rear wall of the cage. He heard Michaela shout his name, perhaps in warning. But it was too late. He felt a familiar stabbing sensation in the side of his neck. He knew what was happening to him, but knowing made no difference. He seemed to be falling. The fall accelerated. Then there was only darkness.

When he recovered his senses, he was in the rear of the van, half folded in an oil-stained sheet, his left arm snagged above him. He looked up and saw he was handcuffed to the grab-rail next to the side door. Michaela lay beside him, still unconscious, handcuffed like him to the grab-rail.

The van was moving fast but smoothly through the night. The only light was from the dashboard display, which he could see through the wire barrier separating him from the driving compartment, and the headlamps of oncoming vehicles, their beams moving at intervals across the windscreen. Chas was behind the wheel, while Dave and Butch sat shoulder to shoulder on the bench seat. The droop of Dave's head suggested he might be asleep. Tina Turner was singing 'I Can't Stand the Rain' on the radio and Chas was accompanying her in a tuneless mumble.

Nick glimpsed an illuminated sign ahead and craned his neck to see what it said, hoping for a clue as to where they were going. *Honiton 15, Exeter 28*. So they were in Devon, heading west. But why? What was their destination?

Chas must have noticed Nick moving in the rear-view mirror. He turned the volume down on the radio and reached up to adjust the mirror. 'Look lively,' he said, nudging Dave. 'One of the sleeping beauties is awake.'

Dave snorted and jolted into consciousness. He half turned and squinted at Nick through the wire. 'Nothing to worry about,' he grunted.

'Where are we going?' Nick asked.

'Shut the fuck up.'

'You may as well tell me.'

'We may as well tell you fuck all.'

'Don't be like that,' Chas cut in. 'We'll soon be saying good-bye, Nicko,' he went on in a louder voice. 'You and the climate queen are going to the seaside. Pity you didn't bring your buckets with you, really. You could've made sandcastles.'

'You're going to release us?'

'Maybe. Maybe not. In my experience, these things don't always go according to plan.'

'Where are you taking us?'

'Like I said, the seaside. I haven't been on a beach in God knows how long. It'll make a nice change.'

'The seaside where?'

'Porthtowan, down in Cornwall. Know it, do you?'

Porthtowan? Why would they be going there – of all places?

'Yeah. You know it. I can tell. That good news or bad?' Nick said nothing. 'Mmm. Sounds like you're not sure. Well, never mind. Not long before we find out. Should be an interesting morning. One way or another.'

TWENTY-NINE

WADA WAS UP BEFORE DAWN, BUT NOT, IT TRANSPIRED, BEFORE MRS Griffiths, her rosy-cheeked landlady. 'Morning, deary,' she trilled from the kitchen as Wada came down from her room. 'You're a bit early for breakfast.'

'Oh, I realize that, Mrs Griffiths. I am . . . going for a walk.'

'Catch the best of the day. Good idea. Birdwatcher, are you? Or hoping to spot some seals?'

'I, er, enjoy nature,' Wada replied noncommittally, drifting towards the front door.

'Got a pair of binoculars? You won't see much with the naked eye.'

'Binoculars? Er, no.'

'Well, borrow these.' Mrs Griffiths lifted a pair off a hook and handed them to her. 'It'll be like you're standing right next to whatever you're looking at.'

'Oh. Thank you. Is it . . . low tide, do you know?'

'Should be. Good as. It was high tide around midnight.'

'Thank you.'

'Be back by half past nine if you want breakfast.'

*

Wada slipped the binoculars into her shoulder bag as she headed along the road towards the beach. The sky was mostly clear, although purple-tinged clouds were massed on the horizon. The sun hadn't quite risen yet. Wada moved fast in the almost mono-chrome light, head down, still cautious about showing herself but aware that the decisive moment in the life of Peter Ellery/ Evans/Driscoll was fast approaching.

Driscoll had said she should go up on to the headland above the western end of the beach. According to the large-scale map of the area helpfully displayed on the wall of Mrs Griffiths' guests' lounge, there was a lane leading up it, which Wada fol-lowed past cottages and holiday chalets whose occupants weren't up and about yet. The beach revealed itself in stages as she climbed, smooth sand lapped by lazy, white-crested break-ers. There was virtually no wind at all. There was a stillness everywhere around her – a stillness of waiting.

She reached the summit, where the lane ended. There was no view from there of the beach directly beneath the headland. For that she had to follow a footpath off to the right. A fence had been erected across it with a sign attached: *Path closed due to cliff instability.* She ignored that, rounded the fence and moved up to the overhanging edge of the cliff, where she knelt down.

Immediately beneath her was an open stretch of sand, dotted with rocks. Away to her right was the main apron of the beach, the sand there furrowed by the rivulets of a brook flowing down the valley in which Porthtowan sat. At the other end of the beach was a cluster of buildings reached by the main road through the village. A black four-wheel-drive was parked at the extreme end of the road, where the land began to climb towards the eastern headland. Closer to her there was a lifeguard station, with a car park behind it, backing on to a bank of dunes. The only vehicle in the car park was a big silver-grey SUV. It looked like the kind of vehicle Nishizaki might have travelled there in.

Wada studied the 4WD and the people-carrier through Mrs Griffiths' binoculars. The 4WD appeared to be empty, while the windows of the people-carrier were tinted and reflective, so there was no way to tell if there was anyone inside.

The sound of a car engine caught her ear. Lowering the binoculars, she saw a black Transit van driving along the road towards the other end of the beach. It slowed as she watched, pitching and rolling through potholes and over humps of sand.

The van pulled up some metres short of the 4WD. Its engine died. Silence was restored. Nothing moved.

Wada checked her watch. It was a few minutes to six. The sun had strengthened in the short time she'd been there. It was casting weak shadows now, including one of herself, zigzagging behind her across the tussocky grass of the clifftop.

A door slammed. It was like a gunshot in the still air. She raised the binoculars and looked at the van. A man dressed in black had got out. He was smoking a cigarette. She saw him cough and thought she could hear the sound as well. He glanced at the 4WD, looked back at the van and shook his head, then moved to the top of the slope that led down to the beach, limping as he went. Wada realized then who he was: the man who'd crashed through the shed roof at Dr Morrisette's house while chasing her. She instinctively dropped from her knees to a prone position. The man wasn't looking in her direction. But she didn't want to be seen. By anyone.

She checked her watch again. Dead on six. Where was Driscoll?

The juddering of the van on an uneven surface and glimpses of the sea through the windscreen told Nick they were approaching their destination. The sun was up, gleaming on the wave crests. They'd arrived.

Timing was obviously crucial. They'd laid up for nearly an hour outside a Starbucks when they'd left the A30 before heading on to Porthtowan. Nick remembered the route from his drive down two weeks before and had been able to tell Michaela they were nearly there.

'So, we're going where it all happened forty-two years ago?' she'd asked in a whisper.

'It seems so.'

'Why?'

'I don't know. But we'll find out soon.'

'Is this shaping up well for us, Nick?'

'I don't know that either.'

'But we'll find out soon, right?'

'I guess so.'

And now here they were. The van came to a halt on a slight slope. Chas yanked on the brake and killed the engine.

A few moments passed. Butch lit a cigarette, opened the door and climbed out. Nick caught a breath of fresh sea air. The door slammed shut. Butch moved out of sight. Nick saw Dave nod, as if acknowledging some signal from him.

Chas turned then and looked at them through the wire. 'You'll be getting out soon,' he said. 'There'll be nothing to stop you making a run for it except this.' He held up a gun and tapped the barrel against the wire. 'We'll shoot you down if you try it. Understood?' He paused. '*Understood?*'

Realizing a response was needed, they both nodded energetically. 'We get it,' said Michaela.

'See, we're in this business full time. If we fuck up a hostage handover, it hits our bottom line. And letting hostages get away before the ransom's paid counts as a major fuck-up. It won't be anything personal, but we won't hesitate. It's just the ground rules. OK?'

They nodded again. 'OK,' said Nick.

Chas looked round at Dave. 'Anyone shown themselves?'

'Not yet,' Dave replied.

'Time?'

Dave checked his watch. 'Six on the dot.'

'Any minute, then.'

Any minute. Nick felt Michaela's hand close round his . . . and squeeze hard.

Wada wriggled closer to the edge of the cliff and peered over. She still couldn't see the beach directly beneath her. She wondered if Driscoll was down there somewhere, concealed from view. She looked to her right. The limping man was standing still, puffing at his cigarette. No one else got out of the van. The waves rolled in. She heard the soft whisper of the backwash on the sand. There was no other sound. She checked her watch again. One minute past six. Driscoll was late.

And then she saw him, out of the corner of her eye. He walked into view from the base of the cliff. He was wearing his dark blue suit, which made him look both out of place and yet wholly relaxed as he strolled across the sand with every appearance of casualness.

He was following a curving route that cleared a line of rocks and took him towards the water's edge as he moved slowly east. He raised his right hand high above his shoulder as she watched, lowering it almost immediately.

She glanced right. A figure had appeared on the footpath leading down from the eastern headland. She raised the binoculars to her eyes. It was Espersen, walking at a steady pace towards the van. Driscoll must have been signalling to him, or acknowledging a signal of his.

She trained the binoculars on the van. A second man had emerged from the cab. He walked round to the side of the vehicle and slid the door open. Wada's view of the interior was limited, but she thought she could see movement inside.

351

Then she heard a noise from closer range. She lowered the binoculars and looked down towards the lifeguard station. The front doors of the SUV were open. Two men who looked like the pair who'd guarded the entrance to the boardroom at Quartizon's London offices had left the vehicle. One of them had headed out to a position in front of the lifeguard station, from where she calculated he could see Driscoll. The other was still by the car. He opened one of the rear doors as Wada watched. And Nishizaki climbed out. He too was wearing his suit. In a sense, she supposed, this was a business meeting. For him and Driscoll.

'Here we go,' was all Chas said. Dave responded by jumping out of the van.

A few seconds later, he slid the side door open. Daylight flooded in. He placed one foot on the sill and leant in. He unlocked Michaela's handcuffs first, then Nick's. 'OK,' he said when they were both free. 'Out you come. Slowly.' He stepped back.

They clambered out of the van. Nick's limbs were so stiff from sitting in one position for hours on end he nearly fell over. He pulled himself fully upright and squinted along the beach past Butch. He could see a figure in the distance, moving towards them, close to the water's edge.

Dave drew a gun from inside his boiler-suit. 'Stand where you are until we say otherwise,' he growled.

'We're going to do exactly what you tell us to do,' said Michaela. 'Isn't that right, Nick?'

'Absolutely.'

Wada lowered the binoculars. She looked down at Driscoll. He'd slowed and turned his head towards the cliff, as if watching something. She tried the binoculars again. He was squinting.

She had the impression he was lining himself up with something below her. Then he stopped and looked straight ahead.

She followed the direction of his gaze. At the other end of the beach, two people had emerged from the back of the van. One of them was Dr Morrisette. The other was a man of about forty. Nick Miller, Wada assumed. She'd never seen him before, but there was something about his face, when she studied it through the binoculars, that reminded her of someone else: Driscoll, of course. He was his father's son.

She lowered the binoculars. Espersen had halted his descent from the eastern headland. It was difficult to judge distance at that range, but she reckoned he was about thirty metres from the 4WD. The van – and the four figures gathered around it – were about ten metres beyond that. A fifth figure climbed out of the driver's side of the van as she watched and looked up towards Espersen, then back along the beach.

Wada switched her gaze to the lifeguard station and the car park behind it. Nishizaki and the second security man were walking slowly towards the beach. Nishizaki pointed to the first security man, who was already on the beach, and directed him to go ahead with a jerk of his hand. The man started moving.

He was heading towards Driscoll, who was standing, arms folded, apparently waiting for him. He looked down at the sand as Wada watched. He seemed to be looking at something close to his feet. She trained the binoculars on the spot. But all she could see was a small pile of mussel shells thrown up by the tide.

Suddenly, Driscoll turned his head and looked directly up at her. In the second before she pulled the binoculars away, he seemed to smile.

Nick stood stock still. And Michaela stood stock still next to him. He was aware – and he knew she was aware – that the next few minutes would determine whether they were going to be released unharmed. He tried not to think about what might go wrong. The figure he'd seen at the other end of the beach had stopped moving now. A white-haired man, wearing a dark suit, standing with his arms folded. Driscoll. It had to be. His father. This was the closest he'd ever been to him. But still they were a long way apart.

Another man, tall and bulky, came into view then, striding across the beach from a building that backed on to some dunes: the lifeguard station. He was heading towards Driscoll, casting a faint reflection of himself in the wetter stretches of the sand, where a brook flowed out to sea.

'Everything look OK?' Dave called to Chas, who'd left the van and moved round to the front of the vehicle.

'Everything looks fine,' Chas replied.

Wada watched the first security man approach the spot where Driscoll was waiting and stop a few metres from him. He said something to which Driscoll replied, then he pulled out a phone and spoke into it. Wada glanced back at Nishizaki. He had his phone to his ear. He was also heading towards Driscoll, leaving the second security man back by the lifeguard station. He was walking fast, impatiently, it seemed to her, water splashing up from his shoes as he strode through the rivulets of the brook.

The first security man closed in on Driscoll, who stretched out his arms sideways. The security man began frisking him. The process lasted no more than thirty seconds and evidently gave no cause for concern. He stepped away and, looking back at Nishizaki, gave a reassuring nod: Driscoll wasn't armed. Nishizaki nodded curtly in response and strode on towards them.

Nick gazed along the beach. A second man was moving towards Driscoll from the direction of the lifeguard station. The first man was standing right next to Driscoll. It looked as if he'd just patted him down, searching for a weapon, maybe, and evidently finding none.

'Who are they?' murmured Michaela.

'Nishizaki and some goon of his, I guess.'

'I don't get how this is supposed to play out.'

'Me neither.'

'Shut the fuck up,' growled Dave.

'It won't be much longer,' said Chas. He gave them a tight little smile. 'Then we'll have to say our goodbyes.'

Wada saw Driscoll raise his hand. Nishizaki stopped about ten metres from him, with the security man between them. Driscoll raised his arm aloft. Switching her gaze to the other end of the beach, she saw Espersen raise his arm in response. She looked back at Driscoll and Nishizaki. Nishizaki raised his phone to his ear. A moment passed. Then there was movement back at the other end of the beach.

Nick heard the beep of a phone. Chas pulled out his mobile and answered. 'Yeah? . . . Yeah, right . . . OK.' He ended the call and looked towards Nick and Michaela. 'Time to move, you two. Walk slowly round here.'

They started moving. As they rounded the front of the van, Nick saw a black four-wheel-drive parked a short distance away, shielded from him till now by the van. And he saw a figure heading down the footpath from the headland above them: a loose-limbed, muscular-looking man in windcheater and jeans, with short-cropped hair and a growth of beard.

'It's Espersen,' murmured Michaela.

'You know him?'

'He works for Driscoll.'

'Walk over to the car,' said Chas.

They headed towards the 4WD. Espersen would have got there before them, but he pulled up and called to Chas, 'I want them inside the car. OK?'

'OK,' said Chas. 'But you stay where you are until I get the word from down there.' He nodded over his shoulder towards the trio at the other end of the beach.

'Good enough,' said Espersen.

'You can get in,' Chas called after Nick and Michaela.

Michaela took the nearside rear door and climbed into the car. Nick walked round to the other side. He caught a glance from Espersen as he did so – blue-eyed and piercing. Something in it made him hesitate.

After watching the movements at the other end of the beach, Wada lowered the binoculars and looked down to the group on the beach directly below her. Driscoll hadn't moved. Nor had Nishizaki, who beckoned for Driscoll to approach him. But still Driscoll didn't move. Nishizaki said something into his phone, then strode forward.

He was within reach of Driscoll when he suddenly pulled up and said something. Driscoll didn't appear to reply. He simply raised both arms in the air above his head.

'OK,' was all Chas said into his phone. Nick glanced up the slope at Espersen, who was looking along the beach. Nick followed the line of his gaze. There was Driscoll in the blurry distance. As Nick watched, he raised both arms in the air above his head. Something prompted Nick to look back at Espersen in that instant. There was an object nestling in his palm. His thumb moved over it – and pressed down.

A massive roar split the silence. Wada glimpsed a fountain of sand and a gush of flame and black smoke. Then a wall of hot air struck her. She squeezed her eyes shut and felt her hair being blown back.

As she opened her eyes, the smoke and the rumbling echo of the explosion rose into the sky above the beach. Grains of sand fell around her in a fine rain. She looked down. Driscoll, Nishizaki and the security man had vanished, swallowed by an eruption from beneath. There was a crater where they'd been standing, filled with smoke.

She couldn't grasp for the moment what had happened. But one thought surfaced before any other. This was Driscoll's doing. This was his plan.

It had been him or Nishizaki. And he'd found his solution. It was neither of them.

A massive roar split the silence. Nick saw a fountain of sand and a gush of flame and black smoke at the other end of the beach. Driscoll and the two men who'd been standing with him vanished into it, swallowed whole by the explosion.

'What the fuck?' Chas shouted. But he didn't move. Neither did Butch. They gaped, like Nick, at the sudden spout of destruction.

Only Espersen was prepared for what had happened. He reached the 4WD in several long strides and leant across the bonnet, levelling a gun at Chas, who turned slowly and stared at him, slack-jawed in bewilderment.

'What . . . the fuck's going on?' he mumbled.

'Your employer and my employer are dead,' said Espersen. 'But you're alive and I'm alive and so are Dr Morrisette and Mr Miller. The explosion will have woken the village. We won't be alone here for much longer. Probably someone is already calling the police. We all need to leave. With no shots fired. Otherwise it ends ugly for everyone. You understand?'

Chas looked as if his reactions hadn't yet caught up with events; as if understanding anything was pretty much beyond him.

357

'You and your two friends need to get into your van and drive away while you still can.'

'Did you . . . set that bomb off?'

'I did what I was told to do. Now you need to do the same. In the next ten seconds.'

'The fuckers have . . . screwed us,' said Dave, stumbling into view from the other side of the van.

'Are you going to go quietly or not?' demanded Espersen. 'The man who hired you is dead. You're not going to get paid. So write the job off. And leave now. It's the sane thing to do. And you are sane, aren't you?'

Chas grimaced, as if swallowing something he didn't like the taste of. 'Fuck it,' he said, glaring along the beach at the plume of smoke. 'Let's go, boys.'

'What the fuck went wrong?' wailed Dave.

'Doesn't matter. We should hit the road.'

Chas headed for the van. Butch, who'd said nothing throughout, followed him. And Dave followed as well. They all climbed in. Chas started up, reversed across the road, then took off in a spray of sand.

Espersen put his gun back inside his windcheater and turned towards Nick. 'We need to go as well. Get in the car, Mr Miller.'

Nick didn't move.

'We really need to go.'

'Driscoll just died,' Nick said numbly.

Espersen nodded. 'Yes.'

'You set this up?'

'I did what he told me to do. I buried the explosive in a water-proof canister under the beach before dawn yesterday.'

'And you detonated it?'

'As instructed.'

'He was my father.'

'So he told me.'

'Why . . . why did he do this?'

'It was the only way to protect you. Nishizaki would never have stopped. This way . . . he's been stopped.'

'But . . .'

'We need to go.'

'No.'

Michaela slid across the back seat of the car. She pushed the door open. 'Get in, Nick,' she said. 'Please.'

'I'm staying.'

'We *have* to go. I need to do some serious thinking about how to handle the whole Emergence thing before I find myself being cross-questioned by the police.'

'I'm not asking you to stay, Michaela. It's my decision. I'm not stopping you leaving.' He started walking towards the beach, and the pyre in the distance.

'You shouldn't go down there,' said Espersen.

'I think I have to.'

'Nishizaki came with two men. The second one could still be a problem.'

At that moment, Nick saw from the corner of his eye a silver-grey people-carrier speeding away from the car park behind the lifeguard station. 'Isn't that the problem going away?' he shouted over his shoulder to Espersen.

'You should still come with us, Mr Miller.'

'Listen to him, Nick,' Michaela called.

But he wasn't listening to either of them. He didn't look back as he reached the beach, and started walking towards the spot where his father had just died.

Wada gazed along the beach and stopped holding her breath. For several long minutes, it had looked as if things were about to get even worse. But the stand-off between Espersen and the kidnappers hired by Nishizaki had ended peacefully. And now they'd driven away.

So had the second security man, as soon as he'd recovered from the shock of what had happened to his boss and his colleague. He'd got most of the way to the site of the explosion when he'd seen something that had caused him to clap his hand to his mouth, hurry back to the lifeguard station and speed away in the SUV.

Wada had a good idea what he'd seen. There was an object lying on the beach, thrown twenty metres or so by the force of the blast. She didn't want to look at it through the binoculars. She was more or less certain it was a forearm and hand, with the burnt sleeve of a jacket still attached.

She'd felt sick for a moment, but the sensation was fading now. At the other end of the beach, Espersen was also driving away, but with only one passenger: Dr Morrisette. Nick Miller had stayed behind and was walking towards the plume of smoke that was rising from the crater in the sand.

She jumped to her feet and started down the narrow, crumbling footpath that led to the beach. She could hear voices away to her right: occupants of the cottages and holiday lets along the lane she'd walked up earlier, roused by the explosion and venturing out to investigate. The village was stirring.

She pressed on down the path, slithering on loose patches of earth, but determined to intercept Nick Miller before he reached the spot where his father had died.

As Nick walked along the beach, he was aware of a growing level of movement on the shore. He could see people standing out on the balconies of houses, craning and pointing. Someone was hurrying down the footpath from the headland ahead of him. He heard the roar of a car engine. A pick-up truck barrelled past the lifeguard station and came to a halt on the sand.

A guy who looked as though he could be a lifeguard himself, dressed in a red wetsuit, jumped out and ran towards the smoking crater.

He'd turned back and was shouting into a phone by the time Nick was within earshot. 'An explosion, that's right. Like a bomb's gone off. And . . . there are body parts. Everywhere. People have been killed.'

Nick looked past the guy and saw in the middle distance something lying on the sand. It was too far away for him to identify. But within a few more paces—

'Nick Miller?'

He pulled up and, turning, saw a small, spryly built middle-aged Asian woman running towards him. She was wearing jeans, an orange and red sweater and a thin yellow anorak. A white canvas bag was looped over her shoulder.

She stopped a few metres from him, breathing heavily. Her hair was short – black streaked with a few strands of grey. Her face was round, her features unremarkable. But something in the way she held herself contrived to convey a strength greater than her slender frame implied. And Nick knew at once who she was.

THIRTY

NOW SHE'S ACTUALLY CAUGHT UP WITH NICK MILLER, WADA CAN'T seem to find the right words to express what she wants to say to him.

While she's still tongue-tied, he says, 'You're Umiko Wada, aren't you?'

'Yes,' she manages to reply. 'I am Wada.'

'If you're here, you must have known' – he gestures ahead of him – 'that this was going to happen.'

'No. But, now it has, I understand why Driscoll-san decided it had to.'

'You knew him?'

'A little.'

'That's more than I did, even though . . .'

'He was your father.'

'Yes. He was.'

'You should not go any closer, Miller-san. You will gain nothing except bad memories.'

People are spilling on to the beach now. The man from the pick-up truck is waving and shouting for them to stay back, but they're not taking a lot of notice.

'The police will come soon, Miller-san. Before they do, you should call your wife and tell her you are free.'

'I don't have a phone.'

'Use mine.' She takes it from her bag and offers it to him.

As she does so, it starts ringing. Holgate, she assumes. Will he never give up? But, when she looks at the number, she sees it isn't Holgate after all. It's the only other person who knows the number: Driscoll.

'Hold on,' she says to Nick, raising the phone to her ear and wondering what exactly she's going to hear.

It's a recording. Of Driscoll's voice. *I'm betting you're at Porthtowan this morning, Wada. I'm also betting everything's gone according to plan. In which case Nick and Dr Morrisette are free. And Nishizaki and I are on our way to the afterworld. In the end, there was no other way to go. To save Nick, I had to guarantee Nishizaki's elimination. And this was the only way to do it. There was no reasoning – no bargaining – with Nishizaki. I should have realized that sooner. His son will take over the business, but there'll be nothing to fear from him. Tell Dr Morrisette Vinod will give her all the assistance she needs to dissociate herself from the Emergence fraud. The evidence he supplies will point the finger of blame at Nishizaki and me. As for Nick, you'll let him hear this message, won't you? I want him to know I'm sorry – truly sorry – that I was nothing as a father to him except an absence built on a lie. I'm sure he had a better upbringing with Caro and April than I'd ever have given him. I take some comfort from being able to make sure he has a life to go on with. It's the least I can do for him. And also the most. I was really looking forward to meeting him, but it wasn't to be. Nanoq will return the* kage-boshi *file to you. I don't think you'll need to use any of the contents to protect yourself, but, just in case, it's yours. Try to get Mimori Takenaga released from that psychiatric clinic her family consigned her to, will you? She's just another innocent victim, after all. Like your late husband, I'm afraid. There's nothing I can do about any of that now. The only thing I can do . . . is what I hope I will have done by the time you hear this.'*

'What's wrong?'

Looking at Nick, Wada has the impression he may have asked her that question several times. She gathers her thoughts as best she can. 'Nothing,' she says, trying to smile. 'You should not delay calling your wife any longer.' She hands him the phone. 'I have often dreamt of hearing good news about my husband rather than the bad news that came. For your wife, good news will not be a dream. So, call her, Miller-san. Now.'

Wada follows Nick as he walks slowly back along the beach, away from the people milling around the crater in the sand, away from the smoke and the gaggle of voices and the dying crackle of the flames. He has her phone clapped to one ear and a hand pressed to the other so he'll be able to hear clearly when his call is answered.

She can tell the moment it is by a sudden relaxation of the set of his shoulders. Then he starts speaking. 'It's me, Kate . . . Yes . . . Yes, I'm free and I'm fine . . . Everything's all right . . . I know, darling, I know . . .'

Wada falls further back. She doesn't want to listen to what Nick is saying. That is between him and his wife. She'll tell him about the message from Driscoll later. How much later she's not sure, but she thinks she'll know when the moment is right.

There'll be quite a few more right moments to judge beyond that. But Wada hasn't yet looked too far ahead. She gazes left at the broad blue expanse of the ocean. The waves are rolling gently in. The rising sun is warm on her face. She's not sure why, but she feels more alive than she has in years, maybe decades.

RE-EMERGENCE

Ten months later

UMIKO WADA ISN'T A PRIVATE DETECTIVE. AT LEAST, SHE SAYS SHE isn't. She says she doesn't even work for a private detective any more. But, strangely, in the process of tying up loose ends in the cases ongoing at the time of the death of her late employer, Kazuto Kodaka, she found herself hired by several of his former clients to deal with their problems in her characteristically discreet, low-key, effective manner.

She's still based in Kodaka's office in the Nihonbashi district of Tokyo and it seems she's now widely regarded as his professional successor. The work keeps on coming. She's never idle.

Mimori Takenaga has been released from the psychiatric clinic her family had consigned her to. It didn't prove as difficult to achieve as Wada had anticipated. She suspected the original arrangements had been made at Hiroji Nishizaki's request and probably his expense. Following his death in England in mysterious circumstances, the Takenagas suddenly found it convenient to distance themselves from his affairs, so they put up little resistance to Mimori being discharged. She's left her husband and moved to Tokyo. Wada's met her a couple of times and told her as much as she feels she can about her father's death, almost certainly at Nishizaki's hands, back in 1977.

What Wada hasn't disclosed to her is the full story behind Driscoll's death in the explosion on Porthtowan beach that also claimed Nishizaki's life. There was speculation in the Japanese media at the time that they'd been the targets of a yakuza assassination. Many who'd have thought twice about saying so while Nishizaki was alive suggested there'd always been a sinister side to his business operations. As predicted by Driscoll, Hiroji Nishizaki junior has shown himself to be a very different proposition from his father, setting the company back on a legitimate footing and emphasizing that in future its activities will be free of the remotest taint of scandal. How he appeased the victims of the Emergence fraud has remained unknown for the simple reason that the Emergence fraud itself has remained unknown to all but those directly involved in it. Wada's made no effort to find out the details. She assumes large amounts of money must have changed hands. Where the Nishizaki Corporation is concerned, she's more than happy to leave well alone.

She entirely understands, therefore, why Michaela Morrisette decided not to report her kidnapping to the police. It's much safer for her if the fallout from Emergence stays between Nishizaki junior and his father's aggrieved clients. They're united in one thing at least: an extreme aversion to publicity.

Nick Miller helped Dr Morrisette stay out of the picture by telling the police he'd been kidnapped and held alone by captors who'd never said who they were working for or why they were holding him, although the fact that Driscoll was his natural father obviously had something to do with it. The British and Icelandic police are still supposed to be investigating the tangled web of connections between the explosion at Porthtowan and the fire at Stórí-Asgarbær, but there have been few signs of progress. Driscoll has covered his tracks well, even in death.

Wada hasn't seen Nick Miller since she returned to Tokyo a week after the deaths of Driscoll and Nishizaki senior. Recently, though, he emailed her with the news that he and his wife were planning to visit Japan. Apparently, he wants to see something of the country where his father spent most of his adult life. She's due to have lunch with the couple tomorrow, before they move on to Kyoto. But she's due to see Nick even sooner, because he's arranged to call round at the office to speak to her late this afternoon.

What about, he preferred not to explain in an email. Which, naturally, has aroused Wada's curiosity.

She won't have to wait long for her curiosity to be satisfied, though. Because it's late afternoon already. And Nick is due to arrive at any moment.

Wada notices the light change over the city beyond the office window. Glancing out, she sees clouds rolling in from the east. They look as if they might be rain-bearing. The time of day and the quality of the light remind her of Mimori Takenaga's visit to Kodaka last spring. She tries to dismiss the coincidence from her mind. But it lodges there, portentously, as she hears the lift rumbling up through the building and guesses Nick is on his way. She can almost smell Kodaka's cigarette smoke in the air, almost believe he's still there. But she knows he isn't.

Nick looks well, more relaxed than when she last saw him, lighter in his mind, perhaps lighter physically as well. There's an awkward moment when she thinks he's going to try to kiss her. It ends with something between a handshake and a hug. They

367

smile at each other a little nervously, uncertain how much of what they shared a year ago still binds them together.

Wada brews tea while Nick makes light conversation about the flight and first impressions of Tokyo. Kate, it transpires, is window-shopping in Ginza. It's not entirely clear to Wada whether Kate knows Nick has come to see her, since he mentions he's just come from a brief visit to the nearby Bridgestone Museum of Art. She doesn't press the point, however. He's here for a reason. And soon she'll know what it is.

'Something's happened,' he says, after the small talk has died and Wada's poured him a cup of tea. 'Something I need your advice on.'

'You did not travel all the way from England to ask me for advice, I hope.'

'I suppose . . . in part . . . I did.' He smiles sheepishly.

'What is it that has happened?'

'About six weeks ago, I got a newspaper cutting in the post. Sent anonymously. Typed address. London postmark. Eerily reminiscent, you might think, of how my mother alerted Martin Caldwell to the fact that my father wasn't dead. The cutting was an article that appeared in a Swedish newspaper, *Aftonbladet*, last October. I didn't know what to make of it. I had to get a Swedish friend of a colleague to translate it for me.' Nick fishes a plastic wallet containing the cutting out of his bag. He lays it on Wada's desk. 'I'm guessing you can't read Swedish?'

'You are correct.'

'OK. I'll give you the gist, then. The article's basically an interview with a woman whose husband disappeared in early April last year. Karl-Erik Fagerholm, aged sixty-four, a retired university lecturer. He left his home in Uppsala, north of Stockholm, supposedly travelling to Malmö to visit an elderly aunt living in a retirement home there. He normally went to see her every six months or so, but this visit was only four months after the last one, which was slightly odd. Odder still, he never showed up at the retirement home and hasn't been seen or heard of since. Nor has he taken any money out of the joint bank account he holds with his wife. He hasn't contacted anyone who knows him, either. And there's no record of him leaving the country.'

'Does his wife have any idea what's happened to him?'

'Well, he'd recently been diagnosed with leukaemia and the prognosis wasn't good. She said he was very strong-minded. Quite capable of deciding he'd prefer to die on his own terms rather than lingering in a hospital.'

'She suspects suicide, then?'

'Yes, but she's puzzled by the fact that a large sum of money was deposited in their bank account a few days after his disappearance.'

'How large?'

'She was coy about that. But a lot, that's clear. And she couldn't account for it. He'd done nothing likely to generate such a sum. He wasn't a gambler or a speculator. She described him as completely unmaterialistic. The interviewer asked her if it was enough for her to live comfortably for the rest of her life and she said it was enough for her *and* their children.'

'Who paid the money in?'

'That's where it gets *really* odd. The money was transferred from an account held by Fagerholm in his name only at a bank in Nicosia, Cyprus. His wife didn't even know he had such an account. He'd been to Cyprus on a bird-watching holiday shortly after he was diagnosed with leukaemia. She said he'd wanted to go while he was still well enough to make the trip. She hadn't accompanied him. It looks like he opened the account

369

then. The Cypriot bank declined to give her any information about it on the grounds of client confidentiality, so she's no idea where the money came from originally.'

'She could think of no explanation at all?'

'Only that it was payment for something he'd done that she knew nothing about.'

'What could that be? And why should someone think you needed to be told about it?'

'Exactly. What? And why?'

There's something in Nick's expression that suggests to Wada he already has answers to both questions. She says nothing, but looks at him expectantly.

He slides the cutting out of the plastic wallet and pushes it across the desk towards her. 'Take a look at the photograph of Karl-Erik Fagerholm printed with the article. It was a recent picture, according to his wife.'

Wada picks the cutting up and turns in her chair so the light from the window is behind her. Karl-Erik Fagerholm, retired university lecturer, of Uppsala, Sweden, gazes out of the photograph, smiling faintly. He's wearing a brown jacket and open-necked cream shirt. He's thin, white-haired and slightly haggard, the haggardness – perhaps a sign of his illness – accentuated by the squareness of his jaw.

'You see it, of course,' says Nick. 'I can tell by your frown.'

She puts the cutting back on the desk and looks Nick in the eye. 'Tell me what you think.'

'I think the similarity would be enough to carry him through the few minutes he needed to manoeuvre Nishizaki into position on the beach. And enough to convince you, up on the cliff, that the man dressed in Driscoll's clothes, behaving like Driscoll, really *was* Driscoll. I think the money was payment by Driscoll to a dying man to die in place of him. Last April, at Porthtowan.'

*

Wada is about to argue with Nick, to point out all the reasons why his theory doesn't make sense. But, glancing down at the photograph, she finds there are no reasons. Or, rather, those reasons aren't sufficient. There *is* a similarity. It *could* have been enough. It's *not* impossible. And what's not impossible . . . is possible.

'If I'd simply come across this story by chance,' Nick continues, 'I wouldn't have thought twice about it. But the cutting was sent to me. The article was drawn to my attention. Someone wanted me to know.'

'You think this came from Driscoll?'

'I don't know.'

'You think he wants you to find him?'

'Maybe.'

'Is that why you are here?'

He smiles. 'I only know one private detective. And she's ideally equipped for the job.'

'I am not a private detective.'

'You could have fooled me.'

'And even if I was . . .'

'Remember, I can prove whether Driscoll really did die in the explosion by asking the authorities to test my DNA against the remains they found on the beach. But if I did that and there was no match . . .'

'They would start looking for him.'

'Yes. And not just the authorities. So . . .'

'Does your wife know about this?'

'Not yet.'

'But you will tell her?'

'If and when there's something to tell.'

'You truly want me to start down this road? It was over. We can leave it like that. Maybe we should.'

'I don't think I can.'

Silence falls between them. There is much Wada could say. But, strangely, there doesn't seem to be much point in saying any of it.

Slowly, she stands and crosses to the dark green filing cabinet in the corner. She opens the bottom drawer, takes out one of the empty manila folders stored there, returns to the desk, sits down and writes in katakana characters on the front of the folder, then again on the inner edge that will be visible when the folder is placed in the cabinet.

'What are you doing?' asks Nick.

'What Kodaka-san would have done,' Wada replies. 'I am opening a file. On Karl-Erik Fagerholm. And the source of his money.'

ROBERT GODDARD

WHERE WILL HE TAKE YOU NEXT?

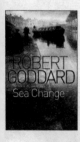

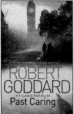

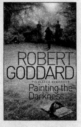

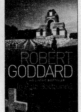

SEA CHANGE   What are the contents of a mysterious package that could spark a revolution in England?

1720

PAINTING THE DARKNESS
The arrival in London of a stranger claiming to be a man long thought dead uncovers dark family secrets.

1880

PAST CARING   Why did cabinet minister Edwin Strafford resign at the height of his career and retreat into obscurity on the island of Madeira?

1910

IN PALE BATTALIONS   Loss, greed and deception during the First World War – and a murder left unsolved for more than half a century.

1920

TAKE NO FAREWELL   A murder trial forces Geoffrey Staddon to return to the Herefordshire country house that launched his architectural career – and to the dark secret it holds.

1930

CLOSED CIRCLE   On board a grand cruise liner, a pair of chancers are plunged deep into a dark conspiracy.

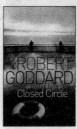

1960

DYING TO TELL   What happened in Somerset in the summer of 1963 that holds the key to a devastating secret?

FAULT LINE   A father dead in his fume-filled car. His young son alive in the boot. Not your average suicide . . .

1970

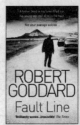

LONG TIME COMING   For thirty-six years they thought he was dead. They were wrong.

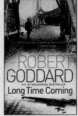

1980

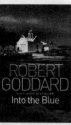

INTO THE BLUE When a guest goes missing from his friend's villa on the island of Rhodes, Harry Barnett becomes prime suspect and must find her if he is to prove himself innocent.

HAND IN GLOVE What long-buried secret connects the murder of a dead poet's elderly sister with the Spanish Civil War?

BEYOND RECALL Dark family secrets are unlocked when a man seeks the truth behind the suicide in Truro of a childhood friend.

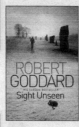

SIGHT UNSEEN A trail of dangerous deceits connects eighteenth century political writer Junius with the abduction of a child at Avebury more than two hundred years later.

1990

BORROWED TIME A chance meeting. A brutal murder. How far will one man go to gain justice?

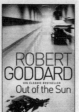

OUT OF THE SUN Harry Barnett must unravel a web of conspiracies if he is to save the son he never knew he had.

CAUGHT IN THE LIGHT
A photographer is drawn into a complex web of deception and revenge following an encounter with a beautiful woman in Vienna.

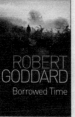

2000

SET IN STONE A house steeped in a history of murder and treason exerts an eerie and potentially fatal influence over its present inhabitants.

DAYS WITHOUT NUMBER
Five Cornish siblings are dragged into a deadly conflict with an unseen enemy as they confront their family's mysterious past.

PLAY TO THE END An estranged husband becomes caught up in a dangerous tangle of family rivalries and murderous intentions while appearing in a play in Brighton.

NEVER GO BACK A group of ex-RAF comrades, Harry Barnett among them, uncover an extraordinary secret during a reunion in Scotland, which puts them all in mortal danger.

NAME TO A FACE When an ancient ring is stolen in Penzance, a centuries old mystery begins to unravel.

FOUND WANTING What connects a dying man's grandfather with the tragic fate of the Russian Royal Family, murdered ninety years earlier?

BLOOD COUNT There's no such thing as easy money, as surgeon Edward Hammond is about to find out.

2010

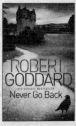
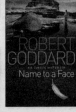
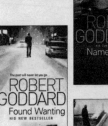
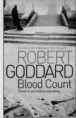

PANIC ROOM
Robert Goddard

High on a Cornish cliff sits a vast uninhabited mansion. Uninhabited except for Blake, a young woman of mysterious background, currently acting as house-sitter.

The house has a panic room. Cunningly concealed, steel lined, impregnable – and apparently closed from within. Even Blake doesn't know it's there. She's too busy being on the run from life, from a story she thinks she's escaped.

But her remote existence is going to be threatened when people come looking for the house's owner, rogue pharma entrepreneur, Jack Harkness. Soon people with questionable motives will be asking Blake the sort of questions she can't – or won't – answer.

WILL THE PANIC ROOM EVER GIVE UP ITS SECRETS?

'Is this his best yet? . . . Full of sinister menace and propulsive pace with twisty plotting'
LEE CHILD

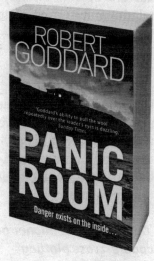

ONE FALSE MOVE

Robert Goddard

What value can be put on a human mind?

How Joe Roberts does what he does is a mystery. He has a brain that seems able to outperform a computer. To a games company like Venstrom, that promises big profits if his abilities can be properly exploited. So they send Nicole Nevinson to track him down and make him an offer too good to refuse.

But Venstrom aren't the only people interested in Joe. His current boss is already making serious money out of Joe's talents and isn't going to let him go without a fight. And then there are other forces, with still darker intentions, that have their own plans for him.

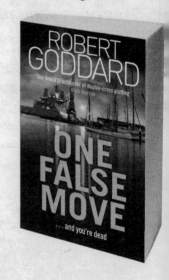

Unwittingly, Joe and Nicole cross an invisible line into a world where the game being played has rules they don't understand. And the battle now isn't just for Joe's mind. It's for Nicole's life.

'Our finest practitioner of double-cross plotting'
MICK HERRON